SILVERHAIR THE

"You will soon be safely home," Silverhair said carefully. "Surely they will welcome you."

Her face grew scornful. "I am their goddess and their slave! I've learned about other things, traveling with you . . ." she added bitterly. "They worship me in Willasfell, but nobody is my friend. And there is no one to make music as you do. Be *my* harper and stay with me! I will give you more gold than any minstrel ever saw. You must come—I *want* you to!"

Silverhair shook his head gently, for a moment shaken by her words, searching for a denial that would not hurt too much. "I am sorry, Thea, but I may not," he said at last. "I'm looking for someone, and until I find her I may give no man my service and call no hall my home."

"Can't I go with you? No one could deny us what we want when I have only to whistle up a wind!"

Silverhair's pity turned abruptly to fear.

About the Author

Diana L. Paxson is a science fiction and fantasy writer living in Berkeley, California. She studied medieval English and French for her Masters Degree at the University of California, and this knowledge has been used as the basis of many of her short stories and novels. She has written a number of fantasies including THE PARADISE TREE, THE EARTHSTONE and WHITE MARE, RED STALLION. SILVERHAIR THE WANDERER is the second in the WESTRIA series, which began with LADY OF LIGHT, LADY OF DARKNESS.

Diana L. Paxson is married with two sons. She spends her spare time playing the harp and writing poetry.

Silverhair
The Wanderer

Diana L. Paxson

NEW ENGLISH LIBRARY
Hodder and Stoughton

First published in the USA in
1986 by Tor Books

First published in Great Britain
in 1990 by New English Library
paperbacks

*A New English Library
paperback original*

*The characters and situations in
this book are entirely imaginary
and bear no relation to any real
person or actual happenings.*

British Library C.I.P.

Paxson, Diana L.
  Silverhair the wanderer.
  I. Title
  813.54

  ISBN 0-450-52091-9

Printed and bound in Great Britain
for Hodder and Stoughton
paperbacks, a division of Hodder
and Stoughton Ltd., Mill Road,
Dunton Green, Sevenoaks, Kent
TN13 2YA (Editorial Office: 47
Bedford Square, London WC18
3DP) by Richard Clay Ltd.,
Bungay, Suffolk.

To Sharon Folsom, harpmistress,
who convinced me my life needed a harp in it;
to Jay Witcher, master craftsman,
who built it;
and to Peregrine, my little harp,
companion of my wanderings . . .

⋙ Prologue ⋘

Before the Cataclysm that restored the Powers of Nature to their old sovereignty, the world was a place of stone and steel. And it was one people, or becoming so, all over the globe.

But in the Cataclysm, the lands shook off the works of men as a dog will shake off the rain, and when humans crept out of their refuges, clutching the scraps of knowledge they had preserved, the world was changed. The great Powers of Earth and Water, Air and Fire, ruled everywhere, along with the Guardians of every kind of beast and tree and flower, and in each region a Guardian who was the pattern of its soul.

Men learned to know these Powers, and as they rebuilt their societies, they were shaped by the Guardians of each land. And so, on the continent men had called America, new nations were born: in the northwest, Normontaine with its peaks of snow and fire; Elaya in the south—an uneasy confederation of races and cultures; and to Elaya's east a greater alliance of old and new tribal peoples—Aztlan. Above Aztlan, as always, were the Barren Lands, with the theocracy of Deseret in the midst of them. Eastward beyond the mountains lay still other peoples and other lands. On the western coast, golden Westria had a King who ruled by means of the four Jewels of Power.

But in the eighth century after the Cataclysm, the

1

King of Westria died, and his lady disappeared with their son. And so the Council declared a search for the lost Queen, and a Regency that should last for twenty years.

CHRONICLES OF WESTRIA, II

☞ 1 ☜

The Hawk Flies Free

Prelude

The hands of the harper settle like nesting birds, and as a branch trembles when a bird alights, so the faintest vibration passes along the strings. In the great Hall of the Hold, sound whispers to silence, and in the act of easing back against their benches the wedding guests grow still, waiting for the harp to speak again.

A single note sounds in the silence, then another. A third forms part of a pattern that is repeated up and down the scale. No one can tell when the other hand enters the music, for already they are forgetting that there is a player, that there is an instrument. Eyes close, as the eyes of the harper are already closed, and there is only the pure awareness of sound.

Now melodies emerge within the web of the music. They are tunes of the north of Westria, of the Corona, with a hint of sadness as they evoke the tangled memories of a time that will not come again. The childhood of the harper flows through his fingertips, and the bride for whom he is making this song finds her eyes wet with tears. For a moment a different tune appears, but the deep chords overwhelm it and it is gone.

Now the music changes as the harper plucks out a rhythm like galloping hooves. The brisk measures of a Seagate ballad mingle with the older harmonies. The songs of the bridegroom's country echo through the room, lifting hearts and bringing reminiscent smiles. In the eight centuries since the Cataclysm, much of the civilization the Ancients made has been lost, and much rejected, but music remains—the old mingling with the new, for in music, man and nature find harmony.

And still the music continues, deepening in chords that cascade one upon the other as they build toward a climax in which the music of the northern mountains and that of the western coasts becomes a single theme. And again that other melody threads the music with bitter harmony, and again it is swept away. The music swells, even the tune disappearing in a triumphant glissando that quivers palpably through the still air. The listeners breathe deeply, saturated by sound.

Then the tempo slows and the shimmer of music ebbs until the distilled purity of single harp notes can be identified once more. The melody soars for the last time, the essence of all that has gone before, and its echoes pass from the air that bears it to the hearts that hear it, so that the listeners do not quite realize when it has gone. . . .

⇛ ONE ⇚

Farin lifted his hands from the harpstrings. His arms were trembling, and when he clasped them around the harp he felt the smooth wood transmit the tremors back to him again. He could still hear the ghostly humming of the strings.

It was done, and he knew that he had never played so well. He had married the melodies of Seagate and the Corona as well and truly as Eric and Rosemary would soon be joined. Yet still that other melody that he had exiled from the music echoed in his mind's ear.

"O Beauty like the Evening Star . . ."

It was no melody of north or west, but his own—the song he had made for his sister Faris.

Had Eric and Rosemary heard it? Had they understood? Rosemary was sitting between her parents, with bowed head and folded hands, her face veiled by her wheat-colored hair. Yes, perhaps she had felt what words could not say. But Eric stared at his bride like a man gazing on the golden hills of his homeland after long wanderings in the Barren Lands.

Farin sighed. Once Eric had gazed at Faris just so, but Faris had married the King of Westria instead, and seen him die, and borne his child alone. And then one day she and the child had disappeared. Her tragedy was the tapestry before which the romance of Eric and Rosemary had been played. Without that background of sorrow, the joy which Farin had just proclaimed with his music could never have flowered.

As the echoes of the music faded, the listeners recollected themselves with a sigh that swept the room as if a door had been opened to let in the wind. But the spell still held them, as if beyond the bounds of hearing the music continued. Their shared reality had shifted, and they were united in awareness of the outer and inner significance of the ceremony that was about to begin.

The Master of the Junipers was already waiting on the broad dais of stone that supported the great hearth. Light shafted through narrow windows set high in the western wall to glitter suddenly on the embroideries of the parti-colored black and white cope he wore and aureole his thinning brown hair. Though he had not moved, something in his presence altered; he focused the attention of the wedding guests as a prism gathers light.

"O my brothers and my sisters, we are gathered to witness the pledging in marriage of a woman and a man—the foundation of a new household in Westria, the linking of two kindreds, and the consecration of that union in the Names of the Lord and the Lady and the Elemental Powers. . . ."

The Master spoke slowly. His voice was deep, almost harsh at times, but it resonated with sweetness like the deep notes of Farin's harp. Sighing, Farin eased the instrument down upon the floor beside him, though he continued to rest one hand upon its smooth curve. Like the hall itself, in which fragments of concrete from the Ancient Days had been mingled with blocks of pure granite quarried from the Father of Mountains, the Master's worn, ugly face had a luminous authority.

It was the mark of the College of the Wise, thought Farin. And yet it was more than that, for after the King's death the Master had been like a blind man in a strange room. But now he was filled with light. And it was not only the Master—in the gentle sunset glow Rosemary's unbound hair shone upon her shoulders like gold, and her blunt features had a sculptured serenity. Farin's sister Faris had looked like a goddess, decked with the four Jewels of Westria, but Rosemary's sturdy humanity mediated that Divine Presence to something that could nourish mortal men. And Eric, wrapped in his green cloak, was like a tree that stands in a forest clearing, rejoicing in her light.

Farin felt tears sting his eyelids, looked down, and was dazzled by the brilliance that flashed from the golden swan that crowned the head of his harp. Swangold . . . He shut his eyes, and his fingers closed on the satiny wood of its curve. He had thought the memories would not hurt any more—it had been over a year since Faris had been married to the King, and four months since she disappeared—but his nerves had been stripped by unchanneled grief and unanswered questioning. He fought the urge to snatch up the harp and dash from the room.

But with the remnants of his control Farin knew that he would do nothing to disturb the ceremony. Shivering, he pulled around him the red cloak upon which Faris had set in exquisite stitchery his emblem of a hawk taking wing from the curve of a harp. As Eric and Rosemary joined the Master and pledged themselves to each other and to the community in which they would found their family, words echoed in his mind like the refrain to a litany—*Faris is gone . . . how can I remain?*

The ritual continued, each section building upon its predecessors like the balanced harmonies of a great piece of music, for no simple promise to share bed and fire would suffice for these two, nor even the public vows with which they had begun the ceremony. Eric was Lord Commander of Seagate, and like the King and Queen, the lord of a Province of Westria and his lady must be priest and priestess to each other and to their land, bound not only in body and fortune, but soul to soul.

Farin shut his eyes in a vain attempt to resist the power of the ritual. How could he believe in all of this when it had betrayed Faris and the King? And yet the beauty of word and image resonated in the strings of his spirit.

"In the Names of Earth, Air, Fire and Water may they be blessed, and in the Name of the Lord and the Lady, and of the One, Unnameable, who is Maker of All!" The Master's voice rang against the carven ceiling and he brought down his arms.

There was a long sigh, as if the room itself had released

its breath—the sigh of a warrior when the battle is over, or of a man and a woman when the act of love is done. Carefully Farin detached his clenched fingers from his harp and sat rubbing them.

For a moment he had not been alone . . . for a moment he had known what it was to be partnered in the Great Dance. And it had been such a familiar feeling! But when had he ever known another human being so intimately? He had slept with Faris's maid Branwen the year before, but that had been a brief thing, a meeting of the flesh only.

He was not remembering Branwen, but someone who was like the other half of his soul. . . .

Then music stirred in him again, words he himself had made at that other wedding, more than a year ago—"*She who was a twin to me in birth, in face, in memory . . .*" He groaned and covered his face with his hands.

This then was the reason he could not accept the idea that Faris was gone—not because of any lust of the flesh, but because of this linkage of the spirit, which he could never find with any other living soul.

And it is forbidden, he thought, *perhaps more straitly than if I had wanted to sleep with her. Marriage should be a union of opposites, but Faris was my twin, like another self to me. She left me behind to marry the King, but I cannot seek another union while I fear she may be alive and in need of me.*

Another music was beginning, at first a ragged trickle of sound, then a great surge that swept away his own song like a river on its way to the sea:

> "*Praise to the Lord and Lady; praise the One,*
> *Who Self-divided is at once Self-known*
> *And from that knowledge manifests the world.*
>
> *In union all diversity lies furled;*
> *Sweet music needs both singer and the song;*
> *By twining separate strands the thread grows strong.*
>
> *It is the darkness that defines the light;*
> *The stars shine best against the cloak of night;*
> *And rest and motion are not paired by chance—*

They are the partners in an endless dance,
As male and female opposites are paired
And in their marriage Unity is shared."

Automatically Farin had joined in the singing. Then he stopped, as if hearing the words for the first time. If marriage was the world's basic pattern, then by clinging to his solitude he might create a disharmony that would destroy him as surely as a wrongly chosen chord could destroy a song. His eyes sought the Master, but the priest was standing with his two hands poised above Rosemary's and Eric's bent heads, his face closed upon some inner harmony.

Dizzied, Farin forced himself to take a deep breath, then another.

Even in the hymn the singer is married to the song—he thought at last. His fingers moved gently across the smooth wood of the harp. *Perhaps there is a Way for me too, Swangold's Way. . . .*

The singing had become a babble of congratulation; someone jostled Farin's arm. He realized that the ceremony was over and they were trying to clear the hall for the feasting. He remembered then that he had promised music for the celebration, and snatching the harp from under the feet of the crowd, almost fiercely he began to play.

Braying insolently, the pipes launched yet another reel, supported by the insistent rat-a-tat of the knuckle drum. Farin opened the flaps of the sealskin harpcase and slid Swangold along the soft fur until the instrument nestled snugly inside. The light of guttering candles glinted on the twenty bronze strings. Then the lifting of the leather flap transformed them to lines of shadow. Farin flipped up the other flap and began to fumble with buckles.

Dancers skipped down the center of the hall. Revelers who still had room for food picked at cakes and fruit piled on platters, or they leaned against the dismantled trestle tables stacked next to the wall. Farin's fingers slipped on the buckle. He swore and forced himself to focus on its silver gleam. He had played and sung almost without break since the end of the ceremony. He wondered if there was anything left of the roast, but his stomach cramped and he realized he did not want food.

"Farin!"

He tightened the final buckle. Rosemary was hurrying toward him with Eric half a pace behind, as if their hands were still linked by the marriage cord. They had been dancing, and Rosemary's face was as pink as the roses that nodded above her brow. She laughed and straightened her wreath as Eric stretched out a muscular arm and one-handed lifted Farin to his feet.

"You're not going to play any more?" Eric asked.

Farin shook his head. "They've been bringing me wine to oil my throat all evening, and my coordination is beginning to go. Anyway, the party is getting too loud for anyone to hear Swangold's song."

Rosemary pushed back a strand of hair that clung damply to her cheek and took Farin's hand.

"When I asked you to play I didn't mean you to miss all the fun! I have not had a chance to thank you, and it was so beautiful—everything I could have imagined music could say. . . ."

Eric nodded. "Yes, it was. You've gotten better. It sounded so familiar, like the music I would make if I had any skill for it, but I knew that it was new." His other arm went around Rosemary and she settled against him.

Something twisted in Farin's belly as joy stamped the two faces before him with its own identity, but he held his tongue. Memory, like a prismed mirror, showed him also Eric's bloodless face after the Battle of the Dragon Waste, and Rosemary's bleak eyes as she nursed him, and later, their faces equally intent as the three of them plotted to trap Caolin the Seneschal, who had betrayed Westria.

"The music was all I had to give you," he said with a half smile. "I'm glad it pleased."

Rosemary's lips tightened in exasperation. "You know it was more than 'pleasing'! Don't you know what your music is worth by now? You could command an audience anywhere. If you won't go study at the College of Bards, stay with us! I've asked you before, but you have not answered me. Come with me and Eric south to Bongarde—if you don't want to live with your father you know you will always have a home with us there!"

"It would be a waste of talent for you to stay in the north—" said Eric. "Bongarde is nearer to the center of things now. . . ."

Now that the King and Faris are gone. . . . Farin's thought echoed him. The line of dancers was advancing on their end of the Hall, and a couple from Seagate, twirling right instead of left, cannoned into them. Laughing, the dancers from the Corona pulled them back into position, and Eric drew Farin and Rosemary closer to the wall.

Farin held his harpcase to his breast. How could he answer them? "I'm not going to live at home with my father, though I suppose I should see the old buzzard while I'm up here." He tried to laugh, though he flinched inwardly, remembering the shadows of a hall whose windows were never opened to let in the sun, and the sour, old-man smell of his father, brooding there like some great moulting bird deprived of prey. It was no wonder Faris had wanted to leave home.

At first he had thought she might have sought Hawkrest Hold after she disappeared with her child, but Faris would never have gone to the old man for sanctuary, and would their father have even welcomed her? In any case Lord Theodor's men had searched there in vain. Farin, who was heir to the few acres of arable land and a hall which his father would not trouble to keep in repair, had no desire to live there now that Faris was gone.

"And when you have seen him will you come to us?" persisted Rosemary.

Farin looked down at his long brown fingers with their nails carefully shaped to pluck the harpstrings. For a moment he wavered. It would be good to live with Eric and Rosemary, as they had lived in the household of the King. He knew the kind of home Rosemary would make—lively and orderly without overmuch formality, filled with convalescent animals and probably with a gaggle of children soon. *Why not?* he wondered, *if I don't intend to start a family of my own?* But for Eric and Rosemary this was a beginning while for Farin it could only be an attempt to resurrect the past.

Instead, into his mind flickered a momentary vision of a hawk soaring across the open road, something he had seen so often when he played the part of a wandering harper the spring before. For a moment his belly tightened with excitement and he could almost taste the pure dawn air.

"I don't know, Rosemary . . ." He found himself answering. "I can't decide that now." He could find no way to justify what he really wanted to do, but he was certain now that it would only give him pain to play audience to Rosemary and Eric's happiness.

Suddenly Rosemary flung her arms around him; then they were both being crushed in Eric's embrace. The heavy perfume of crushed roses and the aromatic scent of the laurel wreath Eric wore mingled with the warmth of their bodies, heated from the dancing. Farin had to look up to see their faces, and for a moment his unhappiness eased, as if the Lord and the Lady themselves had lifted him in their arms.

"Whatever happens, you will always have a home with us. Remember!" Rosemary murmured in his ear.

They had been friends for so long; was she picking from his mind the image of a winding road that bound his soul like a golden ribbon and drew it away? He flushed, as if by the thought she and Eric were somehow betrayed.

"I will remember. . . ." he whispered at last.

The mead tasted bitter, and Farin set his goblet on the stair. He peered down the passageway, blinked, and focused again, a momentary clarity informing him that he would be sick if he drank any more. He ought to be used to the mead his older sister Berisa brewed, but not perhaps to so much of it, on top of so much wine.

The bride and groom had been bedded with a volley of obscene jokes, the worst of them from the women, which embarrassed Farin even through the golden haze of mead. But now the corridor was empty, though sounds of revelry echoed hollowly from elsewhere in the Hold. They would wonder why he was not there to lead the singing, but at the moment it was all Farin could do to hold onto his harp. Instinctively his fingers felt for the buckles, checking that they were closed and the strap secure.

Bed . . . he thought. *Surely I have drunk enough to drown my dreams.* He picked his way down the passageway.

Firelight spilled from an open door across the worn stones. Farin stumbled through it and stood holding to the doorframe while his eyes focused on the grey figure of the Master of the Junipers sitting by the fire.

"Oh . . . forgive me," he murmured. "My room must be farther down the hall."

The Master looked up at him, his dark eyes keen under rather bushy brows, firelight gleaming on the thin places in his greying hair. Farin was aware of a vague wonder that this rather ugly little man should be the same commanding figure who had performed the wedding ceremony.

"Would you like to come in? I won't offer you more wine, but I have some tea simmering."

Abruptly Farin nodded. He was sobering slightly now, and he did not want to go to his cold bed with only Swangold for company, not when he was still too drunk for the comfort of her music.

"Thank you." Carefully he set down the harpcase and lowered himself into the other chair. The Master glanced at him again, frowning a little, and began to busy himself with the teapot.

"Rosemary and Eric want me to live with them at Bongarde. . . ."

Something in the line of the Master's body shifted from the ease of a man by his own fire to the balance of one who takes up the tools of his trade.

"What are you going to do?" He poured tea into a stoneware mug and held it out to Farin.

"I don't know—" the harper began, then shook his head. "No, that's not true. I don't want to live with my father, but I can't settle down with Rosemary and Eric when Faris . . ." The cup began to tremble and he put it down hastily, pain welling through him like long-gathered floodwaters breaching a dam.

"Something happened to her! The night she disappeared I 'heard' her screaming. It woke me, that screaming, though I was miles away. And I had deserted her—it had been so long since our minds had touched at all. . . . It wakes me still, some nights, and I lie until morning wondering where she is now. . . ."

The Master was sitting very still, watching him. "And if you knew what had happened, what would you do?"

"I would kill whoever gave her that pain!" Farin realized that his whole body was shaking now, and he buried his face in his hands. "I love Eric and Rosemary, but it was so hard to watch their wedding," he continued in a muffled voice. "I kept remembering Faris and Jehan. *She* was married too, but what chance did she have to know joy? I have to find her. . . ."

"What makes you so sure she is alive?" the Master asked quietly. "You searched. Everyone searched. Don't you think that someone would have found her if she were still on this earth? Whatever destroyed her life is done with—don't let it ruin yours."

"I heard her agony that night; surely I would feel her dying!" Farin said fiercely. For a moment he saw her face as it had been the last time they were together—dark eyes like his own in a thin face, and a cloud of black hair already streaked with silver like lightning through a stormy sky. But the face he remembered was a furious mask.

"We had quarreled, but the link between us was still there—it has to be there!" Farin shook his head against the black gulf that waited at that thought's end. "I would have felt her final pain!"

The Master's gaze met his for a moment, then slid away.

"What is it? Is there something you're not telling me?" Farin leaned forward, hit the teapot, and reached quickly to still it. His head was clearing now, and he thought there was something strange about the way the priest had refused to meet his eyes.

"It's Caolin, isn't it—" his thought rushed on. "Someone told me you went to the Red Mountain to look for him. What did he say to you? Did he tell you where Faris

is? We know now that he is a sorcerer—did he cause that
freak storm after the Council stripped him of office and he
fled?" Farin was on his feet now, stooping over the Master
with taloned hands.

"Sit down! Drink your tea before it gets cold!" barked
the Master. "You young fool, do you think you will learn
anything by threatening me?"

Farin flinched and subsided into his chair, dashing tears
of anger away. The comforting insulation of the mead had
evaporated, and all his nerves were bare. There was a little
silence, then he picked up his mug and forced a swallow
of tea past the tightness in his throat.

"Very well. You see that I am calm. What did you
learn?"

The Master sighed. "It is true that I went to the beacon
post at the top of the Red Mountain. The earth tremors and
the lightning storm on Midsummer Eve appear to have
centered there."

"Did you find Caolin? He's not dead, is he?" Farin sat
back, feeling as if the ground had given way. He realized
then how certain he had been that Caolin was somehow
responsible for the disappearance of the Queen, and how
much he had counted on revenge.

The Master remained silent and Farin leaned forward.
"Well? Are you going to lie to me?"

The older man's head came up, and Farin jerked back as
if his gaze had burned him. "There are truths and truths,"
the Master said after a moment. "Would you know truth if
I told it to you, or what to do with it? But no—I will not
tell an untruth to you. . . ."

"I'm sorry," Farin murmured sulkily. "But I have to
know!"

"The cabin was in ruins," the Master said carefully,
"but Caolin was not there. I found only that poor mute
woman he had taking care of the place; Margit is her
name. But she was sick and confused—the images I could
get from her mind were chaotic." The Master sipped at his
tea.

Farin settled in place, watching him as a hawk watches
for prey. "But Caolin survived?"

"Barely. Margit tried to care for him, and after a day or two his man Ordrey got there and the two of them nursed him until he could ride. Then Ordrey took his master away southward by the secret paths through the hills. They did not tell Margit where they were going. I have given her a home in my cabin on the Lady Mountain, but it would be no use for you to see her—she knows no more."

"South!" exclaimed Farin. "Then Ordrey must have taken him to Elaya—no Westrian household would receive Caolin now. I'm sure he knows things about Prince Palomon that he could use to buy his aid." He drank more tea without tasting it.

"South," the Master said flatly. "And what are you going to do about it? Fight the entire Elayan army and torture Caolin to get at the truth? What if he does not *know* the truth?" Logs cracked and settled in the fireplace, sending shadows chasing crazily across the ceiling.

"He knows—the snake knows something! He was the last person to see Faris, and he must have caused her the pain I felt. I would seek vengeance on him for that even if there was nothing more!"

"You would go after Caolin even if you knew that Faris was dead?" The Master's voice was very still, but the flames in the fireplace seemed to blaze through Farin's vision into his brain. His harp-trained fingers twitched. Then something in the master's tone reached him and he met the other man's deep gaze.

What have I said? he thought. Farin looked quickly back to the fire as if the Master could read his soul in his eyes. His longing for Faris and for freedom had become a single vision; the flames painted the road to Mist Harbor where the southern trading ships called. *Yes, I'll go after Caolin, but the Master would get Eric or Lord Theodor to stop me,* he realized. *No one must know where I have gone!*

"I don't know what I would do!" Farin answered quickly. "I've had too much wine and my head hurts. I don't know anything anymore."

His lips clamped on the words that trembled there—*I will wring news of my sister from Caolin and find Faris.*

And I will have neither hearth nor master until I can bring the news to Westria!

The Master shook his head. "I should not have told you."

Farin tried to smile. "It doesn't matter. Besides—you are always telling everybody to find their own Way. I'm just stumbling about looking for mine. I should go to bed." He pushed himself to his feet and slung the harpcase from his left shoulder. "Don't worry about me."

But as he went down the passageway he knew that his words had not been true—he felt as if all his tangles had straightened out at last. There was a road to follow and a goal to seek. Like a hawk that finds the thermal that will bear it to the skies, Farin knew where he was going now.

⋙ TWO ⋘

Farin blew on his numb fingers and tugged at the straps that bound his harpcase to the saddle as the roan horse stamped impatiently. Through the stable's narrow window he could see the glitter of frost on the meadow where they had held the war games, and the long ridges that rose beyond it were luminous with mist in the morning sun. Fall was coming early this year—it was just as well he was leaving now, before winter storms kept the trading ships at home.

Blackbirds squabbling over spilled grain in the stableyard squawked protest at some other early riser. Farin forced his fingers to pull the strap tight and reached for the bridle.

"You're up early, lad—"

Farin jumped and dropped the rein, blinking at the tall silhouette in the doorway, which was crowned with silver now as the sun backlit his hair.

"My lord Theodor!"

Rosemary's father came into the stable, his face creasing like an old wood carving. "Is something wrong?"

Farin bent to retrieve his rein, thinking frantically. Had the Master of the Junipers guessed what he intended and told Lord Theodor? But those lean features held only concern. Farin could say he wanted to clear the wine fumes from his head with an early ride, but there were his pack and harpcase to explain, and the heavy cloak and high-laced journey boots he wore. He straightened, forcing a smile.

"I'm off to visit my father, sir. He's getting on, and

18

who knows when I'll have a chance to see him again—''
Farin stopped short, remembering that Lord Theodor, in
his sixties, was a year or two older than the man who
brooded at Hawkrest Hold. But the Lord of the Corona
still stood like one of the pine trees that grew in his
mountains, and the gradual silvering of his fair hair had
been imperceptible. One could not think of him as *old* . . .

"I can't object to that—" Theodor was smiling. "But
they will miss your music. We have barely begun to
celebrate the wedding."

The roan jerked at the rein, and Farin let the horse pull
him along out into the bright sunlight of the stableyard.
"Rosemary understands—" he said over his shoulder, "I
don't have much heart for feasting now."

"Yes. Of course—" Lord Theodor followed and stood
patting the roan's neck. "You are still young and you need
to cherish your grief. The old learn to enjoy happiness
while they can. But don't brood too long, lad. You mustn't
waste your life too." He cleared his throat abruptly and
turned toward the Father of Mountains, whose peak, still
snow-crowned even at summer's end, soared serenely above
the lesser hills.

"I had hoped that Rosemary would marry nearer home,
but who could object to Eric as a son-in-law?" Theodor
was still gazing at the mountain. "But—he is always so
formal with me. Farin, you have fought at his side. Is it
really all right? Will he be good to my girl?"

Farin faced him, uncaring now what the morning light
might reveal. "If you are thinking that Rosemary is a
substitute for Faris in Eric's love, be easy, my lord. He
began to turn to her before Faris—went away—because he
had learned to *know* her. Eric is not like the King—" Farin
swallowed, but made himself continue, for he and Lord
Theodor had been equals in their service to Jehan of
Westria, and no one had served the King without loving
him. He thought the old lord would understand. "But he is
honest and honorable and strong.

"And Rosemary will be good for *him*," Farin went on.
"She needs a man who will take her as his partner, and
she would be wasted ruling anything less than a Province!

I love her too, and I've been hoping for this match. You know she has been better than a sister to me!" He swallowed, afraid he had said too much—he had never had such a conversation with Lord Theodor before. How odd this should happen now, when Farin was leaving him.

But Theodor was laughing. Farin's oldest sister, Berisa, had married Theodor's son Sandremun over ten years ago, and ever since then she had been virtual mistress of the Hold.

A lad carrying wood to the kitchen looked at them curiously as he passed. Farin could hear voices and a clatter of pans; the fortress was waking. The roan butted his arm, and Farin gathered up the reins.

"I've kept you too long talking," said Theodor, "and it will take you all day to reach Hawkrest Hold. Be off with you now, and give Gerard whatever greeting he's willing to accept from me!" Smiling, he gripped Farin's shoulder, then stood away.

Farin pulled himself into the saddle, swinging his leg high to clear the harpcase, but it took all his control to maintain his answering grin. Lord Theodor had been more of a father to him than his own would ever be, and he had not known it would be so hard to leave him with this dishonest farewell.

"You tell Theodor he'll regret letting his daughter go with a southern man!" Lord Gerard's gaunt head turned abruptly to Farin, and the young man saw with disgust that soup was runneling through his father's grizzled beard. Still chewing, Gerard continued his monologue. Daughters were ungrateful creatures who would leave a man to the mercy of strangers. Sons were no better, dashing off to amuse themselves at court or getting themselves killed in pointless wars.

Farin grimaced and took another swallow of thin beer. Hannah Brightapple, who had kept house for them since his mother died, gave him a half smile of sympathy as she set a dish of steaming boiled potatoes next to the stewed chicken and cleared away the soup tureen. It had gone on like this ever since Farin had ridden up the road to Hawkrest

Hold the afternoon before, and he was realizing that the complaints were the old man's inner dialogue made audible. The words would continue to flow in a bitter stream whether or not he was there.

And I won't be! he told himself as his gaze passed over the scarred paneling and the water-stained ceiling of the hall. *Even if I had not sworn to find Caolin I would not stay here.*

"And the rains have been wrong for two seasons now—half the south pasture washed out last winter and I suppose the rest will go this year," said Gerard. "They don't do the ceremonies right at the College anymore—another Cataclysm, that's what we're heading for, you wait and see!"

"If you hadn't kept goats on that land for so many years they wouldn't have cropped it bare!" Farin answered him. "And if you don't repair this roof you won't have a hall to shelter you. You can already see daylight through the ceiling of the tower."

It was not really a tower—more of an observation post built in the days when border raiders still endangered outlying holds, but Farin and Faris had loved it and made it their own. Farin's stomach burned even now, remembering how he had found those rooms with the floor warped and buckling and Faris's bed sagging beneath a coverlet of desiccated leaves. Could his father have torn away the shingles himself to destroy what remained of Faris's presence here? Farin shook his head—if he started thinking that way he would be as bad as the old man soon.

"Let it go—let it go! What matter if an old man is drowned by the winter rains and frozen by the winds?" Gerard coughed and sputtered, sending potato fragments across the table. "You don't care what happens to me any more than your sister did. The men sniffed behind her as if she were a bitch in heat—she couldn't even be satisfied with the King! I never believed that story about how he died, you mark me. She was likely offering herself to his murderer before he was cold in the grave, and don't you think another man wasn't waiting for her when she ran away!"

Farin stared at him, dizzied. Whatever faults his sister

might have had did not include promiscuity, even if she
had flirted with Eric before she realized that she loved the
King. Jehan had died of wounds from a wild boar. Was
this the sort of poison that filled the old man's belly these
days?

"Just like her mother—" the querulous voice wandered
on, "the bitch went away and left me alone. . . ."

But Farin did not wait to hear more. The blood was
pounding in his ears and his hand clenched on his eating
knife as if he would sink it into his father's throat. His
chair went over with a crash as he ran out of the room.

Farin stood in the kitchen yard, his hands clutching
emptiness at his sides. The old man liked his dinner early,
and there was still an hour or two till dark, but the peace
of early evening was quieting the hills. He made himself
breathe deeply, trying to master his rage, resting his eyes
in the familiar contours of the mountains as he would have
rested in his mother's arms. Except for the river bottoms
and holdings like this one where meadows had been cleared,
the mountains were thickly forested with the dark dull
green of fir and pine, splashed now with the warm tan of
the changing oaks and the bright fluttering gold of the
aspen trees. Across the valley the long slopes were turning
purple in the sunset light, below a sky whose clear gold
shaded to rose.

"He can't help it, lad—" said a voice behind him. "He
wept when your mother died, but he could never forget
that she had disobeyed his command not to go out at night
and dance with the apple trees."

Hannah stopped beside him, her broad face crinkled
with concern. Farin nodded and put an arm around her
plump shoulders. He and Faris had been very small when
pneumonia took their mother from them. He remembered
only her shining wings of dark hair and a sweet voice
singing of the spirits of deer and bird and apple tree that
she had seen. She was buried on the hillside beyond the
hall.

"But to say that about Faris!" Farin's voice still shook.
"She looked too much like your mother, and I think it is

almost easier for him to believe that Faris ran off than to accept that—''

''She isn't dead!'' exclaimed Farin. ''She can't be, I would know!'' He stopped short, realizing he had been about to blurt out his plans to search for her. He let go of Hannah and stepped away.

''Ah—I'm sorry, lad—'' said the woman. ''Of course, it would be even harder for you.''

But Farin was already striding across the yard, spurning unseeing the small black and white dog who frisked after him. His anger carried him past the stable and up the hill. When he could control himself again he was in front of the mews.

The first holders of Hawkrest had trained birds for the lords of the Corona. But like everything else on the holding these days, only part of the building—originally as well-built as the hall—was in repair. As he stepped into its dim mustiness, Farin found the balanced tension of the birds beginning to steady him as it had always done.

Talons scratched faintly on wood as the hawks sidled on their perches. Amber eyes glittered in the gloom. Farin remembered that the big peregrine falcon had died the year before and there were only three birds here now. As he stepped toward them the tiercel red-tail began to bate eagerly, wings thundering in the darkness, and he stretched out his arm so that the bird could hop onto it, scolding with an odd quacking sound.

''Aliento, Ali—that's my boy—yes, it's truly me, and I know I've neglected you. . . .'' As Farin stroked the smooth mottled breast feathers the hawk quieted, bobbing his head to preen and then jerking it back as if to make sure Farin was still there. The rustle of footsteps on straw brought the dark head swiveling round, and Farin turned.

''Hullo, Bird—you've grown!''

The boy who had entered grinned, the shadows lending a kind veil to the slick tortured skin that marred his face and, as Farin remembered, much of his body too. Faris had been lucky to get off with no more than a burn on her arm when she had saved that child from the fire.

''Mother told me you were back.'' Bird set down his

pail. "I'm glad. I fly the birds when I can, but they haven't been getting enough exercise."

Farin nodded. Now that his eyes were used to the light he could see that the big female red-tail's feathers were dull, and even Ali had a slightly scruffy air. Bird had an instinctive way with the hawks, but he could not have much time to fly them when he must help his father with the rest of the work of the place too.

"My father doesn't take them out?" Farin asked.

"Him!" Bird snorted. "With all respect, he's gone broody. It's as much as my dad can do to get him out to the fields."

"But the birds can't just stay in here!" said Farin painfully. Abruptly he was twitching with an echo of the panic he had felt when Branwen tried to hold him. Even Rosemary's robust affection made him stiffen and pull free. Aliento quacked impatiently and moved down his arm, and Farin eased the hawk back onto his perch.

Bird was holding the merlin, stroking its feathers gently—he had trained it, and it was his favorite even though the little hawk was good for nothing bigger than mice.

"You're going away again, aren't you—" the boy said abruptly. "Don't worry, I won't tell. But I want to go with you. You understand—with *her* gone, nothing here is the same. . . ."

There were tears in Bird's voice, but though Farin's eyes burned, a stone fist seemed to be squeezing him dry. Bird had been born here, and Faris had saved his life. He was Farin's responsibility, but he could not even guarantee his own survival, much less protect this boy.

"No—" he managed at last. "I have no household, and your gift for the hawks would be wasted. Go to Lord Theodor or Sandremun—they will know how to value you."

For a long moment the boy stared at Farin, his eyes glistening. Then a man's voice called his name and he sighed.

"All right. Now I've got to go. Dad will need me to help get the cows in. Will you feed the birds?"

Farin nodded, but for a long time after Bird had left him

he simply stood. The evening had grown very still. The
hawks moved restlessly, wanting their dinner, and after a
time Farin started toward the coolhouse where the game-
bag always hung. As he reached the door three crows took
wing awkwardly, startled from their scavenging, and climbed
toward the empty sky.

He stopped, staring after them, and thought, *Even the
carrion crows are free to fly. What will become of the
birds I am leaving in there?*

He swallowed then, frightened at the thought that had
come to him. But what else could he do? The hawks were
his responsibility too. Before he could change his mind
Farin strode back into the mews, untied Aliento's jesses
and coaxed the bird onto his arm, and with more difficulty
persuaded the female to do the same. The merlin belonged
to Bird, and the boy could take care of him. Moving
carefully, because he had forgotten just how heavily a six
or seven pound bird could weigh, Farin bore the two
red-tailed hawks up the hill.

They were used to being carried, and through the thin
homespun tunic Farin could feel the minute flexing of foot
muscles that kept them balanced as he moved, without the
help of their honed talons. Without pausing, he climbed
the dusty path that led past his mother's grave and picked
his way among the fallen apples in the orchard until it too
was behind him and he could no longer see the holding
nestled into its fold in the hills. Then at last he stood still,
alone with his birds and the sky.

Farin's breath was coming in harsh gasps and his thoughts
flailed like wings beating at the bars of a cage. He had
brought the hawks here to free them, but would they go?
Could they leave the security of their accustomed home?
Could he? Biting his lip, Farin raised his arm so that
Aliento would sidestep down it to perch on his shoulder,
then fumbled to unbuckle the jesses from the female on his
other arm. She had been captured wild and had never been
so attached to him—surely she would be the easiest to set
free.

She was already bating as he lowered his arm, and then,
with all his strength he tossed her into the air. For a

moment she flapped heavily, as if confused by the absence
of her bells, then she caught the wind and lofted suddenly
into the sky.

Farin was trembling. The tiercel's beak pressed little
hawk kisses against his cheek, and he turned his face to
the softness of the bird's golden-feathered breast. A faint
scent like sun-warmed watermelon brought back memories
of the hawk's weight on his arm on summer afternoons
and his father's harsh voice smoothed to patience as he
helped him to train him.

As if he were still hearing those careful instructions
Farin moved the hawk back down to his wrist, unbuckled
the jesses from around his feet and let them fall, tensed the
lean muscles of his arm and shoulder and propelled the
bird into the air.

Because he was better slipped, or perhaps because he
had seen the female launched and understood, the red-tail
tiercel mounted smoothly into the air. But instead of following her into the trees he circled Farin, calling plaintively.

"You're hungry, aren't you?" cried the young man in a
shaking voice. "There's food all around you here—mice
in the meadow, and ground-squirrels, rabbits even, if you
want to try. Go on, damn you—fly!" Farin flapped his
arms despairingly as the hawk swooped over his head and
soared upward again.

"Please . . . please," whispered Farin, watching him,
"let me go free. . . ."

The female was still spiraling above the trees. Aliento's
swoop became an arc that carried him higher and higher
while Farin craned his neck to see. Then the female's
circle opened into a westward glide. Aliento called once,
harshly, and followed her.

Farin stood without moving until they disappeared. The
world darkened around him, but still his vision was filled
by the image of the two winged shapes, black against a
crimson sky.

It was three days' ride from Hawkrest Hold to Mist
Harbor, where the trading ships put in.

Farin had spent most of his last night at home wakeful,

painting over the golden interlace that marked his harp as a King's gift and darkening the white streak in his hair that marked *him* with leather dye. He had made up a pack, but not a large one, for once he had sold his mount for the passage money he did not know when he would have a horse again. At least the roan gelding he was riding was an animal he had found running loose on the field after the Battle of the Dragon Waste, and it was his to sell. There seemed to him a nice irony in the idea that an Elayan horse should buy his way to Elaya.

And then he had gone into Faris's tower room and packed up the things she had left there, putting them away carefully as if by preserving them he could make sure she would one day return.

No one had stirred in the darkness of the hall as he closed the door; the horse had given no betraying neigh, and if Bird woke and knew the meaning of the hoofbeats that echoed in the grey dawn he made no sign. Farin guided the Elayan horse through mists, which veiled the buildings behind him as if a curtain had been drawn between him and his past, and by the time the sun shone clearly he was many miles on his way.

But it was the second day of his journey before Farin had the heart to uncase his harp and play, and the third was fading before he found himself able to sing. But then, as he crested the last ridge and saw the road uncoiling before him toward the blue glitter of the sea, he found words on his lips that fitted themselves without crafting to a melody with the long slow swing of the wayfarer.

> *"The path is clear before my feet,*
> *I know the way that I must go,*
> *For there's a world that I would meet*
> *And until that world I know,*
> *I will not cease from wandering . . ."*

And as Farin reined the horse down the road, it seemed to him that far overhead a slim shape circled, shot forward, and with a faint sweet cry was lost in the blaze of the sun.

⋙ THREE ⋘

The ship surged and dipped, and the splash of salt spray striking cold on his face made Farin gasp. He clutched at the rail, breathing deep of sea air, and the cry of the gulls tore once more at his heart. Blue sea foamed around him; above was a blue sky where the sea-birds were wheeling. His spirit soared with them, but the shore was near now. The sea had been new to him—now he was sorry the journey was over. Choppy waves broke the rhythm. The boat leaped. He staggered as it settled, then steadied, and the long slow surges bore it toward the shore.

Elaya . . . Farin's eye followed red cliffs that rose like a palisade above the beaches, and beyond them shaggy grey-green hills that swelled into a great half circle around the plain of the Tambara, shimmering in the haze. As he leaned over the rail the wind shifted and he smelled for the first time pungent wood smoke and the sage-scented breath of the hills.

And do those hills shelter my enemy? He spoke the name silently—*Caolin . . .*

Bare masts forested the breakwater, but a sleek rowing craft was bounding toward them. The steersman wore red breeches and the plumes of an officer. Farin stared—he had never seen anyone quite so black before. In Westria the races of men had mixed until people who were completely fair or very dark were rarely seen. His own mother had been the child of a Karok chieftain in the north.

"Hai—what ship be you, and where bound?" came the call. Precise strokes of the oars sent the little craft swirling through the water until it lay alongside, matching the progress of the larger vessel with almost contemptuous ease. Men of every shade of white and gold and brown grinned up at the Westrians.

"This is the *Dolphin*—I'm Will Blacktooth, her master," their captain replied. "We've come from the north of Westria with a load of tarred timber and hides and Seagate wine. D'ye have any use for that here?" Laughing, the captain handed the tiller to his mate and joined Farin at the rail.

"Oh, aye—you be welcome then, 'special the wine!" White teeth flashed as the Elayan grinned. He was speaking the Anglo dialect that passed for a common language in Elaya, though the sailors said there were more native speakers of Spanyol, and Farin had been trying to learn it from them.

"Follow here!" the steersman barked a command and the shell shot ahead, her oars beating the water like pale wings.

"You heard the man—" rasped Will, "two points to starboard and follow him!"

"Oh well," one of the sailors observed as the gap between the *Dolphin* and the Elayan guardboat widened, "we were never meant for speed."

The deck tilted as they changed course, and Farin clung to the rail. They rounded the breakwater and slid into the slack water of the harbor of Sant' Yemaya like a swan in a duck pond as the big square sail came flapping down.

There were two other Westrian ships already moored— biggish, blunt-nosed craft built to endure the open sea. But only the two, for Westria looked inward, and the rivers that flowed through the Great Valley carried most of her trade. The harbor was full of smaller boats—fishing vessels and a variety of oared craft, including one slim, serpent-prowed ship whose oar-ports marked her as an Elayan galley of war. From the Dragon's Head to the southern border the coast was gentle, with long fair beaches and easy anchorage, and Elaya had a brisk fishing industry and sea trade.

The master put the helm over hard as the mates took in

the foresail, and the *Dolphin* swiveled abruptly, green water swirling along her sides. Then Farin helped them to heave the stone-weighted anchor over the side, and the ship jerked like a tethered horse and came to a rocking halt at last.

"Well, lad—we're here."

Farin turned, wiping his hands, and met the captain's gap-toothed smile.

"You're sure you won't come into town along with me? I've been trading here for twenty years, and I can point you to a good inn. . . ."

Farin glanced nervously at his packroll and the piece of sacking that covered his harpcase. The captain's concern for him was exasperating, but he did not dare protest that he was a sworn knight of Westria who had fought beside her King. With the white in his hair disguised he supposed he must look the part of the mountain lad he had pretended to be, out to see the world. It was his own fault if he had succeeded too well.

"I'm grateful"—he shook the man's hand—"but I want to be on my way."

"Well, be careful. There are some here who lost kin in the Battle of the Dragon Waste and have no love for Westrians, and there are some who will take your money just because you are a stranger, and alone."

Farin nodded, remembering Lord Brian's brown beard, stark against a dying sky, and the wailing of his warriors as they lit the funeral pyre. That day seeds of hatred had been planted in many Westrian hearts as well.

But Farin was in little danger of losing his money, for he had none. His treasure lay hid in his harpcase, and his long fingers twitched with impatience to touch the music from Swangold again. The shore boat bumped the *Dolphin*'s side and Master Will turned away to meet the Elayan officials who were coming on board. Gulls squabbled overhead and Farin could hear the babble of mixed accents from the shore. He picked up his bundles and clambered down into the rowboat. He had arrived.

*   *   *

Farin spent most of that day wandering through the winding streets of Sant' Yemaya, wondering at the worn concrete statue of the Lady that had somehow survived the great waves of the Cataclysm, and at the multitude of colors and customs around him. It was not until late afternoon that he found a corner where he could make music, the first few being already claimed by local performers who drove him away. But by nightfall he had made enough coppers to buy a hot meal in an inn near the shore.

After a month on shipboard Farin was used to sleeping in the open, and in the mild southern autumn the beach was preferable to the odors and vermin he was likely to find within walls. He spread his cloak beneath a strange spiky-trunked tree whose feathery branches rubbed against each other all night with a soft rustle that blended with the incessant sighing of the sea.

He woke toward midnight to the sound of women's voices, at first so hushed that he thought them the song of the sea. Raising himself on one elbow, he saw moving figures silhouetted against the brilliance of the moonlit ocean.

> "*Yemaya asesu . . . asesu Yemaya . . .*
> *Yemaya olodo . . . olodo Yemaya . . .*"

One of the women offered a tiny silver ship to the heavens, curved arms and arched back repeating the curve of the moon, of the shoreline, of the wavelets that lapped her feet, then bent like a bending bow to give it to the sea. A sudden larger wave hissed across the sands to take it, and laughter mingled with the singing.

The women were still dancing when Farin fell asleep once more, but their chanting wove itself into his dreams— *Yemaya . . . Yemaya . . .*

And in his dreaming it seemed to him that sky and sea flowed together in a marvelous glittering cloak, whose swirling alternately hid and revealed the form of a woman with hair like night and eyes like twin stars.

"Faris!" he cried out, reaching for her. "Faris, wait for me!"

And it seemed to him then that She smiled, and he heard a voice that murmured, *Surely that is one of My names. Sleep now, My brother, My babe, My beloved, for I will watch over you. . . .*

> *"En los ojos hay un cielo,*
> *En tu boca un paraíso,*
> *Un jardin en tus mejillas,*
> *Tu pecho un cocodrilo . . ."*

Farin grinned at his audience as he finished the song about the lady whose heavenly beauties hid the heart of a crocodile. A sailor had taught it to him on the way south, and it made a useful addition to his repertory. Coins jingled on his spread cloak as he paused to retune the harp, and the crowd that had gathered to hear him began to drift away—two women chattering in Spanyol, a giggling group of dark-skinned children from the farms on the plain, an almond-eyed Nippani fisherman, a Mojave tribeswoman and her child, kilted Anglo miners, cloaked cattlemen from the coastal hills, and horsebreeders from the desert in their flowing robes—a typical mixture for the capital.

It had taken Farin several days to work his way inland from Sant' Yemaya to Los Leones, which sprawled along the crossroads beside the trickle of water in the broad riverbed that bisected the plain. According to local legend, a great city had once covered the basin, but in the Cataclysm a monstrous wave had destroyed all the buildings, carrying most of the rubble back with it into the sea. Thus the lords of the Tambara had built Los Leones on a land scoured clean of the past, and seen it grow into the capital of Eláya.

Farin leaned over to count his money. Twenty coppers and one silver lunaro glittered in the light of the setting sun. The plaza was growing quiet now as people sought their homes or inns. He would get little more today.

The plaza of the cloth-merchants, where Farin had spread his cloak, was on the edge of the Westrian quarter, and

between passersby during the day and customers at the
inns at night, Farin was living reasonably well. But he was
no closer than ever to finding Caolin.

The whitewashed walls of El Castillo, or *Al Kaid*, as
they called it in the tongue of the Tambara, gleamed
mockingly from the bluffs to the south of the city, the color
shading from golden to apricot as the sun went down.
Farin sighed. He suspected that those walls held the key to
his quest, for Caolin had betrayed Westria to Prince Palomon
himself, and surely it was the Prince who would have
given him sanctuary if he had come here.

The encircling mountains were turning purple in the
fading light, their lower slopes luminous in the haze. And
despite his frustration Farin found the hush of early evening easing his spirit. He must locate his enemy, surely,
but for the moment it was sufficient simply to enjoy the
evening air. His hands moved on the harpstrings and he
found himself plucking out the formal measures of a
nightpiece that had been a favorite of the King.

> *"Trailing his robes of splendor from the west,*
> *The weary sun beside the sea would lie.*
> *He draws his coverlet across the sky*
> *And sleeps at last in peace upon her breast."*

A flight of birds winged in precise formation across the
sky. Somewhere a dog barked and was silenced; the clink
of pots and the laughter of women echoed in the still
evening air as families began their evening meals. Farin
sang on:

> *"The children of the daylight seek their rest,*
> *And from the marsh the frog and singing fly*
> *With their many-voiced lullaby*
> *Lull each creature in his drowsy nest."*

A coin tinkled and Farin caught the flash of silver.
Surprised, he looked up to see a tall man leaning on a
stick, his face hidden by the loose folds of a hooded robe
of white cotton such as some of the desert people wore.

Farin smiled his thanks and continued to play, shifting up
the scale for the second part of his song.

> "And now the burning torches of the night
> Are lit, and one by one begin their dance,
> As courtiers revel when their lord is gone;
> Until the sovereign lady, Queen of Light,
> Appears, and stills the heavens with her glance,
> And earth waits, silent, for the voice of dawn."

He finished, looked at his cloak, and realized that the
stranger had given him a double lunaro. He bent forward
to peer at the face beneath the deep hood, but the man
stepped backward, leaning heavily on his staff.

Farin glimpsed scar tissue, slick and pink, on the backs
of the stranger's hands, and understood why he kept his
face hid. Faris had gotten just such scars on her arm when
she saved the boy, Bird, from the fire, and Farin remembered how she hated to let anyone see them. But from the
way this man moved, the flames must have seared his
entire body. Farin repressed a shudder, tried to disguise
the movement by touching the harpstrings, then modulated
into a tune of the desert.

His listener turned to look behind him, his gaze halting
tensely at each of the streets that opened into the square.
His breathing was harsh, as if he had been hurrying. Farin
felt a twinge of pity and continued to play.

"Harper, do you know any other songs of Westria?"
the stranger said huskily as Farin came to the end of the
desert tune.

Farin looked at him in surprise, for the accent had been
that of the north. "I *am* Westrian, friend, and so I think
are you—" he replied. "What would you like me to
play?"

For a moment there was no answer. The hooded man
was staring at the harp, and Farin wondered if the black
paint with which he had covered its insets of golden wire
was wearing away. His arms tightened protectively.
Swangold seemed a part of him, but she had once be-

longed to Jehan the King. It was possible that she might be recognized.

There was a stiff shrug from beneath the robe. Farin frowned and began a Seagate rowing song, wondering if it was he himself who had been recognized. Had this man known him at court or in the army during the Elayan war? Could he have been captured by Elaya at the Battle of the Dragon Waste? He considered playing his lament for Lord Brian, but that might not be wise here.

He sighed then and glanced back at his solitary audience, who had huddled into the curve of the fountain's rim, and launched into a medley of dance tunes and work songs and ballads he had learned as a boy. The coin on his cloak deserved a generous return.

An oxcart creaked sluggishly across the square, its driver gazing curiously at the little tableau, and two children raced by in the other direction, followed by a hysterically barking dog. Then there was silence once more.

Farin's music grew slower and quieter as the dusk deepened, and then, without intending it, he found that he had begun the lament he made after Jehan died. But fog rolling in from the coast was changing the temperature and humidity, and even as Farin realized what he was playing, a string went out of tune and the chord soured. Rather raggedly, Farin brought the melody to a close. The other man sat still, barely breathing, as if he had become part of the stonework.

Farin cleared his throat. "It's late and getting too cold for me to play out here. There's an inn around the corner where they'll welcome me. It's run by a woman of Westria. Why don't you come along?" He stopped, surprised at himself for making the offer. But though the other man did not complain, his shoulders were perpetually braced against pain and, after all, he was a fellow Westrian.

He saw movement then—the fellow's shoulders were shaking—and as he got up to help him he realized that the other man was laughing.

"I meant it kindly—" Farin said a little stiffly. The man in the hood shook his head.

"I know . . . and I will accept your invitation in the

spirit in which it was given. I must admit that food and fire
would be very welcome to me now."

The whitewashed adobe walls of the Golden River Inn
were flaking on the outside, and on the inside they were
stained by smoke to an uneven grey, like most of the other
buildings in Los Leones; but the mistress had hung Westrian
tapestries on the walls, and there was a shrine to the
Guardians in one corner to give it the feel of home. She
was also convinced that Farin needed feeding, and the
bowls that she set before him and his companion were
heaped generously with barley stew.

It had taken them some time to get here, for the stranger
did not walk quickly and paused often to look behind him.
And even when they arrived he had insisted on sitting at a
table from which he could watch the door. For some time,
Farin gave the food his full attention. He noticed that his
companion, though awkward, ate very carefully, and stopped
while half of the stew still remained in the bowl.

"Thank you." The stranger's scarred hands disappeared
back into the folds of his robe.

Farin nodded and sopped up the last of his gravy with a
piece of bread. "It's none of my business, I suppose, but
is someone after you?"

"Yes. But I don't believe they will look for me here."

Once more it seemed to Farin that the stranger's tone
held amusement, although his voice made it hard to tell. It
had a curious husky quality, as if the vocal cords had been
scraped raw by some shout of agony.

Farin shivered slightly and beckoned to the girl who was
bringing round the pitchers of wine. It was not Westrian
wine, of course, but it was honest stuff. He poured a mug
full and pushed it across the table to his guest.

"Have you lived in Elaya long? I am still trying to
understand how things work down here. . . ." Farin tried
again.

"The Elayans don't know either, half the time," said
the stranger. "But that's because they keep changing the
rules. This was once a kingdom like Westria, but the states
kept fighting over the kingship, and now they elect a

Prince-Governor, who is King in all but name. For the past four generations the ruler has been the lord of the Tambaran royal house." He paused for a sip of wine. "Prince Palomon has held the Lion Throne for twenty-two years now, despite the best efforts of assorted cousins and nephews to unseat him. He is an able man."

"I suppose so—" replied Farin unwillingly. He remembered how arrogantly the Elayan Prince and his escort had ridden into Laurelynn for the peacemaking, and he felt himself flushing with anger even at the memory. For a moment he longed to walk out of this place and take the first ship home to Westria. What was he doing here among his enemies?

"Do you want the news from home?" he asked quickly. "Eric of Seagate has married the Lady Rosemary, and—"

"No," the other man's crisp tone cut him short. "Elaya is my home now."

"And what do they call you here?" asked Farin, to hide his embarrassment.

"*El Desterrado*—the Exile . . ." The voice sounded weary, but the wine had smoothed it. "You have been very kind to me, harper. Why?" he asked then.

"I don't know," answered Farin honestly. "Perhaps it is because we are both alone in a strange land. Will you tell me who is after you, and why?"

There was a short silence, and Farin remembered abruptly that it was considered bad manners to ask that question of another wanderer upon the road.

"I am being hunted by the kinfolk of a woman who is carrying my child," said Desterrado.

"Was it they who injured you?" Farin asked more boldly.

"No," Desterrado answered almost bitterly. "They were sheltering me, and the woman was my nurse." As he turned his head the hood fell back a little and Farin caught the flash of pale eyes.

"Did you love her?"

"She loved *me*. She saw me like this, and still she gave me her love. . . ." Desterrado's voice trembled. He lifted his hand to draw the hood away.

Farin was steeling himself not to flinch when there came a thundering at the door. It crashed open. He glimpsed blue plumes and dark faces against the darker curtain of the sky.

Desterrado swung himself from the bench and to his feet with astonishing speed as Farin reached for his harpcase. While the soldiers, dazzled by the light, peered around the room, the scarred man grasped Farin's shoulder and propelled him toward the back door.

"Quickly! They'll want you, too, now you've been seen with me!" he hissed as they stumbled through the kitchen. Farin nodded breathlessly, managed to hitch the strap of the harpcase over his shoulder, and scrambled after the other man out into the night.

Following Desterrado's awkward lead, Farin wove through half the back alleys in Los Leones. If he had had any breath to spare he would have cursed himself for a fool, to befriend a hunted man when he himself was the next thing to a spy in this country, or at least likely to be treated as one if he were recognized. But he had no choice, and as he listened to Desterrado's labored breathing he thought that the other man was at the end of his strength, and had merely been seeking a little human comfort before his enemies found him.

And who will comfort me? thought Farin bitterly. *I will die here like a snared bird and no one at home will ever know what became of me!* They were slowing now, as if Desterrado could go no farther, or perhaps did not know where farther to go, for their flight had landed them in a maze of warehouses, and bales and wagons were parked askew all over the road.

I should leave him, thought Farin. *He can't escape now.*

"Go on!" whispered Desterrado at the same moment. "I cannot run!"

Farin took three steps down the nearest alley and stopped short as torches bloomed suddenly at the end of it. Now light was spilling down the lane from the other direction as well. Shadows ran ahead of it like the vanguard of Prince Palomon's guardsmen. Barred gates and shuttered windows surrounded them; there was no escape.

Desterrado limped toward the illusory protection of a porch and turned. "Give me your dagger—" he said to Farin crisply, "and try not to shame Jehan's teaching when you draw your blade!"

Farin stopped short with the knife half out of its sheath. "What sorcery is this?" he exclaimed, shaken out of caution. "How did you know?"

"If I were still a sorcerer I should not be here—" The stranger plucked the knife from Farin's hand. "But perhaps it is just as well. I shall not be sorry to make an end, and there is a certain irony in the fact that I am with *you*. . . ." He laughed softly and the hair rose on Farin's neck, for he was certain he had heard that laugh before. He drew his shortsword.

"Or would you like to kill me now and save them the labor?" He threw back his hood and Farin tried to read his ruined features in the wavering light.

"Caolin!" the deep-voiced call echoed down the alley. "Will you come out to us, or must we shoot you where you stand?"

The air thrummed and a crossbow bolt thunked into the door behind him. Farin flinched, but not from the bolt—from the name. He had known—he must have known! But how could he have befriended his enemy? He stared stupidly at Caolin with his sword dangling from his hand while arrows buzzed past.

Then a bolt grazed his harpcase, he half turned to protect it, staggered and cried out as something struck his leg like a lash of white fire.

"No," came Caolin's voice beside him, quite strongly. "Not this way—not for me!" He straightened and stood for a moment like a carven image, ignoring the arrows. Then he stepped forward and Farin heard a deep voice cry, "Halt, on my order! What does this mean?"

"Stop, it's the Captain!" someone shouted from one of the alleys, and the arrow fire from that direction ceased. Farin gasped as the first wave of pain rolled up his leg. His vision blurred.

"You gone mad? The Captain is behind us!"

Farin shook his head, saw an Elayan officer standing

before him in the alley, shook his head again and it was
Caolin, then the Elayan once more . . .

"Where he go? That foreign wizard is disappeared!"

"The wizard is among you, and he has his powers
again!" Caolin's voice wavered between hysteria and
exultation. Farin watched him move swiftly down the alley
and reaching for him, clutched air.

"Faris! You never told me about her!" But his cry was
only a whisper, and the movement let loose the pain upon
him as once the tidal wave had engulfed this plain. Like a
wounded bird plummeting from the heavens, his consciousness hurtled into darkness and was gone.

⋙ FOUR ⋘

Farin woke moaning from a dream in which he was surrounded by grinning dark creatures who tore his leg in two. His eyes opened, and after a moment he remembered who and where he was and turned over on the straw. His right leg was throbbing with an echo of pain.

Fighting the sick feeling that comes from having slept in the daytime, he listened to the faint voices and the heavy slam of a door down the passageway. They would be bringing him his dinner soon; another interminable day in Prince Palomon's prisons was almost gone. Through his slitted eyelids Farin could see the obscene comments scratched in the whitewash by his predecessors and the row of twenty-two slashes with which he had recorded the days of his stay. And there had been perhaps a week when he wandered the dark roads of delirium, before the wound-fever left him and they brought him here. It must be the end of November by now.

The noises were getting closer. With another sigh he opened his eyes again and stumbled to the window. His cell was on the second floor of the tower. From here he could see the enclosure where the royal lions roamed, the maze of city streets, and the patchwork of irrigated fields along the shallow river all the way to the blue haze of the bay. The brown mountains surrounding the basin were powdered with snow. Nothing had changed.

Abruptly he turned back to his pallet and picked up Swangold, his thinking stumbling once more along the well-worn track of confusion and despair. Why had they

41

labored to mend his leg instead of leaving him to bleed his life away? Why had they penned him here but left him his harp? And why had Caolin sought him out and told him so much and then betrayed him?

With an oath he forced his fingers into the chording for a Spanyol drinking song he was learning from one of the guards.

The key turned in the lock and he looked up to see the man himself opening the door, but he had no plate of slops in his hand.

"Francisco! Listen to this—is this how the fourth verse ought to go?"

"No, no, not now. You don't want such low songs now." The man shook his head in anxious anticipation. "You suppose' come with me and get washed. New clothes for you too—" He grasped Farin's shoulder.

Farin was halfway down the corridor when he realized he was being dragged along like a child and shook himself free.

"Come on—you hurry. The Prince don' like to wait!"

"The Prince!" Farin stopped short and was jerked along again.

"He says you all fixed up and you play for him—"

Farin was still gaping when they came to the bath house. He submitted to being stripped and scrubbed with harsh soap, rinsed and scrubbed again. Looking down at himself, he saw his sticklike thighs and realized how thin he had become. The pink scar from the crossbow bolt showed livid on his right calf.

When they had dried him and thrust him into clean clothing, Farin was led up another set of stairs into the main wing of the palace. A different guard was there, awkwardly holding Swangold. Farin snatched the harp from him like a mother finding her infant in a stranger's arms and met Francisco's broad grin.

"You go now and play good, eh?"

Then the great door opened and Farin walked unsteadily into the presence of the lord of Elaya, clutching his harp to his chest. It was a rich room, with filigreed shutters to keep out the night air and hanging lamps of worked brass

and silver below the painted beams. Bright rugs were
scattered across the tiled floor.

"You may sit down." The voice was deep, almost lazy,
almost amused.

With an effort Farin focused on the speaker, a dark man
with just a little silver dusting his tightly curled hair and
short beard, dressed in a caftan of bright yellow silk. He
was lying against the cushions of a long, rug-covered
couch next to the little fire.

Palomon . . . For a moment Farin considered defiance,
but that would be a child's gesture. He limped over to a
low hassock, tested the strings and adjusted one.

"What would my lord have me play?"

The Prince glanced at the two women who sat sewing
on the other side of the fireplace. The younger looked up
and Farin saw that her body was rounding with early
pregnancy. It seemed to him that she smiled.

"It is not often that we hear the music of Westria. Play
me the tunes that you used to play for your King. . . ."

Farin stiffened, knowing now that the Elayan ruler was
aware of precisely who he was. *He would not have remem-*
bered me from the peace talks in Laurelynn, thought Farin.
Caolin must have told him. I must not let him see how he
has shaken me.

He bit his lip, knowing that the color in his face had
already betrayed him, and anger brought to his mind a
song which he had heard in Elaya as well as Westria. His
fingers began to pluck out the lilting, bitter chords, and he
sang:

> *"The coyotes are gathered to choose their king*
> *(with a yip and a yap and a howl);*
> *And under the moon the dark hillsides ring*
> *As they vie to see which will the loudest sing*
> *(with a snarl and a snap and a growl)!*

Especially in Elaya, it was a political song, and Farin
knew it was madness to sing it here, but music was his
only weapon now.

*"Now the wiliest chokes all his foes with dust
    (with a yip and a yap and a howl),
Tricks the others to help and betrays their trust
While explaining he does as a ruler must
    (with a snarl and a snap and a growl)!*

*"Oh the king of coyotes is throned on high
    (with a yip and a yap and a howl);
And only the losers will wonder why
As his triumph-song echoes against the sky
    (with a snarl and a snap and a growl)!*

*"But the cubs watch and grin as the king goes past
    (with a yip and a yap and a howl),
And study his deeds, for they're growing fast
And one of them's born for his bane at last
    (with a snarl and a snap and a growl)!*

"The coyotes are gathered to choose their king . . ."

A repetition of the first verse brought the song to a bitter end, but Palomon's eyes still held amusement. Farin remembered the gossip of the marketplace and wondered if the Prince knew that his nephew was plotting against him, or if he cared. His defiance for the moment exhausted, he shifted hastily into a hunting song, and then to a ballad of the northern hills.

"Yes, I begin to see why Jehan valued you," said Palomon when Farin had brought the music to an end. "And you are the brother of his Queen, are you not? You were foolish to leave Westria, but your loss is my gain. . . ."

"Does my lord wish me to continue to play?" Farin managed to say at last.

Palomon laughed. "I do not think so. You still need your rest. But be ready to come to me again."

The chamber to which Farin was returned was different—small, but clean, with a real bed and a chair. But there was still a lock on the door, and Farin understood that despite Palomon's interest in him, or perhaps because of it, he was still a prisoner.

* * *

Sometimes Farin thought that the music was all that kept him sane, as the Prince sent for him again and again. He began to acquire possessions—warmer clothing, oil and spare wire for the harp, even an embroidered band to hold back his hair—everything but freedom. The court musicians taught him the formal music of Elaya, and he took a certain pleasure in transposing the music of the gitarra for his own instrument. He realized that he had not spent so much time on his music since those endless hours playing at the bedside of a dying King.

And then there came an evening when Farin entered Palomon's chamber and saw not the Prince's sister and her attendant, but a man sitting on the other side of the chessboard. This time he recognized him instantly.

Caolin's scarred hands were hidden by black gloves now, and he was dressed in a loose indigo tunic and trousers thrust into soft black boots. A desert headcloth veiled the lower part of his face. It was odd to see him out of the red robes of a Westrian Seneschal, but Farin would never again mistake the poise of that head with its fringe of fair hair, or the deliberation with which he advanced his bishop across the board. Caolin did not look at him.

Farin settled into his usual place midway between the drafts from the windows and the heat of the little fire and began to tune, wondering what he should play. The room had been decorated with branches of red-berried toyon and pine boughs and many little candles in honor of the Feast of Sunreturn.

In Westria, at this time a year ago, had died Jehan their much-loved King.

Remembering, Farin relived for a moment that unbelieving, despairing pain. The men's low voices drifted from the chessboard: Caolin's husky and blandly courteous, and Palomon's with an undertone of irritation, as if he were losing the game.

How can he? thought Farin. *How can Caolin amuse himself in the house of Jehan's enemy as if this day meant nothing at all?* His fingers had moved from an aimless chording to a progression that teased his memory. He frowned, then recognized it and lifted his left hand to the strings to add the melody.

It was the lament he had made for the King.

Did he see Caolin's hand pause? Did he see in his body a stillness of attention that was not directed toward the game? With a bitter smile Farin continued to play—

"The Lord we loved is gone . . ."

"Check and mate!" came Palomon's deep voice in sudden triumph. He had used the Dragon's Tail maneuver in which a transformed pawn lashed back to take the king. He got to his feet, stretching, and went to the side table to pour wine. Caolin remained in place, unmoving, staring at the board. Farin's fingers stilled on the strings and the last vibrations hummed to silence, but his heart hummed with the knowledge that there was at least one memory to which the former Seneschal was vulnerable.

"Here, drink—" The Prince handed one of the goblets to Caolin. "This makes, what—the third time that I have ever beaten you! I only wish I could be certain that you were not letting me win." The crimson silk of his robes rustled as he reseated himself and his teeth flashed a smile.

Farin thought, *I could tell you why you won.*

As if he had heard, Palomon smiled at his harper. "Go on, lad, play. Console this other exile with more music of Westria. . . ."

He is like a cat and we are the birds he is playing with, thought Farin. In sudden revulsion, Farin wanted Caolin to reassert his mastery. He began to pluck out the pavane that Caolin had choreographed for the peace talks where Palomon had conceded victory to Westria.

There was no way to tell if Palomon recognized the music. He turned to Caolin. "The trouble is that you have no stake in the game. If you had not got your sorcery back I would arrest you and make you play for your freedom."

"I have another idea," Caolin spoke for the first time. "Why not let me play for *his*"—he gestured toward Farin.

Palomon lounged back in his chair, glancing from one

man to the other. "But you must realize how it pleases me to own the pet harper of Jehan of Westria. . . ."

"Would not you prefer to have the services of his Seneschal?" said Caolin quietly, still looking down at his wine. Farin gaped. He had thought that Caolin had sold himself to Elaya when Farin was captured, or perhaps before.

"So—the wild bird comes at last to my hand. . . . I cannot hold you to account for your sins against my family, and now you will put yourself in my power?"

"No," answered Caolin, "for then I should be no use to you. But I will serve you if I can make a place for myself here."

There was a long silence. Farin sat staring, afraid to touch the harpstrings. He remembered the pregnant woman who had often listened to him play. He had learned finally that she was the lady Aisha, Palomon's sister, married to the Lord of Campos del Mar and visiting here until her baby was born. Now he remembered what Caolin had told him about the reason for his flight from Palomon's men, and realized that it was Palomon's own sister who was carrying Caolin's child. But Caolin's motives toward himself were still unfathomable, for if he had betrayed Farin in the first place why should he now want to set him free?

"A double stake, then—" said Palomon at last. "If I win I shall decide the manner of your service, and his. If you are the victor you shall serve me on your own terms, and the harper shall be yours to do with as you please."

Only then did Caolin look at Farin, and it seemed to the harper that the cloth that veiled the lower part of his face hid a rather nasty grin.

"And as for you, boy, while I still command you I want you to play—tunes of Westria and Elaya alternately lest either of us be unfairly encouraged," said Palomon.

Farin obediently launched into an Elayan dance tune he could play without thinking, for his confusion had, if anything, grown. An hour before he would have considered anything preferable to captivity, but what in the names of the Guardians did Caolin intend to do with him if he won? He had shot one bolt with the lament for King Jehan,

but he might also be able to shake the former Seneschal
with the lament he had made on the death of Brian of Las
Costas—the song that had turned the people of Westria
against Caolin and brought him down.

But did he want to?

He watched, fascinated, as Caolin's dark-gloved hands
set each exquisitely carved white onyx piece in its place
again. Something in the tension of his shoulders showed
that this time Caolin *cared* who won the game.

But his opening was conservative. The king's pawn
stepped forward, followed by his opposite number from
Palomon's side of the board, like two heralds conferring
before the battle begins. Then the knights began to move
onto the field. Caolin's opening sally with his king's bishop
(as Farin remembered, a favorite piece of his) was drawn
back, and the black pieces began to curl around Caolin's
line.

A glance from Palomon reminded Farin that he was
supposed to be more than a spectator. A lively marching
song he had heard Palomon's soldiers sing jingled from the
harpstrings.

Palomon laughed shortly and Farin looked up. Caolin
had drawn first blood with the capture of a pawn by one of
his own, but now Palomon's dark knight leaped forward to
capture *it*. Caolin's own knight exposed itself to take
another pawn, Palomon's knight sortied out to take it, and
was taken in turn by Caolin's rook, which then scurried
back to its original position again.

Farin let out his breath, seeing that the flurry of action
was over for now. As a warrior, he saw the game as a
substitute for battle, and he suspected that the Elayan
Prince was remembering the excitement of the charge as he
sent his pieces against his foe. But there were others who
saw battle as a live chess game, manipulating men as coolly
as Caolin moved the pieces of stone. He scarcely knew
what he was playing. Tunes of Elaya and Westria tinkled
softly through the stillness, punctuated by the click of
stone on wood and the crackling of the fire.

Then some tension in Palomon drew Farin's attention.
The Elayan was sending out his other knight in an appar-

ently suicidal attack on the white defense of its castled king. He could understand Palomon's frustration, for despite all the maneuvering, most of Caolin's strength was still stolidly entrenched in the left-hand corner of the board. He waited to see what Caolin would do.

The former Seneschal smiled gently, moved his queen to face the invader, and contemptuously refused to take the offering. Now he was threatening the black queen's rook. *Be careful, Palomon,* thought Farin, *he's preparing some trap for you.*

But the Prince, refusing to cut his losses and retreat, ignored the threat and moved his own queen to his knight's assistance. Caolin serenely opened his center by advancing a pawn. Palomon pounced on this sign of weakness, removing it to open a diagonal for his own bishop which could lead to checkmate in another move.

Oh, Caolin! thought Farin, *is he going to take you after all? Must I spend the rest of my life here like a mockingbird in a cage?* Farin applied himself to his music again. The difference in style between the two masters was increasingly apparent. Palomon's pieces dashed to and fro while Caolin played cautiously, always holding something in reserve. But they were both excellent players. What would happen if those two strengths were allied against Westria?

Then Farin saw Palomon pull his bishop back in what was almost his first motion of retreat in the game, leaving his queen stuck deep in enemy territory. Now Caolin began to press him a little, while Palomon played for time. And still the white pieces held their solid formation while the black wore themselves out fruitlessly.

And then, suddenly, the white bishop, who had remained quiescent so long it had become effectively invisible, leaped from ambush to the middle of the board, commanding the field. Palomon advanced a pawn in a desperate attempt to free his own bishop. With an indulgent smile Caolin took it and allowed his own pawn to be snapped up, knowing Palomon's most important pieces were still impotent.

Caolin moved out more of his pieces in careful array;

there was a flurry of action with the pawns, then Caolin's rook swooped across the board to threaten the black bishop again. Farin realized that Caolin had tricked his opponent into fighting his war with only the powers of the bishop and queen, through some mastery of illusion as powerful as any of his shape-changing. He tried to distract himself with music, but his fingers did not want to move. He wondered: *What spell has Caolin cast on me?*

Palomon's bishop took Caolin's remaining knight with a wry satisfaction. Now all the knights were off the board. The warriors had been sacrificed, as they always were in war, and only the politicians remained.

Palomon's pawn inched forward in a last attempt to prepare an escape route for his king; Caolin's pawn continued its inexorable progress toward becoming another queen. Grimacing, Palomon started to move his rook forward, then, with a snort of exasperation, set it down and tipped his own king onto its side in sign of concession, like a defeated wolf offering its throat to its foe.

Even Farin could see that now, any move Palomon might make would lead him to checkmate soon. Masters did not force each other to play a hopeless game out to the end.

"And so I am beaten. . . ." Palomon saluted his fallen monarch. "But you have made me stretch myself, my friend, and you have been pushed also, which was what I desired. Challenge me—fight me always, Caolin. For otherwise I will grow soft, and then I will truly be at the mercy of my foes. . . ." He bent forward, forcing Caolin to look at him, and Farin was uncomfortably aware that more than a chess game was being discussed here.

"Yes. Yes, I know. Why else do you think I asked to serve you?"

Strangely, Farin was reminded of the ceremony in which he had given his King fealty, and despite his own confusion, his eyes stung suddenly with unshed tears. This was no such wholehearted giving as his own had been, and yet he felt that for once Caolin was quite sincere. And after all, he thought with unaccustomed charity, why should the man not build a new life here? He himself had helped to deny him Westria.

Palomon sat back and smiled. "And what about the other portion of your reward?" he asked. "Will you leave the harper with me, or hold him to ransom, or shall I have him executed as a warning to your enemies?"

Farin froze, one hand still poised above the harpstrings. Ransom! Why had he not guessed? He knew only too well that Eric and Rosemary would give their patrimony to have him out of Palomon's hands. And then the sense of the third option penetrated and his stomach grew cold.

If his own feelings were any guide, it seemed to him only too reasonable that Caolin had taken this tortuous route to his revenge. Alone of Caolin's foes, Farin was now wholly in his power. *If my suffering could save them all I would endure it gladly,* Farin thought shakily, but seeing the cold grey eyes of the Seneschal turned full upon him for the first time that evening, he was afraid.

Farin followed his enemy down the passageway as if he were walking through deep water. It had all happened too fast. They had made someone bring his harpcase and his things, and somebody, with unexpected thoughtfulness, had gotten an old cape for him. In December, even this far south, the nights were cold.

His captivity was over. Whether Caolin meant to kill him or keep him in some other servitude, at least he would not be Palomon's prisoner any more. And as he watched the uncommunicative back of the man ahead of him, confusion was gradually diluting the pure intensity of his fear.

It was not until they reached the plaza below the fortress that Caolin came to a halt, not with any air of decision, but rather as if the course of action he had planned was complete and now he needed to consider what next to do. The full moon was settling toward the west, its pallid light checkering the whitewashed walls and tiled rooftops like a chessboard, and casting into sharp silhouette the jagged mountains that edged the plain. In the houses, the candles that were set to burn in the windows each night of the festival were guttering.

Farin's foot brushed a tangle of colored paper left behind by revelers celebrating the birth of the Guardian of Men; his muscles bunched and relaxed as the impulse to run wildly past Caolin into the night was restrained by fear and the habit of captivity. And by curiosity. He shivered; the loose buckle on his harpcase clinked and was still. Caolin turned abruptly, and Farin saw the blind glitter of moonlight in his eyes and his forehead white above the dark cloth of his scarf.

"Why are you still here?"

"What are you going to do with me?" They spoke almost as one.

"I just did it," said Caolin. "You are free."

Farin was shivering more violently now, with cold, or perhaps with relief. There was a long pause while Caolin considered him, then the older man sighed.

"I would have waited till morning, but I wanted to get you out of there before the Prince changed his mind. But you can't stay here, obviously, and the inns are closed. I have a room. You can sleep on the floor. Come."

"I don't understand," said Farin as they made their way past a trio of offering candles set in the crossroads, and dipped into the warren of streets beyond. "It was you who gave me to Palomon in the first place. Why are you letting me go?"

"You were injured," Caolin answered absently. "The only way to make them try to save you was to tell them who you were." He turned into an alley, unlatched a complaining wooden gate in the long back wall, and led Farin along a dirt path to a shack that had been built onto a larger dwelling.

Farin followed him inside and set down his harpcase while Caolin fumbled with the oil lamp. His leg was hurting badly from the unaccustomed exercise. He lowered himself awkwardly to the floor of beaten earth and stretched it out with a sigh.

There was only the single small room, with one window, a battered wooden chest, and a pallet of straw that was little better than the one on which Farin had slept in

Palomon's tower. Caolin sat down on the chest, carefully, as if his old injuries were also paining him.

"I don't understand," Farin spoke at last. "Do you want ransom for me? When we met, I thought you were in hiding. And then there you were, playing chess with the Prince. Why are you living here?"

"Here?" Caolin looked around him as if noticing his surroundings for the first time and gave a short laugh. "It is all I can afford. I have been making my living conjuring in the city squares!" He met Farin's stare and went on. "But I told you the truth when I met you—Palomon's men were hunting me. I thought that I had lost them, that it would be safe to listen to your music, to rest for a little while.

"I was wrong, but I owe you some gratitude. You seem to have been a key that unlocked skills I thought I had lost." He looked at Farin with a hint of angry pride that reminded the harper of the man he had known and hated in Westria. He remembered how Caolin's figure had wavered in the torchlight and then he had seemed to see an Elayan officer there, and gooseflesh pebbled his skin.

Don't trust him, he told himself, *not even now, when he appears to be helping you. Remember what he has done, what he can do . . .*

"And so I escaped them," Caolin went on, "and though my hands have now no skill, still I can make people believe they are looking at what I want them to see—" From the neck of his tunic he drew a silver medallion that caught Farin's eye as it caught the lamplight; it expanded to become a rose, whirled like a pinwheel, then shrank back to the round of the medallion again.

"There is a group of players that will head north in the morning. They could use another musician," Caolin added abruptly. "They are willing to take you with them, and in a few weeks you will be home." The medallion winked like a mirror in the palm of his gloved hand.

Farin blurted, "But we are enemies!"

"I have no enemies," Caolin said very quietly. "You must believe that the man who hated you died six months ago."

Farin stared at him. Caolin believed what he was saying—
Farin was sure of that now, but could he trust him?

"There is a woman to whom I have some responsibility,
and a man who will use me if he can. It is enough to build
a new life on. But I have nothing now to do with
Westria. . . ."

"No?" Farin's voice shook. "Caolin, why do you think
I came to Elaya?"

The other man's swathed head lifted and he surveyed
Farin with a flicker of amusement. "I thought you came
here to kill me."

"I came to question you! You may be done with Westria,
but I am not, and we still do not know where my sister has
gone. You would not answer when they asked you about
her before, but I am begging you now to tell me what you
know!"

Caolin's eyes did not close, but it seemed as if the man
behind them had gone away. Farin, watching him, thought
that Caolin had forgotten to breathe, and then, drawing his
own breath in a deep gasp, realized that it was he who had
not been able to get air.

Whatever had happened, he knew now that it had marked
Caolin as well as the Queen. He summoned his sister's
image to help him resist the impulse to take the question
back again.

"I do not remember. I do not remember. . . . If I
remember, that other man will wake again. Can you not
leave the dead in peace?" The hoarse whisper seemed
scarcely human now.

"Caolin, for Jehan's sake, please!"

After a long time an answer distilled out of the shadows.

"She turned into a demon . . . or I thought she did. I
fought her, and she ran away. I do not know where she
went—if I had known I would have killed her, as I would
have killed you all." Caolin shook his head like a wounded
wolf. "But there was something else . . . a dream . . . in
which she came to me. She came from the east, from the
mountains, and then—" The voice was stopped as if the
laboring memory could not bear the finality of words.

Farin saw tremors move the length of Caolin's body, and

even though the other man had just admitted his attempt to kill Faris, Farin felt, unbelievably, a kind of shocked compassion for an agony which paled his own sufferings. He remembered rumors he had heard in Laurelynn, and the Master of the Junipers' reference to sorcery. Caolin had tried to destroy Westria. Faris must finally have mastered her own powers well enough to stop him.

Caolin did not kill her, he thought. *He does not know where she is now. I can go home. . . .* But that thought gave him no comfort, only an aching weariness that was equally of the body and the soul. *I must sleep now*, he told himself. *It is very late, and tomorrow will be a punishing day.*

Caolin was still sitting on the chest. Farin got up to extinguish the lamp, but as he touched it, the other man suddenly stirred.

"No. Leave it burning. Please, do not leave me in the dark. . . ."

⇛ FIVE ⇚

A mule squealed in outrage, and the air exploded in a tumult of clattering hooves and curses. "Hey, you Westrian wastrel! Are you sleeping there?"

Farin jerked painfully back to awareness of the cheap saddle beneath him, his plunging mount, the gaudily painted wagon ahead of him and the pack mules scattering to either side of the road. He had joined the troupe that called itself *Los Pajaritos*—the little birds—a week ago, but with his muscles and health weakened by illness and captivity, Farin wondered how long he could go on.

With an effort he drove his heels into his bony mount's sides and sent the beast sliding down the bank after the beasts who carried all the extra gear that the wagon could not hold. Two of them were still hesitating at the rim of the road. His whip slashed along their flanks and they turned resignedly back to follow the wagon. But the third mule continued to pick its way down the hill, its pack swaying dangerously.

I should have expected this. . . . Farin tugged his horse's head around after it. *That unnatural beast has been trying to do me in ever since we left Los Leones.*

It took most of an hour for him to catch the mule, persuade it back to the road, and catch up with the little caravan. When he finally resumed his place at the tail of the procession, he had to face the frown of *Maestra* Luisa, who was driving the wagon. In theory, her husband, Jorge the Clown, was the head of Los Pajaritos, but his wife would make two of him—a very big bird indeed, Farin thought glumly.

He tried to catch his breath and scowled back, bending to rub his leg, which was aching furiously. Red Duncan, the son-in-law, who was riding ahead of the wagon, shook his fist and muttered something in Spanyol, which Farin didn't catch. He played the villain, the bully, the swaggering, braggart soldier, when the troupe performed. *A triumph of typecasting*, thought Farin.

They paused to rest the animals at the top of the interminable grade, following the road to the Dragon's Tail Pass. Farin turned in his saddle, gazing back along the way they had come. Below him the long valley through whose orchards they had passed this morning lay dreaming in the afternoon sun. A golden haze half obscured the hills that closed its southern end, veiling the plain of the Tambara. Somewhere, back there, Caolin was beginning his service to Palomon. . . .

Was he telling me the truth? Farin wondered. It went hard to give up hatred that had been a year building. But Caolin had set him free, and the man who had given him his own bed and spent the rest of the night watching by the little lamp had been too hard-pressed by his own terrors to lie to him. He had to accept the knowledge that Caolin had changed, at least for now.

Farin twisted back and forth in the saddle, trying to ease his aching back. The wind that chilled his face spoke of snow ahead. He resisted the temptation to wrap his cloak around him now. Tonight was when he would need it, when they made camp in the upper pass.

By this time tomorrow they should have crossed it and be starting the steep descent to the Great Valley, which was the heart of Westria. Farin closed his eyes, seeking a vision of sunset on the rose-brick walls of Laurelynn, or the Father of Mountains shining in the new day, and Faris. . . .

The agreement had been that he should go with the players as far as Rivered, playing for their performances and helping with the animals, and then he would continue on home.

But I cannot go home! Farin realized desperately. *I still do not know what has become of Faris. She was my twin, my other self—if I go back, her face will be between me and everything I have ever loved!*

"You! Moonling! Are you coming with us or not? I'd leave you here, but you belong in Westria with your half-witted relatives!"

Farin's awareness lurched back to the present; his horse stepped forward as his legs involuntarily squeezed; his hand was already going to his knife. Duncan sat his mount crosswise on the road, laughing at him.

"It's a fierce witling, is it? Save your strength for the mules!" The man tugged at his reins and urged his horse back ahead of the wagon.

Farin took a deep breath and coughed on the chill air, fighting the urge to fling his knife at the man's back. *I am a free man now and no one has the right to mishandle me!* For a moment he saw not Duncan's red face, but the grins and sneers of all those who had guarded him. The world darkened around him and Farin clutched at the saddlebow. *You shall not speak so to me!*

But after a little the anguish passed, like a lion not quite ready to close on its prey, and Farin turned his horse up the trail.

"Eyah, Orfeo—what did you cook this stew in—mule piss?" The little dark man who tended the stock and kept props and scenery cobbled together leaned back, waving his spoon in the air. The cook, a fair young man who was inevitably cast as the romantic lead, wiped his forehead with the back of his hand and grinned.

"Ajili, *mi trasgo,* does that mean you desire to do the cooking now?"

"Who, me?" Ajili shook his head, looking gnomelike indeed in the flickering light. "Did I say it was bad, now? Not me!" Faces creased in laughter as the old joke was trotted out again.

Farin set down his bowl. He knew it was only a joke— the stew tasted of nothing worse than iron from the pot and too much Elayan pepper, but he was sick from anger and exhaustion, and suddenly he could not eat any more.

Orfeo began an interminable ballad from the coastal hills with an obscene chorus that everyone knew. The others joined in, passing around a jug of beer. Farin took a deep swallow of the beer when it came by, but he did not sing. Maestra Luisa's daughter finished settling her baby in the wagon and came back to the fire, smoothing back her shining dark hair. Orfeo directed a particularly ribald verse in her direction, wriggling suggestively, and she responded with a languishing flutter of her eyelashes before sitting down beside her husband. For a moment her smouldering gaze rested on Farin, and he looked quickly away. Duncan's face was redder than could be accounted for by the heat of the fire, and Farin wondered whether the girl really was the mistress of the man who played her lover on stage, or whether she simply enjoyed upsetting her husband.

Ajili, who had been speaking swiftly to Jorge in Spanyol, leaned over suddenly and cuffed Farin on the shoulder. "You so silent, boy—you hurting for some girl you left in Los Leones? Come on, drink and sing! There's plenty more in Westria, and their menfolk don't care what they do!" He showed stained teeth in a grin and held out a skin of wine.

Farin's arm shot out in automatic outrage, sending the wineskin flying. Jorge caught it and clutched it to his chest, muttering.

"Hey, man, that's no way to treat nice wine. . . ." The dark man was still more surprised than angry. "You cheer up now!"

Farin glared at him, breathing hard, not trusting himself to speak.

"Ho, Ajili—you've poor taste in drinking companions!" Duncan was laughing, his face even redder in the light of the fire. "Don't you know the lad is Westrian? Maybe he'll introduce you to his sister when he gets home!"

Farin saw only the actor now. He was no longer cold, and fury shocked through him, burning all the pain away. With a moan that was at once anguish and release he threw

himself at the other man, reaching for the fleshy creases of
his throat.

A blow glanced from his shoulder, but he had the man's
tunic. Someone's hand pulled him backward and cloth
tore. He whirled, swinging wildly at a shape that bore the
faces of all the Elayans he had ever faced in war, felt his
first shock against bone. He scrabbled for balance, fighting for breath as something struck his ribs, struggling to
focus on the face of his enemy. He struck out again.

A sharp slap rocked him, sent fire raging from his cheek
to sear his brain; a loud voice buffeted his ears. He stood
swaying, trying to clear his head to see. Then the noise
faded. Someone shook him until he focused on the broad
face of Maestra Luisa.

"Young man, you are more trouble than that mule! Yes,
I heard what Duncan said to you, but you have been
carrying a bigger load than any beast in our string. You set
it down now, eh *hijo*? There's grief enough on the road
without fighting your fellows!" She gave Farin a final
shake and let him go.

Farin took a deep, shuddering breath. Maestra Luisa
glared at the other man, who was grinning now.

"Duncan, that's enough—you leave him alone." She
turned back to Farin. "And you too, you keep yourself
reined in. You give me some Westrian oath you won't
fight again!"

Farin stared at her, then back at the bully, who still
wore the same insulting grin. Icy anger was hardening his
rage. All the faces turned on him were alien now. What
peace could he make with these?

"I'll hold my hand if he holds his tongue, but I'll not
swear to you!"

"You try my patience, hijo!" Maestra Luisa scowled.
"You give me your oath or you lose your job—we can get
on without what help you've been!"

Farin straightened. The tone, the words, echoed back and
forth among all the indignities he had suffered in Palomon's
prison. He shook his head.

"Lad—I am ordering you!"

"No, not anymore! I'll go now if a slave is what you

want me to be!'' Other words clamored in Farin's imagination, but he was not sure he could trust his voice. Pain washed through him dizzyingly. Silently he gathered up his packroll and slung the harpcase over his shoulder, trying to move as if he had not been hurt. Clinging desperately to his hard-won dignity, he stalked away from the fire.

"I guess Westrians *are* crazy,'' said Orfeo. "These hills are no place for a man alone!''

"Well, Duncan, you'll have to herd that mule yourself, now!'' said the girl.

The night became hideous with their laughter, and Farin quickened his pace, stumbling on loose stones as his eyes adjusted to the darkness. He did not pause until he could hear no sound but the sighing of the wind.

A stone gave way and Farin lurched, clutching at the slipping harpcase, and fell heavily to his knees on the stones.

As his heartbeat slowed he became aware of the voices of the night. In his first anger he had deliberately turned away from the road, not wanting the players to overtake him in the morning. Now there were no sounds of man to irritate him, only the rattle of branches shaken by the wind, the sighing of wind in the brush, the moan of wind prowling about the snow-dappled peaks that glimmered in the moonlight.

Farin sighed and settled back on his haunches, rubbing his bruised knees. His flight had used up his last reserves of strength, and he was trembling with strain. *They were right, I am crazy,* he thought. *I have come alone and afoot into this wilderness. I will die here, and the legend of the lost harper can join that of the lost Queen of Westria.*

It was desperately cold, and the whispering of the wind plucked at his nerves; but his legs would not obey him anymore. For a time he simply sat still, listening to the wind. Then, in a pause between one gust and another, he heard a faint gurgling that made him suddenly conscious of how dry his mouth had become. He licked his lips and began to crawl toward the sound.

The water was seeping from a crack in the rock. It

glistened in the moonlight as it dripped into the tiny pool below. Farin drank thirstily, feeling the wind chill his cheeks as it dried them. The rocks were a partial shelter from the wind; beyond them the ground fell away in a scrap of meadow and then rose again in battlements of stone. He was alone on the roof of the world.

Even if his body could have carried him farther, this was the best shelter he was likely to find. Dry branches had crackled under his hands when he fell. He bent to gather enough together to make a fire. It took all his concentration to strike a spark from his flint and steel, but presently light flickered to life beneath his fingers. He pulled open his bedroll and huddled into it.

And as he lay back, he heard a coughing that was not the wind. He stiffened as it came again, extending into something between a yawn and a roar. He had heard that sound in El Castillo, looking down into the fenced plain where the lions that were the totem of the Princes of Elaya were kept. None of those great golden creatures roamed these hills, but he had heard that before the Princes claimed them, some had wandered into the wilderness and bred with the native cats to produce a creature that was stronger and wilier than either ancestor. Then the wind shifted and there was silence again.

Farin ate a little of the hard bread from his pack, wondering how he would get more food when this was gone. He had only his knife, and he was not good at throwing it. Perhaps if he got really hungry he could fashion snares from his harpstrings.

I would have to be desperate, he thought, shuddering. And picturing the ravaged harp, he remembered how he had fallen, and his vision altered to show a cracked or shattered frame. In terror he fumbled with the fastenings of the harpcase.

The harp was still whole. Reverently Farin passed his hands across its smooth surface, like a man with a virgin bride. His fingertips traced the golden interlace inlaid on the sound box. In the moonlight the strings glistened silver. How long would it be before he could enjoy playing it again?

It was not your fault . . . he thought as an accidental touch brought an answering shimmer of sound from the strings. *You were the Elayan's captive too.*

His arms ached for the weight of the harp, but he could think of no tune that had not been tainted by Palomon's sardonic smile. Then he heard a deep grumbling, as loud as if it were only a few paces away. Without thinking, Farin pulled the harp from its case and into the protection of his lap.

Had he really heard a lion, or was it a fancy of his fear? The skin of his arms tingled with tension, but he could neither fight nor flee. He had no weapons, and the energy that might have saved him had been expended in a foolish quarrel. His body still twitched with exhaustion, and he knew he could not run away.

Then the lion spoke again, and Farin saw a new shadow beyond the circle of firelight.

If he pulled out his knife he might at least mark the creature before it tore his life away. Fear twisted his gut as the shadow moved. He caught the gleam of eyes. Then he realized that his stiff fingers were poised over the harpstrings.

It is well . . . he thought with a moment's clarity. *This is what I am, and this is how I should end.*

The shadow neared, flowing from stone to stone. Farin forced his fingers to curve, to pluck, and into the night's breathing stillness fell a single, humming note. The cat-shadow paused.

O my brother! O my enemy! Farin's fingers moved in sequence, drawing from the harp a new song like the purring of a great cat, and its majestic prowl, and then the antics of kittens at play. He launched himself into the music, using his concentration to fight his fear.

And as he continued, his cold fingers, trained by over a month in Prince Palomon's service, grew warm with exercise, and his extremity shattered the barrier that had shut away his inner music. And the music became a flood that drowned his fear.

Life is pattern, and harmony, and beauty, and I am alive! he thought. The music affirmed it, and the rocks that curved around him amplified the sound. Exulting in the music, he looked up and saw not one but two lions stretched at the edge of the firelight. For a moment the music faltered, then the melody caught him up again and he stared unafraid into the unwinking golden eyes.

Brother! Sister! he thought exultantly. *We are all part of the same harmony!* He bent to the harp. When he looked up again, the two lions were gone.

But still he continued to play, letting the flow of the music carry him to a realm where the thinking mind did not follow. His fingers moved without his will, and the music was both his pathway and his goal.

Images moved through his mind as effortless and changeable as clouds. He saw Caolin's anguished face and Faris's glowing eyes . . . he saw snowy mountains and a dusty road . . .

Caolin thought she was in the east, he remembered. *It is in the Ramparts and the Barren Lands beyond them that I should search for her. . . .*

His thought quested after her and found instead a star-filled sky and a figure robed in light that he pursued until he knew no more.

When Farin came to himself again it was morning. He was curled next to the ashes of his little fire with his fingers still laying across the cold strings of his harp.

Gingerly he moved and found that although his muscles were painfully stiff and he was chilled through, the paralyzing exhaustion of the night before had gone. He was filled by a curious, unfocused joy, but he could not remember what he had dreamed, only that there had been something, or Someone, who had comforted him. But he remembered also his vision of Faris, and it seemed to him obvious now that his next task was to search north and eastward for her. But he would need a way to travel.

Like an echo, a conversation that his self-indulgent anger had kept from consciousness came back to him— *"When we've played the river towns we'll be moving into the mountains—lots of hamlets and holdings there with no entertainment but their own. We should do very well!"*

The territory Los Pajaritos planned to cover was just where Farin wanted to go!

He stumbled over to the little pool to drink. Beyond the lip of the hollow the slope fell steeply to the curve of the road. Farin shook his head and smiled ruefully—his flight had not taken him very far after all! He packed up the harp and, using a fallen branch for a walking stick, began to pick his way down the mountainside.

The road shone below him in the morning sunlight, and a hawk was soaring above the blue ranges. Music stirred in Farin's memory—not the splendid melodies of the night before, but something simpler and more structured—the walking song that had come to him when he left Westria. Now more words were forming, and softly he began to sing:

> *"I have the sun to light my way,*
> *The clear spring water is my mead.*
> *The hills provide me food each day*
> *And while they give me what I need*
> *Why need I cease from wandering?"*

When the brightly painted wagon and the recalcitrant mules of Los Pajaritos creaked and rattled around the bend in the road at last, they found Farin waiting for them by the roadside, playing a music that seemed to make the sun shine more brightly, and smiling.

⋙ 2 ⋘

The Exile

First Interlude

The harpstrings buzz as the harper plucks them, scarcely audible over the babble of conversation in the tavern. The harper continues to play without caring if anyone is listening. He sits on a crimson cushion on a kind of gilded balcony, and he knows that he is there as much to flatter the vanity of the tavern's owner, La Carmina, as to actually be heard.

He strikes the strings again, imitating the harsh jangle of the gitarra. A new melody emerges—a piece from Aztlan that he learned at Palomon's court. The song that goes with that melody is a legend of the Ancient days that tells how the great conqueror, Cortes, refused to stay buried in his tomb. The harper plays fiercely, flicking a sharping lever without missing a beat to strike the great minor chords. Men pause in their conversations to listen, sensing the unvoiced passion in the song.

And the harper smiles bitterly, knowing that he is the real ghost, wandering restlessly across the land. For five years he has haunted the mountains that border Westria, first with Los Pajaritos, and then alone, earning his way by labor in field or forest or by Swangold's sweet song.

And the fruitless years have grizzled his head like a wolf's pelt, until men to whom he will not give his name laugh and call him Silverhair. He tries to find the song that will comfort him or at least let him sing out his longing, but there is no music, there are no words—it is as if his love for his sister and his need for music have become the same, and with his quest frustrated, the springs of song within him have been damned as well.

"You'll be at the market tomorrow?" a florid, heavyset man with a gold earring asks his companion, ignoring the musician above him. He does not need to specify that it is the slave-market he means. Arena is the city where anything may be bought or sold, including the lives of men.

"Need you ask?" the other giggles. "With a shipment just in from Elaya? That new man the Prince has put in charge of internal security is most efficient—those who displease the Prince are arrested, along with their families. Executions would provoke an outcry, but these people simply . . . disappear."

Their laughter makes an obscene harmony, and the harper's fingers fumble on the strings. Caolin! He has been hearing of him more and more often, and always with that shiver of fear. But Caolin knows nothing of Faris, he is sure of it, and there is no reason why they should ever meet again. Only when he thinks of Caolin he feels cold, as the thought of the slave-market makes him flush with rage. If only he could be sure that when Faris fled from Caolin she was not taken and sold! It is why he still haunts these tawdry streets, hoping to pick up some clue, to hear some chance word.

He grits his teeth and forces his fingers to keep moving, to modulate from the Cortes ballad into a sentimental lovesong that he can play without thinking, like one of the Ancients' machines. La Carmina moves through the crowd like a brightly plumaged bird, chirping empty witticisms whose humor never reaches her eyes. For a time her beauty held the harper enslaved as surely as one of the merchants' pens—that is past now, but he does not dare let her know that he has come to his senses. La Carmina thinks he suffers because she has taken a merchant's soft-

skinned son to her bed. He smiles when she approaches him and tries to hide his relief when she passes by.

Two of Arena's more solid citizens have claimed the table below his perch. They call for wine.

"You say the caravan from Radiston has already gone?" asks the dark man. His companion nods and pours out the wine. The harper can smell it and licks dry lips. He is learning to value the oblivion that liquor can bring.

"Damn!" the dark man goes on, "I was hoping to deal for buffalo hides from the Sea of Grass. Why were they in such a hurry?"

"Don't know—" says the other, drinking again. "Didn't seem like they was really interested in trading at all. They had a woman prisoner, or maybe she was the keeper for the child—pretty, from what I could see, with black hair. But they threw me out when I asked if they'd set a price on her—nervous as a coyote with a snootful of porcupine quills, they were, and damned if they'll get any more of my trade!"

A harpstring snaps beneath an incautious finger, jangling across its mates and slashing the harper's hand. He does not feel it. He is staring at the merchant whose words have set the strings of memory resonating more loudly than he could play. A female captive with a child—a woman with black hair! A melody he has almost forgotten begins to sing in his memory.

"Which way did the caravan go?" He leans down suddenly, knocking over the flagon of wine.

The merchant looks startled. "Eastward, over the pass—" he begins; then he sees the dripping wine and begins to swear.

"Here—buy more—" The harper flings a silver coin on the table and slides down from his perch. "You say they left this morning? With the woman and the child?"

The man nods. For a moment the harper stands still while the blood from his wounded hand mingles with the spilled wine on the floor. Then he picks up the harp and strides swiftly from the room.

➤➤➤ SIX ❮❮❮

At the top of the pass the horses paused, heads low, flanks heaving in the thin air. Farin, who had been leading his dun as well as the spotted pack mare, let them be. In the past five years he had learned enough about horses to let them choose their own pace, though he twitched with impatience even now, when he needed a breather as much as they did.

He straightened, shifted his sword back into position at his side, and settled the harpcase more securely on his back. Behind him the road twisted down into the basin that held Arena, city of taverns and slave-markets, and beyond it the jagged ridges of the Ramparts that guarded the way back to Elaya.

He drew a worn woolen sleeve across his face, but his eyes did not leave the broken lands before him. He saw horse droppings and a discarded piece of harness on the road. Surely he had gained on the caravan already. With loaded wagons they would have to go carefully now. He realized that his pulse had quickened, and his weather-tanned face creased in an unaccustomed smile. It would not be long now. . . . Soon he would know if the caravan's prisoners were Faris and her child.

The dun horse snorted softly and nuzzled his arm. Farin turned and slid his hand down the sweat-slick neck. "Are you rested then, old boy? Well, so am I, and it will be all downhill from here. . . ." He gathered up the reins and swung easily into the saddle. The spotted mare stamped and shook her head, but he only laughed and tugged to test the leadrope before turning to the trail again. Delicately the two horses began to pick their way down the slope.

Three days on the trail brought the traveler out of the hills and into a land that springtime seemed to have passed by. But that did not concern Farin—each day brought fresh proof that he was gaining on the caravan. And when at the end of the third day he glimpsed ahead of him a haze of dust that glowed in the light of the westering sun, it was hard to keep from pressing on through the night. But he had pushed the horses hard, and he might need their strength to get Faris and the child away.

Farin slept badly and woke before the sun. In the grey predawn he followed a fresh trail, but it was not until the sun was high that he saw any sign—something darker than dust that rose in a thin column into the still air. He swore and urged the horses onward, knowing it was smoke even before he smelled it. Carrion birds speckled the stained sky.

Then he went slowly, and when he could hear the birds' harsh cries, he tethered the horses and continued on foot, although he already suspected that no one would bar his way.

The charred timbers of the carts smouldered in the road. Farin hesitated, watching the dark wisps wreathe skyward. For a week he had trailed this caravan. Now he had found it, and he was afraid.

Birds cawed resentfully and hopped aside as he approached each still form, peered into its face, and from some instinct of apology straightened the sprawled limbs. Brown-feathered arrows jutted from the backs of the bodies, except for a few who had managed to face their foes. Two horses lay dead in their traces. The others, naturally, were gone.

Farin counted the bodies—five, six, seven, clothed in the embroidered leather the barbarians wear. His face was expressionless beneath the fall of silvershot hair, but his mind tensed against the tug of fear. He cursed himself for giving way to strained nerves—he had seen such sights before—and turned to the next corpse.

He saw long black hair streaming from beneath a black-

ened wagon bed, and a slim, stiffly curled hand. He stood
a moment, heart pounding heavily, then lifted the planks
away. After a moment the boards, dropping from suddenly
nerveless fingers, thudded to the earth and bounced a little
before lying still. Farin gave a long sigh.

"Poor lady, whoever you may be, I am sorry for your
fate . . ." he said softly, "but by the Maker of All Things,
I am not sorry to see your face!"

It was not Faris! His heart sang. Then his newly eased
mind vibrated to an imperious call. He had taken an
automatic step forward before he could stiffen against it.
Softly he drew his sword.

There was no movement from the looted wagons, only a
little vagrant breeze that swirled the dust and blew Farin's
hair forward across his face. But the pressure on his mind
was a better guide. He slackened his defenses, just a little,
as a fisherman slacks his line, and stepped carefully
toward that strange call.

It led him away from the wagons. There was a clump of
brush; he glimpsed something blue. Farin moved around
the bushes and looked down.

It was a child. Not the one he sought—a girl child this,
perhaps ten years of age. Her blue leather tunic was smeared
with dust, but he saw no blood. As if she felt his glance she
whimpered and moved restlessly. He knelt beside her,
stroking back her matted hair.

"Be still, child. Your enemies are gone. . . ."

Abruptly the mental contact ended. The child frowned
slightly, as if in sleep, then her lids quivered, and large
grey eyes, curiously pale, stared dispassionately into his.

"Water . . ." she said thickly. Her eyes closed again.

Farin raised her and set his waterskin to her lips, wondering what he was going to do with her. She drank
eagerly, without opening her eyes. After a little he laid her
down in the shade of the bushes. Then he went back to get
the horses and tethered them nearby. They fell to nosing at
the sparse grasses, only tossing their heads nervously when
the shifting wind brought them the carrion smell.

The girl still slept, so Farin turned to the wagons and
methodically stacked what wood remained to make a pyre.

One by one he dragged the bodies away from the protesting birds. It was as good a way as any of putting off thinking about what to do next. His last clue had unraveled here in the dust. Where in the world should he turn to seek Faris now? The sun was reaching for the tops of the western mountains by the time his task neared an end.

"What are you doing?"

Farin whirled. The child stood nearby, rubbing sleep from her eyes and curling her toes in the warm dust. He grimaced, knowing he should have been aware when she awakened. This was not a land that forgave inattention.

"The dead are too many and the ground too hard for me to bury them," he answered finally. "I have been told your people believe dead men's ghosts will walk if the beasts of prey scatter their bones. In Westria, when we cannot lay men in clean earth, we send them homeward by our Lady Fire."

The girl shrugged. "Do as you please. They are no kin to me."

"No? You traveled with them. You wear their clothes. . . ."

"They stole me from my home!" The girl spat toward the pyre.

Farin looked at her a moment, then lifted the last of the bodies into place. He had already collected a pile of tumbleweeds. Now he thrust them into the spaces between the planks. The girl squatted in the dust, watching.

"Can you ride?" he asked at last. "I would put some miles between us and such a beacon as this will be." Whatever he decided to do, he could not leave the child here.

She nodded. "If you give me more water. I have no reason to stay." She spoke stiffly, as if she had forgotten how.

Farin went back to the horses and got his waterskin. The desert seemed very still. The girl sipped at the water like a bird. He sighed, then went back to the pyre and took out his flint and steel.

"*Into Thy hands, Great Mother, we surrender . . .*" his voice soared suddenly in the funeral hymn. Tinder caught,

and little yellow flames flickered through the brushwood,
tasted the already charred timbers, reddened, and began to
grow. The wood was very dry and the heat already oppres-
sive by the time he finished singing.

Farin stepped back and motioned to the girl. Without
speaking, he untied the horses and swung her into the
saddle before him. The dun danced a little, seeing the fire.
Farin reined him down and looked over his shoulder at the
pyre.

Sunset had veiled the mountains in mauve and blue.
Above them the memory of daylight was fading from the
sky. The pyre was roaring now, as if the sun had decided to
set there on the desert instead of behind the hills. Then the
wind shifted and Farin smelled roasting flesh and glimpsed
the shape of charring limbs against the fire. His heels dug
into the horse's flanks and they moved quickly away.

The brown desert mellowed around them as they went
on. Several hours later, when the features of the land
showed only as dark shapes under a sky brocaded with
stars, he brought the horses to a halt in the lee of a dry
wash.

The girl had made no complaint, but she staggered as he
put her down, and she stood very still until he had heaped
folded saddlecloths into a seat for her. With quick, sure
movements Farin built a tiny fire and poured cornmeal,
dried meat, and water into his copper pan. *I'll have to take
the child back to her own people, or at least leave her
some place where they can come* . . . he thought sourly,
glancing at the pale face on the other side of the fire.

"We should use no more water than this," he said
aloud. "The horses can go dry for a night, but tomorrow
we will have to find a spring. We will also have to choose
a direction. Do you know where your home lies?"

"Willasfell . . . ." She closed her eyes for a moment. "It
is north, north and a little east from here. I do not know
how far, but I will know when we draw near."

Farin frowned, adjusting the pan on the fire. He had
heard of Willasfell, perhaps in some old song. He could
not remember where, or what the song had said. There
was only a sense of richness, age, and something disquiet-

ingly strange. Defenses—that was it—legend held that Willasfell was defended by some unknown power.

"We shall have to try and find it." He wondered if he was being a fool. But one direction was as good as another to him now. And perhaps—if there was some Power in Willasfell, perhaps It could tell him where to seek Faris and her child.

"We will find water, too," the girl said calmly, "a little north of here below a hill. Give me your waterskin again."

Her certainty shook him and Farin found himself handing it over while still seeking words to deny it. He watched her as she drank.

"What is your name?" She lowered the skin at last and looked at him.

"My name?" He felt his face stiffening. Once he had been Farin of Hawkrest Hold, and then Farin Harper, knight of Westria, but it seemed to him that the boy who had borne that name was as dead as if his bones lay in the Dragon Waste. He pushed back the white lock that fell over his brow.

"You can call me Silverhair." Fumbling a little, he dug in his pack for the spoon and took the copper pan off the fire. "Wait a moment till it cools—" he said quickly. "You have told me where you are from, but not who you are—" he added then.

"I am the Wi . . ." her quick reply faded.

"Thea?" he repeated. She gave him a sidelong look, nodding.

Farin doubted that was the whole truth, but if he was going to hide behind the name of Silverhair he could hardly require more frankness from her.

They ate. Farin, who was now Silverhair, rearranged the saddlecloths to make her a bed, and rolled up in his cloak on the other side of the fire. Soon Thea's regular breathing told him that she slept. But Farin lay wakeful for some time, staring up at the wise and distant stars.

A week's travel had brought them into a long valley between two lines of ochre hills. Farin Silverhair stood in

his stirrups and peered ahead. There, where a fold of the
hills extended into the plain, he thought he had glimpsed a
flash of green.

"What do you see?" Thea brought the spotted mare
alongside the dun.

"A settlement, I hope. We need supplies."

"We don't need water. . . ."

He did not reply. They had found plenty of water on
their way, but after a week of Thea's company, Silverhair
wanted to see another human face and taste water he did
not owe to her prophecies.

He could see buildings now, an eyeless square with a
courtyard inside. Earlier they had passed ruins—the work
of the Ancients lasted well in this dry and lonely land
where no one needed to mine them for building materi-
als. But here irrigated fields glowed garishly against the
dull hills. The dun horse stumbled on wheelruts, and
Silverhair turned him toward the settlement.

The clamor of a gong split the air as they approached.
Silverhair smiled. Dogs were barking and a figure appeared suddenly in the gateway, spear poised. The harper
held up his arm in sign of peace.

Soon they were inside, surrounded by people who seemed
to spring from the walls. There was a curious similarity in
the faces turned up to his. Inbreeding, probably, he thought,
though they seemed healthy. He sent a swift glance toward
the girl at his side, wondering if that explained her features. There was something too pronounced about the size
of her eyes, her broad pale brow and pointed chin, her
narrow, thin-fingered hands. But Willasfell was a city—
surely there would be no problem there. Not for the first
time, he wondered about Thea's family.

Inside the courtyard he dismounted, trying to hold his
horse still. The dun shied as a small boy ducked beneath
his belly and seized Silverhair's arm, bombarding him
with questions.

"Hold, lad—I cannot answer everything at once!"
Silverhair said, laughing. "I am called Silverhair, I'm
from the west, and this is Thea whose people were am-
bushed on the road. I'm taking her to her home. We need

food and yes . . . yes, that thing on my back is a harp—"
He got no further. The boy's screech of delight set the
horses to plunging once more.

"A harper! Mama, come see!"

"Tod—be you still and give these people time to
breathe!"

The boy fell silent at last and the commotion quieted as
a big woman in a deerskin skirt and a red woolen blouse
came out. Close up, Silverhair could see the whorls of
tattooing that decorated her cheeks and brow.

"I am Marda, the Mother here. If you come in peace,
you are welcome."

"Lady, it is in peace that I come. May the blessing of
all kindly powers be on you and on this place." Silverhair
bowed.

"It is your presence that will bless us, harper. It has
been long since we had music here." She smiled.

In a few moments their horses were being led away.
People bustled around them, and Thea clutched at Silverhair's arm. "I like it here—" she whispered excitedly.
Silverhair smiled a little, surprised that the place should
make such an impression on a town-born child.

Marda's people killed a sheep and roasted it in a trench
in the courtyard. The fresh meat was good after so many
days of gruel, and the beer excellent. They even managed
to wait until after Silverhair had eaten before they begged
him to play for them.

There was a respectful silence as he undid the clasps of
the harpcase. The golden interlace inlaid in its honey-
colored wood glittered in the firelight. The disguising
black paint had worn off long ago, and he had not troubled
to replace it. He pulled the instrument clear of the bag and
settled it on his knee.

"This is Swangold . . ." His fingers lingered for a
moment on the neck of the golden swan whose breast and
wings capped the headpiece of the harp. He took the
tuning key from its bag and began to test the bronze
strings, adjusting them delicately until he was satisfied.

And then he played for them.

First he chose dance music to set feet tapping, and lifted

the listeners from their seats until half the settlement was skipping in the patterns of dances old before the Cataclysm came.

Thea had risen too, but she did not know the dance. She begged the boy Tod to teach her, but he clung to his place at Silverhair's feet. Thea sat down again, her face closed and pale, but her eyes were glittering.

When everyone was tired of dancing, Silverhair's skilled fingers drew forth a series of minor harmonies that brought them close around the fire. He began to sing then, the old lay of Bryn Blackbrow, whose mother was carried off from Westria and bore him to her barbarian captor before she died. It was not a song they sang much in Westria, for it told how, when the boy was grown and his forehead shadowed with the tattooing of his father's clan, he went back to Westria to kill his mother's kin who had not ransomed her, and thereafter made a terror of the eastern road.

They enjoyed it, as he had expected, but he had scarcely finished before Tod crept moaning to his mother's arms, shielding his eyes and complaining of a demon boring at his brain. Marda held him close, frowning, but Silverhair glanced suddenly at Thea, remembering that mental stab by which he had found her.

She was sitting still, her eyes serene, her lips upturned in a little smile. He eased over to her side.

"Let him go, Thea—stop it right now!" he hissed. She looked at him wide-eyed and he gripped her arm. "Let the boy be or I'll take you into the desert and leave you there!"

She pouted, then relaxed. "He deserved it—he would not dance with me."

On the other side of the fire, the boy gave a long sigh. "It's gone!"

"I'll warrant he sneaked some of your beer, Marda," said one of the men.

"If so, I think he'll not do that again, will you, my love?" Marda gave her son a hug. But Tod did not reply, and though he did not complain again, he sat pale and quiet until someone carried him off to bed.

The harper played on, giving them songs of sadness and songs of joy, while the fire burned down and the stars wheeled toward dawn. He played until one by one his listeners lay down to sleep where they were or slipped away.

After a time he found himself the only one still sitting there. He eased the harp back into its case, shouldered it, and got to his feet, wondering what to do now. Someone had cast a blanket over Thea, who lay stretched beside the fire. Then he felt a hand on his arm and, turning, found the woman Marda close beside him.

"I have a bed for you—" she said softly. "Come with me. . . ."

Silverhair took a deep breath. He had lain alone for a long time, and he felt her nearness as he had felt the heat of the fire. She moved toward the house, and he followed her. A little wind played in the courtyard, swirling the dust and fanning the coals to a new glow. The two figures disappeared through the door.

Over the courtyard the air grew warmer and rose, pulling cold air down from the draw behind the settlement. More air warmed, more quickly, and soon the fire was leaping and a cold wind came moaning down from the hills. Doors rattled and dust blew through open windows. Sleepers turned restlessly and sat up, rubbing dirt from their eyes.

A sudden gust bellied round the courtyard, drawing a shower of sparks from the fire. Outside there was a crack as wood hit the ground, and then a clatter of hooves.

"Dust storm!" someone muttered, and then, "Damn all wind demons, the horses are loose!"

Now people were up and running everywhere. Thea sat up. Down came the wind and sparks sprayed upward, lighting on the wooden porch.

"Fire!" she shouted shrilly.

Someone saw the sparks, ran to the porch, and tried to stamp at them.

"The roof!" came another cry. "In heaven's name put out that fire before more sparks get away!"

The girl retreated to a corner of the yard.

Then Marda's calm voice cut through the confusion and she came out of the house, tying the thongs of her skirt. Firelight glinted bronze on her full bare breasts. Silverhair stumbled through the door close behind her, his tunic awry, but his harp slung securely. His eyes searched the crowd, found Thea.

"You're all right? Good—keep out of the way. I must see what I can do to help."

The girl sat down again in her corner, watching him, and smiled.

❧ SEVEN ❧

Silverhair rode out the next morning in bad-tempered silence. Marda had been generous, and the horses were fully laden, but there had been some strange looks as he and Thea prepared to go.

The country into which they were moving now was even more desolate than the desert to the south. But Thea seemed to be in good humor, and she whistled soundlessly through her teeth as they rode. The days passed. Each night Thea pressed Silverhair to play his harp and he found himself obeying her; and in his music he found comfort and forgetfulness of the mysteries of the present and the sorrows of the past.

"You are free," she said softly one evening when the moon pooled silver light in every hollow in the sand. "You can go anywhere, like a bird."

He stared at her, for the first time in days remembering a time when he had thought of himself as Farin, not Silverhair. Free? He was not free to go home again. . . . She cocked her head to one side and looked at him, reminding him painfully of his sister Berisa's eldest girl.

"You don't understand," he said bitterly. "I did not choose—"

"Did you not?" She shook her head. "Then you are a fool. Who would stay behind walls when he could fly free?"

"There is a freedom in a settled life too—" Silverhair fought against memories of a white road shining in the sun, the first sight of a new mountain peak sharp against the sky, the first notes of a new song that no one in Westria knew, and his words faded. Could he deny those moments that sometimes seemed to outweigh all the pain? "And comfort," he added lamely. "I have heard that Willasfell is a fine town."

"Willasfell rules the trade route. . . ." There was an edge to her voice that he did not understand. "They sell all kinds of pretty things in the marketplace. They gave me a bird once, all red and green with a big yellow bill, they said had come from a land far to the south of Aztlan. But it did not sing."

"Your family is rich then," he began. "Is your father a merchant? They'll be glad to have you home!"

Her laughter interrupted him. "Oh, they will be very happy." She laughed again, and he shivered at the sound, but she would say no more.

Thea curled up in her blankets after that, and soon he heard her regular breathing, but Silverhair lay wakeful for a long time, wondering. How did Thea always know where water could be found? Why did the windstorms they saw in the distance never come close enough to trouble them? And how had the girl gained the power to touch men's minds with or without their will?

In Westria, trained adepts had these powers and more, but it was unnerving to find such abilities in a child. And even though Silverhair had Thea's promise to play no more tricks, he avoided even the few settlements they passed. Upon reflection, it occurred to him that Tod might have accused Thea, and he had no desire to be burned as a witch at her side.

But he could not prevent other humans from seeking *them*, and for some of those who lived in this wasteland their gear and horses would be a rich prize. As the country grew wilder he took more precautions, camping where there was cover and putting out their little fire as soon as they had cooked their evening meal.

Yet he was not surprised one night when Thea woke him in the still, chill hour before dawn. Listening, he heard stealthy movements in the brush. There must be quite a few of them, he thought, or he would not have been able to hear them at all. They would have spears, and possibly knives, and a good supply of the brown-feathered arrows he had seen jutting from the bodies in the looted caravan.

"Who are they?" whispered Thea.

"Nomads who live off the land," he whispered back. "And at the moment, the land includes us. They are afraid of spirits in the night. Unless we try to get away they will not attack until dawn. But this is not a good place for fighting, and I have only my sword. When they do come at us, you must get to that big rock and hide. I will distract them while you get away, and even if they win perhaps they will not find you. Go back and lie down now. . . ."

She crawled back to her bedroll and Silverhair sighed in exasperation. *Even if they win!* he thought. If he made a target of himself for the girl's sake he did not see how they could avoid winning. It would be a good fight, he supposed, and he had heard that these people knew how to appreciate a death song. He would not think about the failure of his quest.

He was cold. He rolled onto his side and stared eastward. Was there a pallor behind the hills? Stealthily he threw off the folds of his cloak and reached for his sword, then stiffened as something moved a few feet away. Already? He peered into darkness and his fingers closed on the cold hilt of his sword.

Thea . . . The girl was bent over, scraping at the ground. Silverhair felt something dust his cheek. She threw again, and in the faint foreshadowing of dawn he saw a cloud. From somewhere there came a faint whistling. Thea?

There were movements around them now. Silverhair tensed, gripping his sword. Why didn't the girl run? As he rose, he glimpsed a swirling in the air, shadow within shadow, a formless something whose shape was neither that of man nor animal, flickering in and out of focus. It was his imagination. It *must* be his imagination!

Then Thea sat back on her heels and laughed, and the thing that Silverhair knew was not there was driven into the brush by a sudden gust of wind. The high thin whistling he had heard was drowned out by screams.

By the time the first thin sliver of sun appeared above

the eastern horizon it was over. Tracks and fallen weapons showed where their enemies had waited, but there was no sign of any foe. Silverhair hoped that in their terror they had simply run away. The sky was pale and clear, but a cloud of dust was moving far down the plain. He stood and watched it until he could see no more.

Silverhair asked no questions as they prepared to move on. But as they rode, the harper began to search his memory for the details of that forgotten song about Willasfell.

After the second week of travel they left the rough hills behind them and entered a wider land. Thea peered at each new formation, but Silverhair did not ask what she was looking for, and he said nothing about the wind that whistled nightly about their camp.

Once they saw horsemen, black specks against the pale sweep of sand, and Silverhair felt upon his cheek the pressure of a rising wind. He looked quickly at Thea. Her eyes were glittering, and as she met his gaze she giggled softly. Ahead of them white dust stirred.

"Thea—stop—we don't know if they are friends or foes!"

"They outnumber us, and I don't want them to see me. Besides, what does it matter? I am the—" She corrected herself, "I can do what I want!" Her voice trembled. "You do not know what I can do. . . ."

Silverhair swallowed, feeling like the man who tried to make a pet of the whirlwind, and used the only hold he seemed to have upon her. "Perhaps not, but I know what *I* can do, and that is to leave you here!"

She gave him a quick glance, found her eyes held. "I don't want to meet them," she said in a low voice.

"There are simpler ways to keep that from happening—" Silverhair led them down a dry watercourse which hid them from view. But he looked over his shoulder as he did so and saw the dust cloud waver and dwindle to a tiny dust-devil that whirled in place for a few moments, then faded away. Involuntarily he shivered, though the sweat was rolling down his face.

After that their journey was even more silent than before. But at last a day came when they camped on a rise from which they could see a narrow glitter of water. Beyond it, some miles eastward where low bluffs extended out into the broad valley, he saw a cluster of walls white as heaped bones.

"Is that Willasfell?" Silverhair looked at Thea. Pale eyes fell before his. "You knew where it would be . . ." he stated. "Don't you think it's time you told me how? And who your family is?"

Her eyes sought the distant city before turning to his face again. "You will not leave me?"

He shook his head. "Start by telling me your full name."

"You did not tell me yours, though I could divine it if I wanted to." There was an edge of malice to her smile. "But I can't tell you mine. I don't have one. . . . I am the Willa, you see, and that is why I knew where Willa's Fell lay!"

Buried memories stirred—a night when the wind had howled round the walls of Laurelynn while the Master of the College of Bards played for the King and sang—

> "A single road leads through the sands
> That blow across the Barren Lands;
> And there a city stands alone
> With walls as white as polished bone . . ."

Softly Silverhair quoted the words, staring at the city beyond the cottonwoods. Now the rest of the song was coming to him.

> "Men say its evil custom is
> That none who passes that way lives
> Unless he pays its guardians well
> To let him go from Willasfell.
> And if a traveler on that way
> Conspires to pass and will not pay,
> The priests go chanting to their keep
> And sing their demoness from sleep,
> Whose whisper can pluck stone from stone,

And skin from flesh, and flesh from bone,
And raise the very winds of Hell
To seek the foes of Willasfell."

He remembered the wind that had driven away the nomads who attacked them, or had it done something more terrible? His gaze moved from the city to the Willa, and watching her still face, he continued to sing.

"Some hail her Spirit of the Air,
And death desired is not more fair
Than she; but some call them beguiled
And say she is a whistling child
Who sees all secrets by her arts,
And whispers evil in men's hearts.
But none the truth of that can tell
Save he who comes from Willasfell . . ."

Silverhair's voice cracked. In the fading light the Willa's face was growing dim, but it seemed to him she smiled, sweetly, maliciously, like a child who pulls on the end of a tablecloth to see if the dishes will fall. And as if the smile had laid a compulsion upon him, his hoarse chant continued:

"He who has seen the Willa knows
Both why and where the deathwind blows;
Speak him no greeting, let him pass,
And if wind hisses in the grass
Behind him, rush to bar your door
And swear to take the road no more.
But if you must, remember well—
Take not the road to Willasfell!"

But he *had* taken that road, in the company of this demon in the form of a child. And yet she *was* only a child, and she had been a captive.

"How could anyone have carried you off? How could they keep you?" he asked, trying to understand.

She frowned. "They drugged me. I was not awake for ten minutes together until you rescued me."

"But who were they? What did they want with you?"

"Willasfell commands the north road, and my priests take payment from all who would journey there." Her words had the cadence of a lesson well-learned. "But the traders of Radiston did not want to pay. Without me, my city has no power. They were afraid to kill me, I think. They wanted the city to ransom me with a promise of free trade. They passed through Westria before they turned back eastward to confuse anyone following. . . . I wish I had been awake enough when they had me—they died too easily!" She finished in a rush. Her pale eyes glowed.

"You will soon be safely home," Silverhair said carefully. "Surely they will welcome you."

Her face grew scornful. "I am their Goddess and their slave! I've learned about other things, traveling with you . . ." she added bitterly. "They worship me in Willasfell, but nobody is my friend. And there is no one to make music as you do. Be *my* harper and stay with me! I will give you more gold than any minstrel ever saw—Willasfell has been taxing the trade route for three hundred years. You must come—I *want* you to!"

Silverhair shook his head gently, for a moment shaken by her words, searching for a denial that would not hurt too much. He busied himself arranging the kindling and starting a little fire.

"I am sorry, Thea, but I may not," he said at last. "I'm looking for someone, and until I find her I may give no man my service and call no hall my home."

She sat back, considering him, warming her hands as the fire caught hold. "Then why should I go back into a cage? Can't I go with you? No one could deny us what we want when I have only to whistle up a wind!"

Silverhair's pity turned abruptly to fear. He could visualize the dust-devil she had raised before grown large, devastating the countryside. It was true—if she had borne the Wind Crystal on her breast she could hardly have had more power.

"Take me with you—I will bring you luck—"

"No."

"You are searching. Shall I tell you what you will find?" She laughed at the hope he could not keep out of his eyes. Worrying about her other talents, he had forgotten prophecy.

"If you can tell me anything that will help me, then speak. I think you owe me that." His voice was strained, but he tried to keep his features still.

Thea gave him her quick sidelong glance, then her face grew slack. After a tense silence her eyes opened again, and he caught a glint of malice in their crystal depths.

"You will wander until your hair is whiter than midwinter's snow, and your search will end beside a lonely grave," she said. "Your own choice will turn a friend to an enemy who will break your harp and then the hands that made her sing. . . ."

Caolin . . . some deep awareness interpreted the prophecy, but he would not allow himself to consider it—not now. . . .

"Have you no more to say?" His voice was colorless. "Threats will bind no better than promises. I told you I would take you home, and I will. . . ."

She smiled a little. "Will you? Do you have a will? I don't think so. I am the Willa, and my creatures will drive you where *I* will you to go!" Her lips moved, and a thin whispering whistle stirred the air.

The night was suddenly colder. The little fire flickered wildly, and Silverhair shook his head at the pressure in his ears. The whistling grew louder, invisible fingers tugged at his clothes and feathered his hair. The horses neighed and plunged in their hobbles and he could hear the sound of rising wind.

He grabbed for the demon child who smiled at him from across the fire. She struggled as he grasped her, and he could feel her heart beating wildly, like the heart of a small bird that had died once in his hands. She whistled shrilly and tried to kick him, and the wind roared in his ears and tore at him.

"Stop!" He tightened his grip. "If you loose the wind on me you'll die too!"

She stilled in his arms. The wind diminished, and for a moment he thought that he had won. And then a voice within his mind commanded, *Let her go . . . Let her go!* He gritted his teeth against the pain as the voice became a roar, and he gripped Thea with all the strength left to him. The agony eased.

Then the pleading began again, but in different voices now—his father's, that of Jehan the King, of Eric who had been his friend. Dimly he knew them for illusions. And then there was a new voice, a woman's clear call that sobbed and begged for rescue. Faris's voice—Faris in danger—Faris sending out the same cry of anguish that he had heard just before she disappeared. . . .

Farin's arms loosened. Before, he had not been able to answer Faris's call. He started to get up and the creature in his arms twisted suddenly. Faris's scream was lost in a cacophony that obliterated all awareness. He moaned and with his last shred of will gripped the Willa's wrist and held fast. Again he heard his sister scream.

That is not Faris!

He forced himself to hear her voice as it had really been. Memories chattered in his beleaguered brain . . . Faris's clear voice repeating the old chants they had learned at their initiations. . . .

Wind and water, earth and fire . . .

"The wind can carry songs as well as spells!" he cried aloud, and jerked the Willa back against him as chaos crashed around them once more. Then Silverhair sang:

> *"Wind and water, earth and fire—*
> *On these four all life depends . . ."*

He repeated the simple rhymes and imagined that he heard his sister's voice chanting in unison with his own:

> *"To balance them be our desire*
> *Nor use their force for evil ends!"*

He ground those words out with venom, and tightened his clasp.

"Earth is the mother of us all
From whom the strength comes to endure;
From sky to sea sweet waters fall
Whose surge revives the world once more."

He could feel the ground firm beneath him now. He forced the words out one by one, imposing rhythm on the pulsing of his brain, imposing order on the world.

"From the air we breathe in power . . ."

His own singing rang in his ears, pulsed in the trembling air . . .

"The wind of heaven bears the Word . . ."

The space around them quivered with balanced forces—

"That spoken, kindles in its hour
Light, and life; the fire of God!"

His voice faded into a great silence.

Nothing moved.

The Willa lay limp in Silverhair's arms, face empty in the light of the rising moon. Only the throbbing of a pulse in her thin throat showed that life was in her still. Silverhair drew a deep breath and looked around.

The embers lay scattered around him. All the brush within a hundred feet of their campsite had been torn up and the earth scoured. Pieces of gear and clothing were scattered everywhere. The horses stood, lathered and trembling in their hobbles, a short ways off.

Carefully, Silverhair laid the girl down and drew his sword. But as she lay there her white face held no more mystery than the face of any sleeping child. Was there another way?

With a sigh he let the sword whisper back into its sheath. He remembered the old tale of the man who had wrestled a spirit in the night and would not let it go until it had blessed him. He bent over the child.

"Thea!"

She stirred a little and moaned. Her face was white as bone. He set his hands on each side of her head and called again. Her eyelids fluttered and she looked up at him.

"Thea—I have given you a name! Give me hope! Tell me if I will find the answers I seek, and the child who should be King of Westria. What will happen to my enemy?"

She looked at him, then through him. Slowly the whisper came. "Your enemy will be his own destruction, and Westria will have her rightful King. . . ." Her eyes welled with tears that left glistening tracks down her cheeks.

Silverhair drew her into his arms like an infant. Slowly he rocked her, humming deep in his throat.

"In Willasfell they rule me with words," she whispered finally. "Since I was born I have answered to the rituals. When the chanting begins I have no choice but to do their will. I don't want to go back there. . . ."

"You have your own name now," Silverhair said slowly. "If you learn to rule yourself you can be free. You know that I must take you to the city when morning comes." He stroked her tangled hair. There would be supplies in Willasfell, he thought, and maybe information too.

"Sing to me, Silverhair. . . ." Thea's voice was low. He had thought her asleep. For the last time, he obeyed.

He sang the Order of Creation that celebrates the hierarchy of all that lives. He sang of Kings and heroes, of lovers and their pains. He sang the lullabies to which he and Faris had fallen asleep. He sang to the Willa until her breathing deepened and he knew that she slept at last. And still he held her, while the heavens moved and the moon set, and the distant walls of Willasfell grew rosy with dawn.

There was no breath of wind.

➤➤ EIGHT ➤➤

"A harper is no liability on a journey, but no necessity. . . ." The big trader looked Silverhair up and down. He was a Dineh tribesman, they had said at the Willa's Temple. He wore a broad hat with silver discs on the band. And he needed men for his caravan.

Silverhair straightened. "I've worked pack trains," he said, wondering what the other man was seeing in him—an already thin frame leaned by wandering, an old man's hair around a face that was gaining some lines of its own. He gestured toward the confusion of wagons and piled bales and the lines of picketed mules and camels that would draw or carry them. "What do you need?"

Hosteen grinned. "Just about everything. Can you use that sword?" He indicated the worn hilt of the blade that hung at the harper's side.

"Well enough," said Silverhair. "I've fought woodsrats in the mountains of Westria and Elayan regulars in the south, and I've come through a good many less formal fights since then." The years had worn away the courtliness of speech he had learned in Laurelynn, and there was no point in telling this man that he had been knighted by the King of Westria. It would only raise questions he had no intention of answering.

The priests of the Willa had given him a new pair of boots, a voluminous hooded garment to keep off the sun, and information. There was, they said, a small but steady traffic in slaves between Arena and the Valley of the Sun in Aztlan. If Faris had ever left Westria she might have

92

been taken there. The memory sent his gaze across the crowded marketplace to the white walls of the Temple with the whirling spiral of the Wind Lord painted in blue. Thea was there. He wondered if she was looking out of some high window, watching him. He looked back at Hosteen. He wanted to find Faris, but at the moment he wanted even more to get out of Willasfell.

"I can also use a bow—" he said quickly.

"If you come with us, you'll have to. And you will practice in the evenings, no matter how tired you are, until I am satisfied."

Hosteen's eyes glittered like black stones, and Silverhair remembered what people had said of him—the trader was a hard man, but a good leader, who got across the desert with his goods intact and his men alive.

"Then I am coming with you?"

"You're on the lean side, but in this heat that's all to the good," said Hosteen. "You look as if you're used to the road. I've no time to seek further, anyway. If you have business left here, finish it now. We leave in an hour."

Hosteen was already turning away, scowling as one of his men poured out some tale of fighting in the camel-lines. Silverhair grimaced wryly and started back to his inn. The money he had got from selling the spotted pack mare would just about pay his score. Perhaps he should have accepted the silver the Willa's priests had offered him, but though he was certain he had done the right thing in leaving her here, he could not quite bring himself to take the reward.

And surely she would be happy. With the water of the little river to sustain it, and the sculptured beauty of the hills to lend interest to the view, Willasfell was as fair a city as one might find in these desert lands. And it was rich. The whitewashed walls of the houses were inset with glazed tiles, and the dome of the Great Temple was covered with a thin layer of beaten gold. It would be laughable to even compare such luxury to the life of a wanderer upon the roads of the world!

When the caravan formed up in the market square an hour later, the place was nearly empty, and the sound of chanting drifted from the direction of the Temple, propelled by the heavy beat of a drum. The priests were losing no time in demonstrating to their people that the Goddess was in residence again. The chanting became a shout, then faded, and Silverhair found himself shivering.

As they crossed the end of the main avenue a flash of gold caught his gaze and turning in his saddle, he saw a decorated palanquin emerging from the Temple.

"Willa! Wil-lah! Wil-lah!" The chanting echoed back and forth from the white walls as the palanquin moved jerkily down the broad steps and began its slow progress, surrounded by ranks of white-robed priests whose shaven heads gleamed in the hot sun. Even at this distance the vibration of so many voices trembled through the ground. Silverhair felt the harp cased at his back thrumming in sympathy.

But as the caravan wound through the city and out into the open lands beyond, and the shouting became a murmur, faint as the wind that blew across the sands, it was the word *Thea . . . Thea . . .* that echoed in Silverhair's memory.

> *"Through miles and years I travel on . . .*
> *Through lands—"*

No, that was not quite right. Silverhair frowned and squinted into the desert glare. Even with the hood of his robe pulled down, the plodding line of wagons and animals shimmered before him, and the undulating surface of the sands seemed to flow like the sea.

> *"Across the years the path leads on,*
> *Through lands where no one knows my name . . ."*

Yes, that was better. All that morning the tune of his old wandering song had echoed in his inner ear while he teased his brain for the right words to a new verse for it. It was frustrating, for the glare was giving him a headache and his ribs hurt where Hosteen had hit him with the wooden practice sword the night before, but at least it gave him something to think about besides the heat and the endless monotony of the road.

> *"And wheresoever I have gone—"*

It scanned, and it rhymed, but it was not what he wanted there. That word, *wheresoever*, that was the difficulty. It used up too much of the line without adding any content, and it was too formal in tone to match the rest.

His horse stumbled, and Silverhair pulled it up, jerking back to full awareness. Guardians, it was hot! And his sweat-soaked breeches were chafing his thighs. They had been traveling south for over a week now, and with every step they took summer gained ground. Springs that had flowed freely when Hosteen Longstep came north the month before were only trickles now. The caravan leader said this would be the last big train to come this way until the winter rains. The mule-wagons groaned and rattled, and the camels were grunting in perpetual complaint against the lot that bound them. And if even the camels complained . . . !

Automatically, Silverhair glanced at the irregular shape of the harpcase tied to the saddle behind him. He had covered the leather with a white cloth in an attempt to shield it, but the heat inside the case must be intense even so. He winced, wondering what the temperature and the dry air were doing to Swangold. It was his own fault. He could have put the harp in one of the wagons, but in six years of wandering it had become almost a part of him. He felt naked, almost painfully anxious, when it was not to hand.

He would oil the harp thoroughly that night, he thought apologetically, and fill the cracks that had formed in the fine wood with glue when they finally reached a town.

If they ever did. Their destination was the City of the Firebird, which nestled among its irrigated fields and canals in the Valley of the Sun; but it was hard to imagine that life would ever again hold anything but this endless riding beneath a burning sun.

"Hold! Aiee!"

At the shout Silverhair's eyelids opened. He glimpsed

frantic motion ahead and thought one of the animals must be down. He was already kicking the dun horse forward when something flicked by him, he heard an angry hum and realized that it was an arrow, that the attack for which Hosteen had been training them had come.

"Circle! Get them around!"

Men and animals scattered before him. Silverhair reined his horse after a camel and shouted to drive it into the circle of wagons that the drivers were trying to form. In the cacophony of braying mules and squealing camels Hosteen's orders were lost, but Silverhair and the others had been painfully rehearsed in what to do. Or at least what to try—it was harder when one had to dodge a steady fire of arrows and the hysterical camels kept dashing toward the desert where they would be easy prey.

He had never *liked* camels, Silverhair thought irrelevantly as he wrenched the dun's head around and kicked him after a sand-colored beast whose pack had slid around to its stomach. Squealing like an oiled hinge, the camel careened in stiff-legged circles as the hanging pack batted its legs. Two horsemen had abandoned the attack and were galloping toward him. They had cloths bound around their heads. Silverhair could not tell if they were tribesmen or desert wolves like those who had looted Thea's caravan.

Swearing, he pulled the bow over his head and fumbled for an arrow from the case at his side. His first shot went wide. He took a deep breath, forcing calm, shot again and saw his target clap his hand to his bow arm with a cry.

Yelling, Silverhair spurred toward the camel, which threw up its head in fright and at last began to buck in the general direction of the wagons. The circle was almost closed now—the last two wagons were being dragged in while the unhitched mules were driven into the center with the rest of the milling herd. Silverhair lashed at the camel's rump with the bow, and it lurched through the gap.

Silverhair was almost crushed against a wagon by one of the mules as he followed it. He tore his quiver from the saddle and found a place with the other men behind the wagons, shooting at any target that was for a moment still. *I was safer outside with the enemy!* he thought, shrinking against the wagon as the herd milled past again. He felt a moment's fear for his harp, which was still tied to the dun's saddle, but there was no way to assure its safety. Or his own.

One of the raiders made the mistake of pausing to take aim, and Silverhair had the satisfaction of seeing his last arrow thud home beneath the man's lifted arm. Then the wagon against which he was leaning shuddered, and he saw someone clambering over the bales with a drawn sword.

Shouting for Hosteen, he tugged his own blade free, but cries were coming from all around the circle as the enemy moved in. There were three men slashing down at him from the wagon now. He ducked, thrust upward at a man's knee and jerked the blade out and brought it down on his neck as the raider crumpled and screamed.

That left only two of them. Silverhair leaped back and forth, desperately wishing for a shield. If they downed him they would be inside the circle and could attack the other defenders from behind. His arm ached as he traded blows with one man, then he saw the other leaping to the ground and dashed toward him, hoping to get in a blow while he was catching his balance.

But these desert wolves had learned to jump on and off running horses as soon as they could walk. The other was already crouched, waiting. His sword was shorter and broader than Silverhair's, but perhaps more effective at close quarters because of that. The harper took a step backward. The plunging animals drove him forward again and he turned the movement into a low lunge that passed through the raider's loose sleeve, grated on ribs and then, as he angled the blade upward, slid between them into the man's chest.

Silverhair wrenched himself to one side. His enemy's heavy sword swept down, obeying its owner's will even now, when the man's eyes were already unfocusing. For a moment the harper thought his own sword was stuck in the sagging body. As the other blade fell past him, he twisted desperately and freed his weapon, staggering back and scrabbling for balance as the second man leaped toward him.

Attention fixed on his enemy, he barely saw the dark shape that was suddenly between him and the sun. Then something struck the breath from his body and sent his sword flying. He hit the hard earth and sharp hooves trampled across his chest and his outstretched hand.

For a long time after, Silverhair knew only pain and fever and an interminable jolting which he understood came from the wagon that carried him because the pain was less at night when it stopped. The air was cooler then too, so that he could tell the difference between the fires that burned in his body and the inexorable heat of the sun.

At night he realized that there were bandages around his chest and swathing his hand. A gash in his leg was festering and his head throbbed from a blow there. But in the daytime he knew only the disjointed images of delirium—Faris's face dancing like a mirage; the Willa, weeping; and once, the Master of the Junipers, striding up a dusty road toward the hills.

> *"Across the years the path leads on*
> *Through lands where no one knows my name . . ."*

The verses he had been composing echoed mockingly, and he clung to them with the last rags of his sanity, as if he could keep himself and his quest alive by continuing the song.

> *"And memory itself is gone,*
> *Yet still my search remains the same,*
> *Nor do I cease from wandering . . ."*

And then there came a day when a sudden coolness brought him to consciousness, even though it was still day. He saw the beams of a ceiling above him, darkened by smoke and age, and heard the confusion of sounds that could only come from a town. A woman was speaking Spanyol in a low voice that rippled like music. He closed

his eyes, trying to see Faris's face, but it would not come
to him. . . . *and memory itself is gone.* . . .

His lips moved soundlessly. Cool hands touched his
forehead, and he forced his eyes open again. He saw a
brown, hazel-eyed face beneath a wealth of sun-streaked
tawny hair. A woman's face . . .

Her eyes locked on his for a moment, then she smiled.
"Yes—" she spoke over her shoulder to someone he
could not see, "I will take care of him."

Silverhair sighed and let the darkness enfold him again,
knowing that, at least for a while, he had no choice but to
cease from wandering.

The woman's name was Yolande. The town was the
City of the Firebird, and the ceiling he had seen belonged
to the Green Turquoise Tavern, which she owned. Silverhair's
harp had come miraculously undamaged through the raid,
though the golden swan that crowned it was battered almost beyond recognition. The harper's fingers took longer
to heal. Afterward he suspected that only Yolande's prag-
matic affection had kept him sane while he waited to find
out if his right hand would ever again make music, and he
learned to compensate for its stiffness. Even now there
was an awkwardness in his thumb that would likely never
go away.

Quite naturally, he came to share her bed, and when he
could face an audience again, to serve as featured enter-
tainer in the tavern. Sometimes the memory of his quest
sent him out with other caravans, always eastward. He
traveled across the deserts to the Sea of Grass, where the
earth was as flat as a giant table, across whose surface men
crawled like ants waiting to be squashed by some huge
hand. There was another expedition, north to the priest-
ruled hegemony of Deseret, in the valley where seagulls
soared above a lake more salt than sea. But he learned
nothing of Faris, and somehow Silverhair always returned
to the Green Turquoise, and to Yolande.

And why not? he thought as he shifted on his bench so
that his back would be squarely to the little fire, and he
picked up the tuning key. If he could find no trace of

Faris, at least there was nothing here to remind him of her. It had been almost ten years since he had seen Westria. They would have forgotten him by now. And it was just as well—here he had a home and a woman and an audience, and if the jagged hills of the Valley of the Sun were not the mist-smoothed hills of home, and if he shared with the woman something that was less passion than a convenient friendship, and if the audience was uncritical of what they heard—how many men had more?

His fingers plucked strongly at the bronze strings, and the drinkers at the nearest table turned to watch him. Tribesmen, they were—Mescaleros and Chiricuas from the southeast and Papago from the Valley of the Sun, and beyond them some men from the Spanyol tribes and a ruddy-faced Elayan clansman as well as one or two Dineh mixed in with the paler folk of the town. All in all, about the usual crowd.

Silverhair grinned at them companionably and struck three strong chords that stilled the room. Then he began to sing.

> *"Oh she sits all alone by her fire in the desert,*
>   *and she wears a red shawl,*
> *And she fingers the fringe without feeling it,*
>   *thinking of nothing at all,*
> *And the men of the caravans watch her and leave her*
>   *alone,*
> *For they all know well how it feels to lose one of*
>   *your own,*
> *So she sits by herself and she pulls the shawl over*
>   *her hair,*
> *And remembers those times long ago and imagines*
>   *she's there . . ."*

It was a new song that he had learned from an old man that last time he took the road, and he knew that now was the time to sing it, before the noise level in the tavern rose too high for anything but raucously shouted drinking songs.

*"It was down in a valley grown over with roses
    that it all began,
With a girl standing still on a hill watching out
    for the Great Caravan.
It had been two long years since the last time the
    merchants came there—
She'd still been a child—she remembered a man with
    black hair,
And she wondered if he would still know her, if it
    meant anything
That her heart beat out rhythms her flesh was still
    waiting to sing."*

The song went on to tell how the girl had followed her
lover and borne him a child; they had prospered, started a
string of their own. The men and women in the tavern
nodded, listening, knowing the desert and its call. They
were mostly caravaners themselves, or herders who followed their sheep and cattle wherever there was grass. Or
warriors—for every tribal chieftain had to be able to lead
his folk in war, though only the paramount chief in Elbarran,
who was called High King for the sake of courtesy, had a
permanent force of fighting men.

*"And they prospered, her man wished to settle down,
    maybe to take up some land—
But she still loved the road and the freedom, the
    sound of the wind on the sand,
'Til the two-legged wolves of the desert came down in
    the night
And the man with black hair and the baby were killed
    in the fight.
But the tears would not come; she cried vengeance
    for losing her man,
And she took the last mule and she rejoined the Great
    Caravan."*

Across the room he saw Yolande standing with her
hands on her hips and her broad bosom thrust forward to

better display the magnificent necklace of green turquoises set in gold from which the tavern got its name. Rumor had it that she had been given the necklace by the old High King when she was still a dancer. Others said it was part of an ancient treasure whose finder died of a curse after he gave it to her. And there were those who sneered and said that the money for both necklace and tavern came from one of old Gut-Pincer's loans, and that the payment was long overdue. Silverhair had never asked her which story was true, as she had never asked him why he left Westria.

Only for a moment, something tightened in his throat, and he wondered how it would be to have a woman who would cry vengeance if he died—as he had sworn it for Faris. Quickly he swung into the last verse of the song.

> *"As the miles and the seasons rolled on there were*
> *raids and she killed when she could,*
> *And when time wore the pain from her memories,*
> *surely she thought that was good,*
> *Until she ruled the Caravan, and of her past she'd*
> *lost all*
> *Except for a memory of grief and the red silken*
> *shawl.*
> *And now control slips from her fingers, but she doesn't*
> *care,*
> *For she dreams of the Valley of Roses and a man with*
> *black hair."*

Silverhair's gaze sought Yolande as he finished the song, shaken by it in a way he had not known for a long while. But she was talking to Hosteen Longstep, just back from a journey that had lasted more than a year. Automatically the harper's fingers modulated chords into a conclusion. There was a little murmur from those around him—half admiration, half unease.

He reached for the tankard of wine and took a long swallow, then resolutely tackled a ballad about a mule-driver and his mother-in-law, which set them all to laughing. By the time he had finished, the wine had begun to work, and he himself was forgetting the odd sadness with which he had begun.

This was the part of the evening he liked best, when his fingers and voice had warmed up enough for a good performance, and the audience was warmed up enough to appreciate it, but not drunk to the point of sentimentality or violence. Drinks were selling well, and the room vibrated with the kind of camaraderie that men would remember later in the isolation of their huts or on the trail.

Firelight gleamed on the copper hood above the central hearth, on the rugs that covered the whitewashed walls, on brown faces that creased in smiles. Silverhair moved easily from one song to another, choosing pieces that reflected the origins of the folk around him, shifting the mood from bawdry to melancholy and back again, playing the audience as he played his harp. Their faces were the book in which he read his music. He could feel the energy he poured out to them radiating back again, more inebriating than the wine.

He finished with a piece that let the harp sing alone, then settled back with a sigh. His excitement began to drain away. The place was getting noisy. The tankard was still at his elbow and he drank deeply, emptying it. Then he waved it at the little Pima girl who was carrying the wine pitcher around, and began to sing.

> "*The lusty wines of Westria are rich and ripe and red;*
> *A mugful of Elayan ale will stand you on your head,*
> *But the very best drink that I have drunk*
>   *(and I have tried them all)*
> *Is the one the barmaid's bringing now to fill my flagon tall!*"

Holding the harp steady with knee and shoulder and continuing to strum right-handed, Silverhair held out the tankard for the girl to fill.

> "*In Normontaine there's cider and Tekelah in Aztlan;*
> *And if you roam the Barren Lands you'll drink whatever you can—*"

That brought a laugh. Silverhair finished the chorus and drank again. He had learned to calibrate his consumption with something of the precision with which he tuned his harp. He never drank until evening, and then only enough to lubricate his throat while he sang. It was only after his performance that he needed the liquor to fill the emptiness he felt when the harp was no longer under his hands, to give him the ready good cheer he needed to circulate like a genial host among the customers.

> *"Good Uisquebagh will ward off cold, chilled beer will beat the heat,*
> *So fill the horn and pass it round when friends and kinsmen meet!"*

He had to play the last chorus twice, and then someone else bellowed out a tune, off-key, but nobody minded that now. Silverhair set down the harp carefully. There was a pleasant buzz in his ears now, and the rough wine tasted mellow at last.

"That was a good song—the one about the boy who hunted the great lion—"

Silverhair turned and saw it was one of the Elayans and nodded, smiling. The ballad of the youth who was first to kill one of the lions of Elaya and became the ancestor of the princely house was one of the songs he had brought away from his time with Prince Palomon. It was a favorite with the people of the Tambara.

"They been hunting men in Elaya, this year—" the fellow went on. "Palomon's youngest brother's son got together an army out of Kilima and the south, and there was fighting all through there and Nippan."

Silverhair swallowed, suddenly shaken by memories. "Who won?"

"Oh, Palomon. Again. He an old fox, and likely foxiest in letting that foreigner, El Desterrado, handle the business for him this time."

"El Desterrado!" Silverhair fell silent, remembering a street in Los Leones and Caolin's scarred hands beneath the white robe. "Do you mean to say this 'Desterrado' fought the battles?" he asked.

"He generaled them." The Elayan shrugged. "The Prince has given El Desterrado the title of Condé and some land up on the northern border." He whistled to the Pima girl, who brought over another pitcher of wine and refilled their tankards.

Silverhair tried to school his expression. From head of security to head of the army—Caolin should be pleased at the promotion. There was no reason why the news should disquiet him. Surely, the more the confederated states of Elaya fought each other, the less energy they would have for troubling Westria, and Caolin had obviously found his service satisfactory.

Caolin made a good servant, but a poor master, thought Silverhair. And after so many years he could even recognize that his sister Faris had had no taste for the role of Queen. If Faris had been more like Rosemary, Caolin might never have gone wrong. He frowned. It was no good thinking of might-have-beens. If Caolin himself had been stronger he could have taught Faris how to be a Queen.

While he sat abstracted, the Elayan had turned to talk to another man. Quietly Silverhair put his harp back into her case and began to move among the tables. Here a trader from the east was describing a new religion that had gotten started on the Sea of Grass, but that was no news—the city-states and wandering tribes of the plains seemed to vie with each other in producing visionary religions.

At another table four men had brought out a board and counters, and were playing Swords and Shields. From the sound of the betting, the stakes were already high. Next to them the two women who dominated the town's dyeing industry were dickering with a trader from Tenochtitlan for a consignment of indigo.

And as usual, some of the patrons were talking politics, for the current High King was an old man, and the Valley of the Sun resented being ruled from Elbarran. It made little difference as far as Silverhair could tell. Chieftains governed their tribes as the Lord Commanders of Westria ruled their Provinces, but the King could do little more than arbitrate when there was conflict between them. Aztlan reacted with gleeful fury when anyone breached its borders, but had never been known to invade its neighbors. After a few sharp lessons even the ambitious lords of Elaya had left it alone.

The harper continued to circulate among the tables, stopping here or there for a word with one of the regulars, or with someone he knew from the caravans. The fire had died down, but the wrought iron lamps suspended from the crossbeams were still burning steadily, and Silverhair's trained ears checked the hum of conversation and recognized the note of content. Good evening—Yolande would be pleased.

And as if he had called her name, the woman looked up from beside Hosteen Longstep and beckoned. The golden curve of her breast glowed in the lamplight beneath the massive weight of the necklace, which hid the embroidery at the deep neckline of her sleeveless white blouse. She was wearing a long flounced skirt, the color of sage in the sunlight, over an orange petticoat, tied at the waist by a multicolored Xicano sash.

Silverhair grinned at her, appreciating her beauty anew. If the evening continued to go well she would want him in her bed that night. He felt the first stirring of anticipation and slid onto the bench beside her, easing his arm around her waist and enjoying the resilience of her flesh through the thin cotton, breathing in the warm, spicy scent she wore as she turned to kiss him.

"Hosteen has a proposition for you—" she whispered as she drew away from him again.

Silverhair straightened and looked from her to the other man. He had heard that Hosteen had once been Yolande's lover—it did not matter, of course, but he wondered how detached her judgment of the caravaner's proposal would be.

"Treasure," said Hosteen simply. His eyes gleamed beneath the red cotton headband.

"Treasure," said Hosteen simply. His eyes gleamed beneath the red cotton headband.

"What does that have to do with me?" asked the harper. "I don't need gold."

"Not gold—at least I don't think so, though it can be turned to gold when we have it in our hands."

Silverhair spread his browned, agile-fingered musician's hands before him—strong hands, despite the batterings of the past ten years. "My treasure is here," he smiled.

Yolande laughed and poured out something from a flagon of green glass into a little blackware cup. "Try this— Hosteen brought it from the south."

Silverhair picked it up—in the cup it was impossible to tell its color. He sensed a sharp, fruity odor as he put it to his lips and sweetness as it went down. Then it hit the glow of wine in his belly like greasewood exploding in a kitchen fire and he coughed convulsively.

"Wha-at, was that?" he asked when he could speak again.

"*Torbellino*—they make it from the fruit of some kind of cactus there," Hosteen explained.

"I believe you. I'll have to add a verse for it to my song!" Carefully he sipped again, letting the fire inside him settle to a steady roar. The air wavered before him like the heat-shimmer from the ground on a hot day. He felt as if one of the mental shields the Master of the Junipers used to talk about had become visible around him and he laughed. This was much better than wine!

Yolande snuggled closer to him, her eyes bright with excitement, or perhaps with the same liquor that was singing in his blood now.

"You know the great cañon, where the gods slashed Earth to the bone? Did you know that there are caverns there?" she asked.

Silverhair had heard travelers' tales of such a place, said to predate the Cataclysm, and knew some of the stories purporting to explain it, though he had discounted most of them. His own wanderings had never taken him that way.

"I found out that during the days of the Cataclysm some of the Ancients hid there with all the treasure they could save," said Hosteen.

"But what did they consider treasure? I have seen ruins from the Ancient times in Westria. It's hard enough to tell what most of their things were used for, much less why they valued them!" Silverhair laughed.

"You would value what they put in the caves," Hosteen said in a low voice. "It was a rich man's hoard—statues, pictures, jewels . . . That kind of wealth has no age."

Silverhair shook his head. "If it is still there. Surely anything worth taking was carried off by some chieftain years ago. Unless—" Abruptly he stopped, frowning at the other man. "Perhaps I *have* heard of those caves. The tribes up that way call it the Womb of the Earth Mother, don't they? They leave offerings there for fear She will shake the world apart once more. You're mad to even think of it, Hosteen. They will surely have guards there."

"Not at this time of year. The Walapai make pilgrimage to the caverns every summer, but they are wintering in the cañon now," Hosteen said quickly. He leaned forward to pour more liquor into Silverhair's cup and his own. "I am bound to take a caravan up to Arena next week, and there are too many people watching my movements anyway. That's why we thought of you—"

"Yes," said Yolande. "No one will wonder if you resume your wanderings. One man could easily carry away enough to make us all wealthy. Hosteen has a map of the caverns, Silverhair . . ."

The harper sighed. "I still don't understand. These things have been there eight hundred years. In one season they will not disappear. Why not take time to plan the thing properly and go yourself next year?"

"Because I don't know who else the man who sold me the map may have peddled it to—" said Hosteen fiercely. There was a short silence, then Yolande sighed and took Silverhair's arm. He looked back at her and saw with surprise that her eyes were filling with tears.

"And because I need the money now—" she whispered brokenly. "I have never told you—oh! it galls me to have to say it even now—but I am in debt badly. It was a little loan Master Santiago made to get me started—I thought I could pay it in a year. But somehow there has always been something that needed doing—last year the rains ruined the roof, you remember, and then blizzards blocked the passes and for two months no one came." Her brown fingers gripped the golden links of her necklace and began to stroke the smooth turquoises as if to reassure herself of their reality.

She caught him looking at the necklace and flushed angrily. "Do you think I should sell the necklace instead? To whom could I sell it? And what would this tavern be—what would I be, if it were gone? Would you sell your harp for bread?"

Silverhair winced. She knew too well where he was vulnerable. He could think of her in the arms of another lover, but not of Swangold in someone else's hands.

"But I have never been in that part of Aztlan, and I know nothing of caves—" he said, less surely. "It can't be as easy as you are making it sound, and I don't understand why you are asking this of me. . . ."

"Have some more Torbellino," Hosteen Longstep said.

Silverhair realized that he was in Yolande's bed, though he had only the haziest recollections of how he had gotten there. He tried to remember, but the whole latter part of the evening was unclear. The flagon of Torbellino had gone back and forth and Hosteen had repeated his arguments. But what had they decided to do?

Yolande's warm fingers were busy at the lacings of his breeches. His tunic was already off and he felt the softness of her breast against his bare skin. He breathed in unsteadily and lay back to give her more room. The oil lamp in the little shrine at the foot of the bed flickered fitfully, lighting the statues of Guadalupe and the Kachina figures there—*los santos,* the Guardians of the diverse heritage of Aztlan.

Now Yolande's lips were moving where her hands had gone. Silverhair moaned and pulled her up against him, his mouth seeking hers while his trained fingers began to

explore the opulence of the full breasts crushed against
him, wanderers traversing the rich landscape of her body
until they reached the sweet haven between her thighs.

But as his urgency flared and he lifted himself over her
a double awareness shook him. He knew her body well,
but he felt as if he were sinking into a dark passageway
that led to caverns where waited a treasure and a terror
greater than anything he had ever known. He tried to
withdraw, but already his body was mastering him, and as
his consciousness exploded in fire and darkness, the woman
beneath him convulsed as if the earth herself were climaxing.

After, he lay spent upon Yolande's still trembling body,
waiting for the strength to pull free. Returning self-awareness
told him that the passion between them had never been so
shattering before. But now he remembered another thing—at
some point during that long evening he had agreed to go to
the caves. . . .

⋙ NINE ⋘

Silverhair hunched over his little fire, shivering and wondering why he had left the Valley of the Sun. And yet at the same time some part of him was enjoying the cold and the loneliness. The sky had been swept clean of cloud by the bitter wind, and the vast sweep of the heavens above him was encrusted with stars. They seemed huge, impossibly near. It had been too long since Silverhair had taken the time to look at them. It had been too long since he had been alone.

Three weeks of steady riding had brought him here—three weeks of wondering where he was going and what he would find when he got there. But wheelruts still showed in the sandy soil, guiding him, and the remains of summer lean-tos marked the entrance to the caverns. They provided the illusion of shelter at least, and a little protection for his fire. He had tied his spotted pony to one of the poles. The steady sound of chomping as the animal nosed at the sparse clumps of grass punctuated the sighing of the wind.

The land stretched flat and featureless toward the circle of distant hills. Other than himself, it seemed uninhabited except for the coyote that had howled intermittently throughout the evening and was calling mournfully now. Silverhair shivered again, rolled himself in his heavy cloak, and lay down next to the fire.

A sensible man would pack up in the morning and move on. But then a sensible man would never have left Westria.

I no longer know how to keep faith with Faris, thought

Silverhair as sleep at last began to conquer the cold, *but I can at least try to keep faith with Yolande*. . . .

There were stairs leading down into the caverns, an endless zigzag of echoing iron treads that descended through a large shaft, past the remains of some kind of machinery. Silverhair shifted the balance of his pack, made bulky by the addition of two waterbags, a bundle of torches, and the harp, and wondered if those rusting pieces of metal had once belonged to some magic of the Ancients for getting people up and down without the labor that made his leg muscles tremble and the breath ache in his chest.

The stair angled sharply, and the harp hit the rail with a painful clunk as Silverhair jerked back. There was a demon! No—he caught his breath—a mask, suspended in midair. He stepped forward again and saw it was not a mask but a huge skull, suspended from the rough-hewn wall. It was something like a lizard's head, but there were no lizards that size alive today. Then the answer came to him—it must be a dragon, whose skull had been set there by the Ancients to guard the shrine.

And if they had taken so much trouble to guard it, perhaps there really was something worth seeing down here after all. The unchanging dry chill of the air began to penetrate his clothing, and Silverhair started moving again. Dark metal gleamed in the fitful torchlight; Silverhair had never seen so much metal in one place, or any artifact of the Ancients so undamaged by time. Everything aboveground had been cannibalized by the survivors of the Cataclysm centuries ago. They had been mighty craftsmen, surely. His skin prickled with sudden excitement. What else was waiting here?

At the base of the staircase was a chamber whose walls were painted with Walapai religious symbols. Silverhair pulled out the map that Hosteen had given him, checked it, and looked back at the wall. There was one design he must watch for—an arrangement of three black triangles radiating from a common point on a yellow field. It was the symbol the Ancients had used to ward their secrets, and it would lead him to the shrine.

He followed the symbols through the right-hand tunnel and paused as he came to the huge chamber beyond it. It was a cavern perhaps one hundred and fifty feet long and almost as wide. Tiered seats had been built around it, of rough stone topped with long boards. The center was broad, flat, with the polish of a surface that has been used for dancing, and in the center he saw the platform where the drummers would sit during ceremonies.

Drums must echo like thunder in here—he tried to imagine it. But the silence around him was almost palpable; Silverhair could hear the rasp of his own breath, the pounding of his pulse in his ears. Suddenly he felt the weight and density of stone. The chill air was fresh enough, but for a moment he felt as if it were congealing around him, that it would grow solid in his lungs and he would become a fossil here.

Silverhair took a deep breath and started around the edge of the dancing floor. Closer to the walls he could see variations in the surface of the stone. The natural walls of the cavern had been smoothly sculptured by some ancient river, but in some places the stone had been sliced as smoothly as a knife cuts cheese. Silverhair guessed that was the work of the Ancients' machines. And then there were other marks, mostly in the side passages, where the rock had been chipped away by the muscle-power of men; no doubt by the Walapai, when they needed additional chambers for their ceremonies.

At the other end of the cavern he found wooden steps and another smooth passage that led deeper into the earth. His torch began to hiss and sputter and he lit another, setting the old stock to burn out in one of the iron brackets set into the wall. As the new flame flared, flickered, and caught again, he realized that light was coming from the other end of the passageway as well. He passed stone formations like clusters of grapes that gleamed in the torchlight, and the light before him grew greater, until he hardly needed his own torch at all.

He stopped, blinked, and then moved slowly into the second cavern, instinctively following the pathway that led past more grape clusters around the cavern wall. Torches had been set at intervals all along it, and they were all burning, but Silverhair was not looking at the walls.

This was the place, then. It had not all been some drunken dream.

It was a holy place, and a treasure house.

And a tomb.

In the midst of the cavern Silverhair saw the Earth Goddess the tales had described—a great image made of polished bronze cast with a rude vigor as if the artist had sought to convey the essence rather than the detail of the female form. Its eyeless face seemed to fix him with a malevolent surveillance unmitigated by the glow of gold chains and sparkle of jewels with which it had been adorned. There were other statues around it, and paintings in golden frames set on ledges in the low walls of stone beneath a canopy of native cloth.

And like a congregation, the mummified bodies of the dead lay upon their biers of cold stone. Cold—yes—even in his shock, Silverhair realized that it must be the dry air and even chill that had preserved the bodies so well. For how long? The hair lifted at the back of his neck.

The bodies that lay closest to the shrine had all grown old, and pale with the pallor of those who never see the sun. They wore the strange dull garments of Ancient times. Beyond them lay others, mostly men. But these were of every age and nation, weathered and brown. And there was another difference—while the faces of the Ancients were drawn in bitter smiles, those of the latter intruders were frozen in grimaces of terror which could not be smoothed even by the slow desiccation of the cavern's cold air.

Silverhair took a step inward, trying to read the riddle written here.

A breath of air against his cheek warned him. Silverhair whirled, reaching for his sword; but, laden as he was, before he could wrest it free he saw framed in the entrance to one of the passageways a young tribesman, who was covering him with nocked arrow and drawn bow. It was a heavy war-bow, he noted as he froze in place, the kind that could send an arrow through a man's leg and the saddle he sat on and into the flesh of the horse he rode.

"Thief! I hope you have looked well. This sight will be your only reward!" The words were only a whisper, but the torches leaped as if something had moved through the cave, displacing the air. The bowman was young, with a brown face and light eyes, dressed in ceremonial buckskins. Silverhair remembered that after the Cataclysm many Anglos had taken refuge with the tribes, but there was no kinship in the eyes that met his.

He let out his own breath in a long sigh, searching for words. The place was guarded after all, as he should have known it would be. Had Hosteen known it? He wanted to tell the tribesman that he would have taken only a little treasure, and done no desecration. Indeed, having seen this place, he might not have dared to touch it at all. Now he would never know what his choice would have been. But it was most likely death for a stranger even to set foot here.

He took a careful breath, forcing tense muscles to relax, balancing himself without visible movement. His burdens were an almost impossible handicap, but if he could get the young warrior to shoot—and to miss—

Silverhair leaped, casting the bundle of torches at his opponent, and the arrow, released by reflex, smashed in instant response through one of the waterskins and scored his thigh so that for a moment he could not tell if the wetness he felt was water or blood.

Awkwardly, trying to shield the harpcase bound to his back, Silverhair grappled with the tribesman, but before he could free his dagger his foot slipped on the slick stone and he crashed onto his side.

When his head cleared he felt the cold edge of a knife at his throat. His hands were already bound. *If I hadn't twisted to avoid falling on the harp I might have taken him,* he thought bitterly. *Hosteen always said it would be the death of me!*

He found his voice. "Are you going to kill me now?"

"Not here—it would make the ghosts too angry. Get up!" The youth was already hauling on his arm. Silverhair groaned and staggered, trying to balance, and with his head still ringing found himself being hurried around the edge of the cavern toward an exit behind the shrine.

There was a shout from the passage through which Silverhair had entered. They stopped, staring. Silverhair saw a dark head, then another, and with a little leap of hope recognized Hosteen and three of his men. But Hosteen was not looking at him.

The young Walapai let go of Silverhair and shouted at them, but the intruders leaped down from the path and ran up the aisle between the bodies toward the shrine. Only when they reached the image did Hosteen pause, staring at the jewels.

"Don't touch Her!" cried the warrior, but the moment of stillness had passed. Hosteen's hand brushed the smooth metallic flesh of the Goddess of the cave.

Silverhair staggered as the stone moved beneath him, and a sudden wind whirled through the chamber, extinguishing all the torches simultaneously. The cave shook again, and Silverhair heard the rumble of falling rock. A hand gripped his shoulder and instinctively he scrambled after his captor toward the relative safety of the passageway.

When the torches went out Hosteen had begun to swear. Then he screamed, a harsh, astonished sound ripped from his throat as if by some totally unexpected and unendurable fear. Then the other men were shouting too; a cacophony of obscene harmonies. Silverhair heard other sounds too, rock thundering, a frantic scuffling, and then nothing but an occasional deep rumble and the clatter as a last fragment of stone fell. Shuddering he clutched at the rock on which he lay.

But the end of the earthquake did not finish his fear. It was not the sound of the screaming but its cause that shook him—palpable waves of avid, malevolent fury that pulsed from the cavern like wind blowing off an endless, bitter sea.

He felt the tribesman trembling beside him, invoking his Guardians. "They woke the ghosts . . . the ghosts are angry . . . they will eat our souls!"

Cold sweat trickled down the harper's spine and he nudged the young warrior. "At least let's get farther down the passage . . ." he gasped, "farther away." He wriggled clumsily backward, hardly noticing the handicap of his bound hands, and as the pressure of fear against his mind grew less he began to breathe more easily. The hoarse gasps of the other man slowed, he sobbed twice and was silent at last.

Silverhair still felt whatever was raging within the cavern as a man waking from a nightmare still shudders with the terror of the dream, but he could think again now. His wrists were throbbing painfully.

"If you are going to kill me, do it now!" he said harshly. "If not, then untie my hands!"

"Kill you and make another ghost to strengthen that tribe?" the Walapai's voice cracked painfully, and Silverhair realized that for all his strength he was scarcely more than a boy. "But I won't have to. Now they are awake, and they will take us. We are both dead men now!" He began to laugh with a sound like tearing cloth, which in its way was more terrible than the screaming because it covered tears. Then he gulped and fumbled with Silverhair's bonds.

Ghosts . . . The harper lay biting his lip as circulation returned to his hands, chewing on the realization that what the boy said must be true. More than falling rock had struck that note of terror from a man like Hosteen Longstep. The psychic violence he still sensed emanated from something more self-aware than stone.

He had always wondered why the tribal peoples of Aztlan had such a terror of the dead, burning a man's possessions or tearing down the house in which someone had died lest he remain there to haunt them. In Westria, the body was returned to the elements, and the soul instructed in the road home. But he had heard that when a man had suffered great pain or fear, or was consumed by hatred, some part of his spirit might remain to trouble the place of his death, especially when his body was not given back to the earth from which it came.

But this was not Westria. If Silverhair died here his body would not disintegrate peacefully and return to its origins but remain unnaturally uncorrupted, desiccated by the cold, dry air until his features had frozen into that awful grimace of terror or glee he had seen on the faces of the mummies in the cave.

"We have to get out!" he said, more loudly than he had intended. "You guard this place—you must know some way back to the entrance that does not lead through *there*—" He started to point down the passageway, but realized that in the darkness his gesture could not be seen.

"Do you think that She needs human guards?" the young man said bitterly. "I came here only for my testing, and to light the midwinter fires. I had been here two days only when you came—hardly long enough to memorize the passageways! Without light I could not find my way. You threw your torches at me, and my flint and steel are back in the other passageway."

"We could burn our clothing—" Silverhair began, then remembered that he had been carrying his fire-lighter with the torches so that it would be handy if the fire went out. They had neither fuel nor any means to make it burn. No light . . . no way out of the caves . . .

He tried to moisten dry lips, then reached for the unpunctured waterskin, drank, and offered it to the other man.

"That is all the water we have." The tribesman handed it back without drinking. "These caves are dry as bone . . . as bone!" The words were cut off as if he did not trust his voice to say more.

"So—we go back, and die of terror, or die of thirst if we stay here," Silverhair said baldly. But he still could not believe in the trap. It seemed impossible that after all he had done and suffered he should be fated to join a company of ghosts haunting a cave in Aztlan.

"The ghosts were quiet when I came—surely they will sleep again. And won't someone miss you when you don't return?"

"What is time to *them*? When the shaman comes for the Midsummer Festival he will know how to quiet them. To him the lands of the living and the dead are the same. But as for me—my family will mourn and blame my death on wild beasts or the human desert wolves. Or they will conclude that I failed my testing and never speak my name again—and that will be closest to the truth, after all," said the Walapai.

After a long silence Silverhair levered himself up so that he was sitting with his back against the rough wall. The harpcase dug into his back, and he got the strap over his head and settled it beside him.

"Well, you can at least tell me where the bodies in the caverns came from. If I am doomed, I'd like to know in whose company I'll be spending eternity."

The young warrior made a sound that was trying to be laughter. "The first ones were the Ancients who came here during the Cataclysm," he said. "They brought their Goddess and their treasures, and enough food and water to last for years. And they stayed here for years—for the rest of their lives. I don't know if the entry was blocked, or if they were just afraid to go outside, but they died here, finally, still clinging to their treasures and hating and fearing everything above ground. They still do. . . ."

Silverhair nodded in the darkness. "And the others came afterward, and met the ghosts, and died and joined them?" The dead cold of the place was seeping through his clothing again and he shivered violently. "We have to get out . . ." he said again, hopelessly.

He felt the Walapai boy shrug. "It is my fate. Each man who comes here seeking a vision of power risks the loss of his soul. But why did *you* come here? You do not seem like those other men."

Silverhair shook his head. Sitting here, with his death waiting all around him, he found it hard to remember why Yolande's pleas had seemed so desperate, and why he had thought it forgivable to invade a sanctuary and steal a jewel. Perhaps he deserved this punishment. . . . But no, it was not just! He had not known what he faced here.

But did anyone ever know what lay beyond the next turn of the road? It all depended on choosing the right way. He tried to picture Faris's face, but he saw only darkness.

The young Walapai heard his groan and touched his arm. "If you cannot kill yourself when the water is gone, I will do it for you."

Silverhair could not reply. Blindly he reached for the harpcase and undid its clasps, pulled the harp free and cradled it against his breast. How many times had he filled the hours when sleep eluded him by lifting the harp from its place beside the bed and playing in the darkness? His fingers had long ago ceased to need help from his eyes to find their way.

Carefully he ran his hands over the smooth wood of the frame, afraid he might have cracked it in the fight. But the thick fur inside the harpcase had cushioned it, and the heavy walnut could endure a surprising amount of punishment. His hands poised. Gently he plucked a string.

His companion sat up abruptly. "What was that?" Panic sharpened his tone.

Silverhair laughed bitterly. "Only my harp," he said. "Did you think this great case on my back was for carrying the treasure away? I only wanted a gold chain or two. But Swangold is a treasure greater than anything in that cursed cavern could be!" He found the tuning key and adjusted the strings, then started to play.

For a time the melodies wandered aimlessly. But one tune kept returning, and after a little he realized what it was and began to sing.

> *"The golden hills of Westria lie dreaming in the sun,*
> *And there, as on a mother's breast, I'll rest when day*
> *is done.*
> *Wherever I may wander, and however long I roam,*
> *My heart still hears the calling of the gentle hills of*
> *home."*

Memory painted an image of the low hills that edged the Great Valley of Westria, the oak-studded coastal hills and the gentle slopes that led down to the bay, and the music faltered. A red-tailed hawk slipped across the blue sky of his vision, and for a moment he could almost smell the pungence of drying fennel on the hillsides, or the salt tang of the sea. He took a deep breath and continued the song.

> *"The sunlight falls like amber through the green veils*
> *of the trees,*
> *And splashes silver sequins on the blue skirts of the*
> *seas,*

> *Like the ramparts of a fortress, the snowy mountains*
>   *stand*
> *To guard the folded valleys of the fabled golden*
>   *land.''*

The vision possessed him now. He was the sunlight, he
was the music. Clearly before him he saw the Lady Mountain, and the Master of the Junipers in his cabin there. He
was working in his garden, and as Farin watched he
looked up, almost as if he had heard the longing in the
harper's song. Then the scene began to darken, and
Silverhair's playing grew slower, as if to hold the shadows
at bay.

> *"The world is wide and wonderful, and I have wan-*
>   *dered far,*
> *With music my companion and with beauty for my*
>   *star,*
> *But the road has grown too lonely, and my weary eyes*
>   *would see*
> *The golden hills of Westria that wait to welcome*
>   *me. . . .''*

He tried to hold the vision, but it was passing like a fair
dream in the dawn. The golden hills would wait forever,
but they would never welcome him home. He could not
even lay his bones in their embrace. Grief closed his
throat, but his fingers moved without thought or volition,
drawing from the invisible harpstrings a lament so poi-
gnant that the youth by his side started to weep softly in
the darkness, his apathy overwhelmed by this last protest
against the dark. The stone around them echoed as if even
it had been moved to sympathy.

Time passed unmeasured, but at last Silverhair realized
that his back was aching from the pressure of the rough
rock against which he leaned, and his fingers were faltering. He felt empty, as if the floodtide of grief had borne all
other emotions with it away. His spirit contemplated its
plight with a fragile clarity.

Images presented themselves unordered and inconsequential—incidents from the road that had brought him here, from his childhood, from his time with Faris and the King. He remembered the mute despair in Thea's eyes when he left her in Willasfell—he was the prisoner now. Stories came to him too, snatches of old ballads and bards' tales. . . . Dispassionately he saw them come and let them go. There had been one tale, he remembered, of a harper whose playing won back his bride from the Lord of Hell. If only he—

Abruptly Silverhair's detachment left him. His fingers tightened painfully on Swangold's smooth curve. Could that legend be based on fact? Could the music that moved his spirit move the ghosts of men and women dead eight hundred years? His heart began to thump painfully. He could not do it—how could anyone go back in cold blood to face the horror in the cave?

But the alternative was to remain in the passageway, clutching his harp to his breast until he died. If he had been a warrior, he would have preferred to go out fighting, and Farin Silverhair was enough of a fighter to hate the thought of waiting meekly for death to come. Only *his* weapon of choice was the harp. With music he had made his way through the world. Did he have the courage to dare damnation with it as well?

Silverhair's stomach churned within him, but he found that he was struggling to his feet, slinging the empty harpcase over his shoulder while he slipped the strap that held the harp itself around his neck like a warrior hefting his shield.

"What are you doing?" The Walapai had heard him move.

"I'm going to entertain our hosts in the cavern. Maybe they'll let us go."

"You're mad—you can't go back there!"

"Yes, probably," answered Silverhair. "But before I was a thief I was a harper, and I have to try. . . ." Wobbly-kneed he took a step and plucked a soft chord. The echoes of the notes shaped the space around him, and though he did not understand how he knew, his trained ears interpreted and guided him.

Step by fearful step he made his way forward. After a few moments a shuffling footfall told him the other man was following. Though his fingers trembled, Silverhair continued to play until he reached the entrance to the cavern, and the dark pressure on his awareness told him that the dead were still awake and waiting there.

"Spirits of the ancestors! I have not come to steal from you, but to sing to you of the world of the sun—" Silverhair spoke as steadily as he could. He struck the first chords of the oldest song he knew, a ballad about a miner that dated from before the Cataclysm, then swiftly shifted to a lovesong, for stories about mines and the ghosts of lost lovers would remind his audience of what they were, not of what they had been.

When he had finished the last verse of "Oh Susannah," he took a cautious step forward and began a lullaby. Though the darkness remained watchful, and horror pulsed just beyond the sound of his song, nothing stirred. Silverhair sang of the desert then, and of the moon shining clear in the sky, and of the long, sighing waves of the sea. He took another step, and another, inching his way along the path around the edge of the pit where the mummies lay.

Though his voice grew hoarse and his fingers weary he never allowed them to falter, for he could feel the music's vibrations like a sphere of protection around him and his companion, beyond which the spirits waited like a moving ring of hungry wolves. But when he could spare attention from his playing to test their silence, he thought he sensed a difference in the emotions beating against his own— hatred and anger were transmitting into confusion, curiosity, and something that might almost be identified as regret.

Silverhair swallowed and allowed the chording to shift from the major key in which he had accompanied a drinking song to a more melancholy harmony. He began to sing of love then—the love of a youth for a maiden, of a mother for her child, of a warrior for his king—the love that lifts the heart with longing and raises the soul to splendor whether or not it is returned. And as the tears slid down his cold cheeks and fell unnoticed to the path, he sensed a change in the presence around him, a perturbation of its density, as if whatever consciousness his hearers still retained was troubled now.

All the grief he had felt for his own lost hopes and distant homeland, his longing for Faris and his love for the King, all of it throbbed in the notes that were released by the harpstrings. And all the longing of the imprisoned spirits for the world that had vanished in the Cataclysm and the friends and kin and lovers that were gone was reflected back again.

Weeping, lost in his music, Silverhair moved onward, and it was only the young warrior's hand on his arm that told him they had reached the far passageway. Silverhair stopped then, standing in the entrance to the other tunnel and facing the murmurous depths of the cavern. But still he continued to play, only now it was a sleep song, a lullaby of sighing trees and sweet-scented fields lying quiet under the stars, a song of warm blankets and soft pillows and loving arms to rock one to dreamless sleep. Softly and more softly he played, and his awareness of his audience faded, faded and finally was gone.

Shaking so that he could no longer find the strings, Silverhair let the Walapai lead him stumbling down the passageway. By the time they reached its other end he had recovered enough to use sound to guide them across the dancing floor to the tunnels that connected with the entry shaft, but he was still racked by tremors that shook his whole body. He touched the cold iron of the ladder, and saw the dragon's head in silhouette above him against a square of golden glowing sky.

Only then did Silverhair dare to replace the harp in its case and strap it tight, and only the fear that the ghosts might yet wake from the sleep his music had laid upon them gave him the strength to grasp the cold railing and pull himself up the endless steps that led to the light.

It was sunset. Silverhair's eyes shut automatically against that painful splendor, then opened hungrily. He ignored the agony as his vision readjusted until he could feast upon the etched line of the mountains on the horizon and the kindling sky. *Light!* His heart constricted in adoration.

Then a touch on his leg recalled him to himself and he
hauled himself the rest of the way out of the entry shaft so
that the Walapai could follow him.

He saw movement around him, heard a babble of voices,
and shook his head in confusion. Who could be here?
Then he remembered Hosteen. The caravan leader must
have left men on guard.

But a woman's voice was screaming. Silverhair blinked
and focused on Yolande.

"Hosteen!" she cried again.

Silverhair stared at her and got shakily to his feet as she
ran toward him. "He—" His voice, worn bare by hours of
singing, cracked, and he had to swallow before he could
finish the sentence. "He followed me. . . . He is still there."
He remembered the horror in the screams he had heard and
his throat closed.

"He laid hands upon the holy things and the ghosts of
the ancestors have eaten his soul." A voice spoke from
behind him, as implacable as the stone of the caves.
Silverhair turned and saw that it was the Walapai, his hair
flaming in the dying light.

"You killed him!" shrieked Yolande. Her eyes were
ringed with white, like a frightened horse. "You ran away
and left him to die!"

Silverhair shook his head. "No. He sent *me* there to
draw off the wrath of the Guardians and give him a clear
chance at the treasure. He needed bait, and there I was,
friendless, a wanderer who would not be missed, a fool
ready to be persuaded by a woman's easy tears and open
thighs. You and he planned it together, didn't you,
Yolande?" The bitterness had grown until it burned in his
throat, and his voice rasped across her muffled sobbing
like the drawing of a sword.

"No . . . no . . . I did not know how it would be!"
Yolande shook her head again and again.

"Or you did not care to find out?"

"What happened?" she cried piteously. "Why should I
believe you? If Hosteen is dead, how did you get away?"

Silverhair stared at her, struggling with the realization
that even now she would have traded his life for that of the

man who had run toward the statue so greedily. Very likely she and Hosteen had never ceased to be lovers, and had laughed at him.

Hosteen's men began to back away from him, making the Sign against Evil.

"I went down into the earth because of love, and Hosteen went because of his lust for gold. His violence woke the ghosts, angry ghosts, Yolande—don't you know what the dead who will not leave the earth can do? But the Maker of All Music gave me the power to play for them, and they let me go. . . ."

Now Yolande had begun to edge backward. Silverhair took a step after her.

"Come here and touch me and see if I am real—" he went on. "Perhaps I am a ghost too, come to send your soul where your lover's soul has gone!" He was laughing now, for it was impossible that he should have survived, having heard what he had heard, and done what he had done. "Come now, love—won't you kiss me and find out if I am still a living man? For I am changed, Yolande—I am changed!" He opened his arms as if to embrace her and the laughter kept him from saying any more.

But she had gotten to her horse and was clambering into the saddle. She whipped the reins across the pony's neck and sent the startled animal bucketing after the two men.

By the time Silverhair's shrieking laughter had turned to sobs, then hoarse gasps that left his throat raw, the Walapai youth had gotten flint and fuel from a supply cache near the entrance and was building a little fire. Daylight was now only a memory in the west, but in the night sky the pale eyes of the stars winked down at the red eye on the desert below.

Still shuddering with the aftershocks of his emotions, Silverhair managed to take the few steps necessary to reach the fire. Carefully he lowered himself to the sand. The Walapai's hair was shining in the firelight as it had shone in the sunset light, and Silverhair realized with an odd pang that in the few hours since they had fought in the cave, all the color in the boy's hair had gone.

And I was already grey, he thought, pulling a strand of his own hair forward. *I am truly Silverhair now. . . .* But there had been too many emotions for him to care. He was alive, and that was all that mattered now.

≫ TEN ≪

It had been snowing since the day before, and Silverhair was lost. He tugged at the reins, and the pony reluctantly followed him down between the dimly perceived walls of the ravine. He knew the tendency of ravines to narrow into solid walls or to fall away in drops that could be negotiated only by a waterfall. But as long as he could follow it, this one at least offered protection from the worst of the snow and the wind.

He knew now that he should have gone back to the Valley of the Sun and faced whatever hysteria might have been stirred up by Yolande's ravings. But he had not wanted to face the fear with which the people of Aztlan might view a man who had returned from the caverns alive. Perhaps he would have done better to winter with the Walapai, but almost equally, he feared the awe with which they would have treated him.

So he had gambled on a light winter and gone west with some vague idea of turning north after he crossed the river and reaching Arena; and now he was likely to leave his bones in some fold of these wild hills. Wet and weather would disintegrate his clothing, and the beasts would polish his bones until only a scattered skeleton and the rotting fragments of a harp remained. It was better than dying in the caverns—at least from here his spirit would find its way home—but he felt a tremor of grief at the thought that Rosemary and Eric and the Master of the Junipers would never know what had become of him.

He took another step forward, slipped on a hidden rock

128

and fell. He could feel more rocks beneath the snow's deceptive blanket, and he lay for a moment, swearing as his bruises began to ache. Wet flakes of snow sifted over his face and eyelids, and he tried to shake them off. Cold snow-kisses touched his lips, tempting him to surrender to the storm's embrace.

The pony shook its head and blew. The dark patches on its white hide were all that made it visible in the snow. Silverhair grasped instinctively for the reins, but the animal was too exhausted to run away. He considered unsaddling it and letting it go to find whatever shelter it could in these hills, but it carried his meager supplies, and when they could go no farther its body might provide a little last warmth and shelter for *him*.

But why was he still struggling? The snow promised an easy death. His face and his fingers ached already and his body shook with cold, but soon all feeling would go and he could sleep beneath the snow's white pall. He grimaced, knowing it was the same perverse inability to accept defeat that had gotten him out of the caves and a thousand other dangers that kept him from taking the easy way. His breath sobbed in his throat, but he grabbed for the hanging stirrup and pulled himself upright again.

The path is clear before my feet . . . a verse from his old wandering song flickered through his awareness, and his face twisted with bitter laughter. He could see no path here, and he could not feel his way any more. He considered that fact with mixed emotions, knowing its warning even as he appreciated the relief from pain.

Even the horse was staggering. Silverhair clung to its mane as they went on. He had thought the snow might decrease if they got lower, but his dead feet told him nothing of what lay beneath it, and he could no longer see through its drifting curtains. But still he kept moving, for he knew that if either he or the horse fell now they would not get up again.

One step, then another . . . he went on while coherent thought dissolved into white eddies like the snow swirls until he was only aware that he was still upright and still in motion.

Then the horse stopped, and Silverhair had no strength to urge it onward. The ground seemed oddly level; he blinked and thought he glimpsed dark humps through the snow. His ears were ringing with cold, deafening him, but the horse whinnied, and for a moment he thought he had heard other horses neighing a reply. Then his eyes must have begun to fail, for he seemed to see shadows dancing through the whirlwind. So he closed them, and finally his legs betrayed him and he fell.

When Silverhair opened his eyes he saw a low ceiling overhead; for one terrible moment he thought he was back in the caverns. But that could not be—his head felt as if it had been stuffed with wool, but he knew that if he had been back in the caves he would not have been able to see anything at all. He blinked, and as his eyes focused he realized that this ceiling was made of brush woven tightly and chinked with red mud, not of stone.

He started to take a deep breath and gasped through choked lungs as his body rebelled. He was burning! Why was it so hot in here? He managed to turn his head and saw brown faces around him, and he wondered in sudden terror if the Walapai had followed him and taken him for punishment because he had entered the caves.

His awareness steadied until he could localize the greatest pain in his hands and feet, though his whole body seemed to be on fire. He had been stripped and wrapped in blankets whose rough weave was almost unbearable against his sensitized skin. He tried to speak, but he could only croak. A woman's face appeared, strong hands lifted his head, and a bowl of some hot bitter liquid was held to his lips.

Silverhair recognized the taste of willowbark tea from his childhood, and understood finally that they were trying to help him. He managed to grimace a smile of thanks, and when he had taken a few swallows they let him lie back again, exhausted almost to unconsciousness by even this small effort.

When he could focus once more there was someone else looking at him. He saw a face seamed and wrinkled by time as the land itself had been carved and crumpled by eons of wind and rain. But there was an ageless vigor in the black eyes that inspected him. The person turned, saying something in the tribal language, and Silverhair saw that it was an old woman, so old that gender hardly meant anything anymore.

Then she turned back to him and spoke in accented Spanyol. "Rest, we will watch over you now."

Suddenly Silverhair was shaking with cold. He surrendered to his weakness then, and let his eyes close, and soon afterward the darkness came and whirled away awareness of who and where he was.

He found himself walking a stony path that led into the bowels of the earth. At first he thought himself back in the caverns, but this path continued downward, as if the caves he had seen had been only an antechamber. And though he had no torch, a curious lavender luminescence showed ribbed stone arching overhead, flecked with crystals and studded with the bones of dragons like the one whose skull had been suspended at the entrance to the caverns.

He did not know why he was walking, or where. He knew only that at his journey's end waited something, or Someone, for which he felt both desire and fear. Reason told him to turn and flee, but his feet bore him steadily on.

And then, when he had walked long enough for Eternity to die and Time to be reborn, he came to a vast cavern filled with whisperings and the cold breath of wind. The sun had never come here. This place had never known the heat of fire. It was not meant for the presence of living things.

But it was not empty. He shuddered, hearing the whispering and a rustle like the movement of many tiny clawed feet, and he turned. But the walls of the cavern were shrouded in shadow. He could not even find the passage through which he had come. And now the sounds were getting louder, and the darkness was studded with glowing eyes.

Step by step he retreated until something high and hard like a table stopped him. Whatever was following was closer now, glimmering out of the dark. He saw little feet

clawed like the feet of rats, and reaching fingers, and faces
with bright eyes and open jaws. A scream exploded in his
throat, for he recognized the faces of the mummies of the
Ancient Ones who had come to claim him, and with them
other faces; Brian of Las Costas, men he had ridden with on
the caravans, Jehan and Faris and soldiers he had fought
beside, Thea, his father even, reaching hungrily.

He understood then that his music had only earned him
a respite, not forgiveness. Unprepared and unpurified he
had seen the sacred things. His life was forfeit to the
ancestors now. Without strength to resist he collapsed back
onto the stone altar, throat exposed and his sinewy arms
with their clever harper's hands outstretched.

"It is just," he said as the sharp teeth closed in his
flesh. "I belong to you."

He lay, his body convulsing in agony and offering, as
the ghosts began to feed. They tore away his genitals and
bored into the softness of his belly, tugging at arms and
legs as they ripped the muscles away, and his lifeblood
flowed freely across the cold stone.

And after a time that body no longer held him. He
floated, less substantial than the ghosts who fed on the
body he had worn, watching curiously as they uncovered
his bones. And then a wind whirled him upward in dizzy
spirals as it whirled the ghosts away from the bones they
had been polishing. It sighed and moaned with an oddly
familiar tone.

The wind tossed his bones and the wind thrummed
through his rib cage, as if they had been the strings of a
harp. The wind grew greater; he seemed to hear the heavy
beating of great dark wings.

"This is my Kingdom . . ." The voice seemed to come
from every direction. *"Give yourself to me and I will give
you a body that will never die."*

He answered, *"Give me a body that can sing with the
wind."*

And the darkness exploded in a shower of stars. The
stars were crystals that fell like snowflakes upon the frame-
work of his abandoned bones and clung, growing as icicles
grow on the bare branches of a tree, or stalactites from the

roof of a cave. They encased the bones in clear crystal flesh that glimmered in the dancing light, sifting down, ever down, with a shimmer of sound like the shaking of countless silver bells.

"But it is not alive—" protested the spark of awareness that had been Farin.

"I can only give you a body—the soul must be your own!"

Confused, the harper felt himself descending in hesitant spirals toward the still form. It was so hard and cold—how could he enter it? There was no opening. He flew at it, beating against the icy surface like a moth against a pane of glass.

Beating . . . beating . . . but now it was he who was beaten. He was being buffeted by great strokes from an eagle's wing. But it was hot here, and the curved walls flickered with red firelight, and many voices were chanting, "Heugh! Heugh!"

Then he was back in the cavern, but the statue before him glimmered as if it were catching and reflecting the glow of the fire. Color shifted and shimmered as if the smooth surface were melting. He cast himself downward, inward, and drowned in that dissolving crystal sea.

Heat seared his skin. He was lying on a drenched blanket; sweat poured from his body as if he were melting. Something hissed nearby and he breathed in steam. He began to cough, loosely, as if his lungs had dissolved too, and strong hands lifted him as he brought up all the liquid in which he had been drowning.

They laid him down again. The chanting continued, and above it one thin voice with the purity of a crystal bell that rose and sank in prayer. After a time the sound stopped; he sensed a breath of cooler air and a stirring around him, and later a pungent scent and more singing in that language he did not know.

When he awoke again he was warm and dry, lying in a bed of deerskins spread over sweet-smelling grass. The ceiling above him was the one he had seen before. It was all he could do to open his eyes, and he was aware of

a general aching and weakness as profound as if he had
been poured back into his skin without his bones.

Black Bird, he thought, *give me back my skeleton!*

He must have made some sound, for the door curtain
stirred and the old woman came into the room. The lines
in her face seemed to have been graven inches deeper
since he had seen her before, but when she saw him
watching her she smiled.

"You come back. That was a long journeying. How you
feel now?"

Silverhair's throat muscles worked, but no sound would
come. The woman came closer and laid a hand on his
forehead. Light shimmered around her. He blinked and
looked at her again, but it was still there.

"Tomorrow we do more doctoring. You'll be better
then, you see."

He was still barely able to move by the next morning,
but his mind was clear. He was being tended by a young
woman and a boy just entering his teens, who knew Anglo. They were feeding him a noon meal, a rich meat-
flavored gruel, when the old woman came in. They had
told him to call her White Bird Woman.

The woman who was feeding Silverhair stood up re-
spectfully, still holding the bowl. When the old one nodded to her, she took it and left the room. The harper turned
his head on the pillow to look at her.

Seen in the light that filtered through the skin-covered
window, she was only an old woman in a shapeless blue
gown and a brightly-patterned wool shawl, though her
many necklaces of shell and turquoise indicated she was a
wealthy one. But when he had seen her before she had
been wearing a skin cap decorated with the tails of many
animals, and her cloak had jingled with ornaments of
metal and bone. White Bird Woman was a Medicine
Woman, a shamaness. Judging by what he remembered,
she must have considerable power.

"Lady, I thank you. . . ." His voice wavered like an
untuned harp.

She considered him for a moment and nodded. "How you feel?"

"The evil has gone from me. But I have no strength. I feel . . . empty," he answered, pausing for breath between each phrase.

"Yes. You lost your spirits. We have to get you some more."

He grimaced. "Maybe the ghosts ate them."

Abruptly she sat down, her eyes fixing his. "Tell me."

Silverhair shuddered, feeling cold at the memory even though he was well wrapped and the room was warm. "I should warn you—I may be cursed." Haltingly he began to tell her about the great caverns of the Walapai, and how in his delirium he had dreamed he was there once more.

"And so I saw my bones and got a new body there, though it doesn't seem good for much," he finished with a sigh.

"That was a shaman's dream," she said. "The ancestors have accepted you and they will give you power."

"I'm a harper"—he shook his head weakly—"I don't want a shaman's power."

"Don't worry. They give you what you need. Tonight we do another sweat to give you strength. Then I find you new spirits so you can get strong again." White Bird Woman got to her feet. "Tell my daughter, anything you need."

"I'm a harper," Silverhair repeated stubbornly. "It would ease me if someone could set my harp on the bed beside me, even if I cannot play."

The shamaness smiled and left him, but her daughter carefully lifted Swangold from the case and laid the harp where Silverhair could touch it. He dozed throughout the rest of the day, comforted by the feel of the smooth wood beneath his hand.

This time, Silverhair was aware when they carried him into the round sweat lodge and laid him down upon the reeds. The lodge was packed with people—every adult in the village must be here. The boy, whose name was Antelope, sat beside the harper, his face shining with

apprehension and pride. There was a blackened pit in the
center of the lodge, and Silverhair, already warm beneath
his blanket, felt sweat bead on his skin as two men brought
in glowing rocks balanced on the tines of deer antlers and
piled them there—one for each direction and one for the
center, until an incandescent pyramid radiated heat into the
room.

The doorflaps were closed. Searing steam rushed over
him as the first dipperful of water was cast on the stones.
Silverhair gasped. He had done this once in his teens at the
village of his Karok grandfather near the Father of Mountains, and he knew that they practiced the discipline of the
sweat lodge at the College of the Wise; but that had been a
long time ago, when he had been young and in full health.

I was half-dead last night, he reminded himself, *and I
survived.*

Chanting throbbed in the darkness, punctuated by out-
bursts of prayer. Silverhair caught the Spanyol word for
harp and realized they were praying for *him.* Something
constricted painfully in his throat and chest, and abruptly
he was weeping hot tears that flowed easily to join the
rivers of sweat that were already drenching him.

You do not even know me! his spirit cried silently. *Why
are you doing this for me?*

The heat increased until his head was swimming, but
just when he thought he would pass out, the doorflaps
were opened and a rush of cool reviving air flowed like a
benediction across his skin. A dipper of water was passed
among the people. The boy Antelope held it to Silverhair's
lips, and it seemed to him sweeter and more invigorating
than the most exquisite wine.

More glowing rocks were brought in. Then the doors
were closed again, and darkness smothered him as water
was cast once more upon the stones and the sweat lodge
filled with steam.

"Grandfathers, grandmothers, hear us! Help our brother
with the silver hair! Grandfathers, make him strong again!"
Antelope's clear voice rose above the others.

"Heugh! Ai-yah!" the people replied.

The stones are earth heated by fire, and the steam is

water and air combined . . . thought Silverhair dazedly.
Surely the great Guardians of the Elements were being
invoked here as powerfully as they ever had been in the
stately ceremonies of Westria. *O you Guardians of this
place and of my own golden land! Help me and strengthen
me and bless these people who are trying to help me here!*

Again emotion swept him away on a bitter tide of love
for the sweating people around him, of grief for all that he
had ever loved and lost, and for all that might be and
might have been. Until now he had been silent, but the
gasping breaths he drew in were coming out in a series of
short moans which grew into a scream, a shout of power
that seemed too great for the wasted body from which it
had come.

He heard the shrill murmur of the Medicine Woman's
voice beside him and jerked painfully as she began to beat
along his body with the eagle's wing. He was pushed
beyond consciousness, beyond control, twitching and crying
out in an anguish that transformed itself into an agony of
longing for a beauty whose nature his senses could not
comprehend, and a union with Someone whose name he
did not know.

The feathers were still sweeping along his body, but the
superheated air in the lodge was swirling in powerful
eddies, buffeted by the fanning of other wings that clapped
like thunder in the confined space of the lodge. The singing intensified, rising to a pitch of passion that seemed
beyond the power of humans to sustain. It was lifting
him—in a moment he would be carried away. . . .

Then the air stilled, and the beat of great wings faded
away. Someone pulled the flaps aside and Silverhair breathed
deeply of the cooling air. His heartbeat gradually steadied,
and he returned to awareness of who and where he was.

There was a third round in which the singing changed to
a slow, harmonic chant of thanksgiving and farewell. The
heat was almost bearable now. By the time it ended and
the flaps were opened so that the Sacred Pipe could be
offered to the elements and passed around the circle,
Silverhair found that he could sit up.

The aromatic smoke of the pipe swirled toward him as

each person puffed. He breathed it in, feeling his blood begin to sing in his veins, and when the pipe reached him he was able to hold it without fear of dropping it and raise it in the ceremonial manner to his lips. The bowl was smooth, cool, carved with designs he could not see, and beads and feathers adorned the pipestem. He drew the smoke in carefully, reverently, feeling it charge his body with new energy, and he found that his fingers were tingling where he had touched it after he passed it on.

His body was recovering from the weakness that had paralyzed it, but his spirit was still empty, waiting like a new vessel for the Guardians to fill. All his life he had struggled to shape his reality—to achieve knighthood, to become a harper, to find Faris and bring her home. Now he only waited, ready at last for whatever the Grandfathers should choose to give to him.

They sweated the next night too, and by the time they were done Silverhair could stand and even eat a little of the ceremonial meal that followed. But still he was bound in the passive state in which he had been left by his illness.

"Next week we do a ceremony, when the moon is new," said White Bird Woman. "You need new spirits to help you or you get sick again."

So he rested, waiting, and even began to practice the harp, smiling when people seemed to materialize from the village around him to hear him play.

The name of the place in Anglo was Red Rock Valley, and the tribe wintered there because the high walls protected it from the worst of the wind and snow. Silverhair's horse had scented the village herds and led him here. The tribesmen did not seem to find this remarkable, but without their woodcraft, Silverhair knew what a miracle his survival had been.

Then came a night when the wind swept the clouds away and the new moon lifted over the white peaks around them like a sliver of pearl. Silverhair, dressed in a new white tunic embroidered in red, joined the other people who were moving toward the largest house in the village, which had been emptied of its usual furnishings for the occasion. There was a festival atmosphere about them; normally this ceremony would be held to give someone spiritual helpers when he came of age. Only rarely did an adult need to have it performed again.

Antelope held him outside until everyone else had entered, then escorted him through the low door and told him to sit on the blanket near the center of the room. The two drummers were already in place, and White Bird Woman sat across from them, talking to her daughter. As Silverhair came in she looked up and smiled at him.

"I still don't understand—" he began, but she shook her head at him.

"You don't do anything. Just sit there and maybe lie down when I show you."

Feeling awkward, he lowered himself to the blanket, noticing with surprise that Swangold was already there. Why had they brought the harp? Did they think he was afraid to be parted from it? Or else— Uneasily he remembered what the Medicine Woman had said about a shaman's tools and her pronouncement on the fancies he had had during his delirium. Did she intend to consecrate him and the harp with some kind of shamanic power?

He wanted to get up, to stop her. The Way of the Shaman was not for him! But her placid good humor made him ashamed. Surely such a thing could not happen to him against his will. . . .

White Bird Woman nodded and the doors were shut, plunging the house into deep darkness. Silverhair twitched, remembering the caverns, but this was a warm and breathing blackness, not the dead chill of the caves. He smelled the pungent odor of sage and knew that someone was using a feather fan to send the smoke of the smouldering herbs around the room.

Softly at first, and then with greater certainty and power, the drummers began. Silverhair felt the vibration through the earthen floor. For several minutes nothing else happened except that he found his breathing steadying to match the beat of the drums.

Then he sensed movement near him and heard the dry scrape of a rattle. Leather fringe brushed his hand and he

realized that White Bird Woman had begun to dance. Soon
she was singing too, short phrases repeated over and over
while the people echoed her. A faint humming came from
beside him—the harpstrings were vibrating in sympathy
with the song.

Silverhair wondered how long it would take for it to
become unbearably boring, but as the singing went on he
found that he could hear new subtleties in tone and pitch
and rhythm; his consciousness was narrowing, focusing,
until the singing was all he knew.

He felt dizzied, as if the tilt of the earth had shifted, and
he blinked as the darkness was spangled with swirling
sparkles of light. He felt his skin tingling, and a sense of
pressure as if the room were filled with almost too much
energy for it to contain.

Then the shamaness ceased singing, and cried out, and
was answered by a deep, sweet calling and a rattle of
ascending wings. Silverhair's hair stirred as something
went by, and he felt gooseflesh on his arms. White Bird
Woman called again, and this time it was a heavy padding
and the soft snarl of a great cat that answered her. Again
she called, and Silverhair heard dainty hooves click on the
hard floor and a moist snorting close by. *Guardians preserve me!* he thought then. *If she calls any more of her
allies there will never be room for us all!*

But after a few moments the physical manifestations
ceased, although the sense of animal presences was still
heavy in the room. Silverhair let out a deep breath, then
tensed as he felt the old woman kneel beside him. Her dry
hand touched his forehead, then his chest, pushing him
down on the blanket beside the harp. He felt his senses
leaving him, and then, as abruptly as if she had pushed
him through a doorway, he was no longer in the dark
room.

He was outside now, in the brilliant sunlight of a summer
morning. But it was cool, for he was high in the mountains
in a meadow surrounded by sighing pines. He looked
around him. Beyond the trees rose sheer walls of grey
stone, embroidered by the silver lace of waterfalls. Famil-

iarity nagged at him; he ought to recognize this place, but he knew that he had never been here before.

A cry came from overhead, like the call of a hawk but more musical, and he saw the dark silhouette of a bird gliding through the clear air, soaring in a great circle that brought it low enough for Silverhair to see the glint of sunlight on bronze feathers before it shot upward again. He forgot to breathe as he watched it, for the bird's flight had the concise beauty of a perfect harmony.

Then it was gone, and he was able to see other things once more. A faint path led through the meadow toward the trees in the direction in which the hawk had flown. Silverhair followed it. The bird was waiting for him when he emerged from the pines into another clearing, perched on an upper branch with its head swiveled to watch him with bright golden eyes. It launched itself suddenly, swooped low over the harper's head and then up over the dome of a circular building of pale granite that glistened in the sun.

No, it was more than a glistening—it was the same kind of shimmer he had seen around White Bird Woman or the Master of the Junipers when he was performing a ceremony. Yet it seemed natural for Silverhair to climb the broad stairs and open the heavy redwood door.

The hush inside was so intense that it was almost audible. For a moment he stood blinking, growing used to the shadowless silvery light. Four long windows spaced around the walls framed oblongs of azure sky.

In the center of the chamber a throne of marble was set into the polished surface of the floor. Silverhair could see no occupant, but he was overwhelmingly aware of a Presence waiting there, eternally patient and immeasurably powerful.

"Seeker, why have you come here?"

For a moment he was at a loss for an answer, then he fell back upon the response he had given when he presented himself for that first initiation in which Westrians took their adult names. *"I seek to learn my goal and my name."*

"Only you can decide who you are and what the purpose of your life shall be." The pressure eased while Silverhair considered this, then words came to him again.

"Choose one of the directions. Your guide will come to you. . . ."

Remembering the orientation of the valley, Silverhair realized that the windows faced the four directions. If he looked north, he would be choosing the Powers of Earth—the stability of Earth's bones, the vigor of the soil and its nourishment. If he looked south he would face the fires of sun and star, of the volcano that destroyed and of the hearthfire that served mankind. There lay the realms of all warm-blooded creatures and the passions that ruled them. The Lady of Love reigned there. He turned to the west, where the moon floated above the kingdoms of the sea, but the powers of the waters were not his to rule.

He turned once more until he faced the east again and the Powers of Air.

And even as he moved a wind blew through the window and he breathed deeply of air like the breath of stars. The light grew brighter, dazzling him, and as he blinked he seemed to see in the window a figure whose drapery streamed away in banners of orange, and he heard the merry laughter of a boy.

Then he staggered as a warm weight settled on his shoulder. Sharp talons pricked his skin, as Aliento's talons had done when he carried the hawk to freedom so long ago.

"Go on—" The communication seemed to come from very close to him. *"What are you waiting for?"*

Silverhair stepped to the window and gazed in wonder at the landscape of sculptured clouds.

"Well, don't stand there gawking—" he heard, *"use your wings!"* Talons dug into his shoulder, then the bird launched itself, and in the same moment the harper realized that he did indeed have wings, great pinions that expanded from his shoulders. He leaped to the windowsill and extended them, felt the wind catch and lift him, and, wings beating strongly, he pulled himself into the sky in pursuit of the hawk that flew just ahead of him.

Of course, he thought as he gained height, sideslipped with a twitch of a feather, and sped forward. *This is how it feels to fly. How could I have forgotten?* For he had seen this landscape before, in his dreams, and in his dreams he had always had wings.

Now the hawk had circled around to fly beside and a little beyond him, and it was communicating with him again.

"*This is our kingdom, the kingdom of the winds that carry to us all the sounds of the earth and bear us wherever we wish to go.*"

Then there was a timeless space in which the hawk showed him the use of his powers, teaching him to soar and plummet, to use the wind to glide and the air currents to lift majestically into the heavens again. And Silverhair followed him, drunk with flight, and the crisp air thrummed and whistled through his outstretched wings.

And all the time they were rising through layers of cloud, pausing sometimes to greet the other creatures who floated there, but always moving upward until gradually their flight became less a physical movement than a perceptual progression through the skies.

"*Where are we going?*" said the winged creature that was Silverhair. The air around them had brightened so that only a bird's eyes could still see. They were drenched with light, suffused with it. It shone through them so that the other hawk glowed like a lantern whose feathers were picked out in gold.

And the hawk had grown larger. It came to Silverhair that this was no ordinary red-tail, but one of the Guardians, and even as he thought this, the other opened its beak and began to sing.

> "*I am the spirit that forever soars,*
> *I am the singer as I am the song;*
> *I am the Light the seeking soul adores,*
> *The harmony to which all notes belong . . .*"

And even as it sang its outlines were being lost in a greater radiance, and its singing in a music that swelled in volume and gathered complexity as first one, then another voice joined the harmony. At first he thought the sounds came from instruments—viols, flutes and brass and a

ripple of harps—and then it seemed to him that they must
be human voices, each in its own range, and then, the
many different voices of birds.

But it was all of those together, the melodies mingling
in a unity which still allowed each single voice its
unique contribution to the whole. It was the consummation
of Music that Silverhair had only glimpsed in those moments when he ceased to control the music and both he
and Swangold had become a single instrument upon which
Someone else could briefly play.

"This is what I am searching for!" The cry broke from
him. *"Give me the power to play the music I am hearing
now!"*

He struggled to beat upward where there was no longer
an earthly atmosphere to support his wings, to hear with
his ears a music which his senses could not comprehend.
But it seemed to him that for a moment he understood the
voices. They were the turning of the earth and the ebb and
flow of the tides, the changing of the seasons and the birth
and death and transformation of all that lived. And then for
a moment he understood that all of those separate things
were only single notes of the music which was being combined into a transcendent melody by Someone who played
the world as Silverhair played Swangold, with strings
made of wind. He strove to merge with that music, but
even now, here, there was still some lack, some barrier.
Overwhelmed, his spirit spun away.

Silverhair opened his eyes, still mazed by a confusion of
images which had recapitulated and reversed his journey.
He groaned and tried to sink back within himself, but the
hands of the shamaness were holding his head firmly, and
her gaze would not let him go.

"You have a powerful helper—it's the red-tailed hawk,
the little eagle," she said. "But I think you know." She
looked very tired, but content.

The doors had been opened and the lamps lit. Around
them people were getting to their feet to go. Their faces
held some emotion like the afterglow in the sky when the

sun has set, and for the first time Silverhair wondered what his experience had looked like from the outside.

Had he spoken in tongues or rolled like a hoop about the floor? Their eyes rested upon him with friendship, or curiosity, but the awe came into their faces when they looked at the harp that was still beside him on the floor.

"Oh yes—" said White Bird Woman, "the vision was not just for you. While you were on your journey, the harp played all by itself in the wind."

⇒ 3 ⇐

The Songmaster

Second Interlude

The harper rides with the reins loose on the pony's neck, his instrument clasped in his arms. Music flows from beneath his fingers, delicate and unconstrained as the wind that stirs his silvered hair. The sun shines shyly, as if not yet sure of its welcome after the winter's cold, and spring flowers jewel the dun slopes where the desert sweeps down from the hills.

All these things are in the harper's music—the playful breeze, the flowing flowers, the azure purity of the sky. The sun sparks gold from the strings as the harper's fingers flicker across them in shimmering glissandos that resolve into single sounds that throb at last to silence in the listening air. Then a chord breaks the silence, followed by another, until the music leaps in a gleeful dance that makes the pony move faster, adding the percussive beat of his hooves.

How long has it been since the harper has played with such delight in the making of music? He cannot remember; at this moment he has no awareness outside the moment and the joy of pure sound. And yet there is still something missing—his fingers are still inadequate to transmit the

147

music his heart is hearing—the perfect harmony he is seeking remains just beyond his grasp.

Still, this is so much more than he has known for many years that the quick tears blur his sight. The face of his sister is becoming a fair dream, but his search for her has become part of a greater quest. Sheltered by the desert's isolation, purified by the touch of death's bright wing, he understands that the goal he seeks now is worth a lifetime of wandering.

⋙ ELEVEN ⋘

"And yet another path I'd find
That leads where Beauty's true self lies,
And where, though now I follow blind,
The singing hawk still soars the skies,
So I'll not cease from wandering . . ."

Silverhair stood at the top of the pass that led from the mountains north of the Tambara down to the long valleys of the Campos del Mar, squinting against the glare of the setting sun upon the distant sea. He felt his heartbeat quicken, and smiled. He was still only halfway to his goal, but the worst of his journey was over. Now he could allow himself to believe he would reach the College of Bards.

He had left White Bird Woman and her people when the brief desert spring was beginning to haze the hillsides with green, and headed westward. It had not been easy to leave the village. During the long winter months they had become like family to him, and they had not wanted him to go away. But he had his strength back now, and the Medicine Woman herself had put the conviction that had come to him in his vision into words—*"The spirits want you to serve them, but music is your power. You find teacher, do it right."*

He had been self-taught even in the beginning, and years of wandering had made him careless and clumsy. And now that he had heard the music of heaven, when he played his harp he winced at the inequalities of tone, the uneven rhythms and faulty fingering, the lack of imagination in his harmonies.

There was only one place where he could learn the technique and the discipline and the musical theory he needed so badly, and that was in Westria, at the College of Bards.

And so he had headed south from the valley, and then he had turned westward through the Iron Hills and made his way across the Drylands of Elaya, earning his way by playing for festivals at the isolated holdings along the way. Sometimes the only excuse for the festival had been his presence there. He had traveled with the couriers, or more slowly with the mule trains that carried ingots of raw iron to the foundries east of the Tambara. And sometimes he had pushed on alone, playing for himself in the evenings, under the immensity of the desert sky.

But the road that he saw uncoiling before him now led through the northernmost state of Elaya and up the coast to Santibar. And beyond lay the golden hills of Westria. Silverhair had no desire to use the name he had left behind him ten years before, nor to seek out Rosemary or Eric or anyone that he had known; yet even so, something deep within him eased at the thought of breathing in the familiar scent of bay laurel on a sun-baked hillside, or hearing the soft speech of his homeland once more.

He smiled and urged his pony down the hill, and the melody of his wandering song began to reecho in his memory. Ahead of him, a single hawk wheeled and called and slid off across the sky.

Saticoy was full of soldiers. Silverhair rode slowly down the main street of the town and across the plaza, avoiding the groups of men-at-arms with sleeveless hauberks of hardened leather and bright steel banding their leather helms. Their officers wore polished breastplates and backplates that repelled the sun in blinding flashes, and their brimmed steel helmets were shaded by dark red plumes. At least they did not belong to Prince Palomon's guard. Silverhair remembered only too vividly those same silver helmets crowned with plumes of bright blue.

There were crowds of townspeople too, hurrying across the plaza laden with purchases, or clustered in front of some craftsman's stall. The broad valley that meandered between the shaggy southern hills and the taller, more starkly sculptured mountains to the north was rich, and the market was full of local vegetables. The cries of merchants hawking their wares echoed from adobe walls, rising above the liquid murmur of Spanyol as people bargained with craftsmen whose smiles showed that they knew the worth of their weaving and leather and silverwork. Clearly, there was no war in this land. Why then were there so many soldiers?

A trumpet rang faintly from the direction of the white-washed fortress on the hill. A red banner was flickering above its tower, too far away for Silverhair to make out its device. The trumpet sounded again and a little anxious stir ran through the crowds. He saw the soldiers straighten, and felt an odd focusing of attention. An almost palpable tension vibrated in the air.

He reined his horse into an alleyway and turned so that he could see. He was in no hurry—the supplies in his saddlebags would see him to Santibar, where he could find a ship to carry him northward or restock and head up the coastal road. He wanted to see this great lord who could throw the busy town into a flutter merely by passing through its streets.

He listened to the townsfolk, trying to learn the man's name, but it was sufficient for them to call him "the Protector," and once or twice a title that sounded like "the Hidden One." A small, dark-bearded man said something about sorcery, but when he saw Silverhair watching him, he made the sign against evil and drew his companion away.

Silverhair shrugged and moved the spotted pony forward. He drew rein beside two men who were standing at the entrance to the alleyway.

"I am a foreigner and have not been this way before—" he said pleasantly. "Who is this great lord you are waiting for?" Over the years his Spanyol had been colored by the accent of Aztlan, and with his soft boots and tribal blanket they would certainly not suspect him of being a Westrian.

"He is the Lord Protector of the Campos del Mar—" the dark-bearded man began.

"He is *El Sangrado,* the Bloodlord, who is afraid to show his face to men," added his companion. "But men do not speak that name very loud."

"Now that the Conde de Las Palisadas is dead, he rules the Campos as if it were all his own. But there will be a reckoning when the Conde's son is grown. . . ."

"Hush!" said his companion, "they are coming now."

Silverhair straightened in the saddle and looked across the square. The steady drumbeat was closer now, and he could hear fifes twittering. Then he saw the musicians— Elayan guardsmen marching in formation as they played, followed by two more pairs of soldiers whose armor was polished to a silver gloss and whose cloaks glowed red as blood in the sun.

They tramped steadily across the plaza, their pikes held at a precise angle so that the honed blades flashed in the sun. The faces shaded by the brims of their silvered helms were emotionless. Silverhair wondered if they served their mysterious leader from fear or blind loyalty.

Behind them, several men in the drab gowns of clerks attempted to keep their mules in some kind of formation. On the left breast of each gown was a red patch with a device—the same device he saw emblazoned on the banner that followed them—argent, a wolf's head caboshed, on a crimson field. He did not recognize it, but obviously its owner understood ceremony.

The leader himself was coming now, keeping a tight rein on a big palomino who pranced and curvetted as the banner snapped in the breeze. Silverhair wondered why they called him the Hidden One, for his face was quite visible beneath the broad red hat he wore. Something about the way he sat his horse teased at the harper's memory. If only he could make out his features—

The procession was very close now. Silverhair saw more attendants and guards marching in close order behind their leader. Then the little dark man in front of him hissed

"Etranjero!" and spat across the cobbles just as the great lord went by.

The palomino snorted and tried to rear, and instantly soldiers swarmed around them, seizing the man who had spat and reaching for Silverhair's bridle rein. The harper hardly noticed. He was staring at the man on the palomino. He could see his face, but somehow he could not focus on his features at all. The soldier pulled Silverhair's pony out into the street, and, startled back to awareness by the movement, the harper's gaze swept back, then fixed on the merry-faced man on a piebald horse who followed the man in the red robe.

Silverhair recognized *him* with no difficulty at all. And then all the little clues fell into place, and he knew who the faceless foreign lord of the Campos del Mar had to be.

The guards grabbed for Silverhair's arm and began to pull him off the pony. The little dark man was already being dragged away. Silverhair saw the anticipation in their faces and knew they would kill him if he tried to defend himself.

"Desterrado!" he cried desperately. "Desterrado, do you remember me?"

The man in red reined in his horse so that it sank back on its haunches. Their eyes met, and for a moment the will that obscured the other man's features wavered, and Silverhair looked into the scarred face of Caolin.

"My guards may at times become overenthusiastic, but you must admit they are effective," said Caolin.

Silverhair turned back from his contemplation of the scarlet bougainvillea vines that spilled over the cliffs toward the valley to look at his host, conscious of a deepening feeling of unreality. At least Caolin had now changed his garments and wore a high-necked caftan of white silk piped in red. It had been unnerving to see him dressed in crimson as if he were still Westria's Seneschal.

He still remembered the hovel in which he had last seen Caolin. The contrast between that squalor and the elegant simplicity of this villa overlooking the valley and the sea, with its subtly patterned tiles and smooth, whitewashed walls, was oddly disturbing. He glanced at his host, then away.

"Thank you for calling them off before they damaged me!" The harper managed a rueful smile. There had been a tense moment before Caolin had recognized him; the guards had already been drawing their swords.

Now that he considered it, he was amazed that Caolin had known him, with his face worn by illness and weathered by desert suns, and his hair gone silver as snow. He cast another covert glance at his host. The older man had ceased to employ whatever magic had veiled his features before, and he had not replaced it with any illusion of perfection. Silverhair saw that ten years had brought some healing, but Caolin's fine features were still blurred and distorted by slick mottled skin.

"I don't understand why that man would"—he sought for a tactful phrase—"would wish to insult you. Are you not the lord here now?"

Caolin nodded and reached to refill the harper's goblet with wine. It was a delicate white wine, probably from Westria, chilled so that one could hardly taste the alcohol. Silverhair lifted it to his lips for politeness' sake, then set it down. He had drunk nothing but water and herb tea since he left the Valley of the Sun, and he did not want to lose control of himself now, not when he was supping with Caolin.

"I am the Regent," said Caolin. "My own lands are in the Campos, in the mountains near the Dragon's Tail Pass. When the Conde died last year, it made sense for the Prince to appoint me to rule until the Conde's son attains the years and health he needs to govern his heritage."

Caolin reached to the silver tray for another tidbit of shrimp that had been baked with butter and garlic in its own puff of pastry. The tray was made of carved silver, and it rested on a stand of manzanita wood that had been smoothed and polished to bring out the rich red and white of the grain. There were little concoctions of spiced pork on the tray too, and pickled rice with centers of hot ginger rolled in thin seaweed. Silverhair had tried one or two when they sat down, but they were almost too rich for a palate used to the simple food of the tribes.

Caolin had never used to care what he ate, Silverhair remembered. He looked more closely at the shape beneath the folds of the caftan and decided there was more solidity there now. Weight as well as scarring had blurred the outline of Caolin's jaw. Silverhair thought, *He doesn't look so much like a mountain wolf now.*

Caolin was looking at him, and Silverhair realized that he had let the conversation lapse for too long.

"But why choose you instead of the Conde's widow?" he asked, remembering how the lady Alessia had taken over the rule of Las Costas after Lord Brian died.

"This is not Westria. The noblewomen here are sheltered, and though the lady Aisha is of the Royal House, she has no experience of government. Her son is in Los Leones with Prince Palomon. She herself remains in Las Palisadas and concerns herself with the education of her second child, a girl."

For a moment he could not imagine why Caolin had added that piece of information. Then he remembered that the Condesa was the sister of Prince Palomon, and suddenly he would have wagered that her little daughter was now about nine years old. He wondered if she looked like Caolin. Afraid his face would reveal his thoughts, he turned quickly to examine the marble statue set into a niche in the wall.

"I see . . ." he said carefully.

"Yes, I am sure that you do." Caolin's voice held a hint of amusement and Silverhair was suddenly certain that the other man had meant him to understand. "Whoever inherits this state will find it prosperous and orderly. Of course the people resented me at first. They have not been used to a strong government, and there was some protest, but I think they are beginning to see the advantages of order, now. . . ."

With the help of your guards, thought Silverhair, but he did not say so. Unthinking, he reached for his wine and swallowed gratefully.

A slender, dark-eyed boy came in to remove the silver

tray, and another, who might have been his twin, replaced it with a new one on which a variety of preserved fruits and sweetmeats had been arranged.

"But what about you?" Silverhair set his goblet down. "What will *you* have when you have given up this stewardship?" He stopped short, aware that the wine had loosened his tongue more than he anticipated and afraid he had angered Caolin.

But the Lord of the Campos was turning his own goblet back and forth between his fingers, staring down into the crystal depths of the wine it held. The harper realized that the slip about the lady Aisha, and the unveiled face Caolin was showing him, were both saying the same thing. Caolin might have superiors, like Palomon, and servants who knew his secrets, like Ordrey, but only Silverhair knew so much of his past and yet was so unconnected with his present. The harper must be very nearly the only man to whom Caolin could talk freely now. Dimly he remembered Thea's prophecy, and discounted it. Thea had been deluded about many things. Caolin was not his enemy.

"My lord Palomon has learned to know my worth," said Caolin quietly. "He understands how to use me, and I believe that I have served him well."

"In the marketplace they say that he is ill, that he's failing—" answered Silverhair. "Will his nephew favor you if he comes to rule?"

"Palomon is an old lion with many years left in him. The reports of his illness have been exaggerated by hysterical fools. But I have been laying my own plans. By the time there is a change in the lordship of Elaya, I will be so strong there will be nothing anyone can do to hinder me."

Silverhair opened his mouth to ask him just what it was that no one would be able to stop him doing, but realized in time that if Caolin did indeed have designs on Elaya, even this openness would hardly extend to a discussion of what they were. And on the whole, Silverhair thought he would be safer as well as more comfortable if he did not know.

"You see how I have risen from the ashes of the past—" Caolin gestured gracefully at the beauty around them. "In another ten years the world will know what I can do. This is what I was born for. . . ."

It was almost dark now. Servants were lighting little lamps with shields of colored glass. Silverhair took another long swallow of wine, then felt Caolin's eyes upon him and set the goblet rather abruptly down.

"But you have not told me about yourself," Caolin said gently. "Were you coming here to seek service with me? In your years of wandering you must have seen many wonders." In the dim uncertain light Caolin's features blurred, or perhaps it was the effect of the wine.

Silverhair shook his head. Remembering the hope with which he had begun those wanderings, his heart contracted with pain for a vanished dream. Caolin had become a lord in Elaya, but he—what had he done?

"When I left you, I went over the mountains into the Ramparts and later to the Barren Lands . . ." he began, and continued, sometimes stumbling, sometimes vividly, as the embers of memory caught fire. It was dark when he finished, and he felt as weary as if he had done it all again.

"And so I have realized how little I really know about music," he said finally. "I will go to the College of Bards not as Sir Farin Harper, but as Silverhair the Wanderer, and ask them to teach me the right way."

He closed his eyes, hearing again in memory the transcendent music of his vision. Then Caolin spoke, and Silverhair could almost have thought there was something wistul in his tone.

"Yes, I think that is what you should do. In a way I almost envy you."

In the morning, Caolin gave Silverhair an escort to set him on his way. By noon he was winding along the narrow coast road where steadily more impressive mountains swept down toward the sea. By nightfall, Silverhair had passed between the twin stone pillars that marked the border of Westria and skirted the proud sandstone walls of the fortress of Balleor to come to the town of Santibar, where he found an inn that would give him a bed in exchange for a few songs.

He was tempted to stay there for a while, for in Santibar the expansive and colorful vigor of Elaya enlivened the more harmonious taste of Westria. He walked along avenues where stately oaks alternated with palms and he understood why the town had so often been the prize of Westria and Elaya's wars. A conflict over Santibar had sparked the war in which he had fought ten years ago, though its great battle had taken place in the Great Valley, not here.

But before three days had passed he was on his way once more, following the road up the coast, where steep hills sloped down to gentle beaches, and only the smokes of scattered holdings spoke of the presence of men. At the fortress of Stonegate he turned inland, exchanging the brushy slopes of the south for the gentle oak-studded hills, green now with spring, which had haunted his dreams.

For this land was Westrian without dispute; the smell of the air proclaimed it, and the taste of the water, and the very shapes of the hills. Alone, he tried to analyze his emotions and found this sense of familiarity made it seem stranger than any foreign land he had seen.

And still he continued northward, through days when the sun shone brightly or the mists drifted like silver veils in from the sea, following the road until it led straight up a long valley through which a little river trickled northwestward toward the sea. He traveled more quickly now, with less care to preserve his pony's strength and his own, for now he was very near his goal.

The valley was rich, with many holdings where he could claim a bed in the barn or a corner of the hearth when evening fell. Silverhair was grateful for the comfort, for the early summer nights were still cold, and though he had known chill in the mountains of Aztlan, there was a dampness in the coastal air that set up a sympathetic aching in all his old wounds. Swangold, on the other hand, seemed to thrive on the moisture. Silverhair thought he had never known the harp's tone to be so full and resonant.

For several days he rode toward the fogbank that blocked the end of the valley like a wall. At the end of May he came to the sea at last and found people who nodded

graciously and pointed toward the forested mountains at the
northern end of the bay when he asked for the College of
Bards.

The scent of redwood bark and needles filled the air
with a dry, spicy perfume. Silverhair rounded the final
bend in the road, drew rein in the gateway, and then
simply sat, breathing it in. He knew then that whatever
might happen to him here or after, the scent of sun-
warmed redwood would always for a moment return him
to this moment, and this place. . . .

After a little while he recovered enough to see other evidence that he had found the College. Snatches of music drifted
from the buildings and the forest, in general the single
repeated lines of practice, but occasionally a choir of
voices periodically interrupted by the exasperated correc-
tion of its master. The gate before which he was sitting
was built of redwood beams. To either side were slabs of
wood whose worn gilding outlined the harps carved there.

It was also a low gateway. After a moment's thought,
Silverhair dismounted and tethered his pony to the fence.
Then he slung the harpcase over his shoulder and went
through. A fair-haired boy in the brownish-purple wool
tunic of a student was raking the pathway. As Silverhair
came up to him he paused in his work and smiled.

"Can you tell me where I might find the Master of the
College?" asked Silverhair, hoping that the last week or
two had gotten him back to talking like a Westrian.

The boy straightened and wiped sweat from his forehead. "Well, no . . ." he said slowly. "Master Andreas
went up to Sanjos for the week, and he's not yet returned.
But I can call his Deputy, if you want to talk to her."

Silverhair nodded and followed the boy to the worn
steps that led up to the porch of the largest of the complex
of buildings. They were all built of redwood so that they
seemed to have grown where they stood. He waited with
no sense of impatience. He had renounced it, along with
his pride, when the hawk that had guided him through his
vision had shown him what music could really be.

Then he heard the boy's voice again pleading with a

massive figure that filled the doorway above him, and he realized that he was about to face the first test to his humility.

"Well, what do you want? I don't have all day!" The woman's voice boomed, then faded, as she turned back to the boy behind her. "Aurel, you should have sent him on his way—I cannot deal with every mendicant who happens by!" She emerged fully from the doorway and Silverhair looked up at a stoutly built woman whose dark gown was so lavishly banded with embroidery that its color could hardly be seen. Only the little golden harp on its chain proclaimed her a Master Bard—that, and the voice whose resonance he could feel even when she was scolding.

"Well?" she repeated, fixing him with pale eyes. He suddenly felt as if he had reverted to childhood.

"I am begging, but not for bread—" Silverhair answered with what dignity he could. "I seek admission as a student here."

For a moment she was silenced, and her mouth opened a little as she looked him up and down. Silverhair winced, realizing how she must see him, with his patched boots and greasy striped blanket, and a stained felt hat half hiding his untrimmed white hair.

"Old man, I am sorry," she said with an effort. "If you love music you can hear it in Montera or Sanjos. That is not what we are for."

"I am glad to hear it," he answered with a little asperity. "And I am not as old as I look. I am a harper, and for ten years I have earned my way by playing along the roads." He threw back his blanket to show the worn harpcase.

"Then go ply your trade there for ten years more!" Her misplaced sympathy had made her angry, and her face was reddening as she drew breath to blast him again.

"This is a school for musicians, not for mountebanks! If you had any talent you should have come here ten, fifteen years ago. But in any case, we accept no one without a recommendation, even when he is young, and none comes without some contribution to pay for his training here!" Her voice echoed against the trees, and even in his anger Silverhair wondered what it would be like loosed in song.

He drew himself up, lips trembling with words she had probably never heard before. But the road had taught him to keep his temper, and he told himself that a man who had survived the Cavern of the Ancient Ones could bear a tongue-lashing from a stout soprano. She was already turning with a final snort of disdain. Silverhair jumped as she slammed the door behind her.

For a moment it was very still. He was unnaturally aware of the constant background murmur of the wind in the trees. Silverhair sighed, and his anger began to drain away. What was he going to do? He had planned as far as this moment, but it had not occurred to him that they would not let him in. Aimlessly he started back down the path, then left it and dropped down to sit with his back to the friendly trunk of a redwood tree.

He could go back, pound on the door, tell them who he was—although he was not sure they would believe him. He could send to Rosemary or Alessia of Las Costas for money and the letter of recommendation they required. . . . Without thinking, he had settled the harpcase beside him and unbuckled it. When he realized what he was doing, he smiled, pulled it open and settled Swangold upon his knees. This was a good place for music, no matter how surly its people might be. Surely they would not prohibit him from playing here, and maybe the music would help him decide what to do now.

Carefully he tuned, then let his fingers wander among the strings, seeking the right melody. After a time his eyes closed and he let his head rest against the tree while his whole being focused on the music.

"That is lovely—where did you learn that tune?"

For a moment the soft voice seemed part of Silverhair's own thoughts. Then his eyes flicked open and he saw a tall man in a dull purple robe sitting on the ground a few feet away. Sunlight falling through the branches above shone on the silver that was threaded liberally through his brush of brown hair, but his dark eyes were those of a little child.

The harper forced his attention back to the melody he had been playing. "It's from Elaya—a love song, with some variations of my own," he said a little shyly. He was still half lost in the music, and all his defenses were down.

"Do you know more music from the southern lands?" the gentle voice spoke again.

"Yes"—Silverhair grinned reminiscently—"and the music of the Barren Lands, and Aztlan, and even some songs from the Sea of Grass. I have made my living learning such things—" The words reminded him of the woman at the door, and he could feel the joy leaving his face.

"Sing—"

Silverhair's eyes narrowed in resentment, but there was something impersonal and compelling about the man who sat before him as if he had grown there, and what did it matter, after all?

> *"Boat, bear me back, over the sea,*
>   *Back to the land where my heart is—*
>   *Weary the soul of the wanderer must be,*
>   *Far from the land where the heart is . . ."*

"Yes, when I saw your harp I thought it must be you," said the stranger. "I once heard you singing for the King. He wanted to send you here—why have you waited so many years to come to me?"

Silverhair stared at him, shock draining all power of expression while his mind raced wildly. Many people had heard him play when the Court was in Laurelynn, and again at Misthall when the King was dying there. There had always been such confusion—he might not have remembered this man. But the King had only spoken of sending him to the College once, to the Master Bard, who was . . .

Silverhair let out his breath and set Swangold carefully on the ground. He must be very stupid not to have realized immediately whom he was talking to.

"My lord Andreas, forgive me," he said slowly. "I had reasons for leaving Westria that seemed good to me then, and in a sense I have still not come home. I am not Sir Farin Harper anymore. But I have learned enough to know how far my playing is from real music, and I was hoping that here, if anywhere, I could learn the right way—" He shrugged helplessly.

"We can teach you some things, certainly, although you may not always find it easy. You will have much to unlearn," said the Master Bard. "But why are you sitting out here? Were you waiting for me?"

Silverhair looked at him in astonishment. "I have just been informed that I am too old to learn, and I have no recommendations, or funds to pay my way. Your Deputy threw me out!"

"Oh. Huldah . . . You must not mind her. She will like you better when she has heard you sing. As for a letter of recommendation—I will vouch for you if you do not wish it known that your sponsor was Jehan of Westria." He was smiling.

"And the payment?" Silverhair responded weakly.

"The songs you can teach us will be worth more to us than gold!"

≫ TWELVE ≪

"Music is mathematics!" Master Sebastian paused, fixing each student with his sharp eyes as if daring anyone to dispute it. Then, satisfied that he had their attention, he hitched up his gown and sat back on the bench. He was one of the few Masters who always wore his deep purple gown. It was so patched and darned that student gossip suggested that he had been wearing it as long as he had been teaching music theory and composition at the College of Bards; very likely since before most of the students in this class were born.

"Mathematics is the purest of the sciences because it deals with Numbers, which are eternal, and whose properties exist independent of the physical world," the Master began to explain. "Music is the purest of the arts, because it consists of pure sound. Both music and mathematics can serve other purposes, but they are most beautiful when addressed for their own sakes alone.

"Now Sound, as you all know, is vibration. You can feel it in your instruments, or in your own bodies when you sing. And what is vibration but number?" he asked triumphantly.

Some of the students looked confused. Silverhair suppressed a smile. He had spent the first weeks after his arrival with Master Sebastian, who had jotted down every melody and accompaniment the harper could remember for him almost as quickly as Silverhair played, until sheets of notation covered the big table. It amazed Silverhair, who had been forced to learn to compose in his head—one could hardly pull out a sheet of music paper while driving a string of mules along the road. But the harper could write that music down only by painfully counting back and forth along the strings of his harp. Fortunately he had only to hear a tune once to repeat it, and he memorized verses almost as easily.

By the time they were done, Master Sebastian had made up a respectable book of the songs Silverhair had learned in Elaya and the Barren Lands and Aztlan, and even the little pieces he had made up himself to shorten the road. And when the harper had run out of breath or had to stop to retune, he had been the bemused recipient of Master Sebastian's Theory of Music.

"I see that some of you don't believe me—" the Master said patiently. "But this can be demonstrated—it is an abstraction that one can see and hear." He stepped over to the table, where a peculiar device consisting of a harpstring stretched between two pegs above a measured board had been attracting covert glances since the lecture began.

"This is called a monochord." He lifted the device and displayed it. "It was invented by a man called Pythagoras, a great philosopher who lived long before those we call the Ancients, in the days when the world itself was young. Now, I want one of you to pluck the string—" He held it out and one of the young women in the class, a flute player, touched it, producing a low, humming sound.

"Now, you see that the board is marked off into divisions, and that there is a sort of movable bridge." Master Sebastian held up the monochord and eased the bridge down the board so that now it held up the string midway between the two ends. "Now pluck the string again—"

Smiling, the girl put out her hand and they heard a dull *ping* an octave higher than the first note had been.

"You see?" said Master Sebastian eagerly. "Now, if I move the bridge again and pluck the string at the one third mark, we hear a *sol*, and at the fifth, we hear *do* once more. There were three notes between the one half and one third in the first octave, but between the fifth and the sixth there is only one. The intervals are shortening, you see—" As he spoke, he slid the bridge along the board and plucked the string. "Thus, the divisions form a mathematical progression; the octave which is the basis for all our music depends upon precise ratios." He put the monochord away, the bitter lines of his face softening as he warmed to his subject. He had given this lecture yearly since he began teaching, but he seemed to find in it an endless source of satisfaction.

"Now, as for the octave, you may think that the notes at the beginning and end of each scale are the same—" Master Sebastian went to the antique piano and played seven C notes, starting with the highest and descending to the deep tone at the bottom of the keyboard. Silverhair grimaced. When the lid was up, the piano looked as if someone had put a big harp in a coffin and attached a keyboard in mockery.

"Listen carefully." The Master repeated the notes. "Each note has half the frequency of vibrations as the one above it. The highest move too quickly for us to hear them, but when I strike the lowest notes the humming is perceptible. There are more overtones and harmonics in the lower notes as well, and the octaves become more complex the lower you go." He began to play a series of ascending chords, striking the keys forcefully to release their full power until everyone's ears were ringing.

"To me the piano is the queen of instruments, because it not only possesses half as well as whole tones, but encompasses the full seven octaves that can be perceived by the human ear." Somewhat reluctantly he took his hands away from the keyboard and turned to face the class. Obviously this analysis reaffirmed Sebastian's faith in an orderly universe. His favorite exercise was to play superbly balanced cascades of sound in which each note fell with precision into its place in a pattern which was repeated with variations in a passion of pure reason incarnate in sound. It was beautiful, but surely, thought Silverhair, music was also something more.

"Now, who can identify the basic harmonies?" asked Master Sebastian.

Aurel raised his hand, his light hair glinting in the sun as he leaned forward. "There's that pretty three-note chord—

you know, the one that goes *do, me, sol*—" He hummed three notes, and immediately Master Sebastian repeated them on the piano—C, E, and G.

"Yes indeed, and that is called the golden chord because of its perfection. It is also the interval called a fifth, because the top and bottom notes are five notes apart. Now if I struck only the first and second notes of this chord what would the interval be called?"

"A third?" a quick dark girl from Sanjos asked as the sound of the two notes died away. Silverhair seemed to recall that her instrument was the horn.

"Very good. You are all undoubtedly familiar with the use of this chord in singing simple harmony—" Two-fingered, he played all in thirds the first verse of a familiar melody. "And who can tell us what the other common interval is called?"

A stocky man from somewhere up north raised his hand. "It must be the fourth," he said. He was one of the older students, whose voice had continued to develop until he felt compelled to leave his holding and come here for training.

"And if you add a fourth interval to a fifth chord, where do you arrive?" the Master continued eagerly.

"At the next octave—" responded Silverhair.

"Yes, you're a harper—of course you would know. That basic pattern can be varied infinitely, and it is one of the most beautiful ways to accompany a tune."

Silverhair smiled back at him. He had discovered that pattern for himself when he was learning to play, but it had never occurred to him it had anything to do with arithmetic.

"Very well—it is almost time for the noon meal, so I had best leave the discussion of rhythm—which also depends on number, you notice—for another day. For now, I want you to go work with your instruments and play notes—not melodies, but thirds and fifths and octaves—simple combinations of sounds—until you can *hear* their relationships!"

Chattering and laughing, the class dispersed, some to their rooms in the dormitories, and others directly to the dining hall to claim a good place in line. Silverhair wandered out into the Masters' Garden, a peaceful arrangement of emerald moss and artfully placed stones with an occasional bench placed before a particularly fine view. He took a deep breath of the cool air. It had been raining, and crystal drops jeweled the redwood boughs and mist wreathed the tops of the trees.

"What did you think of Sebastian's lecture?"

Silverhair turned abruptly and saw that Aurel had followed him. He suppressed his irritation, for the young man had been kind to him in those first weeks when he still looked like the meanest tramp in Westria. Unfortunately, certain unguarded references to his wanderings had given the boy the idea that he was a romantic figure. Why Aurel should take him as a model when there were so many real musicians around was a mystery to Silverhair, but he felt he owed the young man at least some basic kindness.

"One cannot but admire his sincerity," he answered after a moment's thought. "But surely there's more than counting numbers to making music. No one would contend that simply counting syllables makes poetry. . . ."

"That's exactly what I think!" cried Aurel. "Music makes you *feel*, so that when you play, other people feel the same thing!"

The end of his sentence was engulfed by the sonorous reverberations of the noon bell. The two men stood gazing up at the bell tower while the single repeated sound resonated in their blood and bones.

"There! That's what I mean!" exclaimed Aurel when he could be heard again. "Every time I hear that sound I catch my breath, and it's not because I'm hungry, or because a set of mathematically determined sound waves are vibrating the membranes of my ears!"

There was a murmur of mixed sound from the dining hall, and Silverhair smiled and began to move toward the gate. Then he frowned, remembering the vision that had sent him here. He had heard music whose glory pierced his soul, but he had not heard it with his physical ears. Suddenly he wanted the reassuring weight of Swangold in his arms.

*   *   *

Silverhair settled himself on the three-legged stool and leaned the big harp back across his shoulder. After Swangold, its size had been hard to get used to, and he still had to repress a feeling of disloyalty whenever he began to play, as if he were being unfaithful to a devoted wife. But he had to admit that forty strings and four feet of sound box gave him not only more harmonies but a considerably larger volume of sound.

He gripped the sound box firmly between his calves and looked up at Mistress Siaran, who already had her harp tilted back and ready to play.

"Now, I want you to listen, and then repeat this next phrase very slowly, watching out especially for the ornament at the end."

He not only listened, but watched intently as her strong fingers moved over the strings. She was a full-figured woman with shining auburn hair and dark eyes, whose movement had the grace of a swooping bird. He marveled at the precision with which she plucked each string: a swift, clean movement that never produced that nasal buzz that plagued *his* playing. His ears distinguished each note, but hard though he stared, the fingering of the little trill with which she finished eluded him once more.

He took a deep breath and began slowly to echo her, trying to reproduce not only the notes, but the exact pacing and quality of sound. But he could hear the uneven volume of his notes, and when he reached the ornament his fingers would not move quickly enough, and an abrupt twang destroyed the beauty of what had gone before. Swearing, he jerked his hands away.

"Well, that was very nice," she said kindly. "Your tempo was good and you were quite accurate, except for the end."

"Except for the end . . ." he repeated ruefully, still shuddering.

"Let me look at your hands—have you been wearing your gloves?"

"Yes, Mistress Siaran." Silverhair sighed, eased the harp upright and held them out for inspection. At his first

lesson with her she had exclaimed in horror at the state of
his fingers and put him on a regimen of creaming and
massage that would have pleased an Elayan court lady. It
had helped. His fingers were no longer rough and brown,
and most of the calluses were gone, but one could still see
the pale lines of old scars and the distortion where the
bones had not mended exactly after the horse crushed his
hand. Now his hair and beard were trimmed neatly. He
wore sandals and a clean purple gown. But Silverhair's
fingers still ached when the fog came in.

Her experienced hands moved down each digit, probing
and massaging. Then she sat back and released him.

"I suppose they are doing as well as could be expected." She shook her head. "How could you have let
your hands suffer so? They are a part of your instrument—
you should guard them at least as well as you guard your
harp! Perhaps better—a harp can be replaced or repaired!"

Silverhair knew all about repairs. He had spent several
weeks filling cracks in Swangold's frame with glue. A
brass plate now braced the curve and pillar, which had
begun to warp to the left under the tension of the metal
strings. But as for replacement—it would be as easy to
replace his right hand.

"Well, you must just keep working on speed and flexi-
bility, and perhaps in time it will come. Now, let's go
through the rest of the piece, and remember to stop the low
notes as you go."

Silverhair nodded. None of Swangold's notes were low
enough to matter, but on the big harp the strings in the
lower octaves would continue to resonate so long that they
distorted subsequent harmonies, unless he stilled them with
the back of a fingernail. He made a quick run up the scale,
then picked up the tuning key to adjust two strings that had
slipped fractionally out of tune.

Mistress Siaran began to play and he followed her,
phrase by phrase, struggling with an increasing despair.
Her playing had niceties of technique and an ease and
elegance which he could not seem to imitate. Perhaps if he
had started serious study ten years ago . . . if Jehan had

not died and Faris had not disappeared . . . if there had never been a Cataclysm!

His lips tightened as he applied himself to the music once more. He should be grateful that he was not attempting to master the poetic part of the curriculum; the music alone was challenge enough. He had known when he came here that it would be hard, and in some respects his playing had improved. He had mastered a number of ornaments, his technique was cleaner, and he had absorbed some new approaches to harmony. And then of course he had learned a great deal of the Westrian harp repertoire he had not known before.

His hands swept along the strings in a glissando, and back and forth the dialogue between the two harps went on.

"In the College of the Wise, we teach that music is magic—music, and poetry." The slender young woman in the grey robe gestured gracefully. She was a visitor to the College of Bards who had come to instruct them in the use of music in ritual. The glow of the journey to the sacred valley of Awahna, where she had been made an adept, was still upon her like the bloom on the petals of a newly-opened flower. She had taken the name of Mistress of the Waterfall. Silverhair thought it suited her.

"Many of you may be called upon to create hymns or to provide music to support various ceremonies, so you must learn how and why music affects the human soul."

Silverhair sat up and listened more intently, even though her shining black hair and slightly tilted brown eyes reminded him painfully of Faris. Her words sounded as if she might have answers to the questions that no one else here seemed able to understand.

"You all know that the world we see around us is not really solid," she was saying now. Several of the other students exchanged glances and one reached out and ostentatiously patted the bench he was sitting on. "It is just as true to say that everything consists of particles which are being moved by the flow of energy in different patterns at different speeds. The essence of a stone, and of your bodies, and of the air we breathe, is all the same, varying only in organization and density, and they can all be affected by the energies released by a focused will or the vibrations of a sound."

"I don't understand—" A redheaded girl who had married another student last year and now had a baby at her breast raised her hand. "Can I shatter a stone just by singing at it?"

"Something like that. You know how a note played by one instrument may make the others near it resonate in sympathy. If a sound is properly produced and focused, it can indeed shatter stone. That's why we are trained to vibrate the sacred Names at the College of the Wise. But you must not think sound is useful only for destruction. Music can also assist in things like helping plants to grow."

"So that's why we sing hymns at the spring plowing when we go out to prepare the fields," said the man who had been a farmer. Silverhair had heard his singing, and he thought the crops must have flourished on his land.

"Will just any sound help?" asked someone else.

"There are specific sounds and tones and ways of producing them for each purpose," said the Mistress of the Waterfall. "This, for instance—" Everyone jumped as she let out her breath in a resonant *"AUM . . ."* that continued for several seconds and trembled through the floor.

"Now all of you try it with me—project from the belly and keep your vowel sounds pure. . . ." She lifted her hands and with increasing confidence the students followed her lead until sound reverberated through the room like the pulsing of a great bell.

"Do you see?" the Mistress asked when the chanting had spontaneously ended.

"I could feel it all through me, and I think the baby liked it too," said the red-haired girl, "but what does it *do?*"

"The chanting of *AUM* is a very basic way to center and ground the singer and set up a flow of energy between him and the spiritual realms. There are others; in fact the seven octaves are believed to be related to the seven power centers of the body, and the sounds of the vowels and diphthongs are part of this system as well. You must remember that for a spell to work properly, not only the sense but the sound of the words used must be appropriate. In addition, the different musical modes you have studied have different effects upon the mind."

Aurel leaned forward eagerly. "I have heard that there are songs that can control what men do—put them to sleep, or make them happy or eager for war."

"Yes, that is true, though it takes the right instrument and the right musician. An incantation is not a toy to be wound up and set running. It is more like a sword which is deadly in the hand of a master, but which may fail or wound its user when wielded by a fool. The warrior trains his body and his will so that when he fights he and his weapon are one, and he and his foe become partners in an eternal dance."

Silverhair nodded. He had seen great swordsmen, and there had been moments in his own fighting when he had glimpsed that unity. But most of his battles had been haphazard scuffles in which it seemed a miracle that any blows had landed at all. He supposed that many ceremonies were the same.

"But how do you *do* it?" asked Aurel.

"In a way it cannot be described—you simply have to do, to be . . . but perhaps—what instrument do you play?"

"The viol," said Aurel in a puzzled tone.

"Well, aren't there days when no matter how you try the bow squeaks and your fingers fumble on the strings? And then come the other times, when you feel as if something else were playing both you and the instrument, and the music simply flows through?"

Everyone nodded then, and there was a murmur of commentary. Silverhair sat back and let out a great sigh. They had all known those moments in which it seemed that the soul of Music had become their own—it was their worship, the deepest truth of their lives. It was the reason they had come to the College of Bards.

"Magic is like that—" said the Mistress of the Waterfall softly. "It is the activation of knowledge by a focused will. You use your knowledge to choose your means—the tune and the delivery and the words—but once you have started, you let them become the channel through which meaning passes through you and into the listening soul."

"And that is what you are going to teach us to do?" asked Aurel in wonder.

The Mistress laughed. "To master it fully you must come to the College of the Wise. But while I am here I can at least set you on the beginning of that road. . . ."

Silverhair bent until his ear nearly touched the sound-board; he made a tiny turn of the tuning key and plucked the string again, concentrating to hear the note over the barnyard squabble of other instruments being tuned. He nudged Mistress Siaran, who was doing warm-up chords on her big harp.

"Can you give me an 'E' above middle 'C'? I'm not sure I have it right."

She obliged, and he plucked his note while her over-tones were still throbbing. For a moment the two harpstrings vibrated together, swelling the sound.

"It's close enough," she smiled. "This is only a re-hearsal. Don't worry so."

He shrugged and grinned. "I know, but half the musicians in Westria are going to be listening. It scares me." He looked around him. That statement had been an exaggeration, but certainly a great many of the musicians who had been trained at the College of Bards had returned for this concert in honor of Master Andreas's fiftieth birthday. Silverhair had never seen so many instruments together in one place in his life.

Some of the younger students were still hanging garlands of greenery across the redwood paneling at the other end of the hall. Silverhair ran his hands down the smooth surface of the sound box of the big harp, wishing that he was playing Swangold. But her delicate tone would be lost in this herd, like an antelope among the buffalo he had seen on the Sea of Grass.

In front of him a fiddle player finished sawing up and down his scales and turned to the woman next to him.

"You are from Sanjos, aren't you—is there any word from the south? I came by ship from Santibar, and when I left, the city was expecting attack from Elaya at any time."

Silverhair sat up, listening. Was Elaya after Santibar again? And had Caolin failed to prevent the trouble, or was he possibly behind it all? He remembered quite vividly his conversation with Caolin in Saticoy almost three years ago. The former Seneschal had spoken of a great future, and Silverhair knew better than anyone what little cause Caolin had to be loyal to Westria.

"Yes, we had heard something," said the woman. Silverhair seemed to recall that she played the fiddle in the consort at Lady Alessia's court. "They've been fighting on and off for several weeks, but so far the fortress of Balleor is holding fast."

"I don't understand it. We sent to Lord Robert as soon as we knew the Elayan troops were on their way. He should have sent reinforcements on the road by now. What is wrong with him?"

"They say he has been very ill," the woman replied. "And he always was overcautious where warfare was concerned, though a good enough General once the swords are drawn."

The fiddle player sighed, started to lift his instrument to his chin and set it on his knee again. "If he is too cautious now, Elaya will take Santibar, and it will need more than a few reinforcements to get it back again. This would not be happening if we had a King. . . ."

Silverhair shivered, remembering only too vividly the months they had spent preparing for the war Elaya had launched as soon as the King's death was known. Were they going to have to do it all again? He tested his harpstrings determinedly. He was done with war and politics—his life was music now. If there was going to be trouble, he did not want to know.

The din was diminishing as musicians finished tuning and sat back waiting for the rehearsal to begin. The warm afternoon light slanted through the long windows, glowing on the redwood paneling of the hall and on the richly varied woods of the instruments and glittering on highly polished brass and silver as the musicians moved.

Each instrument was a work of art, but Silverhair was glad he was playing a harp, even if it was not Swangold. Like every other student, he had been required to master the basics of each family of instruments, and he could appreciate the skills needed to play each one. The keyboard had been easy for him, though he hated the dull sound of the piano after the harp. He had done well enough with plucked instruments like the gitarra, but the screech of his bow left him with a lasting respect for the players of fiddles and viols. And though he understood the theory of the winds and brass, his lips and lungs lacked the control which years of practice gave to the players of flutes and recorders, shawms and horns.

Ras of Santierra finished his conversation with Master Sebastian and came down the hall, his dark skin glowing like polished walnut in the sunlight. He was now the leader of the city musicians of Laurelynn, a position that had won him the dubious honor of trying to turn this gaggle of players into something that could produce music. Silverhair had been apprehensive when he heard Ras was coming, for he had met the man when he was at court. But apparently he had changed enough not to be recognized. And fortunately Master Ras seemed to be undaunted by his task.

Grinning, exchanging jokes with those musicians he knew, the Master stepped up onto the little dais. He lifted a hand, and the whole chattering mob stilled. *He is the master musician, and we are his instrument*, thought Silverhair. *I hope that he can play!*

"My friends and fellow musicians, I am very glad to see you all. I think that together we may do something that will become a legend here, but we have not much time, so we had best get to work now. You have finished your tuning, and I would like to hear you by sections now. Let us have the fiddles first—"

The Master who taught stringed instruments at the College nodded, and eight fiddles sounded in unison the four notes of their strings and a simple scale. Master Ras

nodded his approval and the bigger viols followed their
example. When they had finished, Silverhair caught Aurel's
eye and smiled. The boy's face was glowing with excitement; Silverhair could feel a growing anticipation in the
room. But it was a pleasant tension, like the first stages of
making love. Now the flutes were calling like a flock of
birds, then the woodwinds, and finally the clarion sum-
mons of the horns. Several times Master Ras made a group
repeat a note, and one or two people had to retune.

Then it was the turn of the three harps, and Silverhair
sagged in relief when their chromatic scales were ap-
proved. He jumped as the percussion section demonstrated
its readiness with an enthusiastic rumble of drums and
clash of cymbals.

"Thank you," said Master Ras. "Now, we may as well
begin at the beginning with the Birthday Concerto which
Master Sebastian has written for us to play. You should all
know your individual parts by now, so it will simply be a
matter of turning those parts into a unity. Are you ready?"
He lifted his arms and nodded to the strings.

Then the dark hand came down, and the fiddle players
began to move their bows to produce a soft shimmer of
sound almost at the edge of hearing that was like the wind
in distant trees. The sound grew as the viols contributed
their deeper harmony, and Silverhair could see his harpstrings
trembling in sympathy. The hair lifted on the back of his
neck. He had known the joy of playing in consort with
several others, but already there was something different
about the quality of this sound.

Master Ras turned in place, and the graceful sweep of
his arm was answered by a single horn call. Then the
flutes began to twitter like singing birds above the deeper
singing of the strings. Master Ras swayed like a dancer;
his hands guided them as if he held invisible reins.

Now the horns bayed loudly, again and again. Silverhair's
heart pounded painfully, but without conscious thought he
found himself reaching for his harp as Mistress Siaran moved
next to him. The three harps tipped back in a single poised
movement like the moment before a charge when light
ripples down the line of lifting swords.

Drums thundered suddenly behind them, then Ras held
them with one hand while his other flashed toward the
harpers and released their fingers in a glissando up and
down the harpstrings that filled the air with a golden
shimmer of sound.

Then the strings were supporting them and the winds
were weaving a counterpoint punctuated by the insistent
calling of the horns and the drumbeat that was like the
pulse that thundered in Silverhair's ears. The music was all
around him, inside him—the vibrations resonated through
every cavity of his body, through the very marrow of his
bones. All of Silverhair's awareness focused on a climax
of pure Sound.

Measure by measure, the great structure of the music
built around him. His fingers flickered furiously, his consciousness more absorbed by the music than it had ever
been in the act of love. Then the tempo began to ease, the
volume to diminish. The chords of the harps sounded more
and more slowly, and then their part was over and they
eased silently to an upright position once more. Now only
the strings were still playing, like wind singing in the reeds
of memory. And then they too were still.

There was a little silence when they were done. People
steadied their breathing and became aware of themselves as
separate souls once more. Then Master Ras relaxed from
his last tense gesture and straightened with a sigh.

"Excellent! Excellent—you are a marvelous group, do
you know? Especially since we have not played together
before. However there are a few places where I think our
pacing might improve. For instance in the second entrance
of the horns . . ." He launched into an excruciating analysis.

But Silverhair lost the rest of his words. The world
seemed to spin around him and he slumped on his stool.

"Well—" said Mistress Siaran complacently. "I think
that all went quite well. We made our entrance precisely—
our practice has paid off. What did you think of it,
Silverhair?"

The harper shook his head, unable to say a word. When
the harps had joined the music he had felt a shock like an
arrow in the heart. The totality of the music was so much

more than its parts—a multiplicity of individual voices joined to become an organic whole, separate pieces intertwining in an intricate pattern which could be felt but not explained. For a moment he had touched the glory he had known in his vision and understood that Music was the Meaning of the universe.

And now he was alone once more.

Mistress Siaran patted him on the shoulder, and he turned his face away so that she would not see his tears.

⟫ THIRTEEN ⟪

They were judging him now. Silverhair turned his back on the shut door and moved slowly into the Masters' Garden, heedless of the fine mist that wreathed and eddied through the trees. His fingers were aching as they always did when it was damp. If the judges found him unworthy, it would be an excuse—how could he be expected to play his best when his fingers felt like some rusted bit of machinery from the Ancient times?

But a true Master Bard would not be handicapped by a physical deficiency. He could not help it, of course, but one did not put a one-armed man in the vanguard of an army just because he had been crippled through no fault of his own. Without thinking about it, Silverhair sat down on the stone bench in the center of the garden.

"Don't look so worried—surely they will make you Master, Silverhair. I thought you played beautifully."

It was Aurel. His golden hair seemed to illuminate the mist like a localized patch of sunshine. Silverhair tried to smile.

"How do you know? No one but the Master Judges are supposed to listen to the performances."

Aurel shrugged and sat down next to the harper. "If you know where to sit, you can hear."

"I wish I had known a friendly pair of ears was listening. It might have helped," said Silverhair. But wherever Aurel had been hiding, he could hardly have heard well enough to notice the fine points of technique the judges would be looking for. Silverhair remembered too vividly the times when a string had buzzed because he did not stop it properly, and the missed ornaments, and the places where his tempo had lagged.

He had not felt really ready, but it was the custom to take the examination when one had been at the College for three years. Why should he have expected to stay here indefinitely? One way or another he would have to leave the College in a year or two. The only question was whether it would be as a Master Bard or with the simple distinction of having studied harping here. Invisible in the mists above him, a sparrow twittered and then stopped, and suddenly Silverhair was wrenched by memories of silver mornings on the road and the dawn concert of the wild birds.

The damp wind kissed his face with a scent of curing grass, and of the sea. Something stirred in him, and he did not know if it was sorrow at the thought of leaving or excitement at the thought of taking the road once more. *But it does not matter*, he told himself, *I serve the spirit of Music*.

Aurel touched his shoulder. The door had opened, and Mistress Siaran was beckoning to him to come in. "Good luck!" whispered the young man as he got to his feet.

For a few moments the change in light blinded him, then Silverhair focused on the figures of the Masters who had judged him, resplendent in their cloaks of purple velvet with the embroidered golden harps on back and breast. Mistress Siaran and Master Sebastian, Mistress Huldah and Master Windwhistle and Master Andreas himself—their familiar faces seemed like those of strangers. He bowed to them and took his seat next to the big harp on which he had performed, thinking, *I would have done better if they had let me play Swangold*.

"First, you must know that this is only the preliminary examination. You will have the chance to try again," said Mistress Siraran. Her voice was kind, but the tactful wording of her opening was enough to tell him he had failed.

"Your playing shows a solid mastery of basic technique, and you perform with a nice sense of style, but you must realize that for us to award the title of Master, a player must be superior in his chosen instrument as well as being proficient in all other areas of music,'' said Master Sebastian.

"Only if a musician shows some extraordinary mastery can these rules be altered, and although your playing is quite competent, you have demonstrated no unusual ability," Mistress Huldah added less tactfully.

How could I, thought Silverhair, *with your eyes like chips of ice and your skepticism chilling my soul. This bloodless exercise is not Music!* He had known men who could barely hold their own in martial games who were a terror on the battlefield. But he would never get a chance to prove himself here.

"We want to thank you for performing for us today," the Master of the College nodded gravely. "Do not be too discouraged—you will have another opportunity."

After the others had left, Mistress Siaran sat him down for an intense half hour's dissection of exactly what he had done wrong. It was surprisingly painful, though Silverhair could have done it equally well—perhaps even better, for there were a few things he had been aware of which she did not mention. But, when he thought she had done, he saw her smile.

"But you won't have a chance to brood on this, Silverhair. We want you to come with us on the annual tour."

Silverhair looked at her rather sharply. Every year a group of Masters and students of the College traveled to some town in Westria to perform in a Music Festival. It gave the students experience in performing in public, allowed the townsfolk to hear some good music, and enabled the College to audition local musicians who might be eligible for training. But Siaran must know that if there was one thing Silverhair did not need it was more experience in performing in public.

"Where are we going?" he asked carefully.

She reddened slightly. "They want us to go to Santibar. Mistress Alessia requested it especially." She continued rather quickly, "The city has been defending itself valiantly, but they are beginning to lose heart. Lord Robert hasn't given them much support, and I suppose she thinks it will give the townspeople confidence if we hold the Festival just as if nothing were wrong.''

Silverhair continued to look at her, and her dark eyes fell. It took some nerve, after having destroyed his self-confidence as the Masters had just done, to ask him to go to a city which was in immediate danger of being overrun by an enemy.

But he could see why they had asked. Siaran did not know who he was, but Master Andreas knew that he had been a warrior, and they all knew that he spoke Spanyol well. What they could not know was how much he feared going where people from his past might recognize him.

''Yes, I know how you must feel,'' said Siaran, misunderstanding his expression. ''But we need you, and I will feel much better if you come.''

''You are going?'' he asked sharply.

''Yes, with the Master of the College, and Tamira and Elli, and Aurel.''

Silverhair took a deep breath. Master Andreas was very stubborn for such a gentle man, and there would be no stopping him if he had decided to go to Santibar. But Lady Alessia owed Silverhair several favors from long ago, and if he had to meet her again, he would damned well make sure she immediately ordered them home again!

The gentle valley of the Danehold was crawling with soldiers. The open fields Silverhair remembered had sprouted pavilions like rows of corn, and the smoke of many cookfires stained the late summer sky. Here was the proof of the news they had heard on the road—Santibar had fallen to Elaya. Neither the garrison of Balleor nor the men Lady Alessia had sent to reinforce them had been enough to defend it, and the troops Lord Robert had brought south had come too late to help at all.

Silverhair looked around him with mingled anger, exasperation, and relief. The musicians did not need his protection—he might as well have stayed at the College of Bards. Instead he was likely to be thrust into contact with a number of people who could be expected to recognize him no matter how he had been changed by the years, and all the fuss he had so far avoided would begin.

Still, he could not help feeling a stir of emotion when he saw the red and black banner of House Battle flapping proudly against the sky, with the purple and gold of the Ramparts next to it and above them all the circled golden cross of Westria on its green field. He had fought under those banners, and something trembled within him when he heard a trumpet call. For the first time in three years he missed the weight of a sword at his side.

There was a buzz of comment, most of it friendly, as they rode through the camp to Lady Alessia's tent, and as they pulled up before it the Lady of Las Costas herself came out to welcome them.

"Lady, I fear we've come too late to help you," said Master Andreas, dismounting stiffly from the rawboned white mule.

Lady Alessia snorted angrily. "Too late! That's the story of this campaign! But the city was falling even as you received my message. It is no fault of yours. No," she continued, "it is others, who were warned six months ago, who will have to bear the blame!"

She had not changed. Her face had hardened, and there were streaks of silver in her auburn hair, but Lady Alessia still walked like a tigress protecting her young. She was speaking with restraint, but the two spots of color in her cheeks and the edge to her voice expressed all she left unsaid. Her husband, Brian, had died to save Santibar, and now it was lost.

The other musicians clambered off their mounts, asking where they should picket them, and where their baggage and, more important, their instruments could be safely stowed. A young man came out of the tent behind the Lady, calling for people from the household to come help. Silverhair stared at the arms on his overtunic and realized with shock that this must be Brian's son, whom he had last seen running across a field at the Naming of Faris's child, thirteen years ago. A heavy ring glinted on the boy's forefinger as he gestured and Silverhair's breath caught. He remembered too vividly the moment when Eric had given to that child the ring he had taken from Lord Brian's dead hand.

And Caolin had been the spider in the web that caught Brian and brought him down, even though the actual killing had been done by the crossbows of Prince Palomon's guard. Silverhair's mind rang with the question that had haunted him ever since he heard of this new war. Where was Caolin now? What part had he had in the capture of Santibar?

Lady Alessia was still talking animatedly to Master Andreas. Silverhair tried to herd the others toward their campsite, but as they began to move the Lady called them back again.

"Alex—what are you thinking of? The musicians will be hungry after traveling. Before they deal with unpacking we must give them a meal."

Silverhair shook his head in resignation and followed the others under the long awning that extended the pavilion. There were benches and a long trestle table covered with a white cloth. After the simple fare of the College, the abundance of meat and the subtle spicing of the rice and vegetables were almost too rich. But Silverhair found himself relaxing as the meal continued, and imperceptibly his speech took on the courtly forms he had learned in Laurelynn. Aurel and Elli and Tamira stared around them in wonder, but Silverhair was remembering that once he had been Sir Farin Harper, and Lady Alessia's peer.

"It is just as well that you arrived too late to go into the city," said the Lady of Las Costas. "It was a foolish idea, to endanger you without cause." Servants cleared away the trenchers and brought in dishes of thick pea soup.

"It is my pleasure to serve you, my lady," said Master Andreas. Silverhair remembered then that although the College trained musicians from all over Westria, it lay in Las Costas, and so in a sense its Master was the Provincial Commander's man.

A boy came around with the soup tureen and Silverhair ladled a second helping into his bowl. With the good brown bread and really excellent Danehold beer, it would have been a fine meal even without the delicacies Lady Alessia had brought along. When he looked up, the Lady was speaking again.

"Well, there *is* something you can do, though I admit it will be mostly a salve for my pride. We have agreed to meet tomorrow with Prince Palomon to negotiate the cession of the city—" She paused, mastering her anger, then went on. "He will be there with a full complement of guards and drummers. Lord Robert says we are not strong enough to fight, but I'll be damned if I'll let that Elayan coyote overawe us with his pageantry. Will you and your musicians come with us and play?"

"Don't you think we should at least be introduced to the musicians, Mother, before you drag them off to meet the enemy?" Alex said dryly.

"You already know Mistress Siaran—" said the Master quickly. "And these are our journeyman students, Elli and Tamira and Aurel and Silverhair." His trained voice spoke the names without a tremor. Silverhair sat very still, his eyes downcast and his fingers clenched in his lap, waiting for their attention to pass.

"Alex is quite right, and you must forgive me—it is a great deal to ask," he heard the Lady say.

"Oh, Lady Alessia, our purpose is to make music, and if we can serve you by doing so, the happiness will be ours!" said Aurel eagerly. *Like a puppy,* thought Silverhair, but at Aurel's age, he would have said the same. It was one of the reasons he and the younger man had become friends.

"And what about the rest of you? Neither your Master nor I can command you in this."

One by one the other musicians expressed their eagerness, and why not—it would make a tale for their grandchildren if everything went well.

"And you, *Silverhair?*" There was the slightest of hesitations as Lady Alessia spoke the name. "You have obviously seen more of the world than these others," she went on, "and I would enjoy some conversation with you. . . ."

He sighed and met her eyes for the first time. "I am at your service and at that of your House, Lady Alessia, as I have always been," he said dryly, accepting defeat at last.

* * *

"She was right—they really do go in for pageantry!" said Aurel in awed tones. Prince Palomon had pitched his State Pavilion on a hill by the road just north of Santibar. It was fashioned of blue and silver brocade that glittered blindingly in the sunlight, and the lions that reared atop the banner poles were of gold. Even at this distance they could see the waving blue plumes of Palomon's guards and the steely glitter from the points of their assegais. It made Silverhair glad he had taken his sword from the baggage and belted it to his side.

But blue was not the only color. Across from Palomon's guards stood a block of men whose polished cuirasses were half-covered by cloaks of burgundy wool and whose cocked helms bore red plumes. Below Palomon's rampant lion hung another banner—a wolf's head on red velvet that glowed like freshly spilled blood.

Something contracted painfully in Silverhair's belly as he faced the knowledge he had been suppressing. There was only one man who could have enabled Elaya to achieve the goal that had always been beyond her power before. Caolin . . .

Silverhair had hoped that some lingering loyalty to Westria might have held Caolin from aiding Palomon in this one thing. He had believed the former Seneschal's assurance that he was satisfied with guarding the Campos del Mar for his child.

And yet I said that all I wanted to do was study music, and he believed me, but here I am in the Lady of Las Costas' train . . . he thought. Then the little procession started forward again, toward the blue pavilion.

Palomon's courtliness was like icing on a cake riddled with weevils. The musicians sat in the back of the great pavilion, playing prettily while the negotiators took their seats around the big, square table and servants brought biscuits and wine.

The Prince was beginning to show his age at last, thought Silverhair as his fingers moved automatically across the strings. His eyes were sparkling with triumph, but his hair had greyed and he was very thin. His nephew sat beside him, smiling blandly and smoothing the turquoise silk of his gown. The golden lion wristlets of the princely house gleamed from his dark forearms, and Silverhair wondered if Ali would be able to take power when Palomon died. And if he did, would Prince Ali also take Caolin? Perhaps not. Perhaps that was why Caolin had tried to win a new territory for his own.

He could not stop himself from looking at the other man on the Elayan side of the table. He was wearing someone else's face, of course—brown skinned, with dark hair and eyes. But the red robe marked him, and a certain poise to the shoulders and turn of the head that were identification enough for one who knew.

"—and I propose that we make the coast between here and the Danehold a neutral area, for Stonegate will be your natural border fortress now. . . ." said Palomon silkily.

Sven Anderssen, who was Lord of the Danehold, glowered through his full, blond beard. His folk had always been the first defense of Westria if Santibar should fall. He looked as if he were hoping that Elaya would test them. Lady Alessia's face was set as if she were in pain.

"Yes, I suppose so . . ." Lord Robert agreed hoarsely. "But you have spoken of payments and assurances. What exactly do you mean?"

Silverhair suppressed the feeling of dismay with which he had first seen the Regent of Westria. Robert's hair was dull and thin, and little remained of his once-powerful frame. The Lord of the Ramparts had never been able to see anything that was not shoved under his nose. Silverhair had no fear that Robert would notice him now, even though he had known him rather well. Robert looked as if it were taking all his strength to remain upright in his chair. The Regent had deprived Caolin of lordship in Westria. How Caolin must be laughing now!

The discussion stretched on, as first one side and then the other proposed compensations and stipulations and arguments. Westria's lordship of Santibar was dead, but its corpse was proving difficult to bury. At last Lord Robert called for a pause. He said it was for consultation, but

Silverhair thought the Regent needed rest before he could go on. *It must be hard for him, too,* thought the harper. *He must be afraid that Brian's ghost will haunt him.*

The musicians were given permission to stretch their legs too, and Silverhair walked out onto the headland. He stood, breathing in the sea air and gazing out across the blue and silver sparkles of the channel. Islands lay like sleeping sea-beasts on the horizon. He thought, *If there was a ship in that cove below me I would climb down the cliff and beg passage on it now.*

Another shadow crossed his own. Alessia's voice broke his reverie.

"Farin, why did you run off? I thought you had agreed to talk to me. I don't know why you insist on this pose of anonymity, but that's your right," she added as Silverhair turned to face her. "I've said nothing, even though it would do Robert's heart good to know you are alive. He blamed himself when you disappeared—he always did look for things to feel guilty for, and now, when he deserves it, even I find it hard to accuse him."

"He looks very ill. . . ."

"He's dying, Farin. But even if Robert were well and had come to my aid when I asked, it might not have helped. It's that other man, the one they call the Protector of Los Campos. He attacked as if he had a map of the fortifications in his head." Alessia gazed out over the ocean, and the sea wind whipped the black veil about her face.

"He does . . ." mumbled Silverhair without thinking.

"What?"

"Nothing—I was thinking of something else," Silverhair said quickly. *Stop, Alessia,* his mental voice went on. *I don't want to have to choose.*

"Farin, what do you know? Who is that man?" Her voice was terrible now. She gripped his shoulder and forced him to meet her eyes.

The city has already fallen, and he is Palomon's right-hand man. What can Alessia do even if she knows? he thought then. He spoke.

"He is Caolin."

Oddly, in that moment it was not the Seneschal's scarred face that flickered through his awareness, but the girl Thea's accusing eyes.

Master Andreas signaled to his musicians to put their instruments away as Lord Robert came in with the other leaders. His cheeks were flushed as if he had taken some cordial to revive his strength for just a little longer.

"Well then," said Palomon, "do you accept my terms?"

"We accept them—" Robert said dully.

"With one exception," Lady Alessia cut in. Everyone stared at her except the Regent, who was gazing resolutely at his clasped hands. Silverhair found his breath gone and had to force himself to draw it in again.

"I defended that city the best I could," Alessia's voice grated like a fingernail scraping steel. "If I must lose it I claim the right to a voice in who my new neighbor shall be! Give the lordship of Santibar to whomever you will, Prince Palomon, so long as it is to someone other than the man who now calls himself the Protector of the Campos del Mar!"

The other Westrians were staring, and Silverhair saw Caolin's features blur as if the suddenness of it had shaken even his control. *Will he be revealed as he is now before them all?* Silverhair wondered in horror. Then the mask hardened and Caolin turned to Prince Palomon.

"My Prince, I won you this city—this jewel, which you have so long desired. Surely I have earned the right to hold it for you now!" he said gently. Prince Palomon frowned and his nephew Ali leaned forward alertly.

"Prince! I swear that if that man stays in Santibar I will stay in the Danehold and never cease to harry this border while I live!" spat Alessia.

"Lady, surely that is a decision for the Lord Regent—" began Palomon, but she interrupted him and turned to Lord Robert.

"You know my reasons—will you say me nay?"

Slowly the sick man shook his head. "You have the right to ask."

"If you are now Lord of Santibar, then the city is in

your gift alone—'' Alessia said winningly. "Why not give
it to a man of your lineage? Give it to the Lord Ali!''

Lord Ali's teeth flashed in his dark face and Prince
Palomon sighed. Caolin had gone very still.

"Lady, will this content you?'' asked Palomon. Unable
to speak, Alessia nodded. Avoiding Caolin's eye, Palomon
said, "Very well.'' Quickly he scratched out one name on
the paper before him and added another, then scrawled his
own signature at the bottom of the treaty and pushed it
across the table for Robert to sign. For a moment the only
sound in the tent was the scratching of the quill.

Everyone else seemed fascinated by the movement of
the pen across the page, but Silverhair, lifting his own
unwilling gaze at last, flinched before the cold fury in
Caolin's eyes.

The musicians were five miles south of Stonegate, plodding along the road beside the sea, when Silverhair heard
hoofbeats behind them. Turning, he saw a red banner
whipping above the cloud of dust on the road. He swore
and kicked at his pony's ribs. He had hoped that by
leaving before Lord Robert's party they would put the
Lord Regent's guard between them and any pursuit, but
Caolin must have brought his men around by some hidden
pathway in the hills. And Caolin's men would be well-
mounted on long-legged Elayan horses that could laugh at
the lethargic creatures belonging to the College of Bards.

The others had heard the noise too and were reining in,
turning in their saddles to see who was riding so furiously.

"It is the Protector of the Campos del Mar!'' said
Master Andreas, recognizing the device on the banner.
"What is he doing here? Do you suppose he has left the
service of Prince Palomon?''

Silverhair pulled his pony around. Caolin's men were
coming so fast—there was no way that they could even try
to outrun them. He urged the horse back through the tangle
of pack animals that were blocking the road.

"I don't think so—'' he began to answer, but how could
he explain? Lady Alessia had given no reason for objecting
to the Protector as Lord of Santibar. Master Andreas and

the others looked back and forth between Silverhair and the approaching horsemen in growing alarm.

"Get back, all of you! They only want me," cried Silverhair. Master Andreas opened his mouth to question and Silverhair shook his head desperately. "Please—it's my fault. The Protector of the Campos del Mar is Caolin, and I told Lady Alessia!"

But it was too late. Two dozen horsemen swirled around them and pulled back into a circle with lances leveled and sunlight glaring from their polished helms. No use to even try to draw his sword, Silverhair thought. Foremost among them was Caolin's servant and pet torturer, Ordrey.

"Farin! Farin Silverhair, come out to me!" The soldiers reined aside to let a rider swathed in red robes come through. Caolin had dropped the face he had worn for the Council, and now his features were obscured only by a kind of mist that pulsed as if his anger had been made visible.

"Did you think you could escape from me?" raged Caolin. "Come out from among those singing rabbits! Have you told them who and what you are? Farin the coward, Farin the ingrate, Farin the drunkard—come out to me!"

Silverhair tried to move past the pack mules, but Aurel grabbed at his rein.

"I tell you, let him go!" cried Caolin. "Give him up before he rewards your kindness with treachery, as he has rewarded mine!"

"I am coming, damn you!" shouted Silverhair, ripping his rein from Aurel's fingers and slapping his horse across the neck till it lurched forward. "These others know nothing—leave them alone! Let them go!"

"Silverhair, you can't sacrifice yourself! We won't leave you in their hands!" cried Aurel, trying to hold his plunging mount still.

"Oh, is he your lover?" Caolin's voice dropped, but each word seared. Aurel went white, staring at him.

"We'll have to think of something special for *him*, won't we, my lord Sangrado—" echoed Ordrey.

"Or perhaps it's the woman—" Caolin turned toward

Mistress Siaran. "See how my men are looking at her, wondering about the white breasts beneath that purple gown. What kind of music did you make together, Silverhair?"

There was a high laugh from Ordrey. The others grinned and urged their horses farther in, narrowing the circle. Silverhair's heart was pounding in his chest. Ever since the Council he had been tormented by speculations about what Caolin might do to him, but he had not thought his rage would include the others as well.

"Caolin, they know nothing. Why are you wasting time on them? I am here, what do you want of me?"

"I want everything! I want my life again, for you have destroyed it a second time!" Caolin's anger blasted like a hot wind.

"I didn't know it would matter—I didn't know what Alessia would do. . . ." Silverhair was pleading now.

"You did not know! But there's so much you do not know, you sniveling strummer! You spent ten years searching for a sister who once offered to be my whore! Did you know that? Or did you know it only too well? Was she your strumpet too, that you've mooned after her for so long? You should have sought her in the brothels of Aztlan!"

Silverhair cried out incoherently and groped at his side; lances lifted toward him and he let go of his sword. His vision was blurred by images of Faris writhing in Caolin's arms.

"Well, you shall seek her in the land of the dead from now on. Ten years ago I dreamed of ways to kill you. . . . I thought I had forgotten them, but they are coming back to me," Caolin added with a menace more terrible than his rage had been. "First, I think, I will break your hands, and then I will destroy your harp."

There was a little silence. Silverhair was vaguely aware of the shocked faces of his friends. Tears were running unchecked down Mistress Siaran's cheeks. The sky was impossibly blue, and the hills richly golden in the sun. Overhead a bird cried harshly and he looked up to see the perfect arc of a hawk's flight across the sky.

I cannot die, he thought in wonder. *The world is too fair.* . . . His hands were trembling.

"If you mean to destroy both me and my music, let me play the harp just once more," he said hoarsely at last. "You were a musician once—at least let me play my own deathsong!"

"O master," cowered Ordrey, "let us hear what the snared bird will sing!"

There was a tense silence. Then Caolin gave a slow nod.

Stiffly, Silverhair got off of his horse and unstrapped the battered case that held Swangold. His hands were cold. He felt as if he were moving under water. But if this was to be his last act he must do it as perfectly as he knew how. Carefully he laid his cloak across the dust of the road and sat down; he opened the case and began to tune the harp, precisely, patiently, like a priest preparing for a ritual.

And as he bent his will on perfecting each familiar movement, fractionally his fear receded, so that he could stand beside it and think again. He settled Swangold against his shoulder and plucked a slow, minor chord, striking carefully in the middle of each string so that the tone would ring true. A lament should be played in the Ionian mode, but what melody could be adequate to this farewell?

Then something stirred in his memory, and he heard once more the Mistress of the Waterfall speaking of the three magic strains of the harp. It was known that they must be played in the Ionian, Dorian, and Mixolydian modes, but no one could say what the tunes should be.

"That knowledge waits within the soul," she had said then, *"but it can be released only by the force of the musician's need and the purity of his will.* . . . *The mode, the melody, and the unique resonance of the harp combine to work the magic, but the most important factor is the focus of the will. You must let the music play you!"*

Silverhair's gaze followed the slow circling of the hawk overhead and his fingers faltered on the strings. Then he seemed to see once more the hawk that had guided him in his vision and the skyfields through which he had flown.

O Thou Lord of all Music; Wind Lord, Spirit of all

songs, hear me now! he prayed. *I can die, but save Your other servants here! O Thou Lord of all the Powers of Air, give me Thy music!*

His hands moved upon the harp, but he felt as if he were being borne upward by mighty winds. And there was a sound. . . . With double awareness he felt himself soaring through the heavens and knew that his fingers were flickering across the harpstrings with a facility and precision that he had always sought without ever attaining. He was the instrument, he was the song. . . .

He heard a lament, and its sorrow was the anguish of all that has ever died uselessly and too young. It was the sorrow of Westria for the death of her King, the sorrow of Caolin for the loss of the city he had hoped to rule, transmuted to a pain that seemed to mourn for the entire world. Aurel was weeping too, and so were the others. Tears ran sparkling into the black beards of Caolin's men.

And gradually the sorrow eased as Silverhair's spirit soared into realms where all pain was transmuted into joy. The harmonies his fingers were drawing from the harpstrings modulated and changed until he was playing in the major, the Dorian mode, which lifted the spirit as if it had been reborn. Music danced from his fingers and a playful wind dried his hearers' tears. Someone laughed like a little child who had just discovered the sun.

And still the great wings beat. The music moved on across vast spaces where there was no distinction between sight and sound, between motion and absolute peace. Silverhair floated at rest in that stillness, but his fingers still moved. Now the harp was making a new music in the Mixolydian mode, which was neither lively nor sorrowful but something other, a serenely harmonious melody that eased the tension from body and spirit and bore both to a healing rest. And in that stillness it seemed to him there were words,

> *"The wind that shakes the world is but a breath;*
> *A moment's rest within My melody,*
> *As that cessation mortals know as death*
> *Transmutes their time into Eternity. . . ."*

"Silverhair, Silverhair, get up!"

Someone was shaking him. He struggled to retain the peace in which he had rested, but his tormentor would not leave him alone. He started to protest, but a warm hand closed over his mouth. Someone detached his harp from hands that seemed without the power of motion, and abruptly he was wholly back in his body again, reaching for it. He opened his eyes, confused, trying to distinguish memories of flight through music from the dusty road, Aurel's frightened face, and the sleeping soldiers around them.

"Come on, before they wake up again!" Aurel whispered hoarsely.

Shaking his head, Silverhair fumbled the harp back into its case and managed to close it. Then the boy was helping him to clamber onto a curiously quiet pony and guiding him past the still forms of his enemies.

Mistress Siaran had already led the others out of the circle. With gathering courage they urged their horses down the road, pushing them to the best speed they could manage until they had passed the towering rocks and stark fortifications of Stonegate and were approaching the Danehold.

Then at last they dared to slow their faltering mounts and draw enough breath for speech again.

"Silverhair, what did you *do?* I never heard you play like that before—I never heard anyone!" Aurel said, his voice trembling. The others nodded. Their eyes were still dazed and wondering.

"It was the extra talent—the other factor that makes the Master Bard," Master Andreas nodded gravely, as if he were somehow responsible for it all.

"Yes, that was the kind of harping one does in dreams. That was mastery—" Mistress Siaran gave Silverhair a tremulous smile.

The harper stared at them. "What are you talking about? That was not *me!*"

"That was the Spirit of Music . . ." said Master Andreas, "and you are its Master."

"Oh, yes"—Silverhair was becoming angry now—"that was true music, but it is not what you were trying to teach me under those redwood trees! Are you trying to tell me you will make me Master because the Lord of Music used me as His instrument to perform a miracle? Keep your velvet cloak for someone who will think it means something! I know better now!'' He reined his pony away from them.

"Silverhair, where are you going?" Mistress Siaran kicked her mare into a reluctant jog after him.

"Everywhere, anywhere, as long as it's away. I tried to follow your rules! I tried until body and spirit dulled and dwindled like a caged bird. And now you want to reward me for something that was not even my doing!'' His heart ached with desire for the harmony that for a moment he had known. How could he ever attain it again, flawed as he was?

He looked fully at Mistress Siaran and felt his anger ebbing before the compassion in her eyes. She had always been kind to him, and she had taught him all he could learn. "I have to go, Siaran—don't you understand? It was my stupidity that put us all into danger. Even if I wanted to stay at the College, it would not be safe for you once Caolin knew I was there."

"My dear, I understand. But you must understand that it is much harder to make yourself an instrument than to simply play one. I have felt it a little, sometimes, and I seek perfection in my playing as the only way I can approach what we are all looking for. Take care of yourself, and try to remember us kindly. Your cloak will be waiting for you if you ever feel you can come back to us. . . :'' She leaned forward and kissed him quickly.

Silverhair tried to smile. "Perhaps one day I will—who knows? I will always remember all of you with love . . . but I have to go on now."

He turned the pony again and kicked it into a weary jog. He did not look back, but he could feel Siaran's compassion following him, and the Master's grave sorrow and Aurel's love and the other students' awe and fear. Ahead of him the road was waiting, and a hawk soared over the rim of the hill.

⇒ FOURTEEN ⇐

The leisurely ride from the College to the Danehold had somewhat hardened Silverhair to the saddle again, but as he moved northward he was painfully aware how long it had been since he had been a wanderer. There was much for both mind and body to relearn. He was not totally without resources—he had stopped in the camp long enough to exchange his tired pony for a fresh horse and to collect the pack that held his traveling clothes. A spare blanket made a cloak to replace the one he had left lying in the road. But it would take time to re-create the spare efficiency of the pack he had carried before, in which each item had been chosen for minimum bulk and maximum efficiency.

He rode northward because the way south was closed to him, and he had never seen Normontaine, but he had heard that harpers were honored there. When he reached the Bay of the Flaming Mountains, he sold the horse and begged a place on a little coastal trader that stopped at every inlet that would give her anchorage. She made a meager living picking up cargoes of salt fish, local weaving and craftwork or tanned hides, and dropping off rolls of fine cloth, wine or dyes or spices that had been ordered by folk in these isolated places as much as a year before. She also carried letters, but there was no one whom Silverhair wished to tell where he had gone.

The weather was fine and clear. The fogs of summer had lifted and the winter storms had not yet begun, and they made good sailing. The captain grinned and said it could not last, but Silverhair paid no attention. He had claimed a coil of tarred rope in the bow of the *Seal Sister*, and there he would sit, drawing music from Swangold that echoed the singing of the wind in the lines and the bubbling of water beneath the bow. The sailors said he brought them a good wind.

Sometimes dolphins played along the side, leaping above the level of the deck as if they were trying to see the source of the music. In the harbors they saw sea otters and the smooth dark heads of their namesake, the seal.

But though the sea was gentle, there were subtle dangers on the land. And one sailor who went ashore at Longbay brought back some strange coughing fever that passed from one man to another of the tiny crew until they had barely enough strength to bring the ship into the shelter of a cove so small Silverhair never even learned its name.

A rutted road led up from the village through the hills to join the north road, they told him. A day or two farther up the coast there was a town with a harbor big enough for twenty ships to anchor there. Silverhair got food in return for a few songs and news of the southern wars; he thanked them and went on. Even when he realized that the fever that had struck his shipmates was upon him he continued to walk. This was a country where even in Ancient times men had been few. There was nothing else for him to do.

"Eh, lad, can't ye get up now? I can nurse ye at me own fireside, but these old bones can't carry ye. . . . Come on now, that's a lad, on your feet. . . ."

Groggily, Silverhair pushed himself upright. He had *been* walking, hadn't he? But here he was sitting in the road while a fine rain slowly soaked him to the skin. He had been alone, too, or at least he had thought so, but here was an old man, tugging at his arm. There must be something he had forgotten.

He smiled politely, tried to get his legs under him, and fell back into the mud. "Never mind . . ." he mumbled, "I'll just sleep here—"

But the old fellow kept pestering him. After a while it seemed easier to force himself upright, instinctively holding on to the harpcase while the old man shouldered his pack, and, leaning on the fellow's bony shoulder, to stumble down a narrow path through endless trees until it became too dark for him to see.

He must have walked the last mile by a subconscious effort of will and fallen into a stupor afterward, for when Silverhair became aware again, he was tucked up in coarse blankets on a mattress of fir boughs, lying in a hut cobbled together out of branches and silvered slabs of wood cast up by the sea. He remembered White Bird Woman's medicine with longing, but the fish soup the old man fed him must have had some virtue, for after a few days the fever left him, though he was still weak and wheezing with a cough that would not go away.

"I haven't thanked you for saving my life. I don't even know your name—" Silverhair had been in the old man's hut for three days. He could hear the steady beat of rain on the roof and the shushing of waves on a shore not far away. The old man looked up from the cook pot and smiled at him.

"I couldn't let ye die on the road like a dog. But it's a wonder I got ye here, wi' ye wandering like a drunken man and me wi' no strength to me arms any more." He ladled broth into the pitch-lined abalone shell he used for a bowl and brought it to the bedside. "Here now—'twill put strength in ye."

"Are you a fisherman?" Silverhair dipped his spoon into the broth, sipped, and blew to cool it before he tried again. No one else seemed to be about. He wondered how the man lived, and what he did here all alone.

"To be sure, lad, and a fish, too, once upon a time! When I was a boy they called me Swimmer, because I was always in the sea. And nowadays men call me Old Fish Feet, or the Merman of Seal Cove. But for a time I answered to this"—his wrinkled lips pursed in a strange, sweet whistle—"and I lived with the People of the Sea."

A merman! Silverhair stared. It explained many of the things that had puzzled him—the strange, makeshift house and his host's stark, bleached hair and weathered skin, as well as the old man's strange manner that was as wise as the Sea herself and as ingenuous as a child's. But he had thought that the mermen—humans who were accepted as companions by groups of dolphins or sometimes seals— were only a wistful legend. Was the old man trying to fool him?

"Now ye must sleep and grow strong." The merman took the shell from Silverhair's hand and pushed him back among the blankets. As the harper closed his eyes he decided that it did not matter whether the old man had really lived with the dolphins or only believed that he had. What stories he must have to tell! He fell asleep to the lullaby of the rain and the sea.

There was a brisk wind off the sea, but a pale, watery sunshine was filtering through the mists. It was enough to give Silverhair the illusion of warmth. He settled himself more securely on his rock and took a deep breath, coughed, and breathed in again. The air smelled freshly laundered by the sea. The harp in its case was beside him. After a little while Silverhair settled her into his arms and began to play, experimenting with odd chords that would harmonize with the sighing of the ocean.

Coming north on the *Seal Sister,* he had tried to mesmerize his mind with the motion of ship and sea. But as he lay, limp as a fish out of water in the aftermath of his fever, it had been impossible to avoid thinking. *I could have died on the road and my life would have meant nothing. No one would even have known what had become of me!* The thoughts repeated like a litany. He did not fear to die so much as to die with nothing accomplished— without leaving a mark on the world to show where he had been.

"But Faris is lost beyond my finding, and her child with her. What on this green earth is left for me to do?" he asked aloud. He coughed painfully and sat very still until the aching in his chest eased again.

He did not want to go home. His experience at the Danehold had made it painfully clear that although there might be a few people, like Lady Alessia, who still remembered him, far from being irritatingly curious, most of

Westria hardly knew he had ever existed, and certainly did not care. Considering it now, he did not know why he had ever expected otherwise.

If he returned to Westria, what could he do? The time when he might have married, started a family, and made a place for himself as his friends had done, was past. At least no one expected anything of an anonymous wanderer.

The mist that had veiled the sea was thinning, drifting in white wisps seaward until he could see that the spot where he was sitting was at the northern end of a tiny cove with a half-moon of white beach in the middle where the little stream trickled down from the forest to join the sea. The hills came down steeply almost to the edge of the water, furred with the loden green of spruce and fir and cypress. Here and there a slope too sheer for tree roots bore grey furze and tough grasses grown tawny with winter. It was a world of silver and brown and green, with now and again, as the sunlight touched it, a lucent flare of tourmaline from the sea.

Music stirred in Silverhair's memory; the harp echoed back the strains of his old riding song as if to reiterate his wanderings. And now new verses came to him.

> *"White hills beneath the moon are fair,*
> *And fair, the silver, sighing sea."*

But the beauty of the world was not sufficient anymore.

> *"But for my grief they have no care,*
> *Nor any song of hope for me,*
> *So why am I yet wandering?"*

Something splashed close inshore. Startled, Silverhair looked up from the harp to see something dark beneath the surface of the waves. Then a brown head broke water, and dark, bright eyes met his curiously. Absorbed in his self-pity, Silverhair had not noticed until now the irregular, hoarse singing that had been added to the ocean's regular melody. Now the lifting mists allowed him to see that the

rocks which broke the first rush of the sea farther out in
the cove were covered with seals.

"What is it? Do you like my music?" Suddenly he was
laughing. "Well, here's a very old song—"

> *"I am a man upon the land,*
> *A Selkie am upon the sea,*
> *But when I'm far from any land,*
> *My home it is the Skule Skerrie. . . ."*

He continued the ballad of the sea-man who loved a
maiden of the land, only to be killed, along with the son
he had by her, by the hunter who became her husband.

> *"And you shall marry a gunner bold,*
> *And a very fine gunner he shall be,*
> *And the very first shot that ever he fires*
> *Will kill both my young son and me."*

"It was very long ago, before the Cataclysm or the
Covenant," he added apologetically. "Land people would
not be so wanton now." The seal was still hanging in the
water as if she were listening.

He had found the ballad in a book at the College of
Bards, whose date set it at two centuries before the Cataclysm. It was odd how some of the older books still
survived, when volumes produced at the height of man's
mastery of the world crumbled to dust in the hand. Surely
some books must have been written in those days that were
worthy of being printed on paper that would survive!

The seal slid beneath the surface without a ripple and
emerged again a few feet away. Silverhair grinned and
returned to his music, experimenting with a tune that would
bind the barking of the seals and the chuckling of the waves
into a single harmony. It was no answer to the questions
that haunted him, but in the sunshine, with the seals
playing before him, the pain was eased for a while.

Silverhair set down his bowl and looked across the fire
at the merman, who was placidly carving bits of whale-

bone into ornaments that he would sell in exchange for the few necessities his cove could not provide. He was like whalebone himself, thought Silverhair, carven with legends by the years.

"And then one day there was a storm, d'ye see," the old man continued his story, "and when it passed I found one of the People stranded on our beach. . . ."

Silverhair nodded. The long winter evenings were good for storytelling, and he had already heard how as a child the merman had tried to swim with the dolphins who came into the harbor of the fishing village where he lived.

"He was afraid, mind ye, but he was dyin', so I got me mates to help and we padded our ropes with rags and got him back to deep water again." His eyes sparkled like those of a man remembering his first love. "That was Waverunner, as our tongue would have it, tho' his name among the Sea People is"—he gave another of the complicated whistles that Silverhair was still trying to imitate— "and he stayed all the summer and taught me his own talk and how to swim his way and some of the stories of the sea.

"That's why the village lads got to call me Fish Feet, ye see. But I paid no mind. I did tell ye that tale of the harper that was saved by the dolphins long ago?" The merman looked at Silverhair in sudden alarm. His mind was unusually clear, but sometimes he did forget and repeat himself. Silverhair thought it came not so much from age as from living so long alone. He wondered how old the man was.

"Yes, the story of Arion of the land of Greece that was before the Ancient times," the harper answered gently. He had been trying to make that story into a song.

"Well, I took that name of Arion in the winter when I went for my Naming, though I never set hand upon a harp till ye came. But it was the name of a man loved by the Sea People, d'ye see. And that winter I made me a little boat, and when Waverunner came again with his tribe I went with them out to sea."

"But how did you live?"

"On the fish they caught for me and the water I could

carry. Raw fish freshly taken has a delicate flavor, mind ye, and the People would tow me little boat when there was a calm.''

The tale went on. In the summers Arion had ranged the seas off the coast of Westria with his dolphin tribe, and when they went off on their migrations they would leave him at some coastal village to live by odd jobs until they came again.

It was a wandering, heedless sort of life, thought Silverhair—in some ways even more rootless than his own—but the old merman did not seem lonely. Perhaps it was because he had loved the dolphins and been loved by them.

"Did I tell ye about the Floating Island, now?" the old man asked abruptly.

"How can an island float?" Silverhair smiled.

"Well it did—five hundred paces long and half that wide, it was, and going up and down in the water like a snake in the grass. It was all seaweed, d'ye see—all twisted and woven together in a big mat, like, with sand on top of it, and shells." Arion bent forward, daring Silverhair to disbelieve him.

"But who made it, and why?" asked the harper obediently.

"Not humans—not the land people. It was the Guardians that made it, lad, for a meeting place in the sea."

"But surely they can swim—why would they need an island to meet upon?" Silverhair tossed another piece of driftwood onto the fire and watched the colored flames lick upward. *Seafire* . . . he thought, *seafire*. . . .

"Maybe they find it easier to talk if they all take man-form, or maybe it's a place to meet with the spirits of the land. I heard that Masters of the College of the Wise go there. . . ." The merman nodded wisely, and Silverhair was reminded suddenly of the Master of the Junipers.

"And why did you go there?" he asked gently.

"Oh, my brothers took me, to show me off, maybe. But I saw wonders too—the Prince of the Dolphin Clans changing into a young man as sleek as water-polished stone, with silvery hair and merry eyes and a voice like a ballad singer

I heard once at a fair." His voice had grown soft, and Silverhair was caught by his vision. For a moment he too could see the beauty of the Guardians who reigned over the sea. He knew their names, of course—Sea Mother, who watched over the ocean's creatures, and the mighty Lady of the Deep Ocean, and all the lesser chieftains of the kindreds of the sea. What must it be to actually *see* them?

"And what about the seals?" he asked then. "I've spent so many hours watching them in the cove, and once or twice I thought I saw a human figure swimming with them there."

"Think ye it was a man-seal from one of your songs?" Arion shook his head. "If such exist, 'tis not here. To be sure, there are some that live with the seals as I lived with my brothers in the sea, but they too must stay on land in the cold season. Maybe ye saw the Seal Sister—the Lady herself, taking her pleasure in the waves!

"Surely all the Sea People who breathe air must love your music—" he went on. "Maybe it reminds them of the time before the great parting when they left us to return to the sea. . . . Come now, I've talked too much and me throat is dry. Now, you take up that harp and make music for me!"

Silverhair hauled in the line, unhooked two small and frantically wriggling fish, and tossed them into his basket. His fingers were aching with cold, but he forced himself to check the rest of the line and replace the bait on several of the hooks tied there. One hook was gone, and he shook his head. It had been one of their treasured iron ones, much stronger than those Arion fashioned from bone. It would be hard to get more.

Squinting into the bitter wind, he drew back his arm and cast the line back out into the surf, wondering, not for the first time, what he was doing here. He had suffered all winter, longing for the heat of the southern deserts as the winds threw storm after storm against the coast. At least once a day he had decided to leave the old man and find lodging in some town.

But he was still here. At first he had been too weak to

leave, and then the weather had been too foul. No ships would ply the coast until spring, so there was no use seeking a harbor. And then Arion had begun to sicken, and he had not wanted to leave him alone. In a way, staying here was a penance for his betrayals of Thea and Caolin.

Silverhair coughed, bending with the force of it without slackening the tension on the line of the long pole braced into the sand. At first he had been laughably clumsy at this, but Arion had taught him the way of it, and where to find edible shellfish and seaweed in the rocks at low tide. He eked out their fare by snaring rabbits—it was a lean diet, but with the sea at their doorstep they would not starve.

At least they wouldn't unless there were more days like this one, when all the fish that usually thronged the waters of the cove seemed to have gone off to some Festival. He peered out over the water, noting the sluggish, powerful swell, and the black, steely wall of clouds advancing from the west. The wind was not too strong, yet, but he guessed that another storm was on the way. Even the seagulls seemed anxious, circling down to the beach and rushing excitedly skyward again.

Yes, it must be a storm coming, and a big one, for most of the seals had already sought the safety of open water. Only one or two were still in the cove, bobbing and diving around the rocks as if they were daring the power of the waves. Fellow fishermen, they had become good companions during Silverhair's months here. He lifted a hand in salute, then pulled in his line and threw back to the nearest of the seals the single fish he found there. The seal bobbed half out of the water, caught the wriggling silver flash in midair, and submerged in a gurgle of foam.

Silverhair grinned, finished coiling the line, and picked up the pole and the basket that contained his meager catch. If a big blow was on the way he would need to resecure some of the hut's rude shingles, and from the feel of the wind he did not have much time.

"No, I don't want any more! Ye must eat it, lad— you're the one that needs the energy. I've lived off your

strength like a barnacle on a whale!'' The old man turned
his head away.

"Come now, Arion"—Silverhair held out the bowl of
broth again—"you fed me when I needed nursing. What's
so wrong about accepting my help now?'' He looked up
uneasily as the hut trembled beneath an unusually heavy
gust of wind, then he looked back at the merman. Arion's
eyes were closed, and he was shaking his head as if he had
forgotten how to stop. Silverhair's heart sank as he noted
anew how the old man's eyes seemed to have sunk in his
head; how transparent his skin had become. He thought,
What will I do if he dies and leaves me alone?

"You have to eat!'' he said desperately. "I need you to
be strong again!''

"Eh, lad,'' said Arion with a glint of a smile, "I'll try it
for your sake, but in the sea, if ye be not strong, ye die. It
cankers my soul to lie here like a beached whale!'' Obediently he opened his wrinkled mouth and let Silverhair feed
him.

It was not yet sunset, but the storm was already shaking
the hut in a giant hand. Between gusts of wind, Silverhair
heard rain clattering against the shingles and the crash of
waves on the shore. He wondered if the rowboat would be
safe—he had pulled it above the normal high-tide mark for
this time of year and hitched the bow line securely around
the stump of an old pine tree, but if the wind drove the
waves high enough it could be torn away. . . .

To calm himself, Silverhair took down the harp and
began trying to match the storm's eerie harmonies. He
fancied he could almost hear the words the wind spirits
were singing to their sisters in the waves.

"Silverhair!''

The harper looked up. Arion was struggling to sit.
Silverhair started to ask what was wrong, but the old
man's finger was at his lips, his head cocked in an agony
of listening.

"It's only the storm—'' he said, but the older man was
shaking his head; and then Silverhair heard it too—the
frantic, metallic clamor of a ship's bell!

Silverhair set the harp on his bed and snatched up his

cloak, trying to wrap it around him while struggling to open the door against the pressure of the wind. Then he pushed, and the wind flung it to one side, tore the garment from his grasp, and sent rain showering across the room.

But he hardly noticed, for he could see the ship, already impossibly close to the rocks and wallowing closer with every swell.

"They'll be aground in a moment," said a voice at his shoulder. "If ye tie one end of the long rope around your waist and the other to the pine trees ye may be able to save some of them without being swept away—" It was Arion, but Silverhair did not pause to wonder at it. Head down, he worked his way around the side of the house, grasped the big coil and fumbled to tie it securely.

As he reached the edge of the water the first wave drenched him. He glimpsed a flash of color, someone jumping from the deck of the ship or being swept away by the sea. "Wait!" he cried out, waving his arms, but his words were whipped away by the wind. Gasping at the cold and the strength of waves that pulled at him like icy hands, Silverhair waded in.

Even over the storm's roar he could hear screaming. Then came a shattering crash and the prolonged groan of wrenching timbers as the ship struck full upon the rocks.

Silverhair forced his way forward. Several times the waves knocked him off his feet, and the light was failing, but he kept on. He saw something struggling in the water, grabbed, and felt cloth. He pulled and small hands clutched at him; he staggered and nearly went down.

"My lady! You must save my lady—" the woman cried hoarsely. He saw another shape in the water beyond her, and knew that if he carried this first victim back to shore, by the time he returned the other one would be gone.

"Can you move?" he shouted. "Feel, here's a rope. Follow it back to shore!" He detached one of the hands fastened to his arm and guided it to the rope, felt the woman's weight shift as she grasped it with her other hand and began to pull herself shoreward. Her weight, added to the complex pressures of wind and waves, made his balance even more uncertain, but he did not know what else he

could have done. Straining, he fought his way toward the
other woman. Her ungainly struggles were growing weaker
now.

Sea Mother! Sant' Yemaya! he prayed to every power he
knew. *Help me get your daughter to shore!* Then, astonishingly, he was beside her, and as he tried to close his
arms around her realized that she was heavily pregnant.

"Did you see my husband? Is he safe?" she murmured
into his shoulder. Silverhair tightened his grip and looked
around him. Dimly he made out other figures struggling in
the water—some sinking, and some thrashing toward shore.
He could not tell one from another and he knew that this
woman had not the strength to make her way along the
rope alone. He would have to carry her.

He began to turn and saw a flicker of movement
nearby—a pale form that shot past with a curious undulation like a seal or a dolphin, or—he gasped as for a
moment splayed human feet showed pale against the waves.

Fish-feet! he thought in wonder and despair. Arion could
never survive this, surely, although at the moment he
seemed to be doing better than Silverhair. His movements let
him slip through the waves instead of fighting them; even
as the harper watched, the old man had reached one of the
swimmers and was pulling him in.

The woman Silverhair was holding stirred weakly. He
took a deep breath and started back to land. He had
thought that returning would be easier, but in the confines
of the cove the waters were boiling like soup in a cauldron, and the waves were trying to suck him out to sea. He
missed a step, lurched backward, and felt something give.
He tried to grab the rope but he needed both hands to hold
the woman. Then he lost his balance and the icy waters
closed over both of them.

The rope was gone. Now there was nothing to hold to,
and in the rainy dusk he could not see the shore. The
waves gave him no direction—in their confusion he could
barely tell the difference between up and down. And he
had no breath to call out, even if he could have been
heard.

He had swallowed a great deal of water. With a dim

horror he felt his strength ebbing—in a moment he would not be able to fight the sea any more. *And why not*—he thought vaguely, *at least I tried, and my life was no use to anyone anyhow. May our souls rest in the mercy of the Maker of All Things!*

Then he felt something smooth and hard rising beneath him; arms clasped him around the chest while other muscles worked strongly and thrust him upward into the air. *Arion?* It could not be, for even in his confusion Silverhair could tell that this body was too rounded and well muscled, the skin too smooth.

Muscles contracted, released against him again, and he and the woman he held were propelled forward. He let his legs dangle and tried to hold still lest he impede his rescuer. He glimpsed a smooth brown shoulder and dark hair that flared like seagrass in the spray. Then they dipped and shot forward again, and he shut tight his eyes as water closed over him.

In moments his feet knocked against the bottom. Their forward motion stopped, and he struggled to stand upright. The strong arms that supported him released. He kicked, staggered, and then found himself crouched splay-legged in shallow water with the woman limp in his arms. He took a step, another, and then turned his head into the wind, looking for his rescuer.

It was almost dark now, but Silverhair's eye was caught by something paler than the waves. Squinting, he made out a face—a woman's face, with long dark hair and a seal's bright eyes. But even as he watched, her head turned, and with a familiar bobbing movement she ducked under the water and was gone.

There was no time for wonder. Cries from the shore told him that others had escaped from the maw of the sea. In a moment they were reaching out to him, taking the woman from his frozen grasp and helping him to stagger ashore.

"I was never much of a swimmer, and I was certain old Seatco, the Sea Demon, would have me when someone grabbed me and pulled me toward the shore. I got a glimpse of him when we reached the sand—an old man, naked as a babe and swimming like a dolphin. I tried to thank him, but he only waved and dove back into the sea.'' The man who seemed to be the leader of the survivors pulled at his draggled, gingery beard and stared at Silverhair helplessly.

The harper nodded. Two other men had been saved by Arion, but he had always gone back to the sea. Now, when night had extinguished all hope of searching even though the wind had begun to drop at last, the old man had still not returned.

They had built up the fire and brought the soup back to the boil. The hut was warm now with the heat of many bodies, and redolent with the odor of sea wrack and steaming wool. Of the thirty souls the ship had carried, five crewmen and three passengers in addition to the lord and lady and her maid had made it to shore. Silverhair's shoulders drooped and he coughed. *Arion,* he wondered, *where are you now?*

"I am Sir Rudiard Applegard, a special envoy from Queen Mara of Normontaine—" the ginger-bearded man went on. "The woman you saved is my lady, Elena. You must know that you have only to ask and all I have is yours—my lady means everything to me, and especially now . . ." His voice faded and he glanced anxiously toward the bed where the maid was fussing over her mistress.

"What possessed you to travel in this weather?" asked Silverhair. "She must be near her time!"

"The weather in the south was fair, and she wished her child to be born at home. There should have been time— the babe is not due for a month or more!" He shook his head. "But I should not have agreed. Only I could not deny her—we have waited so long for this child!"

His attention was already back on the woman in the bed, and Silverhair let him be. If Lady Elena gave birth prematurely there was nothing they could do. *And if Arion does not return,* he asked himself then, *what will I do?*

In the morning they would search the shore for the bodies of those they had not been able to save. But Silverhair did not think Arion's wasted body would be among them.

He remembered how the old man's weakness had galled him, how he had feared to die in bed and be buried on land like shorebound men.

As if he had seen it, he thought he knew how it had been—how Arion, finding his last heroic gift of strength spent, had given himself willingly to the sea.

May the secret currents bear you into the depths, old man! he prayed. *May your brothers the dolphins bring your body to whatever sanctuary holds their bones, and may the Lord of the Waters receive your soul. . . .*

❧ FIFTEEN ❧

Silverhair sat on a piece of driftwood near the door to the hut, drawing a meandering sort of music from his harp and trying to forget what was going on inside. He could hear the hushed voices of the men around the bonfire and the whisper of the waves as they crept toward the high-tide mark, advancing and then falling back again as if the men had frightened them away. That morning had dawned as still as if there had never been a storm—only the smashed timbers and driftwood, the sea wrack and the pallid bodies of those it entangled, bore mute witness to the violence of the day before.

That was not what he was avoiding. Too clearly, he could also hear the moans of the woman who had gone into an early labor around noon and was still writhing on the bed as helplessly as the ship had tossed in the grip of the storm.

"If only there were something I could do!"

Silverhair looked up and saw Sir Rudiard standing beside him, huddling his cloak around him against the evening chill.

"It is my fault, may the Changer forgive me! I should never have taken her south with me! But Elena had never been to Westria, and she said she would have little leisure for traveling once the child was born! I could not deny her—have you ever watched a woman bear your child?" he asked suddenly.

Silverhair shook his head. No woman had ever called him husband, no child would call him father. Even the sister he had loved and the infant she had borne to the King had disappeared into a mystery which he despaired of fathoming.

"No," he said softly. "I am alone."

"I should have told Mara I would not go—" Sir Rudiard went on as if he had not heard. "It was only the investiture of a Regent, after all. It was not as if they had found the little King!"

Silverhair's hand stilled on the strings. "A new Regent?" he asked sharply. "Has Robert died?" But of course Robert was dead, reason was assuring him of that even as Sir Rudiard nodded. The Regent had been dying when he reached the Danehold, and it must literally have killed him to sign away Santibar.

Oh, Caolin, you are revenged upon him at last, Silverhair thought bitterly. *Now there remain of your enemies only Alessia, and Eric, and Rosemary. And me . . .*

"They wished the Lady Jessica to rule in his stead, or even to become Queen," the Montaner lord was continuing, "but she told them to wait out the six years left of the twenty that were agreed and then to choose a new King. They say she has returned to the mountains of the Ramparts to live alone."

A new King! Yes, thought the harper, *if Faris's child had lived, he would now be fourteen*. "Then who have they elected Regent?" he asked aloud.

"What choices did they have? Lord Philip of the Ramparts is still young, and Lady Alessia is still training her son to rule. Lord Theodric has scarcely the strength to sit a horse anymore. They elected Eric of Seagate, over his protests, and he sits now in the chair before the empty thrones."

A wave broke with a rush like distant cheering, and Silverhair sighed, wondering how Eric would deal with the complexities of ruling a Kingdom, and how Rosemary would like living in Laurelynn. It would have been better if Jehan had married her in the first place, he thought bitterly, since it had all come to the same thing in the end.

The hut's crude door scraped open, and firelight flared

across the sand. Sir Rudiard jerked around, paling as he saw his wife's maid standing in the doorway.

"Is it—is she—" he began, but the woman shook her head.

"No, nothing yet, my lord. My lady is resting now, and wonders if the harper—"

"Am I disturbing her? I am sorry, I thought she could not hear." Silverhair started to put the harp away.

"She cannot hear well enough, sir!" the woman corrected him. "She sent me to ask if you will come inside and play for her."

"What?" said Silverhair and Sir Rudiard simultaneously.

"Will you play for her?" the woman repeated. "She thinks the harp music might ease her pain."

Panic at the thought of being so close to women's mysteries warred with the memory of times when his music had soothed pain in the past, including his own. But this woman was no relation of his—he had no right to be there.

"Please . . ." said Sir Rudiard softly. "I am sure that it will help her, and I am so afraid. . . ."

Wordless, Silverhair nodded and went in.

As the hours passed, Silverhair grew increasingly awed by Lady Elena's endurance. She was a strong woman and she wanted the child, but she had been badly battered in the shipwreck, and only her woman could give her any help at all. Silverhair played, hesitantly at first and then with more confidence, songs of Westria and songs he had learned on his wanderings, and sometimes a soothing nameless music that formed around the rhythm of the contractions racking the woman for whom he played. His fingers grew sore, and his arms drooped from the angle at which he should have held them, but while Lady Elena continued to labor, shame drove him to continue to play.

He could hear the patient approach of the waves, and at times his mind sought that regular rhythm as an escape from what was going on in the room. Over and over again a certain minor melody emerged from his random music, and after a little he knew he had the beginnings of a song. Endlessly he played with the form of each new line, and the music grew.

> *"The sea is sighing on the sand,*
> *Upon a dark and rainswept shore,*
> *As tides have served the secret moon*
> *Forever and forever more."*

Now the music mutated into a second verse that summarized—

> *"The ceaseless seeking of the sea*
> *Each wave its own epiphany,*
> *Completed in its company*
> *And yet alone forevermore . . ."*

That said what he felt about the sea tonight, but not what it meant to him. Why was he compelled to express everything that moved him in music? The waves sought their goal on the shore. What was his goal? The woman on the bed arched and fell back again and again, the eagerness with which she had first met the task eroding as time went on. Her husband sat by her now, holding her hand and encouraging her. But Silverhair felt separated from them by an invisible wall.

> *"Within a lonely lamplit room*
> *A harper seeks the melody*
> *That struggles in his secret soul*
> *To find its form and harmony."*

He continued to play—

> *"His fingers fumble on the strings*
> *As each passed hour of darkness rings,*
> *And patient pain the music brings;*
> *He is alone as he must be."*

"No!" exclaimed the woman on the bed. "Rudi—make it stop. I don't want to do this anymore!"

Sir Rudiard looked at the other woman in panic, but the
maid only shook her head with a grim smile. "It's only
natural at this stage of labor," she said. "She is very
tired."

Elena shook her head, stiffened as another contraction
rippled through her belly, then fell back again.

"I want my mother—it hurts, and mother would make it
stop. Where's Mama?" she whimpered.

"Your mother went through exactly this laboring to
bear you, my lady, and our good Mother Earth will help
you now!" snapped the older woman. "So be you still—
don't you see how you're worrying your man?"

For a moment Elena's eyes cleared and she patted her
husband's hand. "It's all right, love," she said, "it's
only—" Then there was another contraction, and her gaze
turned inward once more.

And suddenly Silverhair saw the link between them, and
between them and the sea itself, all striving toward some
unknown goal.

> *"Upon her bed a woman writhes*
> *In rhythms she has never known*
> *To bring to birth she knows not what—*
> *Her body is no more her own.*
> *Her body barriers the brain;*
> *Forever she must strive and strain;*
> *And all the world is made of pain—*
> *Though others watch, she is alone!"*

But the song was still unresolved, the waves still advancing, the baby still unborn. In that moment it seemed to
Silverhair that the conclusion of all three must be the
same. He stopped playing and went to the door. The
clouds had broken, and between them he saw the pale
sliver of a new moon. A pallid light glittered on the
laboring sea. The white line of foam at the water's edge
was up to the jagged rock now. He thought it had perhaps
half an hour to go.

He went back into the hut. Elena's contractions seemed
to have lost the regularity they had had before. She arched

and cried out at random, muttering to herself as each convulsion eased and once striking out at her husband's hand. Silverhair looked up at the maid.

"How long do you think it will be?"

She shrugged. "The lady has done with the first part of labor that opens the gates, and now her body seeks the new rhythm that will push the babe through. This is the hardest part, and the most painful. We can only hope it will be short, because if it takes too long, she may not have the strength she will need at the end."

The harper nodded and sat for a moment thinking, his fingers playing idly across the strings. If harp music could cast sleep upon grown warriors, surely he could play something to ease a woman's laboring! The music he had been playing through the long beginning had been in the minor mode. He needed something different now.

Elena thrashed and cried out as men in battle do when the pattern of the fighting is broken and they struggle without being able to identify the enemy. Silverhair had seen such a tangle straightened by the clear call of a horn. He tried for that simple phrase of music now—a major scale of notes repeated over and over again. And gradually a new melody revealed itself, simple, straightforward, with a strong, regular beat and the cheerful intensity of the charging warrior who sights his goal.

Again he repeated it, and again. And then from the bed there came an explosive "Oh!" and the waiting woman exclaiming, "There, now, my lady—now you understand! Wait now until your body begins to move again, and push with it. Wait—wait—now!"

Her words were echoed by an explosive, guttural cry from Elena, like the sound that might come from a man who was trying to heave a heavy rock from its bed. But Silverhair had heard it also on the battlefield, when men who have been held too long in check are loosed at last upon their foe.

Time after time the woman cried out while her husband bit his lip at the pressure she was putting on his hands and babbled encouragements until he had no breath.

Then came another moment, when Elena's body tried to

move and she had not the energy to move with it any more.

"Come now, girl, you're almost there. I can see the baby's head now. Come on!" The maid was kneeling at the foot of the bed with hands outstretched. For a moment Silverhair saw something bulge between the woman's thighs, then disappear again.

It's the baby! he thought in wonder, and realized that despite all he had ever heard, despite the evidence of the past few hours, he had not really *believed* this was how babies were born! *It's going to happen!* he thought. *There really is a new human being there!* His music rang out triumphantly.

"My lord, get up and hold her half-sitting so that she can push—"

Between contractions, Sir Rudiard scrambled to ease himself behind his wife. His face was red and his hair clung in damp strings to his brow. He looked down at his wife with an expression of mingled fear and excitement and gave her his hands to hold.

Elena's face was contorted and tear-streaked, her hair matted with perspiration, but her expression was one of intense determination now. With a sigh of relief, she leaned back against her husband and gathered a deep breath as her belly began to ridge again. Silverhair heard the sound of the sea close to the house and knew that the tide had almost attained its goal.

He scarcely knew what he was playing. His consciousness had expanded to include the rush of the tide, the struggles of the woman giving birth, all processes that strained to a conclusion now. The moon rode at her zenith; the tide was reaching for the trees; the walls of the hut vibrated with triumphant music, and then there was a shout that rattled the door in its frame as the child burst free into the midwife's waiting hands.

Two voices had combined in that shout of victory, and two faces shone with identical radiance as the waiting woman lifted the baby and settled it on its mother's still heaving breast. Her arms went around it protectively, and Silverhair's sight was dimmed by a mist of tears.

"May Earth our Mother be praised!" said the midwife.
"You have a son."

Silverhair sat back, trembling, sensing that after its
long effort the tide had begun to turn, feeling the joy of
completion that blazed from the new trinity of mother and
father and child, hearing the music beneath his fingers
change undirected from the major to the Mixolydian mode
that brought rest.

> "High tide! Waves wash across the sands;
> Tears ease the harper's harmony,
> Blood bears the babe to waiting hands,
> Man shares his woman's ecstasy.
> Then fades the sea-foam from the shore,
> The music echoes, is no more,
> But cradled close, the child's secure—
> No more alone, now there are three. . . ."

The midwife bustled around the bed, taking care of the
afterbirth, swaddling the child and laying him at his mother's side.

Silverhair let his hands fall from the harpstrings and
heard the last echoes shimmer to silence as he heard the
retreating whisper of the sea. And then the only sounds in
the room were the crackling of the fire and small sucking
noises as the baby sought his mother's breast.

They named the child Arion. Lady Elena had wanted to
call him after Silverhair, but his hair was a gingery fringe
like his father's, and the Montaners did not give their
children "milk-names." Silverhair did not tell them his
true name, partly because concealment had become almost
an instinct, and partly, he realized, because he was in truth
Silverhair now. Just as the child was forgotten when a boy
took his true-name and became a man, the eager young
man who had been called Farin Harper was gone. Somewhere, upon the many roads that the harper had wandered,
he had disappeared.

In the end, they agreed that it would be proper to call

Elena's child after the man who had saved the life of his
father, especially since that was a harper's name too.

When the brief ceremony was done, Silverhair went
down to the edge of the water, where he could look out
over the deceptively gentle sea.

"My old friend, you have not given your life uselessly,"
he said softly, as if the waves still retained something of
Arion that could hear and understand. "You had no child
of your body, but your name will be remembered among
men." A gull swooped past him, and something out to sea
leaped and fell back with a splash—a dolphin, or perhaps a
seal. Silverhair remembered the sleek body which had
borne him to shore, and smiled.

Behind him, men were helping Lady Elena and her child
into a horse litter for the journey to Balena Bay, the village
a few hours up the coast that was as close as the region
could come to a harbor and town. Sir Rudiard had sent his
men there for help as soon as the weather cleared, and now
that the child was a week old, they thought him strong
enough to travel. In the village they would wait for a ship
to carry them north again, for with that last late storm,
winter seemed vanquished at last, and even with its dangers, sailing seemed the safest way to transport a woman
with a newborn child.

And Silverhair would be going with them. They had
been hesitant about asking, but he had made no objection.
Why not? He had been heading north when he fell ill, and
Sir Rudiard could recommend him to Normontaine's Queen.
With old Arion gone there was nothing to hold him here.

"Behold the Mother of Waters, the gateway to Normontaine—" Sir Rudiard gestured proudly toward what
Silverhair had taken to be yet another inlet of the sea. If
the expanse of water these bluffs guarded was a river
mouth, Sir Rudiard was right to be proud. Silverhair had
thought the Dorada a mighty river where it flowed into the
Great Bay, but as the ship came round and began to glide
eastward, he realized there was more fresh water here than
he had ever tried to imagine before.

Conditioned by years in Elaya and Aztlan, where water

was more precious than gold, and brought up in Westria, where a year of drought could ruin a Province, he found this abundance inebriating. Now he understood the significance of the countless streams they had seen flowing into the ocean as they sailed north along the coast. Here was a land rich in water beyond any Westrian's dreams.

Silverhair leaned over the rail staring as the ship moved into the river mouth. Above the little town at the river's mouth, rising hills were crowned with trees, and as the ship continued upriver the high bluffs on the northern side of the river became increasingly clear. He breathed deeply of a landwind that was spiced with pine and cedar and fir, lightened by the sweetness of new grass or spring flowers. In the distance some great bird, perhaps an eagle, circled in the pale sky.

"At least Sunfather has blessed our returning after all our sufferings!" Sir Rudiard spread his arms to the sun. Silverhair remembered standing in just such an ecstasy once in the desert, worshiping the cool, driving drops of a rare summer thunderstorm. Sir Rudiard sighed and smiled at Silverhair, and then at his lady who sat beneath the shade of the big square sail with her son in her arms.

"How long before we reach the capital?" asked the harper.

"If this wind holds, we should make Riverwatch by noon under our own power. From there the galleys will tow us the rest of the way to Antyr Town. I hope we may reach it before night falls."

Silverhair nodded. Sir Rudiard went back to join his wife, but the harper continued to stand at the rail, watching the narrowing banks of the river slide by. The majesty of the cliffs that now rose to either side was almost overpowering, their true splendor all the more apparent in comparison with the gentle fields and low woodlands of the islands that floated in midriver. On some of them people were living; they came down to the shore to wave to the ship as she moved slowly past. On others he saw deer lifting their delicate heads for a moment's glance and then returning to their grazing.

He felt as if he were floating in a dream while all the

troubles of his past life flowed away behind him down the stream. Surely this was a blessed land, where he would be able to make a new life free of ties with the past.

They came to Antyr Town just at sunset, when the clarity of the day was fading to a delicate rose that suffused the sky and glowed on the snowclad slopes of the great peak that rose from the Misty Mountains, which were the spine of Normontaine. Northward across the Mother of Waters he could see other points of white against the tender sky. A wisp of smoke wreathed upward, and he wondered if there was a forest fire there.

But his attention was mostly on the timber- and brick-built town that had grown up on the low, tree-clad hills where the noble river of Vale flowed up from its broad valley to meet the Mother of Waters. There were islands in the river there, and good harborage, forested now with the spars of ships as if the trees had spread down into the riverbed from the hills.

A white road led up from the town to the log and rubble ramparts of the fortress of Norgard, but the heavy gates were open, and everywhere in the town and on the way to the fortress, the bright sparks of colored lanterns glowed among masses of rhododendrons. Lady Elena explained that the great, showy flowers, in every shade of pink and rose, had just come into bloom.

"But why are they hung with lanterns?" asked Silverhair. "Are they celebrating the return of the Ambassador?"

Lady Elena's dark eyes grew more slanted as she laughed. "That would be honor indeed. But the Festival is one we hold every spring, if the weather permits it, to celebrate the return of the sunshine and the flowers. Later in the season, the city will be full of roses."

"My lady will need to rest once we are inside—" Sir Rudiard gestured toward the gate just ahead of them. Its uprights, seen close, were massive, and the crosspiece was flared upward at the ends in a style Silverhair had not seen before. "But I must present myself to my Mistress as soon as I can. I hope that you will come with me, Silverhair."

The harper looked down at his faded purple tunic and

tattered breeches with a rueful smile. "I am hardly dressed to appear in a Queen's hall—"

"Sunfather! What do you think I am? Do you think I would allow the man who saved my wife and child to go about in rags?" exclaimed the Ambassador. "Everything I own would not equal the value of what you restored to me, and if my Mistress values you as I do, you will soon have no need of anything of mine, so let me reward you while I can!" he added more temperately.

Silverhair gazed up at the carved and painted eaves of the palace and wondered. Once he had been familiar with courts and palaces, but that had been long ago. How would he fare with this northern Queen?

Silverhair took a careful sip of cider and set his pewter goblet down. One gobletful had already taught him to respect its power, and the mead which was the other choice at the Queen's table was even stronger. He looked at the Montaner lords and ladies around him with growing respect as they held their flagons out to be refilled. Only a slight flush on some of their faces, and an increasing volume in the babble of conversation at the long table, betrayed any effect from the alcohol.

The Montaners wore garments of brightly dyed wool or leather trimmed with fur. Silverhair was glad he had chosen a long robe of burgundy embroidered with silver at the neck and wrists from among those Sir Rudiard had offered him. He had feared it might look ostentatious, but it was, if anything, understated in this company. Of course he had attracted a certain amount of attention as the story of the Ambassador's shipwreck got around, but the courtiers, while friendly, had restrained their curiosity. He suspected they were waiting for the Queen to show them what his status at court was to be.

Once more his eyes sought the dais where she sat with her officers. At first one noticed her rather spectacular coloring—hair like a dying sunset and eyes the cool grey-blue of the northern seas. A more careful consideration revealed the good bones beneath the high-colored skin, and the sculpturing around eyes and mouth that revealed the unmistakable lines of power. Mara had been just a little older than Jehan, Silverhair remembered, which must put her in her late forties now. However the misty-blue gown she was wearing outlined a figure that was still excellent, and she moved like a woman who knew that she pleased men's eyes.

She was listening to one of her court bards now—Sir Rudiard had said that the art of the storyteller was highly prized in Normontaine. The man had versified a traditional northern tale of the Cataclysm that told how the nearby mountain they called the Guardian had exploded in fire and thunder and destroyed in a single day the city the Ancients had built along the river.

Now the forests around the base of the mountain were sacred lands. A community of initiates lived on its slope to offer prayers and to warn the people if the mountain should become angry again. But although other peaks in the Misty Mountains still smoked or sent up plumes of ash or flame, the Guardian had remained at rest. According to the legend, an ancestor of the Royal House had given his life to the volcano to secure that peace.

The bard finished with a compliment to the Queen and a prayer to the Changer to continue to hold his hand. Silverhair realized abruptly that in Normontaine they had no Covenant between the Powers of Nature and Man. For them the Cataclysm was not the primal disaster from which men counted their history, but only one episode in a history of transformations wrought by that Power who had changed the world and who someday would change it again. The evening was warm, but he shivered suddenly.

And then someone was speaking in his ear and he realized that the tale was done and the Queen had sent for him. He took a few deep breaths to steady his heartbeat, then picked up his harpcase and followed the page to the dais.

"Master Harper, you are very welcome to Normontaine. As you have seen, we value the arts here, but it is rare that we have a visitor with such a varied background. . . ." The Queen's voice was gentle, but Silverhair looked at her narrowly, for he thought he had heard overtones of meaning in it that were not so much malicious as faintly amused. Whether the knowledge came from her own sources of information or from Sir Rudiard, Silverhair was suddenly certain that she knew precisely who and what he was.

He met her eyes boldly, and bowed, seeking a power within himself that might match her own. "My lady is too kind—" he replied with equal blandness. "I have been a wanderer upon the roads of the world, but I am honored to offer her whatever poor skill I have acquired."

She gestured toward the low stool before the dais and he seated himself, extracted Swangold from her battered case, and began to tune.

He gave them first a lively dance tune from the Corona that set feet tapping and drew from courtiers who were prepared to be critical of this stranger an involuntary smile. Silverhair looked up at the Queen, his gaze saying silently, *Yes, my lady, this is where I began.* Then the music slowed and changed, suggesting the melodies of the south and west before it settled into a song of the trail whose minor harmonies sang of the loneliness of nights beneath the immensity of a desert sky. *And this . . .* the music seemed to say, *this is where I have been. . . .*

He continued to play, his fingering becoming more precise and his harmonies more complex as he brought into play the skills he had learned at the College of Bards. He played with authority now, showing them a level of musicianship that might be surpassed only at the College itself, moving at last into a simple, precise accompaniment to a song which he had adapted for the Queen from a hymn to the Lady of Westria. He did not think it was a sacrilege, for now that he had seen her, he sensed that in more ways than the obvious ones, Mara was truly the Lady of Normontaine.

> "Queen most excellently bright,
> Lady of the day and night,
> Thou whose beauty blinds my sight—
> Shine on me still. . . .

> *The verdant mountains are thy breast,*
> *The vales, thy lap whereon I rest,*
> *Thy hair the sunset in the west—*
> *My heart they fill. . . .*
>
> *Thy wrath is like the stormy sea,*
> *But lady, turn thy smiles on me;*
> *Thy loving servant I would be—*
> *And do thy will. . . ."*

He finished and sat still, letting the echoes of the harp fade to silence while the Montaner lords looked from him to the Queen and back again and the ladies whispered behind their hands.

But Mara smiled benignly, ignoring, or perhaps acknowledging, the challenge he had given her, and held out her hand. Silverhair set down the harp and rose, and as he took her hand to kiss it her fingers tightened on his own.

"You have offered me your service, harper, and I accept it!" she said in a low voice, but his flesh was receiving other messages from her warm fingers, and as his heart began to beat faster what Silverhair felt was not fear at all.

⋙ 4 ⋘

The Queen's Harper

Third Interlude

Now the harp tunes itself to lovesongs—sweet, bitter-sweet, or sometimes spiced by a delicate comedy. Precise or passionate, the music accompanies all that Mara and her harper do, until the courtiers of Normontaine joke that they have only to listen for the sweet ripple of harpsong in order to locate the Queen.

At first the harper feels unfaithful, for he has never put all his powers at the disposal of any woman before. He wonders if Swangold resents it when his fingers move from her satiny walnut frame to the warm velvet of Mara's skin. Happiness lies between his two hands, and he is afraid to close them upon it. Mara trusts him more than he can trust himself. Will he betray her, too?

But there is no flaw in his music. Slow airs soothe the Queen after wearing hours in the Council room or the Assembly hall; jigs and reels set her feet to tapping when she needs an outlet for her energy; comic ballads make her laugh; laments give her the release of tears; and sensuous serenades transform the royal bedchamber into a temple of love. The slow sweet chords smooth the air and soothe jangled nerves to harmony. Harpnotes ripple like falling

*water, flicker like darting flame, seducing the spirit and
the flesh away from all care, suffusing them with sweetness
until the harp is laid aside and harper and hearer make
their own climax to the music.*

❯❯❯ SIXTEEN ❮❮❮

Shivering, Silverhair handed his wet cloak to the boy Mikhel, whom they had appointed to be his servant here, and went quickly to the fireplace. For a few moments all other thoughts were lost in the sheer pleasure of feeling the dry heat penetrate his chilled flesh. *The entire year's ration of sunshine must have been used up the week I arrived,* he thought, turning to warm his hands. But at least in this country of forests there was no lack of wood for fires.

He hung his gloves from a hook on the iron drying-rack before the fireplace, and then with a sigh eased into the deep fur of the bearskin that covered the chair. Mikhel knelt to unlace his right boot, drew it off, and hung it on the rack beside the gloves. The odor of scorching leather began to mingle with the reek of wet wool and the spicy warmth of burning pine.

Silverhair drew back his foot self-consciously. Even after three years at Mara's court he found it hard to accept personal service of this kind. But as he rubbed his cold fingers together he was grateful—he would have fumbled with the laces, and his feet were almost numb. Mikhel was the son of a holder from the eastern Province of Normontaine, who had been sent to court to complete his education. And as he said, if he did not serve Silverhair, they would only assign him to some other official of the court, and it gave him status in the Boys' House to serve the harper favored by the Queen.

Even at that thought Silverhair's face grew warm. It still

amazed him that Mara should have given him so much—
and that even after the first novelty had worn off she
should still enjoy him both as a musician and as a man. He
leaned back, appreciating the heat of the fire as he appreciated the artistry of the rich carvings that paneled the walls,
abstract designs of birds and animals in the style of the
coastal tribes.

Mikhel was working on the second boot now. "Have
you heard the news?" he asked as the final knot gave way
and he began to loosen the laces.

"What news?"

"Word came on an Elayan trading ship. Prince Palomon
is dead and his nephew Ali has taken the Lion Throne!"

Silverhair sat up abruptly, his mind racing, as Mikhel
pulled off the boot. The boy continued to talk, but he did
not hear. He had hated the Prince Paramount of Elaya
once, and accorded him a grudging admiration for longer,
and now he was gone. Inevitably Silverhair's thoughts
turned to Caolin. Secure in Palomon's favor, he could
have survived the loss of Santibar, but what would become
of him with Ali in power? Caolin had defeated Ali's bid
for the throne while Palomon lived, and then Ali had been
given the prize of Santibar. It seemed unlikely that Prince
Ali would favor the man who had served both the High
Prince of Elaya and the King of Westria, or that Caolin
would wish to aid his rival. But if Caolin lost power in
Elaya, what would he do?

With a pang, Silverhair realized that if Caolin had been
allowed to rule Santibar, he might have been able to save
himself and serve Westria by restoring the city to its
former allegiance. But Silverhair's own actions had made
that impossible. He thought, *I could not keep his secret,
and so he has no choices now. No wonder he wanted to
kill me!* He had often wondered what had impelled him to
tell Alessia Caolin's identity. He still did not know.

"Is there anything I can get you, my lord?" Mikhel put
another log on the fire and turned back to Silverhair.

"Some mulled wine would be welcome if there is any
hot in the kitchens now—" said the harper, focusing on

the boy and managing a smile. Mikhel nodded and bowed and then left Silverhair alone.

His thoughts moved sluggishly, as if his mind were still numbed by the cold. Where was Caolin now? Ali might have already arrested or executed him, but somehow Silverhair could not believe that had happened. As if he could sense the other man's presence, he knew that Caolin was alive. *Alive, and hating me*—he thought, with a shiver that had nothing to do with the cold.

His feet began to throb dully as circulation returned, and he moved them uncomfortably. He heard the latch click and a step on the boards behind him as the door opened, but he did not look up.

"Master Harper, don't you think you should drink this before it gets cold?" It was a low voice with the richness of warm honey—certainly not the voice of the boy Mikhel!

"My lady!" Silverhair turned quickly.

Queen Mara of Normontaine smiled and came past him to set the copper tray with its paired mugs and stoneware pot on the edge of the hearth. Pulse beating, Silverhair struggled to his feet.

"Sit down, man—we are not in public now!" Mara stood for a moment surveying him and he gazed back at her. Her ruddy hair was braided down her back, and she had belted around her a robe of dusky-rose-colored wool lined and edged with grey rabbit fur.

"And get those stockings off—" she went on. "They're soaked through. If I had known what the weather would be like I would not have sent you out with the hunting party today." She seated herself across from him.

Flushing, he bent to strip off the steaming stockings. He could not conceal from her how he suffered from the cold, and found himself at once irritated and moved by her solicitude.

"It doesn't matter," he said. "We had a good day—a long chase and two fat bucks for your table."

She nodded. "And how did Alyce do?"

He looked up at her quickly, but her eyes were cast down, and she seemed absorbed in the reknotting of her sash.

"The Crown Princess and her lord rode well. In fact, it was the lady Alyce who made the second kill."

"Her father always loved hunting . . ." said the Queen. Silverhair knew the concern that had been masked by that question. Mara's daughter and heiress had suffered a miscarriage a few weeks before.

"I think her pleasure in the exercise did her good." He answered the question Mara had not asked.

"And the Takhoman lords?" Mara poured steaming wine into one of the mugs, offered it to Silverhair, and poured for herself again.

"Boastful—the trees up north are bigger, the deer fatter, that sort of thing—but they seem to appreciate your hospitality. They were saying that the lord McKay ought to talk with you before he does any more trading on his own. Apparently he's sent his greatship off to the Kingdom of the Isles. If you can make terms with him before she returns you may be able to regulate the trade."

Silverhair drank deeply. The wine was hot and sweet, and he began to relax as its warmth penetrated his belly.

"I'll need to send some kind of delegation to their King," said Mara thoughtfully. "Did they know that you were listening?" She looked at Silverhair again.

He shrugged. "I was standing next to him. Either they thought it did not matter, or perhaps they hoped that I would tell you. . . ."

"Why do you think I sent you with them, my friend?" she asked softly. "You are a foreigner with no alliances in the Kingdom and no official responsibilities, but it is known that I favor you," she smiled. "You have been very useful to me—do you mind?"

Silverhair sat up, thinking. It had happened gradually, over the past years, and until now he had not really considered the significance of some of their conversations. But looking at them through Mara's eyes he could see that she was right, and though he would not have chosen such a role, in a curious way he enjoyed it.

She was leaning forward, waiting for his answer, and the firelight warmed her face and hair. *Your hair is like this land*—thought the harper, watching her, *fire threaded with snow*. . . .

"I am happy to serve you in all ways, my lady—" he said aloud, then flushed as he realized the double meaning of his words. But she was grinning, looking for a moment like a girl of eighteen. He lifted his mug to drink again.

"Your tunic is damp as well. If you sit about in wet garments, how do you expect to get warm?" she said severely, but the smile was still in her eyes. She left her chair then and half knelt beside him, her fingers busy on the laces at the neck of his tunic. Her hands were warm and smooth and there was a scent like rosemary in her hair.

He lifted his hand to touch it, let his fingers move down to the soft skin of her neck and the smooth shoulders beneath the gown. She was wearing nothing under it.

She had undone the neck of his tunic and was fumbling with the buckle of his belt. Quickly he set down his mug and moved to help her, then his hands shifted to either side of her face and he held her to receive his kiss. When their lips parted, his skin was burning, and her eyes had gone unfocused as if she had too much wine. Silverhair rose, stripping off the tunic, and began to tremble as Mara's hands passed across his bare chest and around to his back and she began to knead the long muscles there.

His hand slid down Mara's neck to the softness of her breast, parting the folds of her gown and freeing the knot that held it closed. And then in the same confused moment they were both working to slide off his breeches and move to the bed with its heaped furs, and he was lying against her, bare flesh kindling bare flesh to an even fiercer flame.

"I remember the first time . . ." she murmured when for a moment they drew apart. "I had such a hard time convincing you that I wanted you."

Silverhair moved his hand over her rounded belly, still faintly etched by the silver lines where it had stretched when she carried her children—the sigil of the Mother's fruitfulness. Her breathing grew faster as his fingers strayed lower.

"I believe you now," he said. He could tell that she

was ready for him, but he delayed, touching her as he would have touched his harp, with tenderness and knowledge and skill, until she was vibrating like a plucked string.

But still she had not cried out, and as if it were a contest between them she caressed him, until it seemed that the room around them must burst into flame. In the end he could not tell if he had fallen upon her in surrender, or if she had reached out to pull him to her in an agony of need, but suddenly he was the musician no longer, for something else was joining both of them into a single instrument of love.

Later they lay watching the dying embers of the fire, still so warm from the afterglow of passion they scarcely needed the furs. Silverhair passed one finger down the sculptured curve of Mara's brow, touched the laughter lines at the corners of her eyes and tried to smooth the lines of power around her mouth away.

She smiled and kissed his fingers. "Do you know, you have become very useful to me."

"I should hope so!" he grinned reminiscently.

"That's not what I meant," she said in mock severity. "I was thinking of what you told me about this afternoon. People tell you things, or let you hear them, knowing that they will remain unofficial, and yet the word will get to me. But you know how to listen and how to hold your tongue. You are a musician—do you mind if I make you a diplomat too?"

Silverhair was not offended. They had shared the forgetfulness of passion, but now the Queen's mind was once more moving in its accustomed paths. He could not resent it—it was enough to have even for a little while enabled the claims of the woman to take precedence over those of the sovereign.

And as he thought about it, the harper realized that he himself received a certain satisfaction from the work she had asked him to do.

"I am going to send a delegation to the Isles," she said then. "And I want you to go. I will miss you, but I need someone who can pick up the nuances, who can give me the flavor of the place. I need an envoy who will know how to distinguish what is significant from what is merely strange. Will you do this for me?''

Silverhair stared at her, suppressing a quick, unworthy thought that perhaps there was some other man she had her eye on, younger and stronger than him. But even if he stayed here, he had neither the right nor the power, nor even, really, the desire, to prevent her from taking any man she chose. And he had never been to those legendary Isles . . .

"My lady—" He lifted her hand to his lips, renewing the pledge he had made to her before. "I am your servant in all things."

After eight months in the Isles, Silverhair had forgotten that Normontaine was so cold. He found himself shivering, and hurried down the corridor toward the Great Hall, wishing he had worn his cloak. There would be fire in the hall, and the warmth of many bodies. Perhaps that would lift the chill that had plagued him since the diplomatic mission had returned.

Silverhair's memory ran back to endless beaches where the sea whispered stories of lands he could hardly imagine, much less name, and the palm trees rustled like a mother soothing her child to sleep. His skin was still brown from the kiss of that glowing sun. Before he left Normontaine, he had almost been used to the northern weather, but now the acclimatizing must all be done again. He shivered once more. Well, the dinner he was late for was a state affair. They would be serving wine from Westria, and mead. That would get him warm.

As he opened the door into the hall he was struck by a blast of sound—men's and women's voices mingling in a variety of accents, all but drowning out the soft music of the wind consort near the dais.

"The harper!" said someone nearby as the door swung shut behind him. "Silverhair! Silverhair! Give us a song— tell us about the Kingdom of the Isles!"

Mara sat in her chair of state on the dais with her nobles to either side. The harper's low chair was in its accustomed place before her, but someone else was leaning over the arm of her throne, a young man whom Silverhair vaguely remembered hearing praised as an archer. As he watched, the fellow raised the Queen's hand to his lips, and Mara turned her head in the little gesture of tenderness that Silverhair knew so well, and she smiled.

For a moment Silverhair stopped short, then he continued to make his way toward her. In the Isles there had been a girl with skin like honey and hair like the fall of night. It had been very sweet to lie with her in the warm darkness. Why should he have expected Mara to remain faithful while he was gone? He knew too well that the Queen of Normontaine was not a woman to sleep alone.

But however unreasonable, Silverhair's own reactions distracted him so that it was not until he was before her that he realized who was sitting in the two carven chairs to either side of her. He felt the blood leaving his face as he recognized Lord Theodor of the Corona, and realized that the young woman on Mara's left must be his own niece—his sister Berisa's daughter by Theodor's son. He did not even know what name she had taken now that she was grown.

Silverhair turned back to the Queen, his eyes blazing. Mara knew that he wanted nothing more to do with Westria, and above all with these Westrians, his own marriage-kin. Why had she tricked him into this confrontation?

The Queen met his eyes and there was something stern in her face that stayed for a moment the accusations that were springing to his lips. Then she turned to Lord Theodor.

"My Lord Commander—you are fortunate in your choice of a time to visit me. I would like to present my harper, Silverhair. He has been away for many months in the western islands, and is only now returned to us here."

Lord Theodor nodded graciously, and Silverhair, watching him warily for any sign of recognition, saw that his grey eyes were filmed and milky. Appalled, he realized that the old man must be nearly blind. He told himself he should not be surprised. The old lord had been in his sixties when Silverhair had left home almost eighteen years ago. But now that he could really look at Theodor, the harper saw that the strong shoulders were bowed and his

hand trembled very slightly as he lifted it to greet the
younger man. *I remember now*, thought Silverhair painfully, *after the King died, Theodor began to grow old.*

"And this is the lady Elinor, his granddaughter, and
heiress to the Corona—"

Silverhair collected himself, finished the bow with which
he had greeted Lord Theodor, and made another, more
flamboyant reverence to the golden-haired young woman
who was surveying him curiously with her clear, dark eyes.

When he had seen her last she had been called Linnet,
and she had been eight years old. It was unlikely that she
would recognize in this white-headed harper the young
uncle who had disappeared so long ago.

"I had an uncle who played the harp," she said, as if
she had unwittingly read his mind, "and I always loved to
listen to him. I am looking forward to hearing you play."

He looked at her sharply, but her face was grave and
composed. *Well, it's certain I'll not play you anything
from Westria!* he thought wryly.

"I hope to deserve your good opinion, my lady. I have
learned music of the islands which I can play now if the
Queen so wills," he replied in the accent of Normontaine.

Mara nodded, and as the herald called for silence
Silverhair took his familiar position, unlatched the harpcase,
and began to tune Swangold. *She is glad to be back here,*
he thought as one mellow note after another throbbed in
the stillness of the room. *It is only I who cannot stand the
damp and the cold.*

"Here our mountains are volcanoes, but in the Isles the
very land itself is born of the mountain's fire." As Silverhair
spoke, his fingers began to weave the strings into a fabric
of music, testing their harmonies and now and again pausing to make an infinitesimal adjustment. "There are islands where the ruins of the Ancients may be seen, and the
ruins of a people who were old when the Ancients were
young. And there are islands which were born during the
Cataclysm when so much else was destroyed.

"On the greatest of the islands lives the Goddess Pele,
who is one of the oldest spirits, at once Lady of Earth and
Fire. They say that she is very beautiful, but she can be

terrible in her wrath. . . ." He bowed toward the Queen as
he spoke, and those who were close enough to notice
smiled appreciatively, but he thought that Mara frowned.

Silverhair turned to his audience again. He had been
working on this music on the long voyage home from the
Isles, and twenty years of performance had taught him just
how to transform an audience into a single, listening ear.
Theodor and Elinor would not recognize in this accomplished musician the young harper who had fumbled his
way through the songs of the Corona so many years ago.

"There are many tales of Pele in the Isles. One of the
greatest tells how she raged during the Cataclysm until
men thought she would destroy the islands and all that
lived on them. But a young man who had loved her stayed
her anger by offering himself as a sacrifice."

As he began to draw from the harp long, slow cascades
of sound like the incoming combers of the sea, Silverhair
thought that the people of Normontaine, who set commu-
nities of priests on the slopes of each of their great mountains to propitiate their spirits and warn men of their anger,
would appreciate this song. Then the music grew harsher,
vibrating with ominous harmonies and warning thunder,
and he began to chant.

> *"It was in the long-ago days, the days of wrath,*
>   *The days when all of men's ill-doing rebounded upon*
>   *them.*
> *It was in the days when all the gods were angry.*
> *It was in those days that Pele awoke in splendor,*
> *The fire-haired Goddess awoke,*
> *She arose from her mountain, wrapped in flame. . . ."*

Momentarily the harper shuddered, and his fingers faltered on the strings. For he had seen Pele with the eyes
of the flesh when he was in the Isles, and that sight had
seared his memory. But his audience hardly noticed the
pause. In imagination they were already on those faraway
beaches, watching in terror as the sky caught fire and the
red serpents of lava crept inexorably toward their towns.

Men had tried to propitiate Pele with the last remaining

bottles of good whisky—it had been known to work before—but this time the Goddess was truly angry, and lava hissed through the streets of the city. Those who had boats launched them, but there were not enough for everyone, and the unlucky huddled on the sand, watching the fires.

But there was one young man who watched in wonder, not fear. He was not one of the old blood, but a *haole* who had studied the mountain from childhood, and who had seen the Goddess in his dreams.

> *"And then the hero left his people,*
> *He walked, alone he set forth toward the mountain.*
> *'Stop,' they cried, 'the ash will choke you!*
> *Stop! The flames will rise, and char your body;*
> *In the smoke your breath will leave you—'*
> *The people were wailing; the hero stopped, he turned*
>   *to them.*
> *'Staying here will I fare better?'*
> *He put aside the hand of his father,*
> *He put aside the arms of his mother.*
> *'If I must die, then first I'll seek the Goddess.*
> *At least, before I die, my eyes will see her.'*
> *'Stop, I love you!' cried a maiden.*
> *But the hero did not stop; he did not hear her.*
> *Sorrowing, the people watched him climb the*
>   *pathway,*
> *They watched until smoke shifted, smoke-clouds hid*
>   *him.*
> *They wailed, sorrowing, but he did not return."*

But the song followed him in his journey while the harp wove music around it—the fury of the volcano, the terror of the pathway, even the people's wailing, like a distant wind. It followed the young man to the very brink of the crater, where Earth's bowels boiled like a cauldron and molten lava fell about him like rain. And there he stood and called upon the Goddess, commanding and cajoling her by every name by which she had been known to men, until at last the fountain of fire rose in the form of a woman, blazing with wrath and glory. He cried out to her—

> *"O Thou who art beyond all beauty beautiful;*
> *Beyond all terror, terrible,*
> *And full of wonder; Goddess, I hail Thee,*
> *And I beg Thee to spare Thy people—"*

But Pele railed against him, citing the sins of men against the earth and their kindred, and asking why they should not be destroyed. And the young man answered that of all creatures, only men were able to know and adore her beauty, and only humans could offer her sacrifice. And now only a remnant of the men of the islands still lived, for though they had used their magics to send messages to the lands across the seas, neither help nor answer had come. Surely she could spare the lives of these few.

> *" 'And for My promise what will you give Me?'*
> *The Goddess spoke in fire and thunder.*
> *'All the youth and strength within me,'*
> *Came his answer, 'All the passion locked within me—*
> *Myself, Thy sacrifice and lover!'*
> *Then the flames blazed high around Her,*
> *Like a fountain toward the sky the fires were blazing.*
> *'Mortal, do you have the courage?*
> *For if the slightest fear is in you*
> *My kiss shall sear your mouth, to ashes*
> *Flesh and bones themselves will shrivel,*
> *Now say, mortal, do you still dare Me?'*
> *'Yes,' he said, and smiling stepped into the crater.*
> *Though his flesh the magma melted,*
> *Still he waded, smiling, toward the Goddess,*
> *Until at last Her flames embraced him*
> *Until at last the fires of Pele hid him,*
> *Until the man was lost within Her glory."*

Then flame exploded from the volcano as if to sear the sky, and the people on the seashore fell to their knees, certain they were about to feel Pele's final wrath. But the fire fell back into the crater, and the earth ceased to tremble, and after a time even the serpents of lava chilled into twisting snakes of stone.

But long afterward, those who dared to keep vigil on the lip of the crater swore that they could see the Goddess walking, and with her a young man as beautiful as she, whose fair hair flamed like fire.

There was a long moment of stillness while the throbbing of the harpstrings faded to silence, as if those who had been listening were still held by some spell. Then they remembered how to breathe again, and after a few moments they were able to speak and crowded forward to congratulate him, and a babble of conversation and comment filled the hall.

Smiling, Silverhair accepted their compliments, but now that the music was over he felt cold again, and as soon as the Queen's attention was distracted he commandeered a flagon of mead and took it back to his chamber with him.

When he heard the door open at last, Silverhair realized that he had been as afraid that Mara would come to reproach him as he had feared she would spend the night with her new lover. But the flagon of mead was almost empty now, and he had almost ceased to care.

He grinned and motioned expansively toward the other chair. "Welcome, my lady—behold, your throne awaits you!" His speech was only a little slurred.

Slowly she came into the room. "I was afraid of this! But I have had more important things to do than play nursemaid to every sot in Normontaine!"

He frowned at her. That wasn't fair. He had been drinking rather a lot before he went away, but except at the luaus, in the islands he had scarcely touched liquor at all. It was only because it was so cold here—he shivered and drank again—and because seeing Lord Theodor had awakened too many old memories.

Mara sat down on the arm of the chair, watching him. "Theodor came here to talk about cooperation in dealing with the woodsrats. The outlaws were troublesome even before you left, and in the past few months they have become uncharacteristically bold. He thinks there's somebody behind it and wants me to send forces to help wipe them out. You know the southern border—I could use your counsel.''

Silverhair shook his head. "I've been away too long," he said carefully. "And Theodor would have recognized me if I had spoken with him long."

"You fool! Do you think he does not know exactly who 'Silverhair' is? After you left the College of Bards the tale of the wandering harper with the swan harp got carried all over Westria. What's left of your family respects your decision to stay away, but why must you continue to hurt them when there is no need?"

There is need, there is need! his spirit was crying, but he did not know how to explain. The golden glow that had insulated him from the pain of memory was fading. He reached for the flagon again and his fingertips grazed cold metal as Mara snatched it away.

He looked at her. "Please . . ."

"Lord Theodor heard you cough. He was afraid you might be ill." Mara held the flagon against her breast. "In the Changer's Name, he is past eighty years old! What can it cost you to give him the happiness of knowing you still care? Shall I go tell him that you are drinking yourself into a stupor rather than see him again?"

Silverhair could not keep back a low whimper. *I don't care! I must not care! If I cared I would have to go back and tell them all that I have wasted my life—I have failed!* His hand clenched on the goblet and he flung it against the hearth.

Mara jumped at the soft shiver of breaking glass.

"Mara! I will refuse to touch another drop of wine, I will do anything you ask, but do not ask that of me!" he cried, holding his head in his hands. "It has been too long—the man they loved doesn't exist anymore!"

After a long silence she sighed. "Very well. I wish I knew what demons were driving you, but it may be that the day you face them you will leave me, and that's something *I* don't want to face yet." She set down the flagon and came to him, and with a groan he buried his face against the softness of her breast.

"I won't ask you to work with Lord Theodor, but there are strange tales from the south, and someone must investigate them, someone who knows how to talk to the hill people and win their confidence. Will you go there for me and find out what is really going on?"

Her hands were gently smoothing his hair, but he felt no desire. His body ached as if he had been in battle. Silverhair nodded, still clinging to her, needing her warmth. "Yes, I will go."

That night Silverhair dreamed that he was making love to a woman, but he could not tell whether it was Mara, or Yolande, whom he had lived with in Aztlan, or the golden girl who had favored him in the Isles. Many women had wanted him to love them, over the years. But his body was warming as his passion increased, and the woman beneath him began to glow like the Lady of Fire. *Pele!* he thought, waiting for her incandescent embrace to consume him. But as her features became clearer he saw that it was his sister Faris, and he moaned and woke, sweating in the cold air.

⋙ SEVENTEEN ⋘

A bird chirped twice, there was a pause, and then a long, joyous trill. Silverhair stirred sleepily in his blankets, and the fir boughs he had cut for a mattress the night before released their spicy fragrance into the damp air. For a few minutes the harper lay still, listening to the swelling chorus of birdsong, breathing deeply.

The air had the fresh, unused quality of early dawn. He opened his eyes and saw mist veiling the branches above him; soon the rising sun would burn it away. His feet were cold, but the cocoon of blankets had kept the rest of him warm. Muscles unused to sleeping on the ground complained as he moved, but on the whole he felt rested and in a curious way happier than he had been for a long time. The voyage to the Isles had been pleasant, but he had never been able to escape awareness of his mission, and the fact that he was dependent on the ship to get home. And there were unresolved problems that kept him from content in Normontaine.

He heard his horse stamp and the juicy tearing of dewy grass and wondered if it was mornings like this that he had been missing all along. With a horse for transportation, a sword for protection, and Swangold for company, he had all he really needed for happiness. Soon the road would stretch out before him, bringing him to new places and new faces in its own good time. He could worry about his new mission then.

But first he would have to get up. Cautiously Silverhair poked his head the rest of the way out of his blankets. The rough wool sparkled with dew, but when he stretched out his hand to the banked embers he could still feel a faint warmth there. If he was lucky, the coals would still retain enough heat to restart the fire. Shivering, he unwound the blankets, pulled out the wool overtunic which he had kept inside them, and hastily drew it over his head. Then he took dry branches from beneath the top layer of firewood and began to rebuild the fire. Seeing him up and moving, his horse lifted its head and began to paw impatiently. It was a dun gelding, Mara's last gift to him, with a fine turn of speed, yet sturdy enough for the trail.

"Yes, yes, I understand—you're thirsty. Well, so am I." As soon as the fire was crackling steadily, Silverhair picked up his copper pot, untied the picket rope, and led the dun down to the nearby stream. Even now he still marveled at the abundance of water in this land. He remembered desert camps when he had had to share the last of his water with his mount before they could go on.

When they returned from the stream the fire had settled enough so that he could hang his pot above it and heat water for tea. In his pack he had dried apples and jerky and journey bread—not a bad breakfast for a wanderer. Then he found that he was humming the tune to his old wandering song, and began to laugh.

Silverhair had made camp beneath a spreading oak a little ways back from the road. Below the lifting mists he could see down the slope to the noble river the road followed and partway across the valley. There were many valleys in Normontaine, but only this one deserved the title of the Vale—a rich and rolling country of fields and orchards between the thick coastal forests and the snowy peaks of the Misty Mountains that formed the spine of Normontaine.

Drinking his tea, he watched the morning breeze swirl the mists through the trees. Now and again a little sunlight broke through, sparkling on the crystal drops that dewed the long grass. He found himself holding his breath, as if the mists were curtains whose parting would reveal some mystery not meant for mortal eyes.

The patterns of sunlight and shadow increased in complexity as the wind freshened, and then suddenly he saw the slopes of the mountains bejeweled with spring flowers. Mist smoked upward from every fold and hollow, so that each succeeding ridge and range was sharply defined. The mountains were well-named, he thought, for even when the volcanoes were not steaming, mist drifted and eddied among them as if they blazed with cold fire.

And still Silverhair watched, the tea chilling beside him, until at last the shining white summits of Klah Klanee emerged from beyond the farthest ridges, shining in the sun. For a moment there seemed nothing but mist between him and the mountains. Then something dark winked into existence above them; a sharp shape that grew as it came toward him until he recognized it—a red-tailed hawk, soaring straight over his oak tree.

Then it called out once and wheeled sharply southward. Silverhair watched until it was only a dark speck, until it was gone.

"Yes, brother, I understand, and I will surely come . . ." he said softly. Then he got to his feet and swiftly packed up his gear, saddled his horse, and put out the remains of his fire. In thoughtful silence he reined the dun toward the southern road once more.

"I just don't understand it, and that's the truth—" Mistress Gilda leaned toward Silverhair, her broad face flushed with emotion and with the heat of the fire. She was a sturdy woman with her own, well-worn beauty, very much like the home that she and her partner, Raina, had created here. "It's been twenty-five years since Raina and I got permission to clear land for this holding, and though we glimpsed Sasquatch sometimes, and saw footprints aplenty, there was never a bit of trouble with the beasts. Until now, the Sasquatch have been better neighbors than most men!"

Silverhair nodded. The cabin was stoutly built of chinked pine and it was warm inside. He had already taken off his gloves; now, gratefully, he shrugged out of his overtunic as well, still thinking. When he had arrived at the border everyone had been talking wildly about Bigfoot atrocities, but in two weeks of patient investigation, Gilda and Raina were the first he had met who had actual evidence.

"You'll show me?" he asked. "You must understand that most of the tales I've followed up have proved to be exaggerations of gossip about hearsay—"

"Oh, those town people will say anything!" said Gilda scornfully. "But the ground was wet, and then it froze. The tracks have kept beautifully. And then, of course, there's the broken gate—it would take more than a man's strength to do that."

"And I did see one of them running off afterward. There was a full moon, and I was fully awake by then. I heard him whistling too—like this—" Raina pursed her lips and produced a clear trill.

Silverhair had heard that whistle before, when he was a boy, listening to trappers' Bigfoot tales. Obviously it could be imitated, and moonlight was deceptive. He was going to have to go look at the tracks and at the gate, and he shivered, thinking about the cold. The early spring was having a relapse into winter, and he was glad not to have to camp out anymore.

"When you were in town what did they say the Sasquatch had done?" asked Gilda.

"Destroyed fences and run off stock," answered Silverhair, "and frightened people by prowling around their holdings. There's a woman who says she was raped by one of them," he added reluctantly.

Raina's eyes grew round. "And she lived? The one I saw was eight feet tall, and if everything about him was in proportion . . ." She blushed as her companion burst out laughing.

"She didn't seem to have been harmed—" Silverhair said quickly, "but she described the incident very vividly."

"Well, maybe their feet are the only thing big about the Sasquatch," said Gilda, still grinning, "or it wasn't a Bigfoot at all. A hysterical woman will say anything!" she added with all the scorn of a mountain woman for females who huddled under men's protection in the safety of a town.

Silverhair sighed. It was true that the woman had seemed

to be enjoying the sensation she was creating, and her story had been long on impressions of weight and fur and rank breath, but short on real detail. But he was sure that she believed it had happened. At least she believed it by now.

"You had better show me the gate." He got up and pulled his tunic on again. And when he had followed Gilda there, beneath the box she had put over it he saw the clear print of a manlike foot eighteen inches long, sunk deeply into the ground.

Three days later Silverhair was standing in a muddy stableyard, staring at the immense head and hide nailed to the barn wall.

"We heard Owen screaming," said the farmer grimly. "He yelled something about monsters, and then there was a roar. . . ."

The farmer's younger son nodded. "We came running, but when we got down to the pasture Owen was dead with his throat ripped out. But there was blood on his ax, and those big tracks, and when we followed them we found this fellow dead in the forest. At least Owen got the beast that killed him—I wish he could have known."

Silverhair looked around at the ragged blue-green ridges of forest that surrounded the holding in the river-meadow, as if they could give him some answer, then turned to the farmer again. Something was bothering him about the story, but he could think of no flaw. Here was the evidence before him—the skin of a seven and a half foot Sasquatch, an old one, from the white hairs that threaded the darker mane. But the coat seemed healthy—if the creature had been driven mad by illness or hunger surely his pelt would have shown some signs of it.

"This one was dead when you got to him?" Silverhair asked.

"Oh he was dead, all right; more's the pity!" said the father. "We stopped to see to Owen, of course, but the trail was clear and the flies were already thick on the carcass when we got to it."

Even if I were an expert tracker, by this time, everyone

in the holding has trampled all over the trail, Silverhair thought dismally. *There's no way I can read the truth in it. What does Mara expect me to do?*

"Have you sent to the College of the Wise?" he asked aloud. Technically this was Normontaine, but the folk around the river looked equally to the north and to Westria, and were as likely to serve one as the other when there was need. Men from the north had fought behind Sandremun at the Battle of the Dragon Waste long ago.

"If the Sasquatch are attacking men, they are breaking the Covenant. The College should be told. The Sasquatch must have a Guardian like every other kindred. The Masters of the College could contact him and put a stop to this—" he went on.

The farmer laughed. "Those holy fools? We sent to them for sure, but there's been no answer, and you've been long away from Westria if you think that any will come. They sit on their mountain and meditate and that's all they do as far as any of us can tell. They've no care for what happens to the rest of the world as long as they save their own souls, not anymore!"

Silverhair stared at him. He remembered vaguely that there had been some criticism of the policies of the Mistress of the College, long ago, but he could not believe that things had degenerated so far. With a sinking at the pit of his stomach he realized that however far he had wandered, and whatever dangers he had survived, he had clung to the memory of Westria the golden land where man and nature lived in perfect harmony. But was that still true, now that there was no King?

"We've sent to Lord Theodor as well, and to your Queen. He's said he'll meet with us in a week at Spirit Falls. The Queen sent you, to be sure, but we think that she should come as well. We have held back so far, but we know where to look for the monsters, and we mean to destroy them if we have to burn the forest down!"

Silverhair recognized the tone—half hysteria and half a kind of brutal glee. He had heard it before, in the Barren Lands, when the caravaners wanted to hamstring a man they had caught stealing from his mates on the trail.

But there was more than a single human life at stake here. If somehow the Sasquatch were *not* guilty—unlikely though that seemed now—to exterminate them would violate the Covenant. And if in accomplishing that, men harmed other creatures as well, what would the Powers of Nature do?

"Be patient just a little longer, until you can take counsel with Lord Theodor," he told the farmer. "We'll find a way to deal with this—we must!"

Silverhair did not stay the night at the holding, though they had been insistent in their offers of hospitality. He did not think he could bear the continual stink of hatred he sensed from them, or the intermittent stink of the thing that was drying upon the barn wall.

He kept remembering the words of the Master at the Initiation ceremonies where he had taken his adult name— the Guardians cared little if humans killed each other in their wars, and to save his life or to feed his family a man had a right to slay one of the other kindreds. But to threaten an entire species with extinction? There was no greater blasphemy—and the Sasquatch were special, almost sacred, for they were the unfallen cousins of mankind.

When night fell, the harper made camp in a clearing in the forest. The weather had warmed a little, and there was new grass for his horse and old wood for his fire. He would do well enough here, he told himself, though as it grew darker he found himself jumping as the fire popped, and black shadows darted among the trees. He remembered the stories he had been hearing much too vividly. His mind could not accept those tales, but it was night, and he was alone in the forest, and his imagination was beginning to gibber with fear.

Biting his lip, Silverhair settled back against a tree with his face to the fire and Swangold in his arms. There had been little time for music these past weeks. The weight of the smooth wood against his breast was curiously comforting. Carefully he put the harp back in tune and then sat for a moment, his fingers wandering across the strings.

Then he grinned, recognizing in this his inevitable reaction to fear. *When I die,* he thought wryly, *it will probably be with Swangold in my arms!*

But it was not enough to simply hold the instrument. He needed to play. After so many years the accent of Westria had come back to his speech, and now he found himself remembering old tunes of these mountains that he had learned when he was a boy. This was his own country, and not only because his father still brooded somewhere to the south of here in Hawkrest Hold. His maternal grandfather had been a Karok tribesman from a village near the Father of Mountains, one of the Edge People who had lived in this land since long before the Cataclysm.

I belong here! he said with his music. *This is my home too, and I don't want to see it destroyed!*

And after a time he realized that the harp was making a new music, a lament, the hurt and wistful song of a creature that does not know why it must die. But there was an incompleteness to the harp music—it needed something, not a human voice, but some other, purer, sound. Silverhair pursed his lips and began to whistle a thin thread of counterpoint to the strings' music that resolved itself into a brief, trilled phrase that he found himself repeating again and again.

A branch fell somewhere in the forest, and abruptly Silverhair remembered who he was, and where. With a shudder he realized that what he had been whistling was the Sasquatch call. He played strictly human music then, until his fingers were tired, and then he rolled himself tightly in his blankets and willed himself to sleep at last.

He woke with a cry as hard hands closed on his arms and legs. Through sleep-blurred eyes he glimpsed demonic shapes that leaped between him and the dim glow of his campfire. Awaking from nightmare to nightmare, he knew them—monsters, demons, the dark shapes that stalk the primal soul!

He yelled and struck out as he was lifted and crushed against a strong-smelling furred chest. His captor whistled, and a chorus of grunts and whistles answered. The dun horse squealed in terror, and Silverhair heard the

branch to which he had tied it break, branches crashing,
and the fading clatter of hoofbeats. He hoped no brush
would entangle the beast's dangling leadrope before it
found food and water, or some dwelling of men.

*And if my horse is found they will at least guess what
has become of me*, he thought bitterly. *What a fool I was
to doubt the evidence! The Sasquatch have declared war
on men!*

Then they began to move, and terror overwhelmed rational thought again. He realized that he had begun to hope
when no teeth closed immediately in his flesh. But perhaps
they were carrying him off to eat later, when the whole
tribe could share.

The creature bore him as easily as if he had been a
child. If this Sasquatch was as big as the one whose hide
Silverhair had seen, the harper's five feet eight inches of
height and hundred and fifty pounds would indeed make
the human seem like a Bigfoot child. *But there's enough of
me for a good meal*, he thought dismally. He wondered
whether Swangold had been broken by huge feet as they
attacked, or whether the harp would remain where he had
set it to become a mute monument of rotten wood and
corroded bronze wire.

I am not afraid to die, he told himself as the strange
journey in the dark continued, *but not this way, for no
reason at all! Guardian of Men, have mercy on me, and
Lord of the Winds, if I have ever served you, help me now!*

Hard muscles bunched and eased against him as his
captor leaped over a tangle of fallen branches and settled
into a steady loping run once more. Silverhair felt a kind
of dull wonder at the creature's strength. *They could break
us easily if they had a mind to*, he thought then. *Why have
they never attacked humankind before?* Wildly he wondered if things in Westria had already gone so wrong that
the Covenant was broken, and dominion had been trans-
ferred to the Sasquatch by the Maker of All.

And still they ran on through darkness, until Silverhair
was so sick from the constant lurching motion he would
have almost welcomed death to make it stop.

It was still dark when they came to a halt at last, and the

Sasquatch dumped the harper unceremoniously on a pile of leaves. When his breath came back to him, he struggled to hands and knees and tried to scramble away, but a large hand reached out of darkness to thrust him back. He did not try again. Later, half-conscious and shivering in the greatest cold just before dawn, it seemed to him that furry bodies had moved protectively around him, but when he was awakened by sunlight shining into his face he was alone, and he thought it must have been a dream.

Silverhair groaned and struggled to sit up, rubbed his eyes and looked around. He was sitting in a hidden hollow in the mountainside, probably part of a complex of ravines and canyons leading to the larger river he could hear below. A trickle of water glittered on the cliff face nearby, and, suddenly thirsty, Silverhair pushed himself to his feet and staggered over to it, cupping his hands to catch the water.

His thirst eased; he stood looking at the water dripping through his clasped hands. The mud on which he was standing was stamped with the printings of many giant feet. He looked up then and saw a dark shadow against a tree trunk and the gleam of bright eyes watching him. There was another at hidden guard on the hill. With a sigh, Silverhair let the escape plans that his mind had been forming slip away as the water escaped from his fingers. Maybe later, in the heat of the day, they would relax their guard. He was still alive, anyway, and that was more than he had expected the night before.

He splashed some of the water on his face and smoothed his hair; then he went back to the pile of leaves in which he had spent the night and sat down on a fallen log nearby. The ground all around him was worn by the passage of large feet. Sticks stripped of their leaves, with tattered ends as if they had been used to dig into something, lay here and there. But where were all the Sasquatch?

Silverhair sat very still looking around as the sun lifted above the rim of the gully and shone full upon him. The blue sky overhead promised a fair day, and the warmth of the sunlight eased his aching bones. Once he heard a faint squeal, abruptly cut off. He tried to trace the sound and saw a shadow in the cliff face, then more shadows—there

were caves in the hill. Something rustled overhead and a
leaf drifted down to settle upon his hand. He looked up
and saw that what he had taken to be thick foliage was a
pile of branches woven into a kind of nest in the crotch of
the tree. Bright eyes peered back at him for a moment,
then disappeared.

He was reminded of the puzzle pictures one of the
craftsmen in Lord Theodor's household used to draw—
"How many bears can you find in this tree?" the man
would ask, and then you would realize that what had
seemed to be leaves and branches were heads and ears and
eyes. It all depended on what you were looking for.

With altered vision, Silverhair saw more patches of
brown among the leaves; he felt the attention of many
pairs of bright eyes. The hollow must be full of Sasquatch!
Abruptly he was glad that he had not tried to run away.

But if there were so many of them, why were they
hiding? Did they fear to frighten him, or, despite the
ferocity with which they had carried him off, were they the
ones who were afraid?

Taking a deep breath, he whistled softly, the Sasquatch
whistle he had been weaving into his music the night
before. As if it had been a Word of Power, brown heads
popped into visibility all around him. Some retreated after
an instant, but others remained to stare at him. Tentatively,
he whistled again, then began a simple tune. His fingers
twitched, wanting his harp, and then he stopped, for he
had just noticed the familiar worn shapes of his pack and
his harpcase set neatly on the other side of the log.

Heads disappeared as he moved, then poked shyly out
again as he got out the harp, tuned it, and started to play.
It was fair enough, he thought as his tension began to ease.
He had been harper to a King and a Prince and a Queen. If
the Sasquatch were to be man's new masters it seemed just
that he should play for them as well!

And presently, as if lulled by his music, his neighbors
began to emerge from their hiding places. He thought there
were one or two family groups of perhaps four or five
individuals each. The young ones were the shyest at

first, but once used to his presence, the most bold, sidling up to peer at the harp and cocking their heads to listen.

I have played to more exacting audiences, he thought, *but never, even in the ghost-ridden caverns of Aztlan, to a stranger one! Or to one more dangerous?* He was beginning to wonder, now. The rising sun had dispelled much of his fear. He did not think they would kill him as long as they enjoyed hearing him play, and perhaps they did not intend to kill him at all. He remembered hearing tales of lost human children who had been raised by the Sasquatch, though they were never able to make the transition back to being men.

> "*There is a land where the trees clothe the mountains*
> *And canyons cut deeply,*
> *Men farm the meadows, but their numbers are few,*
> *For the hills rise up steeply.*
>> *In all of that land there is rarely a man who*
>> *can tell*
>> *Where the Bigfoot dwell. . . .*
> *There was a storm and the high waters flooded*
> *A small valley holding,*
> *Drowning the folk who were out in the fields*
> *And the dwellings enfolding.*
>> *And no one could know what had happened but*
>> *one who could tell*
>> *Where the Bigfoot dwell.*
> *Buildings and bodies went under the waters,*
> *By mud they were buried,*
> *But down the swift stream to where Bigfoot were*
>> *fishing*
> *A cradle was carried.*
>> *And who knows what came to it then but the*
>> *man who can tell*
>> *Where the Bigfoot dwell?*"

Singing, Silverhair looked at the bright dark eyes of the young creatures around him, and all his earlier doubts of the horror stories began to return. They had not harmed

him, and they did not *feel* hostile. The music he had
played the night before must have sounded like an invitation, an audition for the post of harper-to-the-Sasquatch.
He wondered what that whistle-call meant in their language—
"Come and get me I'm lonely"? or *"Here I am and I'm a
friend"*?

> *"They heard the child's wailing and soon plucked*
> *him free*
> *From where he was lying,*
> *And a female with young put him quick to the breast,*
> *And silenced his crying.*
>> *And how he grew then's known to none but the*
>> *man who can tell*
>> *Where the Bigfoot dwell.*
> *Years passed, and a party of travelers were lost*
> *In the mountains and starving.*
> *And the child saw and pitied, brought food in the*
> *night*
> *And they ate of it, marveling.*
>> *None knows how he led them back home but*
>> *the one who can tell*
>> *Where the Bigfoot dwell!"*

One of the younglings, creeping closer, overbalanced
and sat down with a thump. Suddenly Silverhair wanted to
laugh. As long as they showed no signs of eating him, he
did want to be their friend, and to help heal the breach
between his kindred and theirs, as they had preserved the
human child in the tale.

> *"They coaxed him to stay with them then, and he*
> *knew*
> *His own kind he was seeing,*
> *But their walls and the reek of the woodsmoke were*
> *frightening,*
> *Soon he was fleeing.*
>> *And the life he lived free in the hills is a story*
>> *they tell*
>> *Where the Bigfoot dwell. . . ."*

And if the Sasquatch had their stories, then perhaps this was a tale they knew, he thought, finishing the song. He watched, still making music, while the life of the place went on around him—young ones wrestling or chasing each other around the hollow, females nursing infants, older individuals basking in the sun. He saw one male take a stick and poke with it under a rotting log, then eagerly lick up the white grubs that clung to it. He was not disgusted—he had roasted grubs himself, when on the trail, and been glad for their nourishment.

A young male came into the hollow with an armful of fresh, leafy branches, whistled at the opening to what appeared to be the largest cave, and waited there. Silverhair had already concluded that the Sasquatch communicated through signs and grunts and whistles, and wondered what was going on. Presently another one appeared at the cave's entrance, threw a load of old, dry bedding outside, and took the fresh greenery in.

It was noon before Silverhair understood what had happened, or received any overt notice from the adults at all. He saw movement at the cave mouth, and two young ones assisted out into the sunlight what must be the oldest Sasquatch any human had ever seen—so old that its sex was uncertain and its great frame bent like a storm-racked tree, its fur frosted all over with silver that shone in the sun.

Silverhair was already on his feet when the two large males appeared beside him and urged him forward. He looked up at the massive heads and the sharp teeth, bared, as he appeared to hesitate, and he began to move. As he approached the elder, who was now seated on an outcropping of granite worn smooth with use, he saw something in the faded eyes that reminded him oddly of the Master of the Junipers.

He stopped in front of the elder and made a reverence as if he were being presented to a King. "In the Names of your Guardian and of the Guardian of Men, I greet you, old one, and in the Name of the Maker of All Things!" he half sang, knowing that the Sasquatch would not understand him, but hoping that other powers might hear, and aid.

The elder made an unmistakable gesture, and Silverhair
sat down. For a few moments nothing happened, then a
gnarled finger reached out to touch first the harper's silver
hair, then its own. *The old one thinks I'm an elder too!*
thought Silverhair. He shook his head, then pointed from
himself to one of the males. The elder appeared to sigh,
then pointed to its chest and made a peculiar grunting
sound. Silverhair repeated it and the other seemed to
approve.

What shall I call myself? he wondered then. *They cannot form human words.* He thought for a moment, then
whistled the first notes of his wandering song. The elder
tried it, and then the others, and furred faces twisted in the
grimace that Silverhair had deduced must be the equivalent
of a smile. There followed another sequence of grunts and
whistles, but Silverhair could only shrug helplessly, feeling stupid for failing to understand. The Master of the
Junipers could have reached them with his mind, even
Rosemary could have—she always seemed to be able to
communicate with wild things.

There was another wait, then the elder spoke again and
one of the others went into the cave. When he returned, he
was carrying two objects that made speech unnecessary,
and all the confusing evidence Silverhair had collected
became abruptly clear. For what the Sasquatch was showing him was a piece of wood carved into the shape of a
Sasquatch foot, and a fragment of red cloth to which was
attached a familiar wolf's-head badge.

Silverhair dropped his head into his hands and groaned.
Caolin! He did not know what the former Seneschal had
been doing since they had last met near Santibar, but it
was clear that he was making trouble now. Knowing Caolin,
he feared that this must be some part of a larger plan. In
his despair almost twenty years ago, Caolin had tried to
destroy Westria. Now, it appeared that he was trying
again.

Is it my fault? the harper asked himself. *Could I have
saved him if I had acted differently?* But in truth the
answer did not matter. He had no choice but to fight
Caolin now.

Later that afternoon, as he followed the bulky figure of one of the Sasquatch through the forest, with the torn badge in his pouch and the carved foot under his arm, Silverhair found himself remembering his wandering song, hearing a new set of words fit themselves to the familiar tune—

> *"But on this road that I must go*
> *I see the doom of many men—*
> *The dark o'erwhelms us all, and so*
> *Until the daystar shines again,*
> *I cannot cease from wandering . . ."*

He sensed that it would be a dark and weary business, dealing with Caolin, and though he had given up his search for the daystar who was the child of Faris and Jehan, he had to hope that the Guardians of Westria would find him, or raise up another to take his place and save Westria.

White Bird Woman had tried to tell him, but he had not understood her; the Queen of Normontaine had told him, but he had not believed her—his wandering had not been a quest, but a flight, and the falcon was finally being forced home. Old mistakes, old loyalties, he was bound by both equally; the Bigfoot had taught him what no man or woman he had met had been able to do—his own responsibility.

The golden hills of Westria may be fair and welcoming, he thought, *but this is not the way I wanted to see them again. How will I tell Mara?* his thought went on, and then he found tears in his eyes and shook his head so that he could see his way.

First I must find Lord Theodor, he told himself firmly then. *If we cannot stop Caolin, it will not matter what Mara feels, or what I feel, about anything!*

⇛ EIGHTEEN ⇚

There were nine people in the long, rough-paneled upper chamber of the Pine Maiden Inn, men and women from both sides of the border, Lord Theodor and his granddaughter for Westria, and Silverhair, representing the Queen of Normontaine. The harper sat by the window, half aware of the wind in the pines that had given the inn its name as he was aware of the murmur of conversation and the scrape of benches as people took their seats.

They were looking expectantly at Lord Theodor, but it was Elinor who spoke first, briskly and freely with only an occasional glance at the old lord for confirmation. Silverhair watched her covertly, wondering whether Lord Theodor was letting the girl lead to save his strength or merely to give her practice.

"I want to thank you all for coming here. I am aware that for many, leaving your homes was a hardship. I hope that our meeting may reduce the danger we share."

"That we share?" asked a stout holder from the west— one of those who had given Silverhair information about the Sasquatch when he arrived. "Have those hairy demons moved east and south as well?"

"There are other kinds of demons, that go ahorseback and fight with swords!" said a woman from the north.

"I don't understand."

"Let us take things in order," said Lady Elinor briskly, reminding Silverhair of her mother. "We first learned of these troubles when messengers came to warn us of raiders in the badlands that lie between us and the Barren Lands.

My father took a force to seek them and chased them toward the Ramparts, but either they have split their forces or there are more of them than we dreamed, for the north has suffered as well.''

"We were lucky to escape with our lives—'' said the woman who had spoken before. ''I got my children to safety; they and my man are with our kinfolk now, but the raiders burned our home and trampled the newly-sown fields—all that we had labored for so many years to build!''

"That makes no sense—such folk loot and kill, but why spoil the crops when they might return again at harvest time and steal them too?'' asked one of the western men.

"Sense, or nonsense, that is what they have done!'' Another man spoke harshly. ''The ashes of my family are mingled with the remains of *my* home. If any here can find a reason for *that*, speak, and I will follow you. I am now a hearthless man, with a very thirsty sword. . . .''

The harper felt hair lift on the back of his neck at the tone. He wondered bitterly, *How many others will claim a like vengeance before all is done?* He felt Theodor's eyes upon him and knew the older man was remembering another time when the woodsrats had attacked with a viciousness that passed reason. But that had been only one band, bribed by one man's gold. What coin could pay men to set the entire north ablaze?

Others spoke, and the pattern began to make itself clear. In the east, the threat came from human enemies who struck swiftly and moved on. So far the forces of the Corona had always come too late, and men whispered that there must be some traitor at the Hold who kept the enemy informed of Theodor's plans. Silverhair had heard other whispers as well. Men said the old lord was failing but would not admit the loss of his powers, that he had sent his son into danger while he leaned upon the untried strength of a girl.

Watching Lady Elinor, Silverhair did not think she looked untried. She was dressed in well-worn riding clothes, and with her fair hair braided down her back she reminded him of Rosemary, who would have been competent to take on a kingdom. With every moment it became easier to put aside his memories of the child he had known and to see in Elinor the strength of another young woman, who eighteen years ago had joined in the plot that had brought Caolin down.

And now a new generation has it all to do again . . . he thought. Suddenly he felt very tired.

"In the west, we are not fighting human enemies, but beasts who have turned to demons to haunt our doorsteps. The Sasquatch have broken the Covenant, and I claim your aid against them, my lord and lady! We have fought woodsrats before—we know the evil of men, but this is something new, and we are afraid!" The stout man glared around him as if daring the others to accuse him of personal cowardice.

Silverhair cleared his throat. "And what if the Sasquatch are victims too? My friends, I fear this tangle is greater than you know. Will you hear me now?"

There was a mutter as those who did not recognize him asked the others who he was. Silverhair got to his feet, avoiding Lord Theodor's gaze. He reached down for the sack he had brought with him and waited until they were silent again, watching him.

"I came here as the envoy of my lady of Normontaine," he said softly, "but I am the envoy of the Sasquatch now—"

"He is bewitched!" exclaimed one of the men.

"No, wait," said another. "Let's at least hear what he has to say."

"Yes, hear me!" echoed Silverhair. "And perhaps you will believe the proof of your eyes even if you doubt the words I say." With the vividness trained into him by years of storytelling, he told them how he had been abducted by the Bigfoot, and the mission with which he had returned. "And when you consider the evidence," he went on, "can you be absolutely sure that everything is what it seemed? There was no witness to the rape and the killings, and a bear seen in the distance could well be mistaken for a Sasquatch once people were alarmed."

"And what about the tracks? We live in these mountains— do you think we cannot tell the print of a Sasquatch from that of a bear, or of a man?'' asked Master Jeremy, whose brother had been killed.

"Can you tell the tracks of a living beast from those laid down by the artifice of a cunning mind?'' Now Silverhair pulled from his sack the carved foot the beasts had given him, and set it clattering on the table before Lord Theodor. Suddenly everyone was talking, grabbing at the thing and passing it from hand to hand.

"Your brother was not killed by Sasquatch, but by men, the same men who killed the beast whose skin is now nailed to your barn door, and left him for you to find. It was cleverly arranged, and you saw what you expected to see,'' he told Jeremy.

"Master harper, are you telling us that the Bigfoot attacks have been simulated by men, perhaps by the same men who have stirred up the outlaws against us here?'' Lady Elinor's clear voice cut through the babble.

"Men? Yes—men led by one man who has both the knowledge and the will to destroy us,'' Silverhair said tiredly. "The Sasquatch gave me one other piece of evidence, and I may be the only one among you who knows what it means.'' From his pouch he drew the tattered badge with the wolf's head and set it before Lord Theodor.

"My lord,'' he spoke directly to the old man for the first time, "the last time I saw this badge it was borne by the guards of the man who captured Santibar for Elaya. They called him the Bloodlord in that southern land, but we have known him by another name—Caolin!''

Watching Theodor, Silverhair knew that he had feared the old man would succumb to the dread that had dogged *him* since the moment he saw that badge. But Theodor was straightening and beginning to smile like a child who has found the answer to a riddle.

"I knew it was not finished!'' he exclaimed. "Not so long as that man is alive! I could not pursue him eighteen years ago in the south, but now he has come to me, and I will not rest until I have made him answer for what he has done!'' The table shook as Theodor's fist crashed down.

"Grandfather, be careful!'' Elinor half rose to steady him. "Save your strength for the fighting. We will have

plenty of it, if what this man says is true." She gave
Silverhair a sidelong, faintly accusing, glance.

"I have known Caolin nearly as long as Lord Theodor
has—" the words were dragged from Silverhair's lips,
"and I have known him more recently than any man in
Westria. I swear that I speak truth. Caolin has both the
skill, and the will, to do what has been done here. I do not
know why he has begun with the north, but I believe that
he means to shake this land until it is ripe for the taking, or
else to destroy it. . . ." *And may the Maker forgive me*, his
thought continued soundlessly, *for it was I who set him on
this path!*

"The Sorcerer-Seneschal?" said Master Jeremy. "I've
heard the tale—he'll rue the day he ever came here!"

"We're not so easily overcome here in the north,"
another echoed him. Silverhair sat down by the window
again, forgotten. It was done, and he was caught up in it.
His choice was made.

"I am happy to see such spirit among you—" said
Elinor tartly, "but I think we had better apply some intelli-
gence to the problem as well, if this Caolin is as wily as
you say."

The hubbub stilled, and with question and answer Elinor
and her grandfather began to lay out the tasks to be
accomplished if they were to allay the fears of the folk in
the west and marshal the forces on both sides of the border
to find the source of the evil and to destroy it.

"I've had word that the Queen of Normontaine is bringing a troop south to reinforce the border watch on her side
of the Spirit River," said Lord Theodor. Silverhair sat up
abruptly. Mara had sent no word of this to him, but then it
would have been hard for any message from her to find
him during this past month of wandering. Reinforcements
would certainly be useful, but why was she coming with
them? Did she feel a need to coordinate action with Lord
Theodor in person—surely she could trust her commanders
to do that—or was she coming out of some half-admitted
concern for Silverhair?

As Theodor began to go into specifics of which forces
were to go where, the harper sat back against the wall,

wondering. There was an aching in him at the thought of Mara that was not of the flesh. He had missed her as he had not thought he could ever miss any woman. But the thought of her here, within reach of Caolin, made him afraid.

"And as for myself, while Elinor takes half of my household guard west to track down those who are trying to frighten us with such toys as these"—one long finger flicked the carved Sasquatch foot on the table—"I will take the others and all the riders we can gather here and circle northward to meet the Queen. If we move quickly we may be able to trap the woodsrats between us. If we are lucky, we will find bigger game running with them."

Silverhair realized now that his own dread came from his guilt—but it did no good to wonder what would have happened if he had not revealed Caolin's identity to Lady Alessia in Santibar. Or was he anxious because he had betrayed the former Seneschal yet again, just now? In each case he had been forced to make a choice, but Caolin must have had to make choices too. And what road could lead a man to seek the destruction of the land that gave him birth?

With a start, he realized that Lord Theodor had already sent most of the others away with their orders, and now Elinor, with one sharp backward glance for Silverhair, was taking the remainder out with her, leaving him and the old man alone in the room. He swallowed, thinking that if he had been more alert he could have found some excuse to leave with the others. But he had not, and now he realized that he had made another choice by remaining here.

"Farin?" said Theodor softly, when the silence had begun to weigh almost palpably in the room. The harper looked up quickly, hearing in the old man's voice a hesitation that wrenched his heart, as if Theodor were afraid of being rebuffed if he said more.

"Yes . . . I suppose so, though I hardly know how to answer to that name anymore . . ." he answered, forcing himself to meet Lord Theodor's eyes; they were cloudy. Theodor peered at Silverhair from beneath his drooping white brows, straining to see.

He is old! thought the harper. *Seeing Elinor made me*

*feel like an Ancient, but my lord has lived twice as long as
I!* And then he realized that he was thinking of the old man
as his own lord again, as he used to when he was growing
up at Hawkrest Hold, before ever the King came north and
made his sister Faris Queen of Westria.

"I would not have spoken—we feared that we had done
something to anger you, and I would have respected your
silence, lad, but now we will be working together so
closely, and I could not bear it any longer—" Theodor
said apologetically.

"Oh, my lord, don't say that!" cried Silverhair. "Surely
you and your house have never been anything but kind to
me—kinder than I deserved. And though you are too
courteous to ask me, I will tell you that I have done no evil
so great that I would fear to face you again, not that I have
lived stainless, but—" He shook his head, not knowing how
to go on.

"My boy, there's none of us that could say more," said
Theodor more strongly. "But if neither shame nor anger
have kept you away, why in the name of the Father of
Mountains have you not let us know what became of you?
Your sister counted you dead these many years until the
tales came north from the College of Bards and we began
to hope again!"

My sister! For a moment his breath stopped, then he
realized that Theodor must mean his older sister Berisa
who was married to his son Sandremun. That must be
where Elinor had gotten her knack for taking command,
Silverhair thought irrelevantly. It had certainly not come
from the more easygoing Sandremun.

"If I could explain why to you now, perhaps I could
have written to you then!" he answered wryly. "But the
miles and the years rolled on, and after a time I found it
hard to remember where I had come from, or who I had
been. When I hear the name Farin, I look around to see
who else is in the room. Farin of Hawkrest Hold was an
eager boy who loved and hated and wanted to be a hero.
He is gone. . . ."

Theodor chuckled. "To me you are still a boy, despite
your head of white hair! I remember when I turned forty

and thought I had seen all the world had to show, and now I am past eighty, and if the world has anything new for me it had best hurry to display it, for I will not have many years more!" He laughed again. "But if you wish me to call you Silverhair, I'll do so, though it does seem strange."

Silverhair thought back over some of the things that he had seen, and though he would not insult the old man by saying so, he thought they might well have changed him more than twice as many years spent at home.

"Thank you," he said aloud. "I know it must seem foolish. Once I feared you would fetch me home if you knew where I was, but the only people who mattered have always known who I am, and it matters little what the others think of me."

"Perhaps you are right," said Theodor, surprising him. "I still think of Elinor as a little girl, and even Sandremun sometimes seems a boy to me. It is hard for the old to realize that the rest of the world changes too."

"Oh, my lord, you may call me anything you please! Only remember that for almost half my life I have been alone, and if I seem cold or strange, forgive me. It is not that I do not want to belong to your family—it is just that I no longer know how. . . ."

"As soon as there is time I must write to Rosemary," Theodor smiled. "She has worried about you more than any of the rest of us. She has three sons and a daughter, did you know? The oldest took his name last year. He is called Frederic now, and he is studying at the College of the Wise."

Nieces and nephews had grown to adulthood and Silverhair had not been there to see. He felt like the man in the legend who slept one night on a sacred hill and awakened to find himself a grandsire and all his friends grown old. *What have I missed?* he wondered, and then, *What have I gained?*

He spread his hands helplessly. "I make no promises, except to help you fight Caolin. I have seen enough of warfare over the years that I don't think I'll disgrace you, though it is a long time since I wore a knight's belt and chain."

"And will you harp for us, too, in the evenings when we rest after a long day on the trail?" Theodor looked at Silverhair oddly. "I have heard tales of your harping. . . ."

Silverhair felt his face growing warm. "That was not me . . ." he said softly. "It happens sometimes, when there is great need, and there were those with me who did not deserve to die. But as for Caolin—I am no adept, Lord Theodor, and I do not think Caolin will be susceptible to that trick again. . . ."

Silverhair stiffened, listening, then finished making the slight shift of weight in the saddle that would ease muscles wearied by over a week on the road. He had thought he heard something above the soft thud of hooves on the muddy trail, the creaking of leather and the musical chink of mail, but no one else seemed to have noticed anything odd. Rumors of Caolin's raiders had been everywhere, but the only evidence they had discovered was days old. But men did not call him Caolin, here. He was the Wolfmaster, or sometimes, the Bloodlord, in more fearful tones.

Silverhair felt a feather touch of air on his cheek as the wind shifted, and with it a whiff of smoke and a sound—yes, that was certainly a scream. A lifetime of practice in self-preservation brought him instantly alert. The smell of smoke grew stronger and now the rest of Theodor's men noticed it too. The old lord straightened in his saddle, barking out the commands that brought the men into close formation. They shifted forward in their saddles and swung their shields forward onto their arms.

Someone let out a cheer as their pace increased, and was roughly hushed, although it seemed to Silverhair that the thunder of forty cantering horses must have swallowed up the sound. His harp thumped against his back, and he was momentarily glad he had thought to have an extra rawhide cover made for the harpcase when he got his own hauberk of cuir-bouilli. With his harp at his back, at least he need not wonder what was happening to it, and any foe who could damage it would probably have his life as well. It gave him an odd, humpbacked look in battle, but Silverhair did not mind if he frightened the enemy.

He settled his own shield more securely on his arm, shortening his grip on his reins, and realized that his mouth was dry. For so many days they had followed a cold trail—the thought that in a moment they would be fighting for their lives seemed curiously unreal. Or perhaps it was the fact that after all those years of haphazard scrapping, he was riding fully armed behind the ravens on Theodor's white banner once more. The last time he had followed that banner he had been a boy, mad for glory and panting to play the hero for the King.

That was my first battle . . . he realized with a slight shock. *Will this fight that is coming be my last?* he wondered then. The thought had a certain attractive symmetry. Then he shook his head, knowing that such fancies could kill him more surely than any fated doom. He fixed his eyes on Theodor's straight back.

"He looks twenty years younger than he did this morning—" he found himself saying to the man at his side.

"Oh, aye—and with Lady Elinor away, there is no one who can make him take care. He's been a great warrior in his time, and now he's getting strength from the excitement, but when that goes, where will we be?" The man swore as his horse stumbled, and pulled it up again.

"We'll be taking his body home again with the shame of it on our souls—that's what—" said another. "I'd thought we would meet with the northern Queen before we came to this, and she could have kept the old lord quiet. But there's no help for it now—we must follow and protect him as best we may!"

Silverhair nodded. Wrapped in his own worries, he had not thought how Theodor's men must feel. They were mostly young—sons or nephews of the men Silverhair had fought beside—and to them, Lord Theodor must seem as old as the Maker of All Things. No doubt they were right, but if he had been Theodor he would have done the same. Far better to go out fighting than to waste away into miserable old age as his father had done. *And when I am that old, is that what I will do?* he wondered grimly, but he could not imagine surviving to an age where such a choice would have to be made.

The road curved through the last of the trees and past the pastureland at the end of an oval valley set into the hills. The smell of smoke had grown stronger as they rode; now he could see it, wreathing up from the stockaded village to stain the clear sky.

Time telescoped and extended oddly as they urged their horses into a full gallop. Theodor's trumpeter sounded a challenge and the air shimmered with the light of drawn swords. Silverhair clenched his teeth against the jolting as they hammered onward, knowing that it would not be long now.

Dark figures were milling around the gate. With the town still fighting strongly, the raiders had decided to meet Theodor's forces in the open where their numbers could be used. With every moment there were more of them, and the confusion was resolving into an ordered mass of horsemen that moved toward them with ever increasing speed.

Theodor's riders urged their horses past him to form an elongated wedge the width of the road that would protect him and his banner bearer. Silverhair moved his own mount forward until he was riding at the old lord's flank. If this were a ballad, the brightness of Theodor's eyes would have destroyed his enemies, Silverhair thought warmly; and then the two forces met, and he could think of nothing but tightening his grip on his reins and his sword.

The Westrians passed through their opponents, and both parties struggled to turn their mounts and come to grips with their foes, spreading off the road and trampling the newly-sown fields. Red splattered Silverhair's boot as a raider sliced at the thigh of the man who had ridden beside him. The dun horse snorted and bucked at the scent of blood. Silverhair hauled on the reins to turn him, wishing that he had been able to find a battle-trained mount, and braced himself in the stirrups as the raider's next blow jarred his shield.

His horse was still turning; he swung, slanting his blow beneath the other man's lifted arm toward the gap in his riveted jerkin. The sword bit, with all his strength behind it; he held hard to the hilt as his horse moved, and it came free, and he ducked as his enemy's sword escaped from suddenly powerless fingers and wheeled past him through the air.

Silverhair kicked at the dun's sides to urge it back into the battle. The white banner was bobbing furiously in the midst of the fighting, and he heard Lord Theodor's battle cry. A rider turned to meet him, and the shock as his sword hit the man's upflung shield nearly jerked it from his hand. He reined the dun squealing back onto its haunches, twisted and swung, slicing through the fur robe bound about the man's body, without touching flesh.

A horse screamed nearby, and the dun began to plunge hysterically, whirling him away from the midst of the battle. Silverhair saw loose horses running and knots of men fighting afoot. *I should have dismounted to begin with,* he thought disjointedly, kicking his feet from the stirrups and reining the animal in tight circles until for a moment it held still enough for him to drop the shield and slide from the saddle.

Someone was running toward him. Silverhair fumbled frantically to get his shield back onto his arm, and, still on one knee, lifted it to receive his attacker's first blow. For a moment he had only his shield to defend with, then his groping fingers found the hilt of his sword and closed around it. He brought the blade back and around before the other man could jump backwards, and felt it cut through leather and muscle and the bone of the man's leg and heard his roar of outraged anguish as he went down.

Breathing hard, Silverhair gained his feet and, knocking his enemy's shield aside with his own, plunged the point of his sword into the man's throat, leaning on it until the struggles stilled. Not elegant, he thought, but it had saved him. He straightened, settling into a proper fighting stance and lifting his wet blade to guard as another opponent came on.

By the time he had a moment to look about him, most of the other fighters were dismounted as well. He glanced toward the town and saw a flash of white as the banner

with the two ravens swayed and went down. He cried out
Theodor's name and began to run.

Shouting with rage, the men of Theodor's own guard
were driving a knot of raiders back toward the town where
the villagers who had not been killed in their first assault
waited to welcome them. But men were still clustered
where the banner had fallen. As Silverhair reached them
someone set it upright in the ground, but he saw only the
sprawled body of Lord Theodor lying across the muddy
road as if someone had cut the Great Redwood down.

"How bad is it? Where is he hurt?" he asked the boy,
Theodor's squire, who had taken the old man's head onto
his lap.

"I don't know—I don't know—" The boy's cheeks
were wet with mingled tears of fear and rage. Another man
finished straightening Theodor's legs and looked up.
"There's no wound on him—the banner bearer was struck
down, and my lord slew his slayer, and then he gave a
great cry and fell."

Silverhair found himself shivering despite the sweat that
drenched him. He knelt beside Lord Theodor, laying his
sword down and reaching for the old man's hand. The
pulse was weak and thready, and he could see how errati-
cally Theodor's chest rose and fell.

Somebody had been able to find a water bottle, and
Silverhair held it to the old lord's lips as his eyes opened.

"My arm . . . am I wounded? It is like a great hand
squeezing my heart!" Theodor tasted the water and his
eyes focused on Silverhair. Then he began to cough, gasped,
and the harper snatched the bottle away.

"Keep him very still," Silverhair muttered, trying to
remember what he had heard of these symptoms and how
to deal with them. One way or another he had learned a
fair amount of battlefield medicine, but Lord Theodor had
not been struck down by any mortal hand.

"My lord, my lord—try to relax! Breathe deeply and
steadily—don't try to fight the pain. . . ." His hand was
still on Theodor's wrist. He felt the pulse flutter wildly,
then steady again.

"Farin . . ." Theodor's eyes were still closed, but his breathing had eased.

"I am here," Silverhair answered as steadily as he was able.

"Put . . . my sword . . . into my hand."

Silverhair gestured and one of the other men lifted the great sword from where it had fallen and laid its wire-wrapped hilt in its lord's palm. For a moment Theodor's fingers tightened around it, and he smiled with the satisfaction of one who has completed a difficult task.

"I always hoped to die holding my sword, and on a battlefield." The blue eyes opened then, and they were clear. Silverhair started to deny it, but Theodor gave an almost imperceptible shake of the head. "No," he said, "in a moment the fist will close again. Tell Sandremun and Elinor that I am content to have it so. And to Rosemary, you must say that I am the first of you to fall in this war that Caolin has begun. I hope that I may be the only one, for I have outlived my time. But you must keep on with it, Farin—he nearly destroyed us once before, do not let him succeed now!"

"No . . . no! Theodor, forgive me, I—"

"Forgive what?" whispered Theodor. "Remember me . . ."

Silverhair began to stammer some reply, but Theodor was not listening. For a moment his eyes clouded as if in surprise, and then he smiled. His chest rose and fell once, twice, and then was still, and Silverhair realized that it had been no great fist but a feather touch, this time, and yet enough to call the old man home. When he looked at Theodor's face again, he saw that the eyes were empty.

Weeping, the squire leaned forward to close them. Silverhair released Theodor's hand and sat back on his heels. *In a moment I will weep as they do*, he thought, *or I will cry out in agony. I will make a lament for him that will wring tears from men who never knew his name. . . . That is what I always do. That is all I can do now. . . .*

But instead, he found himself picking up his sword and getting to his feet, walking away, and then beginning to run, without answering the questions of those who huddled about the still body of the man who had been the Corona's lord. By the village gates men were still fighting, and to his darkened gaze, they all seemed to wear the face of Caolin.

❧ NINETEEN ❧

"How could you risk your hands, Silverhair? I thought harpers were supposed to take care of them—I did not send you south to be a one-man army!" Mara shook her head in exasperation.

Silverhair squeezed the dun's sides to bring it level with the Queen's red mare and sighed. "Mara, I'm all right. It was a month ago—let me be!" He held out his gloved hand and flexed the fingers.

He did not remember what had happened after Lord Theodor died, but apparently he had charged the remaining raiders and killed several, until one of them smashed his left hand with the flat of a sword. Despite his words to Mara, he had to repress a shudder when he thought of what would have happened if the blade had been properly aimed. A fingerless harper? As bad as a legless horseman, that would be. He might just as well kill himself and be done with it if his hands were gone.

"If you plan to do this sort of thing often, you should wear mailed gauntlets," she said tartly. "I will see to it."

Silverhair looked up the winding road. There were only a few fluffy clouds in the sky, and each pine tree seemed outlined in clear light. It was hard to believe that somewhere in the slopes ahead of them, Caolin was waiting. Would they manage to bring him to bay? *If we do, it will take more than fancy gloves to protect me!* the harper thought grimly.

But that reminded him of the fear that had been haunting him all day, and he turned to Mara again. "Is there any way I can persuade you to stay back when we catch up with them?'' he asked.

She shook her head. ''I'm not good enough with a sword to be any use in close fighting, but I can command, and there may be some work for my bow. When we get there you and the trumpeter must stay with me—I want to do my own negotiating, and that way I can make sure you don't go berserk again!''

Silverhair wanted to tell her not to be silly, but he did not know himself why he had gone fighting-mad when Theodor died. He had seen men he cared for killed before, and borne it. He wondered if perhaps at some level he had been seeking death himself to expiate his failure to save his lord, or perhaps because from the land of death no one could expect him to go home again. But for Theodor, death had been a triumphant conclusion, and he would turn his face away from one who sought it because he was afraid to live. He sighed again, and Mara reached for his hand.

''I love you, you know. I would help you if you would only tell me what I can do!'' she said softly.

He looked at her, seeing how the sunlight picked out the silver in her copper hair and the fine lines of experience around her mouth and eyes. Her skin had ripened like an apple during these days in the open air, and her eyes were as clear as the sky.

''I have never been able to understand why you do care for me—'' he said slowly. ''I drink, I sulk, and I strike like a new-caught falcon at the hand that would ease me. And yet you still can say you love me. . . .''

''If you could understand it, perhaps I would not love you so well,'' she grinned at him, then sobered. ''I know that one day you will leave me. When you do, I will weep, but because I love you I will let you go.''

Unable to meet her eyes, Silverhair stared down into the gorge that for some miles had paralleled the trail. Sculptured pumice walls fell steeply away to a little marshy valley, carpeted with new grass and wildflowers. He could have dropped a stone into it, but its virgin beauty was safe from him or any other creature without wings.

I wish I was safe down there, and Mara with me, he thought, then turned to her.

"My lady, please go back while you can. I will go more than fighting-mad if anything happens to you!" he said hoarsely.

"No," she answered gently. "We will fight this battle together, Farin Silverhair."

In silence they continued to push upward. Soon they were among the snowbanks, though bare ground was beginning to show in patches away from the trees. The trail was pocked and marshy where horses' hooves had trampled mud into the snow—many horses had passed this way, and not too long ago. Silverhair felt his pulse beat more heavily, and knew it was not the altitude. The sun was warm, but a chill breeze blew off the snowbanks, and yet when he shivered, it was not from cold.

And then suddenly there was no more slope above them, only the white rim of the crater against the deep blue sky. Nicolas of Vale, who was Mara's commander, lifted a hand, and they halted in the black shadow of the last of the pines. He signaled again, and two men dismounted and slipped away through the trees. After a time Silverhair thought he saw movement against the slope, but both men had covered their riding clothes with white cloaks, and he was not sure.

He is there, I know it! Even now, the cold churning in his gut was telling him what the scouts would say when they returned. He wished now that they had been able to get someone from the College of the Wise to come with them, or one of Mara's priests. There was a tension in the still air that made his skin prickle, and he did not think it was only the shadow that made Mara look pale. Legend said that once sorcerers had battled on the island in the lake that filled the crater. Now perhaps a sorcerer was there again.

Something moved among the trees. He saw the scouts pulling off their white cloaks and speaking swiftly to Sir Nicolas. The commander nodded, then reined his mount back down the line to Mara and Silverhair.

"Well, we've found their encampment—on the rim of

the crater, as we expected. My scouts killed the lookout and got fairly close. They say there are cabins for maybe fifty men and corrals for their horses. But there were only a few beasts there. . . ."

Mara nodded. "Do you think they've abandoned it?"

"Not abandoned, my lady, but maybe the main force has gone off again. When we get up there we can check the tracks. There's one other thing, though—my scouts said they saw smoke on the island," said Sir Nicolas.

Mara's knuckles whitened as she gripped the reins, and the mare's head tossed nervously.

"I should have known," the Queen said softly. "I should have expected it! If someone is there, we must get him off immediately!"

"But why?" asked the harper.

"The island is the center—the power point of the mountain, and Mount Mazama is linked to every peak in the Misty Mountains. If someone were to use the place to do sorcery—"

"He could make every volcano in Normontaine explode!" Silverhair finished for her.

"And not only Normontaine—" Mara pointed southwestward. "The peak you call the Father of Mountains is in the linkage too. From here, Caolin could destroy the College of the Wise!"

Behind them a bowstring twanged like a harp as one of Mara's women strung her bow.

"We'll move out now, then—" Sir Nicolas saluted and turned his mount. They all began to move, and Silverhair blinked as they came out into the glare of the snowbanks. The horses grunted and slipped as the muddy trail grew steeper. Between the dark clumps of pine trees, the white rim of the crater shone like a knife blade against the blue throat of the sky.

And then they were over it. Silverhair struggled to sort a confusion of images—the impossibly perfect round of the lake below them, a deep cobalt blue with purple shadows where the steep red walls of the crater were reflected in the water, and the pointed grey island with its wisp of smoke; the whiteness of the snow around the rim fantastically

sculptured into ice traceries by the sun; and finally the flat
shelf of land before them where the dark figures of many
men were now emerging from within the cabins that had
seemed so empty, and from behind the wind-tortured stands
of trees. Silverhair's hand moved to the hilt of his sword,
but Mara held his arm.

Mara's trumpeter blew three clear notes and Sir Nicolas
and his men kicked their mounts into a canter, leaving
behind them the Queen and her two women, four men of the
guard, the trumpeter and Silverhair. As the Montaners
swept toward the enemy he had a sudden sense that he had
seen this scene before, many times before, in the past
weeks' fighting. Surely they had been misled, and this was
just another band of outlaws brought to bay.

He shortened his reins, ready to ride after the others,
when he saw that it was already over. Caolin's men were
running, some over the hill to the hollow where they had
hidden their horses, and others to the very edge of the
crater where a skin boat was already hanging in a winch.
Men scrambled into it and others covered them while it
was lowered down the cliff to the water.

They brought up the cradle and were trying to fit another boat into it when Sir Nicolas's men brought down
the last of them. Mara released Silverhair then, and they
moved down to the edge to join Sir Nicolas. It seemed
very still suddenly, except for a buzzard that had material-
ized in the blue bowl of the sky and the skin boat that
crawled across the blue bowl of the lake below.

The Queen's voice broke the silence. "There are still
two boats here. We will have to go after them. It does us
no good to cut off the arms of this monster if the head is
still there to direct them and grow more. And he is on the
island. . . ." Silverhair remembered what she had said
before.

"Very well, my lady," said Sir Nicolas. "I will divide
the men, and we—"

"No. You will remain here. Send a party after those of
the enemy who escaped down the mountain, and cover our
rear. I will take guards and go to the island."

"But my lady!"

"Mara!" Silverhair and Sir Nicolas spoke at once, but after a moment the commander held out a hand in appeal and shut his mouth again.

"Mara—my Queen—this was too easy! Caolin has set a trap for us on that island; he will be waiting for you down there!" cried Silverhair.

She sighed. "Of course he will, but isn't that why we have been chasing him so long? It is my duty to face him now. Can't you understand? He is on the sacred island, and I am the Queen of Normontaine. I have no choice—he can crush the heart of my kingdom in his hand!"

Silverhair stared at her, remembering how he had seen her first, as Lady of the Land. And he remembered also how, long ago, he had seen the King and Queen of Westria wielding the powers of the elements to fight a forest fire. Just as his harping was to him a kind of priesthood, Mara had also her mystery.

"I am going with you," he said then, ignoring Sir Nicolas. His gaze was on Mara, and he saw the quick, instinctive denial flash in her eyes and fade again. And as if she had spoken, he heard the words that in that public place she could not say, for they were his words too—*Why is it so much harder to face your death than my own?*

And he realized then that now he truly believed in her love for him, for perhaps the first time. But there was no space to savor the wonder of it, for stern orders from the Queen had silenced Sir Nicolas's protests, and the commander was assigning men to the boats and to guard, placing the first one in the cradle, and preparing to winch it down.

Six men went swaying down the cliff in the first boat, and then the second one was ready for four more armsmen and Silverhair and the Queen. Someone asked if he wanted to leave his harpcase with the rest of the baggage, but he did not even bother to reply.

The skin boat was an unwieldy craft, but fortunately they had men from the long lake above Spirit Falls who could manage it. The other boat waited for them, and then together they paddled the half mile across the deep lake to the island. And as they drew closer, the water seemed to

darken. Silverhair looked up and saw that from somewhere
dark clouds had invaded the sky. A cold wind ruffled the
surface of the lake and made the skin boat rock uneasily.

There were armed men waiting for them on the rocky
shore. The other boat grounded first and the Montaners
scrambled out of it and made a wall of shields to protect
the landing of the Queen. But the enemy did not attack
them. They stood waiting while the air continued to darken
and the wind grew colder.

The wind was moaning; Silverhair shook his head in
irritation, then realized it was not the air but a sound that
the air carried that was disturbing him—an odd, droning
hum. He blinked, not sure whether his sudden dizziness
was a trick of the shifting light or that sound. Both eyes
and ears seemed to be betraying him—the shapes of the
enemy warriors seemed to shift and double, and there was
something behind them, like the shadow of a Sasquatch, or
the Great Bear . . .

"Silverhair, what is happening?" whispered Mara. "Is
it your renegade sorcerer?"

"A shapeshifter!" hissed one of the men. "They can
appear in any land when a man of power turns bad. We
must burn him!"

Silverhair shook his head. Caolin had been burned by the
Jewels, but those fires had been only a temporary cauteri-
zation. He knew that the ex-Seneschal had regained all of
his old powers in Elaya, but this shadow that wavered
before him was something else. This was some new and
more terrible sorcery that Caolin had learned since their
last meeting near Santibar.

Mara reached for her bow. "I don't like this. Perhaps
with an arrow—"

"No, put that away," whispered Silverhair. "You would
not be able to hit him in this light, and if he sees you
unarmed he may think you are harmless. . . ." Surely,
Caolin would not be so foolish as to harm the Normontaine
Queen if he knew who she was!

He filled his lungs to call out to Caolin, but one of the
Montaners, maddened by the humming, broke ranks with a
cry and charged across the stones toward the enemy. Oth-

ers followed him; swords gleamed in the cold light and
men cried out as humans battled. But where the shadow
behind them stalked, men fell without a sound.

The sound of the sorcerer's singing buzzed in Silverhair's
head. It was a power song, like the one White Bird
Woman had sung, only this chant seemed to be summoning
quite another class of spirit helpers, and its very harmonies
were an obscenity.

Abruptly he shrugged the harpcase off his shoulder and,
sitting down upon a boulder, fumbled it open. Ignoring
Mara's question, he settled Swangold in his arms. Even
with his ear bent to the strings he could hardly hear—he
could only hope that the harp was reasonably close to
being in tune. He was trying to remember something the
Mistress of the Waterfall had said at the College of Bards—
something about the effects of vibration, and how one
sound could be countered by another in harmony.

Striving to hear Caolin's notes without being mastered
by them, he reached for the strings that would answer
them, plucking single notes and then chords until singer and
harp were linked in a strange duet. His own confusion
began to ease; he heard Mara sigh with relief, and after a
few moments the dark shape before them paused, and
turned, and he knew that Caolin had heard it too.

Smiling grimly, Silverhair began to play louder. The
single battles around them stilled, and the shadow that was
Caolin came down the slope toward them. A few paces
away it stopped, and, as if veils of mist had parted, they
saw the man himself, his ravaged face undisguised above
the folds of the dark red cloak he wore.

"You are Caolin whom they call the Wolfmaster?"
Mara's voice was almost steady.

"Indeed, my lady, I have had many names, but that is
what they call me here."

It was almost shocking to hear that well-remembered
voice, so cool and almost charming, and realize this was
the same throat that had produced that *song*. Silverhair's
fingers twitched above the strings as he waited for Mara to
reply. She had wanted this confrontation, and he must let

her have it, though every nerve screamed with the need to fight, or to flee.

"I have come to negotiate with you on behalf of Westria and Normontaine. I assume that you have demands. What do you ask in return for peace? It would be more just to destroy you, but I do not wish to spend more time and lives. If you will be reasonable, I will settle with you now." Mara's back was straight and her lips were white with anger, though Caolin might take it for fear.

Caolin looked from her to Silverhair and back again. Then he laughed.

"My dear lady, what do you have to negotiate *with?* You would all be dead already, except for my need to settle a particular and personal quarrel with your pet minstrel here. Do you find him a useful bedwarmer? I should think it would be rather unsatisfying to sleep with a man whose first instinct in danger is to reach for his harp, but perhaps you can get no better. . . ." He shrugged disdainfully.

"I will take the harper," Caolin went on, "and perhaps when I am done with him I will keep you alive for a while. The Queen of Westria once offered to be my whore. It would make a nice symmetry thus to use the Queen of Normontaine!"

The Montaner men who could hear him began to growl in outrage, and Silverhair felt Mara stiffen. His own clenched fists were whitening, but he had heard the insult to Faris before. They should never have left the rim of the crater, he knew that now. Neither of them had the power to face what Caolin had become.

"Mara—" he whispered, "run for the boat—I'll try to hold him—"

"Stay where you are!"

Silverhair's muscles stiffened in spasm, then relaxed as the sorcerer's tone gentled, leaving him weak and trembling.

"I am not shocked out of self-control by your treachery now, Silverhair, and I have learned many things since I saw you last. . . ." There was a note of utter self-assurance in that cool voice that was far more terrifying than any threat or bluster could have been. "If your lady moves I will take her anyway, but I will break her mind as well as her body, and through her I will rule Normontaine. Or would you prefer that I ruled the north directly? It does not matter. From here I can rule both Normontaine and Westria. . . ."

Silverhair felt the involuntary movement of fury begin in him, but his muscles scarcely quivered. Indeed, none of them had stirred since the sorcerer's command.

"Indeed, I have learned much, harper. None of you will move until I give you leave. I suppose I should thank you for depriving me of Santibar, Silverhair. If you had not thus wrecked my life a second time I should never have found the man who was for a time my master. I have gained full mastery of all my powers, and no one and nothing can limit me now."

"Everyone has limits, even the Guardians!" Silverhair managed to reply.

"Men are limited by their own beliefs, by their acceptance of other men's laws, by their refusal to pay the price of power. But I make my own reality, and I am bound by no law."

Caolin's eyes blazed. His face was very white beneath his scars. Perhaps the Master of the Junipers might have had an argument to counter him, but Silverhair knew only a wordless, despairing conviction that he must be wrong.

"Besides my death, what is it that you really want, Caolin?" he asked hoarsely.

"What have I ever wanted?" the sorcerer answered him. "I was born to rule, and no ruler can be secure without absolute power. Though I may trifle with Normontaine, it pleases me to exercise that power over Westria. I am grateful to you for setting me on my way, but you are an annoyance to me now, harper, and it is time to be rid of you."

"And how will you kill me, Caolin? I still have a sword, and you will lose your control of these others if you struggle with me—" Silverhair heard his words ring hollowly against the stones. A pulse thudded threadily in his throat, and his arms had hardly strength enough to hold the harp, much less lift a sword.

"Will I? I do not think so—but I have no need to use a weapon on you. I told you that I have learned new powers, and I shall give you the memory of having been bested at your own art to take into the dark!" Again that mirthless smile chilled Silverhair's soul, and then Caolin began to sing.

The song was similar to the one he had sung before, but with an odd repeated half-interval that jangled the nerves and disjointed coordination. But Caolin had loosed his hold on the harper's muscles, and he could hear his singing well enough to try the counter-harmonies he had used before. But as vibration met vibration, Caolin kept subtly shifting. The harp echoed the overtones of the sorcerer's voice as well as its own notes, and their distortion was beginning to put the strings subtly out of tune.

Valiantly Silverhair adapted his manner of playing, plucking high or low upon the strings to raise or lower the tone. And still the distortion increased, until one string snapped, and then another, drawing blood as the broken end whipped across the top of his hand. Playing with more skill than he had known he possessed, the harper strove to use the remaining strings, but he was sickly aware that Caolin might well be able to do just what he had described.

He could hear Mara murmuring some invocation to the spirits of her land, but he knew she had only the training to perform the seasonal rituals—could she tap into enough strength to resist the sorcerer? Desperately he looked up and glimpsed movement—the buzzard? No, it was a hawk, circling lazily out over the water and back above the trees. *Maker of Winds and Words!* he thought. *Help me!* Perhaps he could seek refuge in that cloud country to which his spirit had flown before, if only he could be sure that Mara would be safe from Caolin!

Abandoning all rational strategy, he began to play an invocation that he had learned from the Mistress of the Waterfall, and as soon as he could hear the tune, he started to sing:

> *"Maker of Words and Winds and Wisdom,*
> *Wings to carry me, ways to follow;*

> *Hear my prayer, my plea is given*
> *Out of my suffering and my sorrow—*
> *By Thy winged feet do I call Thee,*
> *By Thy staff and wand of power,*
> *By Thy feathered cloak of splendor,*
> *Do I invoke Thee in this hour!"*

Caolin was still chanting, but Silverhair could not hear
him. Without effort, more words were coming to him,
words he had never learned, though still he followed the
same simple tune. By all the Wind Lord's sacred names
Silverhair called Him—all the names he had ever heard for
the Prince of the Powers of the Air, who was also lord of
magic and of sound and the spoken word. On one level, he
was painfully aware of who he was and what he was
doing, but at the same time he found himself surveying the
scene from somewhere else. He was in the temple of his
vision, and from both places he summoned his lord with
all his will, and through Him, the One who rules over all.

And after a time that was no time, he saw a luminous
figure taking shape before him. As it became clearer, a
little indrawn sigh behind him told Silverhair that Mara
had seen it too. Did Caolin perceive it? Or was he still
deafened by the clamor of his own song? Passionately the
harper continued to play, or rather, to allow some other
power to use his voice and fingers. A crisp wind lifted the
cloak of the vision like great wings and played through the
harper's hair; he took a deep breath of new air and felt the
blood tingle through his veins.

Harder and harder blew the wind. Now Silverhair could
not hear Caolin's singing at all. Then, out of the wind
came a Voice that vibrated through every cell in his body,
though the only word he could distinguish was Caolin's
name. For a time there was speech, and the harper saw the
sorcerer stop and turn as his features contorted in wonder
and rage and pain. Then he hid his face in his scarred
hands, shaking like a tree in a storm. The speech became
singing, a melody that Silverhair had heard twice before,
and words his heart could understand.

"My song is in each stirring of the air,
Who speaks with heart or lips has called on Me,
And I shall turn their cursing into praise,
And transform discord into harmony. . . ."

The harper felt himself dizzied by a joy almost too intense to bear, but the sorcerer gave a great cry, ran awkwardly down the slope, and cast himself into one of the boats, his cloak flapping behind him like bloodstained wings.

The whirlwind still roared about the island. It swept Caolin and his boat away. But Silverhair continued to play. Even if the Lord of the Winds should slay him, it would be better than the feel of Caolin's unclean hands upon his soul. *Maker of Winds and Words*, he prayed, *I am Thy servant, and my life is in Thy hand. . . .*

The winged figure drew closer. Silverhair took a deep breath, ready for a sharp parting from the existence he had known. He was not afraid, for he had never been closer to the essence of his desire. Then the wind scoured through his body and spirit for one moment of tumult during which he knew nothing at all except a Voice that answered him.

"You have served Me, but you are not yet My servant. You will be tested. Strengthen your spirit, that I may dwell with you. . . ."

After a time, Silverhair realized that the Presence had departed. His fingers were still moving on the strings of the harp. Shaking, he lifted them, but the strings continued to vibrate as if played by invisible hands, or by the wind. The harper rested his forehead on Swangold's smooth curve and felt the bitter sting of unshed tears. He had been face to face with the goal of all his striving, and it had rejected him. Through the smooth wood he could feel the harp's vibration, like a memory of music. Then finally that eerie humming faded as well, and the only sounds were the ringing in Silverhair's ears and the lapping of the lake against the shore.

*   *   *

As she had prophesied, Mara wept when she and
Silverhair parted, but even now he could find no tears. His
throat ached with words he could not say. He could not
even promise to return to her. The men they had left on the
cliff had seen Caolin's boat beach itself at the northeastern
end of the crater, where a path led up the cliff from a
narrow strand. When they searched, they found no trace of
him, but his power was broken in the north, at least for
now. Someone must go to the rulers of Westria to tell them
what had happened, and who better than the man who
knew most about Caolin?

But Silverhair rode southward slowly. The duel with
Caolin had left his throat raw and his muscles aching, and
he was not eager to give this news to Eric and Rosemary.
Traveling in easy stages, he made his way back down the
long valley to Spirit Falls, and then uphill again around the
base of the Father of Mountains to join the south road.
And so it was that on the fourth day of his journey he
found himself at the turnoff to Hawkrest Hold.

He told himself that there was no other place near
enough to reach by nightfall, and that it would be oddly
appropriate for him to end his wanderings by revisiting the
place where they had begun. But a sick churning in his
belly suggested other emotions for which he had no names.

Every tree and rock, every turn in the road, was at once
familiar and utterly strange. Silverhair felt as if he were
tracking the ghost of the boy he had been. There was the
tree he had dared Faris climb and then had to get their
steward to help rescue her when she could not get down.
And there, a little farther on, was the rock on which he
used to stand to catch the first sight of the riders when
Lord Theodor or Sandy visited them.

But the fences along the road were lying in pieces in the
grass, and there was small sign of wheeled traffic having
passed that way. Was his father still there, or had Berisa
finally persuaded him to go live at the Hold? What if
nothing dwelt there now but mice and owls?

Then he saw a thin trail of smoke above the stand of
oaks at the end of the pasture. Ghosts did not light fires.
Whoever lived there now would at least let him tend his

horse and give him shelter for the night. He kicked the horse to move faster, then reined it in again. What if his father was still there? What could he and the old man possibly have to say to one another now?

Silverhair rounded the oaks and saw the confused mass of timber and granite that was Hawkrest Hold. Shingles were missing from the roof of the hall and the windows were boarded up in the tower where his and Faris's rooms had been. Last year's dried leaves lay thickly on the stone steps that led up to the great door. He felt an ache of apprehension in his belly, but he had noticed goats in the pasture, and part of a garden could be seen behind the kitchen wing. He reined the dun around the corner and pulled up short as a small black and white dog rushed out of the house barking furiously.

"Brighty! Brighty! Be still and let me see! I can defend myself if I need to, so be still!" The door swung open and Silverhair saw an old woman, bent but still sturdy, step out onto the porch with a drawn bow in her hands.

Silverhair sighed, and some of his tension eased. At least Hannah Brightapple had not changed.

She took a cautious step forward, and then another, staring at the tired man on the tired horse who waited patiently for her to recognize him. Seeing her ruddy cheeks grow pale, he realized that he must seem the ghost to her.

"It's all right, Hannah, it's only me. I've come home. . . ."

She peered at him. "Farin? Master Farin, with your hair like a snowcap and your poor face all worn to the bone, is it really you?" The dog had stopped barking and was waiting with its tongue lolling in an expectant grin.

With a grunt Silverhair swung down from the horse. "That must be one of old Raven's pups—" he nodded toward the dog.

"A great-grandson," Hannah answered automatically, then dropped the bow and bustled toward him. "Oh, Master Farin, what have you done to yourself? Near eighteen years it's been, and we thought you were dead for sure, for we never got any word. I would wallop you as I used to for not writing to us, but that I'm afraid you would fall to pieces here in the yard. Come in, come in—I have a good broth simmering on the fire.''

When he had stabled his horse in the only stall still usable, Silverhair followed Hannah into the big kitchen and settled his harpcase beside him on the stone-flagged floor. Here at least, things seemed much the same. He could almost believe that at any moment Faris would come laughing through the door.

He had intended to have her by his side when he came home again.

Abruptly he turned to Hannah. "And my father? Is he here?"

"Oh my poor lad," she turned to him, her face wrinkling in sympathy. "Did no one tell you? Your father died ten years ago, that winter when the snows stayed so long. My own man died the year after."

For a moment Silverhair sat very still. He had braced himself for this meeting, and now it would not come. Whatever he and his father might have had to say to one another would remain unsaid.

"Lord Theodor did not tell me"—he scarcely realized that he was speaking aloud—"but if it happened so long ago, he might have forgotten, or assumed that I already knew."

"Ah, the old lord—now that's a terrible thing, for a man his age to die in battle after all these years!" Hannah babbled on as she ladled broth into a bowl, but Silverhair hardly heard.

My father is gone, and Theodor is gone, and Faris is gone. . . . I am alone, he thought.

"And so we buried him up on the hill underneath the apple trees beside your poor mother's grave—" Hannah had returned to talking about his father. "Do you know that in those last years he used to go up and sit there on the stone? I think that he forgave her finally, so we felt that would be the best place for him to lie. And there was no one to take the holding here, your sister's children being well provided for by their father's kin, so the old lord said I might as well stay. Bird is hawkmaster to Lord

Sandremun now. He married a girl from near Elder and they have two boys of their own.''

Silverhair sipped at the broth. He supposed it must be good, but he was too preoccupied to notice its flavor, trying to readjust the image of the home he had somehow assumed would always stay the same.

"I suppose that after you've eaten you'll be wanting to go up there to see," said Hannah, setting out the end of a loaf of brown bread and a wedge of goat cheese.

Silverhair nodded. Yes, he supposed that was the obvious thing to do.

It was sunset when Silverhair reached the shadows of the untended apple orchard, where a little circle of stones surrounded the clipped grass that covered the two graves. Without that it would have been hard to find them, for the mounds had sunk level with the earth, it had been so long ago.

He sat down on the big rock that jutted out from the hillside, watching the folded ridges change from green to blue and purple as the sun sank through the golden sky. Even the wind had ceased blowing, and it was very still. The only movement was the circling of two hawks in the sky, and he wondered if they were descendants of the pair he had freed eighteen years ago. For a moment he wished that he had brought his harp, but the stillness was too profound even for music.

They are gone—the litany continued to echo through his consciousness. *And Faris must be gone too, if nothing has been heard of her in so long*. Here, in this place where they had been closest, he recognized at last that the tie which had once bound them was no more. He could not even tell when it had faded away.

I have failed, he thought bitterly, *and all the brave oaths I swore mean nothing. And it does not even matter that I failed, for hardly anyone is left of those I swore to prove wrong*. . . .

And there, in the stillness, he felt something inside him loosen, like a rusted lock giving way. His eyes were burning, and when he reached up to touch them he felt something wet on his skin. Tears! Even as he recognized them, the grief he had for so long locked up overcame him, and he wept in great racking sobs that shook his body, with his blanched head pressed against his knees.

It was from grief for Theodor that he was weeping, the lord he had found only to lose again; and for the father whom he had never known how to love; and it was grief for Faris, whose loss had taken part of his soul; and above all, it was grief for the boy Farin, who was lost forever now.

⇒ TWENTY ⇐

It was the third week of June before Silverhair reached the southern, more populous portion of Seagate and turned up the coastal valley that held Eric's own fortress of Bongarde, where he had been told the Lady of Seagate was in residence now. He rode along an empty road through dusk-shadowed rolling hills that were already ripening to gold. He had hoped to find a holding where he could spend the night, but it had been a long time since he had been this way. Perhaps his memory of the road was faulty, for he had seen no sign of habitation for many miles.

There was no help for it—he would have to find a campsite. His horse was tiring, and he had no wish to arrive on Rosemary's doorstep at midnight. If there was no water, he could make do with what his waterbags held. And then the wind shifted, and he scented burning laurel-wood, as aromatic as some ritual fire. It was two days past midsummer, so this was no fire of ceremony, but perhaps some herder had made his camp nearby.

Silverhair clucked to the dun and urged it over the hill. In the fading light he saw a pale line of trampled grass where a horse had been ridden across the meadow and into the shelter of a copse of laurel trees. He reined his mount off the road, and the dun, scenting another horse, lifted its head and began to jog. Silverhair smiled to himself as he realized that, like the animal, he wanted company. Tomorrow he would have to face Rosemary and possibly the Master of the Junipers as well. A companion might distract him from the memories that could overwhelm him if he spent this night alone.

Dismounting, he led his horse to the edge of the circle of firelight. A young man sat within it, watching his approach with an expression in which hope and apprehension were combined. Then that look was replaced by a simple smile of welcome, and Silverhair wondered if the other look had been a trick of the firelight after all.

"May I share your fire?" Silverhair asked at last.

"Oh, I'm sorry," said the young man. "I'm not usually so behind in courtesy! Of course you are welcome. There's a little water at the bottom of the ravine, and I've hobbled my beast near it, down behind the trees."

The harper nodded, dropped his reins, and unsaddled the dun. Then, leaving his gear by the fire, he led the animal around the laurels to settle it for the night. When he returned, the other man had a kettle simmering over the fire.

"Rabbit stew—" he gestured toward the pot. "I've boiled some barley with it, and there should be enough for two."

"Thank you," said Silverhair. "I have some bread and dried fruit, and a little wine."

"It will be a feast then!" the young man grinned and bent forward to stir the stew.

As Silverhair draped the saddlecloth over the saddle to air and laid out his blanket roll, he had time for a covert study of his new companion. He was younger than the harper had at first thought him—a boy-man with thick, earth-brown hair, tied back with a thong, and straight, thick brows above dark eyes. His shoulders were unusually well-muscled, as if he had spent his boyhood chopping down trees, but as he reached over to add more wood to the fire, Silverhair saw on his shoulder the badge of the Ramparts, and by his pack a very serviceable looking sword.

"You're in Lord Philip's service?" asked Silverhair, remembering, after a short struggle, the name of Robert's heir.

"Yes. I have never been in Seagate before. They told

me that this was the right road for Bongarde, but when the sun began to set with no sign of a town I started wondering. Do you know if the fortress is far?"

"Ten miles or so, I believe, though it has been a long time since I rode this way." Silverhair ignored the unspoken invitation to tell his business there.

"Well, I suppose in the morning we can seek it together. It will be harder for two together to get lost!" The young man grinned, and Silverhair found himself returning the smile a little unwillingly. He had wanted company, but this fellow's openness grated on him after so much time alone.

"I am Julian of Stanesvale, one of Lord Philip's squires," said the boy. He sniffed at the stew. "I think it's ready. Do you have a bowl?"

Silverhair nodded and held out the little copper pan that had accompanied him for so many years. Julian ladled stew into it and then into his own wooden bowl. "And you are a harper?" Julian nodded toward the harpcase as he sat back again.

"Yes. They call me Silverhair." No doubt the lad had messages for Eric from his master, and if he thought Silverhair just another wandering bard seeking employment with the Regent, so much the better. He owed no explanations here.

"And are things going well in the Ramparts?" he turned the conversation back to Julian.

The squire shrugged. "As well as anywhere, these days. We've had trouble with raiders back in the hills. I was on border duty for a year, and we had a time restoring order to some of the villages—well, that's too long a story to tell here, but from what people say, there's been trouble on all the borders this year. We were shocked to hear of the death of Lord Theodor. From all accounts he was a good man."

Silverhair nodded without answering. That grief was still too new for discussion with a stranger. He had the feeling that there were topics that the younger man was avoiding too, and perhaps that was just as well.

He finished the stew, which had been surprisingly tasty

despite rather too much use of the convenient bay laurel for seasoning, and automatically reached for the harpcase.

"Ah!" said Julian, "I was hoping you would play, but I feared that you might want a rest from performing."

"Playing Swangold *is* my rest . . ." answered Silverhair as he drew out the harp and began to test the strings.

"Oh, it is beautiful! I have no talent for music myself, but I've always loved to listen, especially to harping, which seems like music I have heard in a dream . . ." breathed the young man. He leaned back against the trunk of a laurel tree, watching the harper's preparations intently.

Silverhair gave him a sharp look, for the boy's words had triggered a distant recollection of someone else saying something like that, a long time ago. He frowned, but he could not place the memory. No doubt many people had said the same, especially in the back country where trained musicians seldom came.

"What would you like to hear?" he asked indulgently. The food he had eaten had improved his temper, and he recalled that Robert of the Ramparts had never been much of a patron of music, while border duty had probably not given the lad a chance to hear much more. "I have played in taverns and palaces from Aztlan to Normontaine," he continued with the performer's practiced introduction. Julian's eyes widened slightly, and Silverhair realized how boastful that must sound, though it was all quite true.

"Play whatever you like," the boy said quickly. Silverhair smiled, and began with a tune he had learned when he was still searching the Ramparts for Faris, continued with a song of the Barren Lands, and then the ballad of the Willa that brought back so many memories.

He realized that he was performing a musical recapitulation of his wanderings, and decided that was curiously appropriate, now, when they were almost done. He went on to the music of Aztlan, and then, out of order, he played some of the court pieces he had performed for Palomon. Julian continued to listen intently, his face a little averted so that the harper could not see his eyes. Beyond him, the eastern sky showed the brightening glow of the rising moon. Silverhair's music grew softer then, as he moved into a sonata he had learned from Mistress Siaran, and then to one of Arion's songs of the sea.

By the time the harper got to the robust music of Normontaine, his companion had eased down into his blankets and was asleep. Julian's face seemed curiously vulnerable in the firelight, as if all the carefully acquired lines of manhood had been smoothed away. Something tightened in the harper's chest as he watched him. Once he, too, had been innocent and untried. What would the future hold for this boy?

Though his audience was not listening, Silverhair continued to play, songs without words, music that the harp made without his will. And as he played, he found the familiar chords of his wandering song emerging from beneath his fingers, and after a while a new verse came to him, expressing the longing that had come to him here, beside this fire—

> *"Yet if this path could have an end,*
> *The quest complete, the task all done,*
> *And I might pause beside a friend*
> *And lie down with the setting sun,*
> *Then would I cease from wandering."*

But for the present, neither the road nor the quest was at an end.

When Silverhair awoke in the dawning, wincing as he tried to use muscles cramped by a night on the hard ground, he cursed himself for a sentimental fool. The life of a wanderer had lost its romance long ago, and he wished very much that he had found someplace, no matter how humble, with a bed he could have slept on.

Julian was already awake, whistling tonelessly as he boiled water for tea and neatly strapped up his bedroll. The harper eyed him balefully, but the tea was comforting, and by the time they were packed and ready for the road again the sun was high enough to bake some of the ache out of his back, and he found himself almost cheerful again.

But not quite, for ten miles on fresh horses was not much of a journey, and all too soon he saw the well-tended stone

and timber walls of Bongarde rising from their knoll at the
northeastern edge of the valley. He and Julian rode between apple orchards and pastures filled with fat cattle.
Now and again they passed wagons whose drivers saluted
them with a grin. Julian responded in kind, but Silverhair
kept silent, recognizing the leaden weight in his belly as
fear.

There was a guard at the gate, but no one questioned
them. The place seemed full of people, all busy, and they
had to stop a towheaded lad who reminded Silverhair of
Sandremun as a boy in order to get directions to the hall.
Now that they were here, Julian seemed to be as nervous
as Silverhair.

"If you are hungry, go on to the kitchens—" said the
boy. "There's always something extra there."

"So your mother is still feeding people—does she still
keep a menagerie as well?" asked Silverhair on impulse.

The boy looked at him in surprise, then grinned. "Two
hawks and a crow and a mountain cat's kitten, right now.
And if you want to count them, our hound bitch has just
whelped again. We did have a bear cub," he went on
wistfully, "but Papa made us take it to the mountains at
the beginning of the spring. Papa's away now, but he'll be
back this evening, if it was him you wanted to see. . . ."

"And the Master of the Junipers—" asked Julian abruptly.
"Where could I find him, that is, if he is here?"

"Oh yes, the Master is staying with us now. He has
rooms in the West Tower." He pointed. "Is he expecting
you?"

Julian nodded, for a moment looking much older. "I
hope that he is. . . ."

Surprised, Silverhair watched his temporary companion
move off toward the Tower, then dismounted and started
to tie his own mount to the post in front of the hall.

"I'll take your horse to the stables if you are going to
stay—" offered the boy. "I hope you will—my mother
loves harp music."

Everyone likes harp music here, thought Silverhair grimly
as he watched Rosemary's son lead the dun horse away. *I
wish they were going to like the news I bring them as well.*

Slowly he climbed the broad sandstone steps and moved into the relative darkness of the great hall. As his eyes adjusted, he saw that a young woman was sweeping. The steady rasping strokes of the broom sent puffs of golden dustmotes swirling in the long bars of light that came through the western windows. Except for her, the place was empty, though the long tables and benches stacked to one side and the array of weapons, pictures, trophies, and hangings on the walls suggested that this was the focus of communal life here.

On one side of the dais, well away from the fireplace, was a large standing harp. Silverhair's lips twitched and he walked over to it, set his own harpcase down on the floor and put out a tentative hand to the strings. It was almost as tall as he was, with a great carved horse's head where curve and pillar joined. The gut strings were badly out of tune.

The girl had finished her task and gone. Instinctively, Silverhair reached for the tuning key that hung from one of the pegs and adjusted the strings, then sat down on the stool, tipped the instrument back against his shoulder, and began to play.

"To catch a hawk you throw up a lure, and you set a harp to catch a harper, I suppose. . . ." The words were ironic, but the soft voice trembled. "Farin—*is* it you?"

Silverhair looked up and saw Rosemary. Carefully he lifted his hands from the harpstrings, looked down at his long brown fingers with their calluses and scars, and then up at her again. He thought she looked older. There was white in the golden hair, and lines around her blue eyes. Then she smiled at him, and he saw that she was still the same.

"Where did you get this monster, Rosemary?" He nodded at the harp. "It has volume, all right, but the tone reminds me of a clothesline in the wind!"

"It was a wedding present—" she said in a voice that wavered between tears and laughter, "but Eric thinks it's beautiful, and when anyone can bear to play it, it is useful for accompanying group singing in the hall."

She is going to make it easy for me, thought Silverhair,

getting to his feet. Then he winced as her strong hands closed on his shoulders. She shook him, then held him tightly to her as if she feared he would fly away. He could feel her weeping against his shoulder; awkwardly he put his arms around her, patting her reassuringly.

"You wretched man!" she said in a muffled voice. "I should skin you, but skin and bones is nearly all you are. I'll feed you and *then* skin you, for making us all worry so!"

After a moment she straightened and stepped back a little, holding his eyes. "Where in the Maker's name have you been?"

In spite of his emotion, Silverhair began to laugh. "How many years have you to listen to me telling you?" Then he sobered. "But most recently, I've been in the Corona and Normontaine. I was with your father, Rosemary, and I promised him I would come home. . . ."

She swallowed, and he saw new tears in her blue eyes, but she nodded and motioned toward the bench beside the hearth. "Tell me—" she said.

The full story of Caolin must wait until Eric could hear it too, but Lord Theodor's death was a tale that belonged to his daughter alone. When Silverhair had finished, Rosemary sat knotting and unknotting her damp handkerchief for a little while and then sighed.

"I know that he had what he wanted, and now he's at peace, but sweet Lady, I miss him!" Rosemary exclaimed. "I suppose I had assumed he would live forever, somehow. Well, at least the Master of the Junipers is still with us, and he has been like another father to me. Come on—he will want to know that you have returned."

Silverhair stiffened. Having gotten over the hurdle of his reunion with Rosemary, he had forgotten that he would have to face a sterner judge. But it was like going into battle—it must be done, and waiting would only make it worse.

"How is he? Has he changed? Does he always live with you here?" he asked quickly as she led the way across the courtyard to the Tower. At the doorway she paused to answer him.

"I think he is much the same—perhaps he smiles more and speaks less than he did when we were young. He lives mostly at his place on the Lady Mountain, although there are times when he disappears and no one knows where he has gone. He came to me when we heard that my father had died, and stayed without explaining why—not that anyone would ask him. We are always glad to have him here." She looked at Silverhair and managed a smile. "Perhaps he was waiting for you!"

The towheaded boy came running up to them and caught at Rosemary's arm.

"Mother!" He focused on Silverhair and added, "There you are! Did you get the Master's message? He wants to talk to you!"

Silverhair exchanged glances with Rosemary and repressed a shiver. "Perhaps he *was* waiting for me," he said with an attempt at lightness. Then he realized that the young man, Julian, must have mentioned him. That would explain how the Master knew he was here. Silverhair took a deep breath and trudged up the stairs.

It was a different season and a different room, but suddenly Silverhair was reminded painfully of the last time he and the Master of the Junipers had met. The kettle of tea on the hearth could have been the same, and to Silverhair's eyes, so was the little grey-robed man in the slatted chair. No—what hair the Master had left was thinner, and it was all silver now, but there was no change in the brown eyes whose gaze held his own.

For a moment Silverhair hesitated in the doorway, dizzied as if he stood upon the edge of a precipice. Then the Master beckoned, and he stepped into the room.

"Would you like some tea?"

Wordless, Silverhair nodded and sat down.

"So, Farin Silverhair—you have come home." The Master, pouring, peered at him from beneath bushy brows. "Why?"

Silverhair took a deep breath. "I have come to warn you that Caolin has fallen into evil a second time, and arisen possessed by some dread power and dedicated to our

destruction . . ." he finished in a rush. "And I have come
to confess to you that it was my meddling that set him on
that road."

Or perhaps my responsibility began even earlier, the
thought came to him, *when I left that child, Thea, to the
captivity of Willasfell because I could not be burdened
with her.* His head was ringing with pressure, but he could
not tell if it was internal or from outside of him, now. *I did
not think that anything I could do would matter, but it all
matters, and I cannot evade it any more.*

"Caolin!" The Master looked at him sharply. Then he
sighed and shook his head. "I hoped so very much that he
could be healed, and I still believe that one day he will be,
though perhaps not by you, or by me. But we must all
make our own choices. If Caolin seeks to destroy himself
again, it is by his own will, no matter what you have
done."

"I thought that I had chosen my own way. . . . Time
after time I chose it again," muttered the harper. "But
now, after all my wanderings, here I am, talking to you
once more. Was I running toward something, or away?"

"Have you learned anything from all that traveling?" the
Master interrupted.

Silverhair frowned. The pulse in his head was like the
beating of great wings. "I have learned a little about
music, and about music's Lord—" he answered, staring at
the floor. Even here, he could not speak of his prayer to
the Wind Lord. If only he could have died at that
moment—if only the Lord of Song had remained with
him! He looked up, wondering suddenly whether *that* was
what he had been seeking all this time.

But it did not matter. The Wind Lord had rejected him,
and the Master of the Junipers was waiting for him to
continue.

"If anyone alive knows Caolin as he is now, it is I,"
Silverhair went on. "And I have learned the songs of half
a dozen lands, and more about rough fighting than I care
to remember, and how to find my way through a strange
countryside. . . ."

"Not a bad preparation," said the Master softly. Silverhair

closed his eyes. *"You will be tested,"* the Wind Lord had said. Was this what he had meant? Then the Master spoke again.

"Did you never wonder why I did not stop you when you decided to run away?"

Abruptly Silverhair's eyes opened. He stared at the older man, the Wind Lord for the moment forgotten.

"There is another reason I came back here, a question that I did not think to ask you eighteen years ago. . . ." he said abruptly. "Do *you* know what happened to my sister Faris and her child? Did you know then?"

How could one face at the same time hold so much pain and such joy? Silverhair watched, not breathing as the Master nodded and nodded again.

"Faris is dead. I was with her when she battled Caolin in the spirit and destroyed his power. But her body was already weak, and she had been out of it too long for it to survive. Each year I have tended her grave."

"I don't believe you," said Silverhair. "I would have felt her final agony." It was the one surety he had clung to during these long years.

"There was no agony, Farin," said the Master gently. "She went out willingly, to fight for her child, and for Westria. And she had her victory."

The harper looked down at his empty hands. Faris had conquered her fears and gone on, leaving him alone. He ought to rejoice for her, but he felt only emptiness. Then the meaning of the Master's second nod came to him, and his fists clenched.

"If you have known this for eighteen years, why have you told no one, old man? Why didn't you tell *me?*" His voice broke like a harpstring stressed beyond its power.

"Because Faris herself required my silence until the appointed time should come. I swore that oath to Faris and to Jehan!" Unmoving, the Master faced the harper's rage.

"And this is the appointed time? This is the time because now I am wise enough to see through your deceptions, and your life is in my hands?" Silverhair stood over him, his strong harper's hands closing and unclosing convulsively. "Old man! Half my life is gone!"

"If you had known that Faris was dead, would you have stayed peacefully at home?" asked the Master. "You did not want knowledge—you wanted revenge! And do you think that as you tried to take it you could have resisted telling Caolin what you knew?"

Breathing hard, Silverhair tried to call up the memory of a dingy room in Los Leones, and Caolin's scarred face in the lamplight, twisting in pain. Caolin himself had thought he came to kill him, he remembered, and even then, beaten and repentant, there had been a power in him that made Farin afraid. He would have tried to take his vengeance, he knew, but he wondered if he could have succeeded, even then.

"But how could it matter?" he asked with a last protest. "If Faris were dead already, why did it matter who knew? Caolin could not harm her anymore."

"No . . ." said the Master very softly, "but he might have harmed her child. The child lived, Farin. He lives still!"

Legs gone suddenly strengthless gave way, and Silverhair found himself sitting down. The air grew dark around him and he fought for breath as he fought to understand what he had heard.

"You swore to tell no one until the appointed time—" he repeated painfully. "Why are you saying this to me?"

"Farin," the Master said patiently, "when you play a phrase of music, how do you know what the next phrase will be? That is your craft, but seeing the pattern in events is mine. . . . Farin, listen to me—you are the second person to whom I have told this news today!"

Silverhair was still shaking his head. Had he gone mad, or had the Master? "I don't understand."

"My fault, I suppose. I have obscured the truth so long I find it hard to be plain. But I hoped that you might have suspected somehow—man, you rode through that gate elbow to elbow with him today!" The Master sat back and took a quick swallow of tea.

"That lad from the Ramparts . . . Julian . . ." Silverhair had to struggle to remember the name. Caolin had said that Faris was in the east—Silverhair had scoured the Ramparts, seeking her there. It could be true. Painfully he reviewed this morning and the evening before. Was there any sign by which he should have known? Perhaps he ought to have recognized Faris's eyebrows, or Jehan's smile.

"You are sure?" The words came out as a groan—the death cry of despair, or the birth pang of hope? He did not know.

"I have watched him grow from infancy," said the Master. "There—he is walking in the garden now—"

Silverhair levered himself out of the chair and went to the window. In the little garden below the Tower he could see movement, a dark head bent in thought as its owner walked up and down. Once Julian stopped as if to pluck a rose by the path, then pulled his hand away again.

It was still hard to see in this boy any link to Jehan or Faris, but that could wait. What mattered was that he was here. Silverhair felt something twisting within him and remembered abruptly how the lady Elena had struggled to birth her child. He had thought his life ended in failure, but there was his link with the future, stalking the roses as if he no longer quite knew where or what he was.

Unwilling humor twisted the harper's lips. He knew that feeling well.

"Do you find it hard to accept this?" said the Master. "Think what it must be like for him—"

Silverhair nodded, wondering if his face showed what he was feeling. And what *was* he feeling? His emotions were buffeted by the beating of great wings. His ears rang with distant music and he straightened, his hand moving instinctively to the strap of his harpcase.

"At least we have this much in common," he managed to say. "I too would like to find some place to be alone."

The Master smiled gently. "Those stairs lead to the roof of the Tower. No one will disturb you there."

Silverhair nodded. His whole being vibrated to the music he was hearing now, as if the sight of Julian had unlocked a door that only the touch of Death's wing had been able to open before. He swung the harpcase around so that Swangold's weight filled his arms. Could not the Master hear the music?

The old man's touch upon his arm released him, and then he was springing up the staircase as lightly as if he had been no older than the boy in the garden, into the sunlight and the pure air, where a red-tailed hawk spiraled up the slopes of the sky.

⇉ Postlude ⇇

The hands of the harper poise and settle upon the strings. A single note distills from the air, then another, in a tentative shimmer of sound that scatters sunlight from the bronze wire in a golden shower. Amazingly, the harp is in tune! The harper breathes deeply—the breeze brings him the scent of curing hay, and, from somewhere nearer, the sweetness of roses. His heartbeat is shaking his chest with an irregular pounding and he strives to steady it, controlling his breathing as he strives to steady the beat of his song.

He is holding the harp too tightly, clinging to it as if he fears the gift of hope he has just received will be snatched away. He forces himself to straighten, to let the harp rest lightly against his left shoulder and give his arms free play, maintains the melody first with the right, then with the left hand, while he flexes and shakes the fingers of the other.

Now it is better—slow steady chords emerge from the sound box, the deep notes throbbing one upon the other in continuous waves of sound. It is a march whose rhythm he is playing, but he cannot find the melody. The left hand tries first one combination, then another, seeking the song that began to whisper in his ear in the Tower room.

Words have never been his craft, though at times he has made verses to go with his melodies. The pure beauty of sound has always been his means and his end, a way to express the desires that struggle within him and to invoke

309

the power he serves. It is the only way he has to deal with the confusion of longing that shakes him now.

He tries fragments of musics he has made in the past—a phrase from his lament for Jehan linked to Faris's melody. But those are completed; their conclusions vibrate in the still air and are gone. Julian will need a new melody, and the harper does not yet know what it will be.

He sits upon the top of the Tower, unshielded from the winds of heaven, for he has finished with running away. The music is growing clearer now, and he begins to recognize its theme. It is the song of the Maker of Music, the Lord of the Winds. He has seen Him in dream and vision. Twice now he has been pushed by the dread of death to invoke Him.

Now is the third time, and no force from outside threatens him, only an internal pressure to admit the ending of his quest and to enter into his power. He trembles with fear and desire, but his fingers are beginning to move of themselves in the symbiosis of player and instrument from which the great music comes.

The chording deepens, commanding attention. The line of the melody leaps and trills, as agile and brilliant as the darting of a bird through the skies. Clear comes the music, mightier than the wind that shakes the trees, imperious and compelling, proclaiming the Divine Name. Wind whirls about the top of the Tower, humming through the golden harpstrings, making a silver banner of the harper's hair.

Faster and yet faster dances the music; his fingers fumble, trying to keep up with what he hears. Wind roars in his ears, taking his breath away. His hands lift from the harp in homage to the brilliance that blinds him, but the wind in the harpstrings continues the song.

"Maker of Winds and Words—" He can say no more.

"Maker of Music . . ." replies the Voice within his soul, "your offering is accepted. My child, I have been with you in all your wanderings. Now I welcome you home."

The harper sits still in the heart of the whirlwind. But from the harp that lies against his breast the music continues to flow in a song that has no end.

DIANA L. PAXSON

LADY OF LIGHT, LADY OF DARKNESS

Being the First Book of the Chronicles of Westria.

The four Jewels of Power had been created by a priestess in the days when the Covenant between the people and the Guardian of the land had been threatened. The heirs of her line held the Jewels – one of each of the sovereign elements – and through them, ruled Westria.

And in the sixth century of the Covenant, the Estates of Westria petitioned the King to marry, so that he might have an heir. So the King and his companions set out to find a Lady for Westria – a woman who would become both the mistress of his heart and the Mistress of the Jewels ... Queen ... Healer ... Sorceress ...

'This might be an authentic legend of another time and place. Truly it holds one spellbound in the old meaning of that word'

Andre Norton

POST A LITTLE HAPPINESS

Post·A·Book

A Royal Mail service in association with the Book Marketing Council & The Booksellers Association.
Post-A-Book is a Post Office trademark.

DIANA L. PAXSON

WHITE MARE, RED STALLION

Their future was bound by fate and magic

The Lady of the Ravens

Maira lived in the land that someday would be called Scotland, in a time when magic hung heavy on the hills and the Old Gods were revered with pageantry – and with blood.

The soldiers of Rome had claimed the island for their own, but the Celts would never surrender their homeland for they were a fierce and warlike people. When they were not warring against mighty Caesar, they warred against each other.

Daughter of a chieftain, Maira was as fierce and proud as any Celt, trained in the arts of war as well as the mysteries of women. She was of the White Horse clan and her beauty shone like the sun itself. Carric had loved her since he'd first seen her. Even though she was of an enemy tribe. Even though she had vowed to kill him . . .

HODDER AND STOUGHTON PAPERBACKS

DIANA L. PAXSON

THE WHITE RAVEN

A story of the still-living past

Set in an ancient fantasy world, in a time when King Arthur is still remembered, *The White Raven* magically recreates the epic love story of Tristan and Iseult – and of Branwen, healer and destroyer, servant and Queen of the Otherworld . . .

'A lovely blend of legend and realism'

Marion Zimmer Bradley

HODDER AND STOUGHTON PAPERBACKS

MORE FANTASY TITLES AVAILABLE FROM
NEW ENGLISH LIBRARY PAPERBACKS

DIANA L. PAXSON

☐	50938 9	Lady of Light, Lady of Darkness	£4.99
☐	43054 5	White Mare, Red Stallion	£3.99
☐	50251 1	The White Raven	£4.50

FREDA WARRINGTON

☐	41903 7	A Blackbird in Amber	£2.95
☐	40161 8	A Blackbird in Darkness	£3.95
☐	05849 2	A Blackbird in Silver	£3.50
☐	48908 6	A Blackbird in Twilight	£3.99

JEAN M. AUEL

☐	26883 2	The Clan of the Cave Bear	£3.95
☐	39311 4	The Mammoth Hunters	£3.95
☐	32964 5	The Valley of Horses	£4.50

All these books are available at your local bookshop or newsagent, or can be ordered direct from the publisher. Just tick the titles you want and fill in the form below.

Prices and availability subject to change without notice.

Hodder & Stoughton Paperbacks, P.O. Box 11, Falmouth, Cornwall.

Please send cheque or postal order, and allow the following for postage and packing:

U.K. – 80p for one book and 20p for each additional book ordered up to a £2.00 maximum.

B.F.P.O. – 80p for the first book, plus 20p for each additional book.

OTHER OVERSEAS CUSTOMERS INCLUDING EIRE – £1.50 for the first book, plus £1.00 for the second book, and 30p for each additional book ordered.

Name ....

Address ....

....